SURVIVAL

SURVIVAL

You can't outrun a nightmare

Eve Morton

Sapphire Books
Salinas, California

Survival
Eve Morton
Copyright © 2021
All rights reserved.

ISBN - 978-1-952270-18-5

Editor - Tara Young
Book Design - Lori Reynolds
Cover Design - Fineline Design

Sapphire Books Publishing, LLC
P.O. Box 8142
Salinas, CA 93912
www.sapphirebooks.com

Printed in the United States of America
First Edition – February *2021*

This and other Sapphire Books titles can be found at
www.sapphirebooks.com

Acknowledgements

Survival is a novel that I could not have written without the help of numerous authors, researchers, teachers, coworkers, and family. I had always been aware of the case study of Kitty Genovese, but it wasn't until the film The Witness and the book Kitty Genovese: The Murder, the Bystanders, the Crime that Changed America by Kevin Cook that I fully grasped the numerous complexities of her story. I have to thank these authors, along with my science and communication class from 2018-2019 who were my captive audiences as I lectured about both of these texts and the real-life case of Kitty Genovese. My classes were also tasked with sorting through the primary documents of this famous case, categorizing the subsequent research in The Bystander Effect, and then fleshing out their own ideas on how scientific research—especially that involving human subjects or the real lives of others—should be conducted. We had a lot of discussions on Stanley Milgram, Solomon Asch, and ideas surrounding ownership; I had many of these same discussions with other graduate students and professors at the University of Waterloo, so they are also to be thanked.

I also wanted to draw attention to the multiple works on true crime I read while writing and editing this story. The works of John E. Douglas, Roy Hazelwood, and Robert Ressler were imperative to understanding the inside perspective of law enforcement; Rites of Burial by Tom Jackman and Troy Cole, In Cold Blood by Truman Capote, Killer Clown by Peter T. Maiken and Terry Sullivan, Paul's Case by Lynn Crosbie, Rampage by Lee Mellor, and The Man with the Candy by Jack Olsen were all true crime books that dealt with specific narratives about singular killers/crimes that haunted me much like Mona is haunted by Kitty's death; and The Red Parts and Jane: A Murder by Maggie Nelson informed Mona and Kerri's perspectives as survivors of crimes and their ability to craft their own narrative from that survival. I also want to acknowledge the Canadian magazine The Puritan and its blog series on true crime, which I was able to edit and write for during October 2019. The authors who contributed to this series (R. Travis Morton, EmmaJane McBride, Emily-Jean Diamond, Derek Newman-Stille, and Chris Martin) were talented and insightful. Editing their work allowed me to think through multiple issues and avenues of true crime as a genre, recent digital trend, and ongoing ethical issue. I lastly want to mention Last Podcast on the Left; though a comedy podcast about true crime, their work never once valorizes the criminals who commit these acts, but rather works on taking the venom out of their ridiculous schemes and always violent actions. I certainly needed their rather blue or gallows humour when I was spending so much time researching these aspects!

The documentary The Nightmare, Matt Walker's research on sleep, and Jungian research on dreams and their meaning informed much of Mona's perspective (as did my own sleep paralysis). My arts first classes from 2019-2020 also helped me to flesh out my own thoughts on sleep, dreaming, nightmares, and their effects on human psychology and motivations.

Finally, RTM's enduring patience as I read, reread, and made him listen/watch movies and podcasts about these topics should be mentioned as I do not think this novel would have been written without his support. Thank you all so much!

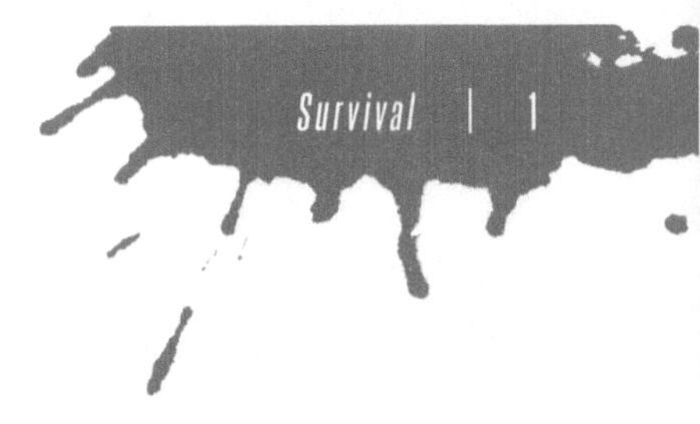

CHAPTER ONE

Kitty Genovese was all Mona saw. As soon as Kitty's dark eyes emerged from the distance and became a fully formed, haunting stare, Mona knew she was dreaming again. Her body went rigid in anticipation of the tableau of pain she was well familiar with:

Kitty Genovese would walk down a New York City street to her apartment building in Kew Gardens. Winston Moseley would approach from around the corner and yell. He would produce a knife. Stab Kitty. Leave Kitty. Then come back again and finish stabbing her inside the stairwell of her apartment building. While Kitty screamed, thirty-seven people in the surrounding apartment buildings would do nothing.

At twenty-eight, Kitty would die.

In her death, Kitty Genovese became an icon, a quick cultural shorthand for modern apathy and the danger of the city. And for Mona Ouellet, Kitty's image was so commonplace she'd become a latent dream symbol to decode.

Sometimes, the variables in her nightmares changed. The streets of New York were replaced with Montreal. The Kew Gardens apartment building would become a basement rented room. Moseley would become Gabriel Côte, a white kid from Mona's second-year Renaissance poetry class (ENGL 245, she would still remember), and not a black man with a criminal record.

Kitty Genovese, though, would always be the same. She would always be there.

Tonight, the knife that Moseley used was replaced with a .44 magnum. It was the only kind of gun that Mona knew, and it grew three sizes in her mind. Kitty spotted Moseley and ran down the street and around the corner. The sun that had once been high in the sky now set with unnatural speed, making the dream landscape pitch black. Mona wanted to wake up, already knowing the ending, but she was frozen. Her body was stiff. She could not breathe.

A shot fired.

A woman screamed.

No one did anything.

Blood mixed with the blackened sky, a bruise on the landscape and behind Mona's eyelids. When she thought it was over, another shot rang out.

Mona awoke in her apartment in Peterborough, Ontario. Her desk light was still on across from her single bed. She blinked once to adjust to the brightness, so she could survey her apartment. The closet was still open. The bathroom at the end of the hall was visible; it seemed untouched. When she rose from her bed to check the bolts on the front door, they were still fastened.

Nothing was amiss, nothing askew. She placed a hand over her chest and breathed heavily as she slumped against a wall.

Another shot rang out.

Mona ran to the window, careful not to become too visible behind glass. Light cascaded in the sky. Another gunshot in her mind became a firework in real life. Reds and blues exploded across from her apartment, over residential streets towards the Otonabee River.

"Of course."

She checked her phone and saw it was Victoria Day. The long weekend in May had completely slipped her mind. She'd gone to her office on campus early on Thursday, exhausted from not sleeping the night before. She'd napped periodically, between trips to the grocery store and the library, and prepared the last few paragraphs of her final comprehensive exam. The weekend had been a blur of Dewey decimal numbers and ramen noodles, then potential brainstorming for the dissertation proposal that would follow. The holidays in Ontario were still new, her mind still perpetually fixated in Quebec, though she'd been here for nearly two years. Time had already slipped to Sunday night before Mona had even noticed.

She watched a few more fireworks burst over the city. Her hands shook. There was no way she could go back to sleep after being jolted awake like this. Each blink brought back the nightmare in full colour, still fresh like a scent in her nostrils. The scream from Kitty at the end always felt like it was her voice, but her chest was so compressed that there was no way she could yell, let alone breathe, during the nightmare. She ran her hands through her hair to steady herself. She counted from one to thirty-seven, in an attempt to reach one hundred, before more pops and bangs disrupted her.

"Fuck it."

Mona disconnected her laptop from her desk and placed it inside her shoulder bag with the charging cord. She grabbed her notebook and a few of the selected titles on Stanley Milgram and Solomon Asch before getting dressed in the same clothing she'd worn the last three days. If she couldn't work at her apartment, there was always the library on campus, where not even the threat of a holiday would interrupt the grad students in their study carrels.

As she rode the elevator down, she splayed her

keys in her hands as if they were brass knuckles. It was only nine at night, but it felt so much later through her disrupted sleep. Before she stepped outside the elevator, she checked around each corner. She did the same as she exited the apartment building. As she walked to the bus stop, she suppressed each time she wanted to jump from a firework. They were starting to become background noise—like car engines, the hum of a washing machine—when someone shouted at her from a passing car.

"Nice legs, sweetheart!"

The rest of the voice and its slurs were blurred away by speed. Mona clenched her jaw. Her face flushed with heat. She'd jumped at his words, though they should not have been a surprise. Her mother's lecturing tone always emerged, like another hidden relic underneath her skin, when men catcalled her. *You are pretty, Mona. You must get used to this.* She thought she *had* gotten used to it, but it took moving to Ontario to realize she'd only built walls around comprehension. She hated the bus stop near her apartment building because it was close to a bar; she would have merely skipped this street in the past. Now she had to walk by it with a stone face and keys between her fingers. She checked the time and decided to risk walking another two blocks to the earlier bus stop by a community centre. She nearly missed it when the bus arrived, but she ran to catch it.

The bus driver was a woman, blonde and smiling. Mona flashed her student card and finally felt the tension ease away. She took a seat close to the back of the bus.

And like always, she reviewed her dream again.

She tried to focus on Kitty Genovese's story, not on her own. Through her three-day research fest, Mona had been surprised to learn that Kitty was a lesbian. She had always thought Kitty was murdered by an ex-boyfriend, a spurned lover, someone who had been tangled with her in some way. That had been the version of the story Mona's mother had told her—yet another reason to understand that she was pretty and had to be kinder to strangers who envied it. When Mona had attended university, a professor brought up Kitty in the Intro to Psych class, but he focused on those witnesses who may or may not have done something or nothing and the legacy they wrought. When Mona took criminology the next year, that professor focused on Moseley, who hadn't been a lover but a criminal who had already committed another murder before Kitty but was never prosecuted for it. It was only now, decades after the crime, that the other details—such as Kitty's roommate, her sudden break from her first marriage, and the gay bar where she worked—made her life stand out as a lesbian. Maybe Moseley had seen Kitty coming out of a gay bar and followed her because of it. Maybe this was a hate crime.

There were so many distinct ideas about Kitty Genovese and what had happened that night. None of them would ever come close to the truth—but that was why Mona was so attached to her. Maybe by examining the life and death of Kitty Genovese, Mona could stop the nightmares and get a PhD at the same time.

Maybe it would also stop her from focusing on Gabriel.

Mona was about to Google Kitty's girlfriend's name on her phone when the bus took a sudden turn. Mona had grown so used to the express student schedule, it had become like a lullaby to lure her into research mode. Instead of driving up towards the western part of campus where the river and Bata library converged, the bus bypassed the exit entirely and drove down the road closer to the environmental studies area, close to a wooded ravine.

"Where are we going?" Mona stood on shaky legs and wandered up towards the driver. The scenery passed as fast as her elevating heart rate.

"Detour stop. We can't go to the library."

"Because of the holiday?"

"Construction around. All summer. Just started." The woman examined Mona in her mirror. "But the library is open. You can walk from our last stop."

Mona mumbled a thank-you before she headed back to her seat. The idea of walking by herself across campus at night filled her with dread. But for research, for a chance to pass away the time until it was dawn and easier to sleep in her apartment, she was sure she'd try it. She always had her keys, and if need be, pepper spray at the bottom of her bag. Her mother may have taught her to accept being pretty and to blink back the affronts of the world, but she didn't have to be stupid or naïve. Her father had taught her that.

The last stop of the new bus detour was past the forested area bordering the campus, closer to a residential area. A strip of bungalow houses sat next to a strip mall so common in Peterborough, containing a cluster of cheque-cashing places, a pawn shop, a run-down convenience store, and a diner. The sign for Mel's Place was fluorescent green. It seemed from another time period, like Mona had walked too far away and accidentally lost herself in time and place. When the bus stopped, a surge of people got off and trudged toward the campus.

Mona found herself heading to the diner.

A bell rang when she stepped inside. A woman at a cashier station with curly, dark red hair smiled brightly. She gestured to a bank of booths to the left or a series of small round tables closer to the counter.

"Take what you like. I'll be right with you."

Mona headed to the booth. The smell of hash browns and eggs became overwhelming; she realized she'd slept through dinner and hadn't eaten much for lunch. The menus were vinyl and easy to read. There wasn't too much choice beyond the standard diner fare, but everything there seemed utterly wonderful.

"How you doin'?" the woman asked. Her accent seemed forced, as if she was trying to sound more like a country homebody than she really was. Her sharp nose and flat cheekbones gave her an aged quality, but Mona was sure she was younger than she was. She was also so much smaller than she had once seemed behind the cash register. Mona was barely over five feet four inches, making this woman barely five feet and less than a hundred pounds.

"I'm good, thanks." Mona ordered eggs and a cup of endless coffee that she could already smell. The woman smiled again and left her in her booth.

As Mona's computer booted up, she surveyed the area and all the easy exits. A man in the back with a bandanna over his forehead seemed to be the short order cook, while only a handful of other employees were around. The woman who had taken her order dealt with all the tables present, most of which were men in plaid shirts and weather-worn faces. Farmers or construction workers or truck drivers. It was a dive diner, a place that Mona would typically avoid because of the clientele. There was a sense of safety and tranquility here, though Mona was hard pressed to say how or why it seemed that way against her better instincts. At the counter close to the coffee machine, a black man and a white woman with blond hair in a ponytail had holsters on their waists and badges right next to it.

Then Mona understood. She'd seen enough police and plainclothes detectives to recognize them, even if this was a completely different province.

She sank into the booth, feeling better about her choice to study here. If the cops came here for their midnight snacks, then at least robbers, drug addicts, and stalkers stayed away.

That was the hope.

By the time her computer booted up, she was drinking her second cup of coffee. Whenever Mona worked on a longer project—like her first dissertation or her comp exam questions—she reverted to her old-school ways of tackling a project. She became the eager know-it-all in sixth grade and sprawled out with her research on the floor, tackling every last interesting piece of data with Post-it notes and flags. She used spiral notebooks and wrote everything by hand. Her computer only made an appearance in these kinds of sessions for email, the occasional e-book, and quick fact-checking online. Even when she was at McGill University and studying in the English Department, she'd always defaulted to writing all her essays out by hand before typing a single word. Sometimes in both languages, too, as if in the process of translation she could hone facts that much more. It was this habit of dual writing—or writing by hand at all—that was why it was taking her forever to finish her degree. Well, that and the rather large topic shift from English to psychology.

She sighed, feeling only a small pang of nostalgia for her old discipline. English was history. Psychology was the future, and it was one that was filled with fewer ambiguities. There were clear answers and results here. Hypotheses and conclusions rather than thesis statements and speculation. In many ways, English lit and psychology were the same—both dealt with how stories were told and to whom—but one dealt with real people and real events. Which also meant that its perfection into a dissertation had very real consequences.

Mona pulled up a photo of Kitty Genovese on her laptop. It wasn't the famous photo that had been reprinted in dozens of magazines afterward—the one with a closeup of her face with her half-open-mouthed gaze. That had been her mugshot, when she was arrested for a small gambling infraction. Mona didn't want to remember her through the lens of crime. Instead, she'd found one of the few colour photos of Kitty there were. She wore a green dress and stood outside next to a backyard fence. The image was haunting, too, but for different reasons. Mona recognized the excitement in Kitty's expression, the formal wear for an event that was supposed to represent a rite of passage, yet Mona also saw the distant dread before Kitty's eyes. Mona gazed at the image for another moment before diving into her work.

"Here you are, hon," the woman said. She glanced at all the books spread out in the booth with a casual smile. "Where shall I put these in all this?"

"Oh. Sorry." Mona pushed two books to the edge of the booth that was vacant, freeing up space beside her elbow for the eggs. The woman placed them as Mona's stomach rumbled.

"Is that your mom?" The woman gestured to the photo of Kitty.

"Oh. Oh, no. Not even close." Mona was about to laugh heartily at the thought when she re-examined Kitty's features. Kitty was Jewish and Italian, while Mona was from two Irish Catholic parents who were Francophone to the core—but there were overlaps in their looks. Kitty's dark hair mirrored Mona's, though Mona's hair was well past her shoulders and as straight as a pin. Their skin was both pale, their bodies small but sturdy.

"I think it's the smile," the waitress said. "You and the woman seem to be smiling at the same thing."

"The woman's Kitty Genovese."

"Oh." The waitress took a moment to process the information. "Well, that certainly changes things."

"How so?" Mona glanced at the waitress's name tag. *Kerri*. She liked the name and the simplicity of it. "Do you know who she is?"

"Yeah. Most people do, right? Considering how she died...this photo is just sad. Before, it looked like someone going to their prom. It looked like something nice. Something that someone would look at when they're nostalgic. Hence, your mom."

Mona glanced at the photo again. This photo could never ever represent nostalgia for her since the Greek root of the word meant a longing for home. Mona couldn't go home, not even to see her mother, because Montreal had been twisted into a place unrecognizable, except in her dreams. She suspected that Kitty had felt the same way, especially given the new revelations about Kitty's sexuality. To go home was to confront expectations about your life that were not fully lived out how everyone thought. So, you didn't go home. You got an apartment in the village and you called your girlfriend your roommate. Maybe that was the distant dread in her eyes, even in spite of a happy green dress. Kitty knew there would be no going back.

"So, why do you have Kitty on your computer," Kerri asked, "if she's not your mom?"

"I'm...I'm working on a dissertation. My dissertation. It's going to be on her. I think."

"You think?"

"Well, I haven't had a chance to start it yet. And then it still has to be passed. There is so much hesitation about even declaring what you're studying before it passes a committee."

"Kind of like speaking about the dead?" Kerri asked. "Like sitting shiva?"

"Exactly. Or like you don't want to jinx it. A curse."

"Sounds like a committee of witches."

"Sort of!" Mona said, chuckling easily along with Kerri. "Except it's a bunch of psychology erudite men who you hope have some kind of understanding of your specific subfield."

"And your subfield is...the bystander effect?"

Mona beamed. Someone knew who she was talking about. She wasn't just reading and reading and reading anymore; she was engaged in a debate. Research was a communal thing again, even if that community was only located in a diner at the end of a bus route. Her supervisor, Roger Conlin, would obviously know who Kitty Genovese was. Everyone seemed to know her story. But whether or not they knew one version or the other, or used it for their own narrative, was another aspect entirely and nearly impossible to predict. At least Kerri, in some way, seemed to be on the same page as Mona.

"I don't know what part of her story yet I'm going to study, honestly. I think I'm trying to explore what she means in as many different ways as possible before putting pen to paper."

"Huh. Well, good luck. Sounds interesting."

"Thanks."

Mona shared an extended look as Kerri departed. When Kerri migrated to the next table, she seemed to fall into another conversation just as easily and effortlessly as she had with Mona. Mona's heart sank as she wondered if her connection had actually been one as strong as she felt it or if Kerri was just good at her job. Being a waitress must have been like play-acting all the time, mirroring people's emotions so they knew you were there for them. It seemed like nearly as much emotional labour as sex work or therapy—which Carmen Nguyen, Mona's officemate, would know more about. Mona made a mental note to ask Carmen if she was studying service work in her own research for more insight.

Mona's gaze drifted to Kitty Genovese again. *She could be my mom. She could be my friend. She could...be my girlfriend.* Each statement came in a rapid succession, but not one felt intrusive. They all felt true. In another lifetime, perhaps, all of them were true at some point. The photograph wasn't one of someone who was dead anymore. It was of someone who was smiling with a secret, a secret that would never come to pass.

Mona ate the rest of her eggs across from Kitty, wondering about home.

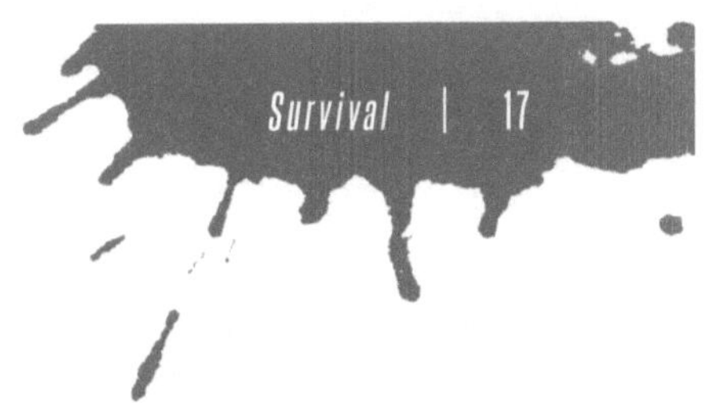

CHAPTER TWO

Kerri set another plate of hash browns and scrambled eggs in front of Absalom Lincoln and Sandra DeVos. Absalom cooed at the unexpected boon while Sandra shook her head.

"Kerri, you shouldn't do this. We didn't ask for this."

"On the house." Kerri gave them a wicked grin, the kind she reserved for only them. "You know cops get free coffee."

"Since when is this coffee?" Sandra asked.

"Since I decided that you keep this place safe."

A few weeks into starting her job at Mel's Place, there had been a homeless person who never left a booth at the front. Kerri sympathized with the man— but knew that Gerry, the supposed owner of Mel's Place, would be livid since the man was also scaring away customers. She'd made the difficult decision to call the police and spoke to Officer Lincoln on the phone. He'd still been working his way up the ranks, not yet a detective, and he was eager to take the call. As soon as Kerri expressed her reservations—the man was homeless, with no place to go, not ostensibly violent but perhaps mentally ill—he had been immediately sympathetic. Instead of drawing weapons and making a scene, Absalom appeared with a social worker, and the three of them left together.

Ever since, Absalom (and whoever his partner was) not only received free coffee, but whatever food Kerri could give them without alerting Gerry. Since he was mostly an owner in name only and it was Kerri and Roy, the short order cook, who kept the place going, which meant a lot of food went to Absalom's regular spot at the counter.

He lapped up the hash browns happily, talking in an animated voice about how many more carbs he needed today anyway after all the running he'd done this morning, while Sandra continued to shake her head. "I thank you for the sentiment, but unlike my partner here, my belt does not appreciate potatoes. I'm going to pass."

"Suit yourself. You want the eggs or...?" Absalom soon took Sandra's unwanted plate as she stood from the counter. She excused herself to the bathroom while Kerri wiped down her spot and the surrounding counter.

When the front bell rang, Kerri noticed the

woman from the front booth had left. It was nearly one in the morning, when the last bus would run back into town, so she figured the woman was trying to catch a ride. It was clear she was a student, though much higher in ranking than most of the other kids who came in here for coffee to water down their hangovers. The woman's books and computer had been open the entire time she was in her booth, utterly consumed by her work. Each time Kerri had filled her coffee cup, though, she had smiled and whispered a thank-you in a faintly French-accented voice.

Kerri walked over to collect the dishes in the booth and a few dollars in tips. Underneath a stack of napkins was a printed-off photo of Kitty Genovese. Kerri couldn't decipher if the photo was left by accident or on purpose, but she settled the image into her back pocket either way. The woman really did remind her of Kitty, even if Kitty had met a terrible fate. Kerri hoped the woman would return for a study session, if only to reaffirm that she would not meet the same end.

"Hey, Ker," Absalom asked. "You got a minute?"

"Sure." Kerri dropped the dishes by Manny's dishwasher station and headed back over to Absalom. She topped his coffee as he fidgeted with a file half in and out of his briefcase.

"I was wondering if I could get your opinion," he began, his voice hovering in a lower register.

"Without Sandra?"

Absalom gave an uneasy smile. "You don't know any of this."

Kerri gave a zipper motion across her lips. "Secrets are always safe with me. I'm basically a priest at this point. Or a psychic. Probably a psychic, right? Do police still use psychics on the down-low? Or is that a seventies thing that has now faded out like hypnosis?"

Absalom rolled his eyes. Their banter was a long-standing routine, established to no doubt make Absalom feel better about soliciting her help. When she'd known exactly how to deal with the homeless man in the restaurant and then been able to suss out what kids entered the diner had fake IDs, he'd understood that she was good at reading people. She revealed she was a writer then; it was part of her job to imagine people's actions from different perspectives and for not-so-common motivations.

"So, hit me with it," Kerri said. "What do you have?"

"A couple really strange break-ins."

Absalom and Sandra were part of the burglary crime unit—the "property patrol" as he dubbed it—and most of their cases were cut and dried. A house was robbed of a laptop and DVDs, all to be pawned within forty-eight hours, and then that money was used for drugs. Peterborough's population was made up of mostly retirees dependent on social assistance, along with transient students who only lived in the area from September to April when the school year was in full swing. Then there were the long-standing, tenured professors who made the university possible and lived in the much better side of town under heavier lock and key. The summer months were the worst for petty and property crimes since the university staff with fancy houses went on vacation and the drug community became desperate without the students to prey on. The crimes were as standard as animals waking up from hibernation in early spring; a new wave of break-ins was surely coming and made even worse because of the recession. Kerri had only been able to help with one of Absalom's cases before, when a burglar had also taken women's underwear and clothing in addition to the typical things snatched. Absalom had been stumped because the clothing had no pawning value, so he considered the burglar a woman until Kerri saw the sentimental value in the stolen object. This wasn't a woman—but a boyfriend or ex-boyfriend who wanted to get back with the intended target, perhaps even a stalker unknown to the resident before now. As it turned out, the victim had rejected a co-worker a week before her house was hit. When they checked his residence, the computer had been there—not pawned—and loaded with a bunch of violent pornography with the woman's face superimposed over top.

So, when Absalom wanted Kerri's help again, she expected another panty raid. Instead, he presented her with a house that had nothing stolen at all.

"Are you sure it's actually nothing, or is it something that the people don't want you to know about—like sex toys or porn?" she asked.

"We considered that. But there's more here. The residents don't exactly have much shame." Absalom gestured to the file but didn't open it. For confidentiality, he couldn't show her anything with information on it. Talking in hypotheticals like this was risky, too, but worth it from his vantage point. "First of all, these were students. A frat house, it seems, but I didn't even know Peterborough had frat houses. There were porn DVDs on the shelf like they were Oscar winners. So, when I asked twice, and they still said no, nothing was stolen, I tend to believe them. And that house, like the other two on the same block, was definitely broken into. The locks were smashed. Books tossed."

"What about insurance scam? You know, report a break-in and make it seem real to get some kind of repair damage while not actually risking losing anything?"

"Sandra thought of that. It's a good thought. But this has happened in more than one house, and there are no commonalities among the landlords or tenants or anything like that. There wasn't even insurance on one of the houses hit. The frat house. Also, those guys insisted there was food eaten."

"Hmm. Like the person was living there?"

Absalom nodded.

"Yikes. Creepy." Kerri thought back to the underwear case. The co-worker had later admitted he'd stayed in the house for a while, wearing the underwear over his face and on his body, as if he wanted to live the woman's life. He'd probably eaten food, too. This kind of behaviour sent all her red flags flying, but she still didn't know what she was looking at with these cases. She asked again if there was anything stolen—like underwear—but still came up negative. "So, how many places are we talking about here?"

"Since April? Maybe four. Five at most."

"Huh. If it was in the winter, I would have figured someone was trying to avoid the cold. They broke in to keep warm. Made a mess of it but mostly done out of need rather than sadism or something creepy."

"It could have been winter. We don't know. One of the houses had been rented out, but the student never showed, so the break-in we found in April could have easily happened in February. There's just no way of formally knowing."

"Huh." Kerri folded her arms across her chest, considering the details. "But the break-ins now are happening in the spring. So, maybe it's a mix of necessity and…something else. Was anything else disturbed? Just books tossed? Or was there, like, maybe writing on the wall?"

Absalom shifted in his seat. He glanced to the bathroom doors where Sandra had not yet emerged. He took out a single photo, face down, and slid it across the counter. He still kept a finger over the image, pinning it down like a bug. "Be warned. This is a gory photo."

"Oh?"

"A cat was killed at the latest crime scene. It appears to be a stray—the owners never had a cat—but it's pretty gruesome. Do you want to see it or have me describe it to you?"

"I'd rather see it. It's always going to be far worse in my head."

When Kerri wrote her horror novels, she kept the monsters hidden as long as possible. Only at the very end could you reveal what was actually making the walls bang and the floorboards shake. In real life, though, you had to stare monsters in the face. It was why she and Absalom got along so well, and why Sandra—who would rather monsters never existed in the first place—would always react with anger at these events, rather than curiosity.

Absalom removed his finger from the image. Kerri took a breath as she flipped the photo over. *Let the fear wash over you*, she reminded herself. *Don't let it stay*. A black and white cat had been completely eviscerated and hung from two clothing lines. The organs were removed and sat in a pile on the grass. Some of the meat from the cat appeared to have been sliced off. After blinking off an initial wave of nausea at the gore, Kerri grew focused.

"Is that...?" Kerri pointed to a black spot in the corner. "Is that a fireplace? A barbecue?"

"A barbecue, yes. Some of the blood was in there."

"Oh. Oh." Kerri placed the photo face down again, her mind reeling. She took a couple of steadying breaths. "He was hunting."

"Hmm?"

"The person breaking into these houses, if he is doing all of them, is hunting for food. He's trying to survive on the bare minimum—like a survivalist. He killed the cat and strung it up, not for taunting or for some sick sinister joy, but for food. He just didn't finish what he started. Someone probably scared him away."

Absalom wrote as Kerri spoke. He asked a couple of questions about hunting, which Kerri answered the best she could, balancing her conviction with enough personal distance. She liked Absalom, she really did, but she didn't want him to get too far into her head or her past. After their first meeting about the underwear house, Kerri had panicked she'd revealed too much and Googled herself. She had no criminal record, so she'd not come up there if he went looking, but her proximity to crime always made her visible in other ways. She stared at the Google search with her heart in her throat—then settled into relief when nothing was there. Not even when she paired her name with her last name of Reznik did anything about her—or her father—come up. Unless someone knew too much and really went digging, her past was her past. If any of her ordeal had happened ten years later, she knew there would be no escaping the internet recognition and absolutely no way to scrub it clean.

She gestured to the other side of the diner where Jim, one of the regulars, often spoke about his hunting trips. "He's not in right now, obviously, but he's talked to me before about making venison jerky. He knows a lot about this kind of thing. Owns a shop even, up in Lindsay. You may want to ask him about the technique displayed in the image or ask him if anyone has come by his shop trying to learn it. My knowledge is limited on the topic, as you can see."

"You know more than me," Absalom said. "City boy at heart. Scarborough isn't much for hunting, and sometimes, I don't even see the parts of Peterborough that cater to that kind of thing. So, what is it? You hunt? A family of brothers? Grew up in the country?"

Kerri gave a thin smile. "Something like that."

"Well, this is great," Absalom said, writing

again. "Not *great* great, but I was so worried I was dealing with a psychopath. Animal mutilation is always the first sign, the experts say. But I don't want to be on a new Bernardo case. I don't care if it would make my career. No, thank you."

Kerri chuckled as lightheartedly as she could. "Psychopaths are rare. It's why horror novels with them don't really hold me. People try to make the monster into a person, thinking it's far more lifelike. But I don't want to be scared by something real because it's not a fantasy then. I'd much rather read Stephen King's scary car monster. Even if it's a ridiculous idea, at least it's an idea I can escape into, you know?"

"Not really." Absalom grinned playfully. "But I'm not a horror writer. How's your latest book coming?"

Kerri brushed off the question. She, like the woman earlier, never liked to talk about projects until they were done and the ink on the contract was sealed. Sometimes, even until the book was on the shelf. Then she knew for sure that the company wouldn't fold or the e-book wouldn't be delayed endlessly. Publishing nowadays offered so many more twists and turns, surprises and disappointments, than in Stephen King's and Clive Barker's days. Speaking too much about anything intangible really did feel like a curse.

"New book is still too new. But I think what I

meant is that when I read a horror novel, I want to be scared by something, of course, but I don't want that fear to bleed into my daily life. The monster in the pages has to be close enough to the present world that it's terrifying—but also far enough away that when I close the book, the horror is over."

"So, you don't get scared when you see a Chrysler? Or whatever *Christine* was?"

"Absolutely not," Kerri said, laughing. "But man, when I'm in that book, I'll piss my pants every time I see a headlight. That's the real fun. And *Christine* was a Plymouth Fury, by the way."

"Ah, okay. Well, I can't wait to see what you come up with next. Aliens? Ghosts? Scary lamp monsters? Whatever is there, I'm there."

Kerri gave Absalom more coffee, and then hash browns, as a way of saying thank you. Sandra came back from the bathroom holding her phone, as if she'd been waylaid by a pending case. From the hushed tones she spoke to Absalom in, Kerri guessed that was exactly what had gone on. Kerry felt no resentment as she heard fragments of her own theory come out of Absalom's mouth moments later. He would have been able to figure out the cat's meaning if he had thought beyond shows like *Criminal Minds*. The cat was food for someone who was starving, for someone who was scavenging and squatting in abandoned student housing. Why someone would need to—instead of going to a shelter—she had no idea. But that was not her job to figure out.

As the night wound down and the flow of people into Mel's Place decreased, she threw herself into her shift-changing tasks. As soon as six a.m. came around, Daniela would arrive and take over for the day shift. Kerri still had to clean out the coffeemaker, help Manny with the dish drying since the machine broke, and count the food in the back for the truck order. As soon as Absalom and Sandra left (with a big tip, of course), the rest of the people at the counter were truckers who didn't need much attention. It wasn't until Kerri took the garbage out at the back of the diner when she remembered the bloody insides of the cat, like a fracture that had yet to heal and smarted with pain at the smallest touch.

She shook her head. *It's because you smell tuna right now. That is the only reason you are thinking of it again.* Garbage was always a rich, heady mix of smells it was so easy to fall back into bad memories. She told herself to stop it, but more came. The strong odour of the inside of a deer when she'd cut too deep and punctured bowels, her father yelling at her for hours because of her error, Lee stepping up and begging for the sound and smell to stop.

Kerri swallowed and pushed the memories away. She never had to go hunting ever again. She never had to go into the woods or live in a small town ever again. But whatever knowledge she'd gleaned from her father made her an incredibly good asset now—either with Jim and the rest of the hunters, with her novels, or with Absalom. She was skilled at working her way in between men with power, contorting her voice into a familiar drawl, and telling them what they already knew. Hunters and cops—while intimidating and scary in the abstract—were nothing but soft men in camouflage clothing. She knew how to handle them because at one point, she'd handled far worse in her father.

It was women, though, especially the quiet bookish types, who she couldn't always decipher. But she wanted to. She really did.

After closing the dumpster, she took out the photo of Kitty Genovese from her back pocket. She smiled and wondered what the bookish woman would discover and if Kerri could be a part of that secret knowledge.

A loud rattle—like the sound of a paint can or the scraping of dumpster wheels—made her jump. She waited on the balls of her feet, wondering if something was trapped inside. Another cat or a rat or even...

The rattle continued.

"Hello?" Kerri asked.

Nothing. Silence.

Kerri peered around the corner of the diner.

The night stretched into the morning horizon, the sun peeking over the trees. *Nothing but the changing temperatures.* Metal expanding, creating something else—that was all that made the noise.

Yet when Kerri wandered to the side of the diner to stare at the dawn full-on, she felt like she was being watched. There were no cars in the lot that she didn't recognize, all truckers and Roy's rusted Mazda 3 accounted for.

"Hello?"

Nothing again.

She spoke in Czech. She asked a question her stepmother used to teach her and Lee the language, folding a pun inside the verse to make them both smile. It was a game, a rhyme call and response. She waited for the answer.

There was nothing.

Kerri completed the answer herself. She pocketed the photo again, thinking only of her stepmother in place of Kitty. The talk of random acts of murder and burglary were just screwing with her head. She had to go back and serve coffee. To mop the floors and then go home. She needed to save all her fear for her next novel, so she could keep the real monsters at bay.

CHAPTER THREE

Absalom liked to chase the sun. Every morning before work, no matter how late he stayed up the night before on dating apps or out at a bar, he always rose just before the sun did so he could start his morning run in the dark and usher dawn into existence.

The family house he'd grown up in was at the top of a hill. He'd started each one of his runs—back then, all in preparation for the high school track team—in the early dawn when his father was returning from his night shift at the hospital and his mother had just woken up to make coffee. Dawn in his parents' Scarborough town house was a magical time; his parents kissed and caught up while he shot from his sneakers in a fury.

Running down the hill was easy. The speed made him feel like flying; he'd often imagine ambient clouds behind him marking his pathway. The uphill climb, though, showed him what he was really made of. His legs throbbed like an open wound; sweat covered his brow. But the feeling of elation, the sun peeking over the edge of the hill, was enough to make him stick with it.

His mother sometimes called the hill they lived on "the mountain." With her bad back becoming worse every year, each slight incline took on an Everest-like quality, each step in their house a nightmare, a mountain inside of a mountain. Soon, she didn't leave at all. Young Absalom, "Abby" to her, doubled his efforts to run in the morning. He'd climb the mountain for her, just to prove that he could.

When Absalom moved to Peterborough, the hardest adjustment was its flat and narrow roads. Almost no hills, save for the one in the centre of the city. Part of the university campus was set on top of Parkhill Road, making it the ideal spot to run whenever he could. The area was almost forty minutes away from his place on foot, though, so it was a once-a-week indulgence. Until those mornings, Absalom contented himself with chasing the sun in the blocks around his town house. By mid-spring, that meant rising at approximately five in the morning, so he could start in darkness.

He'd already taken one corner by the time sweat beaded on his forehead. His lungs ached. He and Sandra had broken up a bar fight the night before when the cops on duty had needed backup. There had been so much smoke in the place, the cloying kind from cigars and the sweet kind from vapes. Absalom still tasted the fuzzy scent of strawberries on his tongue, even though he'd brushed his teeth at least three times before heading to bed. He spit as he ran. He pushed himself. Harder and harder. Dawn was just breaking. He needed to feel this sense of accomplishment before going back to the unit and staring at his case files of unclosable robberies.

Because that was what they were: unclosable. Not merely unsolvable or cold or anything else that encoded hope in its very naming. Robert Stack wasn't going to emerge and beg for audience help in solving these mysteries. There was nothing that a stranger through a TV or a switchboard could give him because there was no solution here. Was something really taken if nothing was reported missing? Could you steal *potential* objects? How did you take something no one owned?

These were existential questions, not legal ones. In all his other cases, he'd run a description of stolen goods through pawn shops and hope it turned up. Maybe find a geographic profile and stake out the next obvious house. There was nothing to do for these ones, and even if they found the person breaking and entering, it was a weak case. They would never be able to link him with the other breaking and entering cases because there was nothing to link him to. Taking something revealed motive. Taking something illuminated a criminal mind—and with nothing missing, there was nothing there. Kerri's insight had helped—at least they weren't looking for a budding psychopath—but it still left Absalom chasing ghosts, or even worse, chasing concepts. At least on his runs, he could chase the sun and catch it by morning. Sure, it wasn't real, but it felt real, and that was good enough for now.

By the time dawn finally emerged in full bloom, Absalom was only a two-minute run from Parkhill.

Elation and adrenaline coaxed him towards the steep incline. It would be murder on the way up; the lactic acid in his limbs already made him ache. He told himself he'd walk up, pace himself, and not fly down like he had as a kid. But he smiled as he launched down the hill, knowing that his youthful memories would win out. He may have been thirty-four, his mother may be dead and his father washed up in a home in downtown Toronto and the house on the mountain gone to decay, but Absalom was still that fourteen-year-old "Abby," and he still wanted to dream.

At least until he got to work.

His heart was swallowed and smothered in his lungs by the time he reached the bottom. The crosswalk lights at the bottom of the hill told him to wait, so he swerved into the trail behind a community centre. Lush green trees provided him shade as he took a respite. Some of the old university dormitories blocked him from traffic and acted as a sound barrier. For a long time, all he could hear was his own panting and elevated heart rate.

Then the rattling sounded.

He'd been breathing with his face between his legs, but now his back was straight. Cop instincts kicked in.

Another rattle came from behind one of the old dorms. Could just be racoons, garbage being collected, homeless men looking for change. All not uncommon and all not crimes. But a sinking feeling plagued Absalom. He stepped towards the dorms.

A man popped out, sudden and tall as if he was squatting before. He wore all black. His dark hair was ragged, definitely in need of a cut. He had a bit of a twitch to him, too, a facial tic as if he had Tourette's or was continually singing a song under his breath without realizing it. In every other circumstance, Absalom would have thought the all-black attire meant he was a burglar in the middle of a job. Early dawn, in spite of what people thought, was actually the most common time to hit a house. So many people were busy on their way to work and willing to turn a blind eye if something looked strange. But missing were the tools of the trade—a crowbar, a hammer, bolt cutters. The man had nothing in his hands. His palms were open, facing upward, as if in supplication. This man was in the middle of something, but Absalom was sure it wasn't sinister. He was about to turn and run back up the hill when the two of them made eye contact.

"Hello," Absalom said. His voice was booming. *Cop voice.* He didn't mean to sound so authoritative, but he couldn't help it. "Can I help you? Are you having trouble getting inside the building?"

The man tilted his head. They were far enough away from each other that his face remained obscured, only a composite of dark features and kinetic twitches. The man turned away just as suddenly as he appeared. He grabbed a bag from behind a trash can and darted into the woods, a rattling sound as his echo.

Absalom stood in the centre of the pathway for a long time. Red flags waved in his mind, but he wasn't sure what to do. There was fear in the man's movements, but fear for what? Absalom may have spoken like a cop, but he wasn't in uniform—yet the guy had been spooked. *Maybe it was a black man running.* He rolled his eyes. His mother had always warned him in Scarborough. *Black men don't go jogging; they run from the police.* He'd become the police to prove her wrong, but he still saw the way some people freaked out as he ran down the street. No amount of Adidas headbands or gym shorts would change that.

Absalom examined the garbage around the dorm's back entrance. Nothing had been jimmied, no windows broken. *Nothing.* One garbage bag had been torn open and quickly discarded. Since the holes were tiny slash marks, it seemed more likely to be animals than humans. Newspapers had been delivered on a back porch, which had also been torn apart. Long strips of newsprint remained on a step, like makeshift streamers.

Absalom paused. That didn't seem right. It was one thing for garbage filled with all kinds of smells to entice animals, but newsprint? *Odd.* When Absalom looked through the torn shreds, he found the remains of paperback novels also tattered among the detritus. Brightly coloured covers were written in, undecipherable, and the spines of other books had been snapped in half. When he nudged one book with his hand, he found half the written pages inside looked to be redacted with long black lines. *Odd, sure. But nothing illegal.*

Absalom wandered around to the front of the dorm building, memorizing its name and university affiliation. The sidewalk then connected him to the lights, which now said it was safe to walk.

So, Absalom decided to walk home.

The entire way, he repeated the strange interaction in his mind. He glanced over his shoulder periodically, swearing he felt a set of eyes on his back. No one was there. By the time he had arrived home, showered and changed into his plain clothes, he was nearly ten minutes late.

"You okay?" Sandra asked when he got into work. She set down a black cup of coffee for him. "You look spooked. Bad date last night? Any teenagers where they shouldn't be?"

"I'm fine." Absalom sighed as he regarded another case file for an unclosable burglary on his desk. The address was ten minutes away from Parkhill. The mountain was heading towards decay, like all mountains did. "Let's just get to work."

CHAPTER FOUR

I've read your proposal," Dr. Roger Conlin stated. "But I don't think it will work."

"Wait," Mona said. "What?"

Two weeks had passed since the fireworks had driven Mona from her apartment. She'd spent the bulk of those weeks at the booth in the diner or a caddy in the library, researching Kitty Genovese and writing her dissertation proposal. She'd narrowed her focus on Kitty's story to New York City itself as a place of refuge and anonymity for queer people. Though Kitty's relationship with women had been covered up in the press and her live-in girlfriend, Mary Ann, referred to as only a "roommate" in court testimony, Kitty's death actually led to a stronger connection in the LGBT community and then later visibility—or so Mona believed.

In her research, she'd found out that Mary Ann had come to the city because she'd read about

New York in pulp lesbian novels of the time period and thought it was a refuge, a gay mecca like San Francisco. After Kitty's murder, though, Mary Ann had left New York and never returned. Meanwhile, a former barmaid at the bar where Kitty had worked had died in a violent hate crime, and a neighbour who overheard what had gone on that night with Moseley never came forward because he was gay and didn't want to be outed. The city that was supposed to be safe for people like them suddenly became a beast that kept them down and forced them into silence. Their despair wasn't just with the thirty-seven witnesses who had done nothing that night, but at a city within a city, a marginalized group that still did nothing but knew the real version of the crime and the private lives of those afflicted.

For Mona, Kitty's story was the perfect analogy for the prototypical queer closet and how that psychic interiority and silencing of desire affected modern queer people. It took Kitty's death for the community to finally understand their boundaries and that they were still in hiding. Thus, five years later in 1969, when police kept invading bars in Greenwich Village, the Stonewall riots could occur, and the community could emerge from years-long suffering and silence as a distinct entity. In a way, Kitty's death led to freedom and rebellion because no one wanted another icon to be emptied of meaning again. Mona's dissertation was going to be a critical exploration of all these issues and how it related to modern psychological ideas of community and apathy, using Kitty Genovese and her lesbian relationship as an anchor point.

It was some of Mona's best work. Even more than the essays she'd written out several different times in several different languages until it was just right when she'd been at McGill. Writing about poetry in translation could never be as exciting—and as terrifying—as this proposal had been. Talking about translation was talking about beauty, about style, about sonics and ideal forms. It was something lovely—but it wasn't real.

Kitty was real. The city was real. Mona had spent so many hours in these details, marvelling at how she could pull some type of order from this horrendous chaos. It may not stop her nightmares—she was convinced they actually got worse during these weeks of late nights and black coffee—but she still felt that she had created something to resurrect herself.

Dr. Roger Conlin, however, was telling her no.

"I'm sorry…" Mona combed some of her dark hair behind her ear in a nervous tic. She realized she was displaying all her cues and weak points, but she didn't care. "I don't understand why my project won't work. I completed the literature review and have found enough sources that follow the department protocol. I followed the guidelines for the proposal on the department website. It's formatted correctly. I even compared it to some of the earlier work from former PhD students here. In the early 2000s, Katja Brenan proposed a similar topic on apathy in the Mormon community, and Chris D. Russell examined HIV status within the LGBT community and shunning."

"Yes, but Brenan's work was over a decade ago. Scholarship practices can change so much in that time period. Her supervisor was also Marla Krenshoff, who was more a theological scholar, hence how it was approved so fast. I also believe that Chris D. Russell never finished his dissertation. So, even if his proposal passed, it doesn't mean very much without the follow through."

"But these still passed. So, there was something in their research that the department saw as useful. Perhaps my work can fill a similar role. I'm studying a figure who is well known in psychological research—effectively exploring the ramifications of the bystander effect from another perspective. I...I just don't understand how it's not going to work."

Dr. Conlin sighed as he rubbed a hand through his grey beard. He shifted in his seat, the chair creaking as he crossed and uncrossed his legs. His foot tapped. Each sound was like a small drop of water on Mona's forehead. When she'd taken his graduate class a year earlier, he was the same kinetic ball of energy—but she'd interpreted his ministrations as excitement as he explained theories to the entire grad class of eight. A week into the class, she and Dr. Conlin had bonded over a translation mishap in one of the texts he'd been teaching them, and she'd spoken French in the class to correct the verbs. Though she was still in the process of transferring her graduate English credentials to the PhD program in psychology at Trent University, he'd said she already had enough experience at a PhD graduate level, so he'd be more than happy to take her on as his student. She was probably far more advanced than all other students who were going at their PhD for the first time. While she was nearing thirty, most other people in the program were barely twenty-five. Her maturity in scholarship was obvious. And because he'd seemed genuinely interested in her past work, even in another discipline, she'd agreed to work with him.

Now Mona's stomach felt nailed to the floor. Each one of their previous conversations came back like a jagged piece of glass, shattered from the inside out. Had they ever gotten along? Or was she always correcting translations, before becoming lost?

"Look, I know you're transferring from another discipline and you're still learning how we do things in psychology," Dr. Conlin went on, his voice pedantic and disappointed. "But in psychology, we focus more on the hard data and facts. Even in applied psychology, where we take that research and do something more interpretive with it, we still always orient ourselves around something we can prove. We can't rely on Freud anymore—and we don't want to associate with him anymore. Take a history class about him. Take an English class again. But his data is bunk, so we don't use it here."

"But Kitty Genovese was a real person," Mona said. "So was Mary Ann. None of that is bunk."

"I know. As much as Kitty Genovese has become a figure in psychology, her legacy has also been disproved. Even the bystander effect is a very first-year observation. Most of your proposal is still based in that first-year observation combined with fairy tales about the city and lesbians. It's just...not going to fly. It will never pass a dissertation committee. I tell you this now before it gets torn apart by a committee. I don't want to see that happen to you."

"I see."

"This is not over, though. Not even close. I see your experience in your writing—quite excellent writing, let me tell you—and I think you're a valuable asset to the department. I always thought so, from day one, when the committee wasn't sure whether or not to admit someone with only a minor in psychology in their undergrad. But I insisted: you were adaptable. That's really the whole point of a psychology degree, too. Adaptability. Progress. Change." Dr. Conlin's kinetic energy boiled over as he stood from his seat and sat on the edge of his desk, inches away from Mona in one of his chairs. "You're very accomplished in whatever you do. I just think you need some direction."

"I see," she repeated, keeping her voice as calm as she could. "Forgive me for being too forward, but I thought that was what comprehensive exams were for—making sure I had the correct direction. I passed those. One not too long ago. So, I find it hard to believe that I've already suffered from misdirection."

"Those exams are far more about separating the wheat from the chaff. They're about making sure you did what we asked you to do. And now we know you've done that, we know you can do more. Hence now, more than ever, is the time for direction."

"Okay," she said. *D'accord*, she thought bitterly. *D'accord, d'accord, d'accord.* It was what she'd say to her mother when she was thirteen and upset, not wanting to reveal anything of herself, so she simply agreed. "So, what should my proposal be about?"

"Well, each proposal must have a stronger direction and clearer focus. Take my research." He rose once more from his desk and darted towards a bookshelf. He pulled out a volume that he'd contributed a chapter to, and then several academic journals he'd also written for. Seeing his kinetic energy in academic form—complete with citations, footnotes, and titles of more than fifteen words—was another rush of sudden emotion that Mona didn't know how to process. Her arms were rippled with goose pimples. Her heart raced, and she let out a breath she didn't realize she was holding.

While Dr. Conlin spoke of his research, Mona suddenly realized that they never spoke about her own. It was Mona's *experience* that he had gravitated towards. He asked her for translations. French words. Questions about Montreal and the best places to go to eat. *Experience*, not academic thought. Her memories morphed. Dr. Conlin's kinetic energy became circling, following. He was not there to praise her body of research knowledge, but her experience in that body of knowledge. Suddenly, her work on the queer city—fairy tales, as he called it—was more like a confession. It felt like he was getting under her skin, and it was her visceral body, rather than her intellectual rigour, that was being attacked.

Mona's gaze flicked to the door in his office. Closed. She stared at him again and tried to focus on what was happening. He was droning on and on about consent forms for experiments on human subjects. They took too long to pass. People took too long to hand them in. But they were integral to his study on ownership since humans could provide the most insight to their thoughts on the concept. "It's not that the animal kingdom doesn't have ownership rights—there have been fascinating studies on crows in this regard—but they are the few who can possibly articulate how and why they believe in its presence."

"Ownership?"

"Yes," he confirmed. "We orient ourselves around what we think is ours. For instance, I don't open your purse because if I do, you'll be upset. And you don't take these journals unless I give them to you because you know I own them."

He extended one of the journals to her. When Mona reached out to grab it instinctually, he pulled it away. With a smile, he remained stationary as she grabbed them again. When she tugged, he held on tighter.

Finally, she let go and folded her hands over her knees.

"See?" Dr. Conlin smiled too wide, half-hidden by his beard. "So much of our behaviour follows this idea of ownership. It makes for a very specific form of study and provides me with enough hard data to write papers and talk concretely."

"So, you want me to talk about owning something?"

"Perhaps. I want you to read these journals and get a sense of what could be a viable, and very profitable, area of research. Currently, it's only myself and a handful of other scholars examining ownership. If you did want to study this topic with me, I have lots of work you can continue to do as a research assistant, and that work could easily feed directly into a dissertation topic. You produce a dissertation in a couple months and get out of here."

For the first time since the meeting started, Mona liked what he was saying. "Only a couple months?"

"Sure," Dr. Conlin said. "Dissertations don't actually take as long as people say they do. Most people fuck around. Don't write. They're in love with the idea of writing, so they waste years being in love. But you're not like that. If anything, this proposal has shown me what a hard worker you are, even if I don't think it's a viable topic in this discipline. You did this in two weeks while also finishing your last exam. It's exceptionally well written and researched. You also converted graduate courses from another institution, in another field, in a matter of months only a year ago. You're adaptable, like I said. No reason to not get you out of here as fast as possible."

Mona nodded, the praise suddenly too much and too close to her skin. A flash of heat rolled over her body, one she recognized as from sleep deprivation. She'd been staying up too late to work—though how that was different from any other time, she wasn't quite sure. She wanted to get out of academia with her degree, especially since this was her second time around, but she also needed something to do to stave off her anxiety. She needed to fill the sleepless nights with *something*. Who cares if it wasn't Kitty Genovese anymore? *Why bother giving yourself nightmares during the daytime in the library stacks, when you can just follow along in someone else's shadows, for a piece of paper?*

"So yes, I think that once given correct direction, you will bloom." Dr. Conlin put a hand on her shoulder. She wanted to recoil, but she couldn't. "And soon enough, you will move on from here. And do much better things."

"Thank you," she said quietly. His hand was warm, pulsating. When he finally removed it and sat across from her, she lifted her gaze to his. They stayed, lingered, and challenged. He slipped the journals across his desk, finally letting them go.

"Is that all today, sir?"

"Yes. Any questions, please reach out."

"Okay," Mona said. *D'accord.*

⁂

By the time Mona reached her office on campus, her eyes were red-rimmed with tears. The keys trembled in her hand as she slid them in the lock. When she was met with resistance—the wrong key— she nearly crumbled to the floor.

"Shoot. Shit. Motherfucker…" She slipped into French as she continued to curse. She rotated the key ring around so she could select the right one. Before she could, Carmen opened the door and aborted any further attempts. Mona walked right past her officemate without a word, plopping her bag on her desk. The psychological journals cascaded out and onto the floor. Mona let out a small cry of helplessness that was louder than she wanted it to be.

"Whoa now," Carmen said. Her tone was languid and lucid, as if she'd been drinking honey all day in an attempt to mask her sometimes too-deep voice. "What's going on here? You're about to lose my mind."

"Lose *your* mind?" Mona furrowed her brows. "Why not my mind?"

"Oh, don't worry, honey. You got the English phrase right. But your mind is already gone, so I figure we'd moved on to me."

Mona only shrugged. Carmen's humour was normally welcomed, especially in relation to the bureaucratic minefield that was academia. She and Carmen had both been transfer students who got the shittiest picks for offices, but Carmen's interests also happened to coincide nicely with Mona's. Carmen was an MA student, doing her degree so she could go into counselling and therapy, but her academic career had been put on hold for a while because of her gender transition. She often joked that she had started her undergrad as one person and emerged into her MA as another; each one of her degrees would have separate names, as if she was attempting to collect verification of each part of herself. Carmen's transition had helped put her research on counselling into better focus, allowing her to draw on her experience as much as hard data in her own project. Mona thought she could do the same—or at least use Kitty Genovese as a proxy—but she had been wrong.

Mona's skin still felt too hot, too fresh and raw from her rejection, for any kind of joke. When she bent down to pick up the journals, glimpsing Roger Conlin's name made her teeth grind. Her hands trembled. She set the journals on her desk and stared at them with the same vexation she would have once given a lover. The words were too close. Her body was her research, and her research was now a wound desperate to become a scar.

"I…can't do this."

"Sit."

Carmen gestured to the chair at Mona's desk. Her long, thin hair framed her face and made her pointed stare seem far more severe. She wore a purple sundress and purple painted nails; she looked as if she was going out for a farmers market date, rather than staying in at the office and doing data entry for an experiment. Carmen's computer hummed from her desk, and her dark teapot signalled her working regime. When Mona finally sat, Carmen retrieved another mug from her desk and set it in front of Mona. The tea was tepid, with no steam rising off of it, but the smell of camomile combined with a fermented sweetness made Mona's stomach ease. Carmen dragged her chair across the tiles—making it shriek in resistance—and both of them grimaced. When Carmen caught Roger Conlin's name on the academic journal, she let out a tsk-tsk under her breath.

"What has this cranky man done now?"

"Nothing."

"Bullshit. Tears like that don't come from nothing."

"Just assigned me some reading material."

"And I say again: Bullshit."

After a couple more prods from Carmen and sips of her tea, Mona opened up. Each time she described the atmosphere of the room, she paused and shifted. Rewrote and retranslated. She didn't want to come right out and say, *I feel violated*, but there was no other way to put it.

So instead, she took the onus on herself.

"It's my own fault," Mona said. "I should have picked a topic that was better. Kitty Genovese is so blasé now. It happened half a century ago. Winston Moseley is dead. So, what's the point? I only wanted it because I wanted it. That's not academic. And besides, it's not like I should be offended. He wants me to work with him. It's a compliment."

Mona's mother's words—*you are pretty, ma petite joliecouer*—came to her again. That was why she felt such discomfort. She was pretty, so she had to get used to being looked at. Dr. Conlin didn't care about her interior dreamscape featuring a murder victim. He just wanted live bodies doing work. And she was good at working, in addition to being more than a pretty face. At least he could see past that.

When Mona met Carmen's gaze, however, she was shaking her head. "No, honey. You are not wrong. You've just been fooled."

"Fooled?"

"Fooled into thinking you got a supervisor who cared. Your proposal was probably fine. He even said it was fine—but he threw it out because he didn't want to do it. Find a different person, and you change your world."

"I can do that? I'm not stuck with a supervisor?"

"Oh, no. Not at all! The paperwork is here, so let it be so." Carmen pushed her chair back to her laptop, wincing once again at the squeaking. She typed in a few commands and pulled up the admin change of supervisor form. She printed and gathered it for Mona.

"Just add your student number. Sign your name on the dotted line, and voilà. Find a new person. You're done with Roger fucking Conlin."

Mona shuddered. *Fucking* as an adjective made

her stomach do flip-flops again. She took the form with a muted thank-you, tucking it into the academic journals. Carmen eyed Mona with a critical gaze. In a sudden hushed voice, she asked, "Don't tell me the rumours are true."

"What rumours?" More than ever before, Mona hated transferring late into the school. It meant she wasn't privy to this kind of gossip that had surely been spreading since day one at orientation. When Carmen only shook her head, Mona repeated with more insistence, "What rumours?"

"Only that Roger likes to roger anything that moves. Yeah, shitty joke. But if it's true, then it's a hell of a warning to anyone around him. He didn't hurt you, did he? Because I will harm him."

"Don't." Mona reached out to stop Carmen, who had swerved on her chair, as if to post something online or gather a posse in a flash mob. "He didn't do anything. He just…got too close to me. He leaned too far on the desk, said I was adaptable and capable with a strange insinuation at the end. I don't know. That's nothing, right?"

Carmen shrugged. "It's shitty. If it makes you feel shitty—"

"A lot of things make me feel shitty. Doesn't mean someone harmed me." Mona sighed. Her back ached. Her neck was stiff. She was overtired. All of that was shitty—but Gabriel, no, that was the real source of pain. And Dr. Roger Conlin was no Gabriel. He was barely a fly in her periphery if she thought long and hard about it. "I think…I think I just realized he never liked my research interests, he was only interested in me."

"Shitty indeed." Carmen eased into her chair, some of her anger cooled. "But there could be a germ of truth in this whole thing. Rumours don't just emerge—and stick—like that. So, be careful. You haven't reached the point of no return. Cut the creepy bastard to the curb. And sign the form."

When Mona picked up the change of supervisor form and withdrew her student ID from her bag, Carmen seemed delighted enough to go back to work. She listened to music out of only one of her earbuds, just in case Mona needed her. Mona appreciated the tiny gesture more than she could fathom.

Mona was halfway through filling out the form when she stopped over the new supervisor placeholder. She knew no one else at the school. Some of the other profs seemed interested in similar materials, but when she pulled them up online, she discovered they were either on sabbatical or contract workers, meaning they couldn't supervise her. Her heart swelled in her chest. The suffocating feeling from her dreams crept up on her.

"Carmen?"

"Yeah?" She tugged out the earbud right away.

"You need a buddy to take the form in?"

"No. I just…I have no idea who else could supervise me. Don't I need a meeting with them? I can't just put their name down."

"True. But I know Jenny would be more than willing to help you."

Jenny O'Connor was Carmen's supervisor, a stunning blonde who mostly studied various therapy practices, but was also well-versed in queer history and its complicated relationship to psychology. Perhaps for a dissertation on Kitty Genovese and the queer city, Jenny could work. When Mona looked her up online, she realized she had reached a critical threshold with students.

"She's out."

"What? How?"

Mona explained the rule she'd just cross-checked on the website. "Staff can't be overburdened. The only other people left are either outside my discipline and area of expertise entirely or Dr. Conlin."

"Shit."

For once, Carmen was silent when faced with a problem. Mona stared at the nearly completed form and the stack of journals. She swallowed hard, knowing that if she switched supervisors, her source of income could change, as well. She'd have to go back to teaching, not being a research assistant who entered meaningless numbers in a spreadsheet. Each time she blinked, she saw the outline of a classroom filled with shadows. She was not a teacher anymore. Apparently, she was barely a scholar.

"It won't be too long," Mona said, trying to brush off her concern. "I've been working for Dr. Conlin long enough now that if I just devote my own academic area to his field, I will probably get out of here much faster. Switching causes too many problems, you know? I just want a piece of paper. I want a degree. I don't care what it's in anymore."

"But is it worth the risk?"

Mona couldn't answer. Her thoughts fused in her head, too many of them trying to get through at once. Carmen asking if a PhD was worth the risk seemed so strange because everything was a risk. Going outside her apartment meant she could get catcalled. Abducted. Shot at. Going to a meeting meant her personal feelings could be shattered or that she could be molested when her guard was down. Even running her own experiments Dr. Conlin did meant she was the one taking advantage, and she could be thrust into this matrix of power where she was the teacher again—or at worse, the abuser. Sleep, not even sleep, could allow her to get away from the oppressive machinery of normal life. Because this was *normal.* One risk led to another led to another led to another. What was the point in asking if it all led to the same overwhelming conclusion?

"What's going on?" Carmen asked. "I mean, really. What's going on in your head right now?"

"Too much. Not enough." Mona rubbed her eyes. Her body faltered with exhaustion. "I don't sleep at night anymore. I stay up and work, then I crash and sleep during the day. But since I had a meeting with Dr. Conlin at eleven, I just stayed up all night." Mona yawned, sudden and fierce. Her stomach quivered, too, empty of food. She wanted the eggs from the diner so badly in that moment, along with Kerri's smile and coffee. "I should just go home and sleep. Everything will seem better then."

"Mm-hmm. Usually does." Carmen folded her arms across her chest, and then nodded resolutely to an unheard argument she seemed to be having in her head. "I have something, if you need."

"Something?"

"Calm down. Just sleeping pills. If you ever just want to go to bed at night again, I can get you there faster."

Je ne sais pas. "I don't know."

"They're legit pills. Prescription from my doctor, but I don't really use them."

"I see," Mona said. She thought: *Peut-être.* She'd already tried a dozen other ways of beating her insomnia. Melatonin, tea, over-the-counter sleep aids, exercise, eating and not eating before bed. Nothing worked. Or if it did, she considered it a Band-Aid solution. It wasn't sleep that was her problem so much as the dreams. There was no way not to dream. Even the pot that Damien suggested to her, and then left in her mailbox, only helped for so long. When she awoke from the blackness that it brought on, she just felt fuzzy the next time. Time morphed and memories came back anyway. So, accepting the offer from Carmen seemed to be yet another offer of fool's gold. "I still don't think so, though I appreciate the offer."

Mona gave a wonky smile. Though Carmen nodded, she seemed disappointed. Mona folded the change of supervisor form in half and tucked it into her desk drawer. Her computer buzzed to life—but since there were no emails and nothing else to do, she stared at the academic journals.

"You know," Carmen said, "I won't be here that much longer."

"You won't?"

"No." Carmen smiled, wide and elated. "Just finished a huge data set before you came in. I sent it to Jenny, and there will only be a conclusion to write and then...I defend."

"Congrats. We should have a party."

"Oh, honey, already have the pub booked for the end of July. And that's well and good for me, but it also gives you an opening."

Mona tilted her head, suddenly wide awake.

"When I'm gone, Jenny's free. You get a new

supervisor, and you can do whatever project you want. Just hold until July, maybe August at the latest. That's two months, which feels like a lot but—"

"Not when I've been getting a degree, in some form or another, for almost ten years." Mona let out a slow breath. It didn't seem like that long in her mind. She had been in her third year of her first PhD when Gabriel happened. She took a leave for one year, and then dropped out for another before deciding to move and transfer her credits. Now a year and a half into this program, and things were finally shaping up. Two more months to wait didn't seem like anything.

"Good perspective. Yeah. Jenny'll love you." Carmen wrote down Jenny's contact info on a bright pink Post-it note and stuck it on Mona's desk. "Maybe you'll want to give her a heads-up before then or keep doing what you're doing so Roger's not suspicious. Whatever lets you sleep at night."

"Maybe," Mona said, laughing. The laugh turned into yet another yawn, one that Carmen soon repeated.

"Just try to sleep at some point, okay?" Carmen said, her voice getting maternal. "And if you still can't, then you know my number. And what I can offer."

"I do," Mona said. "I really do."

CHAPTER FIVE

A ttention, attention. Special delivery!"
Roy stood in the front foyer of the diner, a cardboard package in his hand and a devious smile on his weather-worn face. He waved around his checked bandanna, the one that kept his prematurely grey hair tied back as he cooked, to obtain the diner staff's attention after their monthly staff meeting.

On Mondays at two p.m., the diner's slowest time (other than the three a.m. slump), they closed down Mel's Place and put a "back in fifteen minutes" sign on the door. Though the staff meetings regularly lasted at least an hour, most of the diner's regulars knew to stay away on the third Monday of every month. If they forgot what Monday it was, then Gerry's Volkswagen in the parking lot was another dead giveaway that the coffee was no longer for them. In between sips of her own drink, Kerri had already watched two university professors from the Geology

Department come into the parking lot, then double back and try another place. When she glanced towards Roy and the scene he was making, her heart stopped. The logo on the side of the box was well familiar to her now. Her publisher. Her new novel had been shipped.

Roy gave Kerri a sly smile and stepped towards her. The staff parted ways like the Red Sea, only to then fixate their attention on her. Blush already bloomed underneath her cheeks; she wondered if her limited childhood freckles were glowing like embers against her skin.

"Hello, K.T. Stellar, famous horror author extraordinaire. Your books have arrived! Which means that we're having a party tonight."

"Oh. I don't even know where to begin correcting things in that statement," Kerri said with a laugh. She took the package that Roy offered and ran a long fingernail against the tape that sealed it shut. "First of all, if I was a famous author, I definitely wouldn't be hanging around with you bums anymore."

"I resent that remark," Roy said, his smile never wavering. "But I understand your right to make it, as an author and all. You gotta get creative inspiration somewhere. So, tell me, what character am I in this one?"

Kerri sighed. Other staff members spoke in hushed whispers among one another, wondering where their proxy figures were. When Kerri's writer status had been exposed nearly four years ago, it had been a relatively painless experience—definitely not as showy as Roy was making it now. Her books had come to the diner—after she had asked Gerry if she could get packages here, of course, since finding the delivery notice slips was nearly impossible in her apartment—and she'd opened them on her break. When someone recognized the author photo, they had put her pen name to her face and made the appropriate responses. *How wonderful. Must be nice. Tell me where you get your ideas. I think I can write my own story, what do you think?* She'd answered the queries in kind, and the chatter faded to a muted acceptance.

Then, she thought, everyone forgot about it.

As it turned out, a handful of people—like Roy and some of the temporary hires from the university— had gone online and found the back copies of her work and read them cover to cover. When one of her earlier titles mentioned a diner, they were convinced they found their proxy selves on the page. She had tried to insist it was nothing; she had worked at diners or as a service person for decades at this point. But it was to no avail. People read her stories at work, and they were going to look for themselves between the lines. When these characters died in gruesome ways or were spooked by ghosts and monsters, she quickly realized that they seemed to like it even more.

Especially Roy.

He stared at Kerri eagerly as she withdrew the first book from the package. Though she had approved the cover design weeks ago, seeing it in real life always shocked her. The colours were so much sharper, the wrap-around image so much starker and better realized than the pixelated emailed image. When she first started publishing, she'd judge each potential publisher by its former covers. If the publisher could not do the most basic Photoshop, she was not submitting. There were a dozen other pulp places out there that specialized in horror or the new weird or whatever people were calling her niche genre now. She knew she'd never make any kind of real profit off her writing—did anyone but J.K. Rowling do that anymore?—but she could at least have pretty books she could hold in her hands.

"*Danny In Ice*," Roy said, mangling the title as he read it upside down. "I love it already."

"*Dante Under Ice*." Kerri flipped the book so Roy could see the black-coloured ice on the front that cracked upward into a deep purple and intersected the title. Her pen name K.T. Stellar was in the same shade of purple. On the back, below the summary, were several blurbs praising her past work, all from reviewers in the genre. Kerri never liked to see reviews in the first place, so being confronted with them in such a stark manner made her heart stop, and then start again at a faster clip. She was doing good work, apparently. She had the right to be proud.

"Here," she said, handing the copy over to Roy completely. "Tell me what you think."

Roy fawned over the book, spreading his large hands over the spine. Dana, another server, stood next to him and swooned over his shoulder. Soon, Kerri handed out all six of the author copies her publisher had given her. Some people in the crowd passed them off to the next person—like Marla, who hated the "ghosts and goblins" that Kerri wrote about—but others snapped them up and seemed to work out a way to share the book until they could get their own.

"What about you?" Dana asked. "Did you keep a copy for yourself?"

"Please. I've already read it myself like six times. I'm utterly sick of me."

"But a shelf in your apartment, man," Dana said. "Don't you want to keep it and gloat?"

Kerri shook her head. She gestured to the people around her. "This is honestly all I need for my ego. Too much and my head will become too big for my body."

"That's a good story idea," Roy said. "Right?"

"Sure, Roy. I'll do my best to name that character after you, too. As far as author copies go, I think I can spare all of them at this point, especially since I know Roy also has a cake in the backroom to celebrate this."

Roy disappeared into the backroom while a

handful of workers cheered. Many others doubled back from their hasty exit once they realized cake was involved. Gerry was already long gone, his Volkswagen leaving an empty space in the lot. Marla and Dana spread out paper plates and napkins among the staff, while Kerri discarded the packaging her books had arrived in. She soon spotted a handful of other letters in the front area for the restaurant. Her name was on two of them.

No return address. Her skin was marked with goose bumps. She opened one addressed to Ms. Kerri Reznik, which turned out to be a pamphlet for a charity. *Junk mail.* She shredded the envelope that bore her name and the restaurant address, trying to stomp down the fear of how anyone—other than her publisher, who had a strict confidentiality agreement in regard to personal information—got her address here. She tucked the other letter into her back pocket just as Roy came out with a cake. It was shaped like a heart, with roses and other sickeningly pink candy on top of it for decoration.

"The tell-tale heart?" Kerri joked.

"Hey. Be kind. You don't exactly make getting a cake for these events easy," Roy explained. "You keep all your book releases so secret—meaning I then have to rush out to the grocery store and buy the first one I see."

"I don't want to jinx it. That's why I keep it to

myself. I've had too many publishers fold after signing the agreement that I simply don't believe I'll hold a book in my hand until I hold a book in my hand. And then I give it away anyway." Kerri shrugged. "Horror isn't the booming business it once was."

"Sure, sure. But you have to get better at revelling in your fifteen minutes of fame. Do interviews. Have book release parties, not surprise board meeting parties. Be a ham."

"Come on," Adrian, a weekend busboy, said. "Just cut the damn cake."

With a laugh, Roy handed Kerri the knife. "Oh. Make it like you're stabbing the cake—like that hotel victim in your first novel."

Kerri cringed. "Oh, my first work was a failure."

"Your first one is always the hardest. So, stab it out."

With a sigh, Kerri play-stabbed the cake. When she pulled back the knife and saw red on the tip, her mouth opened in shock. Roy let out an uproarious laugh as he clicked her photo on his phone.

"Red velvet cake. Oh, this is priceless. Please use this as your author photo from now on."

Kerri laughed, but it was a harsh, wheezing laugh. Her mind had gone somewhere else—back to the woods of her memory, the setting for her first real novel, where she'd tried to write about a murderer and not a monster. Where the tools of the trade had

been banal and everyday—a knife, an ax, a hacksaw—
and not supernatural hexes and enchanted objects.
The novel had been a failure because she'd written
about the horror of the real world, not the fantasy of
horror. She'd written about herself and not someone
else.

She shook off the moment before memory
latched on to her too strongly. Adrian and several
other younger workers were getting too antsy for
cake, so their excitement gave Kerri direction. When
she glanced up at the storefront window, the meeting
sign was still up, even though potential customers
had started to step down from the detour bus stop.
Kerri recognized the woman with long dark hair. Her
bookworm. Her heart immediately beat fast once
again but not out of fear.

"Hey, Roy," she said, stepping away from the
cake. "How about you take over and show me how it's
done? I need to let our customers in. And then we all
need to get back to work."

A few groans drowned out the excitement. As
Kerri walked to the front and unlocked the door, she
wished for the first time in a long time that she didn't
give away all her author copies. For once, she actually
wanted to share.

CHAPTER SIX

Mona read the same sentence at least five times. She rubbed her eyes and let her fingertips hover over the pressure points of her skull. She tried to imagine her brain as the writer of the article would see it: skin pulled back on a slab to reveal the frontal lobe. In one of the articles on ownership Dr. Conlin had given her, the author discussed an obscure disease called Diogenes Syndrome, named after the Greek citizen who lived in a glass jar. The syndrome was characterized by an obsessive need to hoard (often items with little to no value, like garbage or stray animals), depression, sometimes catatonia, and extreme self-neglect. The syndrome appeared more frequently in those with frontal lobe injuries.

Don't all psychological syndromes, especially ones with aggression and lack of boundaries, have frontal lobe disturbance? Mona was sure Gabriel's lawyer had tried to claim something similar—to no avail, thankfully. Mona's eyes snapped open. Her brain on a slab disappeared from her mind's eye. *You are not here to think about prosecution. You are here to think about psychology. Ownership. Diogenes...*

Mona recited the names she was learning from the journals, coupling it with her knowledge of other psychological case studies, but she was still coming up with nothing. Dr. Conlin's work wasn't that hard to follow, in theory. Our lives were dictated by what we owned and who we thought owned other things. Even with this obscure syndrome, its relationship to ownership was clear and obvious: with a poor self-perception, the subject hoards items that are also poor substitutes. Their things reflect the self, and that self, more often than not, has been damaged biologically. Talking about ownership was a spatial conception as much as it was about identity—just like her idea of Kitty Genovese and the city. Mona understood this easily enough. In practice, though, these academic journals hurt her eyes. They were dry and boring. To write within this genre felt as if it was sucking the life out of her, and she'd only gone through a handful of them so far.

"You look like you needed this."

Mona glanced up to see Kerri holding a piece of red velvet cake on a paper plate. She'd been filling Mona's cup of coffee every half an hour since she arrived, without saying a word. Now she smiled even wider than the first night they had spoken.

"Oh. Um. Thank you."

"Not a problem. But where should I set this down?" Kerri gestured to the stacks of journals and Mona's laptop that was still open and taking up space.

"Oh, shoot. I'm sorry. I should..." Mona stacked the journals and closed the laptop. She added them to the same pile, clearing space in front of her. Kerri set down the cake, along with metal forks that she'd once cleared away from Mona's booth.

"Was it someone's birthday?" Mona asked. "Or should I leave a really good tip to cover this, too?"

"Nah, no birthday. But it's on the house. Like I said, it really seems like you needed this."

"Well, thank you. You're probably right." Mona rolled her eyes, laughing rather harshly. She tried the first bite of the cake and relished the heavy scent of vanilla and the sweetness on her tongue. Her stomach growled. She struggled to remember when the last time she ate was. "Thank you for this—seriously. I think I should also get...lunch, too."

Kerri didn't baulk at the fact that it was almost six p.m. and Mona was calling this meal lunch. She wrote down the order and then disappeared behind the counter once again. Mona devoured the cake, fighting off the urge to lick the paper plate for the frosting. She had eaten a corner piece, unable to tell if there had been any writing at all on the cake. It wasn't a birthday cake, but did people celebrate random Mondays? Was there an Ontario holiday she'd not been aware of? When Kerri brought out her grilled cheese sandwich, she was about to ask what the celebration had been—but Kerri was already chatting.

"Here you are," she said, sliding the food in and adding more coffee. "I don't think I've seen you here this early before."

"Early, huh?"

"Yeah, though I suppose the time is relevant. You usually come in at night, though, am I right?"

"Am I that predictable?" Mona tried to laugh off the concern as nothing much, but the observation made her feel on edge. If a random waitress could pinpoint her schedule, what did that say for everyone else? Was she sinking into a routine again, making herself vulnerable? She recalled one of the journal articles she'd read about geospatial profiling and how we almost never vary our routines. We always go to the places we know—unless something drastic happens. Like the bus detour that led her here to the diner in the first place, which she had now made into a regular routine.

"I suppose it's the bus stop. You must be getting an influx of people."

"Not too many."

Quiet spread out between them. Mona traced her hands along the side of her coffee cup. She made a mental note to go grocery shopping in a different store later in the day. She thought of all the ways to vary her schedule so she could keep coming to the diner. "It's funny," she eventually said. "I never wanted to come here, but now it's like a diner at the end of the world. I can't imagine going anywhere else."

"Well, thank you. I'm going to assume it's the food and will pass on the compliments to Roy, the short order cook who likes to believe he's a chef. But do you mind me asking…why the end of the world?"

She thought of Diogenes in his glass jar in Agora—the place where the root of the word *agoraphobia* came from. In spite of the syndrome named after him, Diogenes was a minimalist. He liked wide open spaces and being able to see everything. The diner windows became her own glass jar, where she believed she could see everything coming. "Oh, I don't know. I read so much that the world seems to have fine edges, maybe, and I've teetered too far away from my schedule when I'm here. Feels like the farthest place I'm allowed to go before my research pulls me back." Mona tore a napkin, realizing she'd said too much. The edges of her dreams were blurring from lack of sleep. "I should get some variety."

"Maybe." Kerri paused. "If you don't mind me saying, you're usually far more…engaged in what you're doing."

Mona chucked again, more bitterly than before.

"Forgive me if it's none of my business," Kerri said quickly. "I was just curious. End of the world sounds so final, you know? Sounds like the title of a horror novel."

Again, Mona laughed. But it struck a chord with her, too. This was a horror novel, wasn't it? The nightmares were becoming more real each time she went to bed. She was at the diner, not because she desperately wanted to research, but because sleeping during the daylight was hard now. But coffee was easy. Eggs and grilled cheese and now cake were easy. So was Kerri because, for a while, she had asked no hard questions. Kerri had been a presence she could count on without actually counting on her. Kerri didn't even know Mona's name, and there was so much safety in that.

But she had still noticed her. Even to strangers, Mona feared she was coming apart at the seams. She feared they could somehow see everything about her—as if coming to a diner, full of glass windows, wasn't the very point.

Mona swallowed hard and touched her cheek. A single tear had rolled down.

"Oh." Kerri reached into the diner's napkin dispensers and pulled out a couple. She left them on the table for Mona.

"Fuck." Mona dipped into French for a minute before regaining her focus. "Look, I'm sorry. You don't care about any of this. I'm just having a hard day."

"We all have shitty days. But you're wrong about one thing: I do end up caring about the people I meet, even if only incidentally."

Mona caught a glimpse of Kerri from the side of her gaze. Her dark red curls framed her square face, softening the harder edges of her jaw. Her nose was sharp but her cheekbones flat, which drew more attention to her wide and open blue eyes. Kerri couldn't have been more than twenty-six or -seven, a few years younger than Mona at most. For a brief moment, Mona thought she caught a glimpse of desire in her eyes. A flick of a gaze from Mona's face to her boots to her body. *A cruise.* It hadn't happened to her in such a long time, not since Montreal and the club scene there. Definitely not since Gabriel. Kerri's gaze, while hard and penetrating, wasn't like the men who catcalled her from the street. It wasn't violent—but it was probing. She wanted to know, for whatever reason, what was going on with Mona. And Mona was getting tired of fighting the anonymity of the city.

"I'm Mona," she said. "I think your name is Kerri, right?"

"Yeah." Kerri smiled and extended a hand. "Nice to meet you."

"You too."

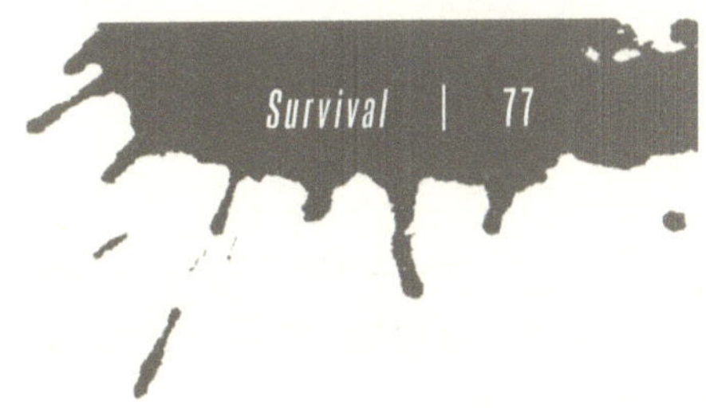

CHAPTER SEVEN

Absalom muted the alerts on his phone. Then he unmuted them to tell Sandra that he was going dark for a while, just in case she tried to reach him. She was never too insistent and tried to play her emotions off as "unnecessary twitches," but she would worry if she didn't hear from him. During those five minutes—at most—while he was looking at the screen, Becca texted him again. A string of emojis spelled out what she wanted to do. He only needed to glimpse the colours before he understood. The memory was like a bruise. His desire was transparent.

But he had to get to work. He'd already been late earlier in the week because he saw Becca just after his run. The two had met at a gas station between her place and his and broke a baby-changing station in the process. He'd barely had time to shower before showing up for his shift; Sandra chastised him for still smelling like a teenager after gym class. He didn't want to do that again, so he'd ignored Becca's flirtatious texts earlier this morning. He'd made his legs ache with how fast he ran. He thought he exhausted himself. But like a teenager, he was ready to go again.

He already regretted adding her to his phone. It was easier to delete a string of numbers, rather than a name. Even worse, Becca was a nickname. A sign of affection. Absalom was caught between wanting to block her so he wasn't tempted to leave in the goddamn middle of the day for this type of shit and sexting with her until Bill Neilson was done with his meal break, and Absalom could finally consult with him.

Absalom liked the second idea more.

He sent Becca a few suggestive texts, anticipating her responses and egging her on. When an image attachment came—unsolicited by him—his stomach roiled. *Not here, not now.* God, he wanted to toss his phone in the Otonabee River to avoid making the choice. He even considered it for a large section of time this morning while smoking after his run. But— like his cigarettes and his jogging—he would have to make peace with the need for something that was bad for him because it also led to the good. He needed his phone for work. For communication with his father and that half-brother who sometimes came around. Without a cellphone, where would he be? Without a cellphone, who would he be?

Absalom went into the bathroom at work. He opened the image. He was predictable, through and through. He used it for what he wanted and needed— then he deleted her number from his phone. Blocked it to be sure. He closed out his dating app account and uninstalled it from his phone.

His mind was clear. That feeling of relief, coupled with the conviction of purity, was enough to keep him going. Superiority over past iterations of himself was a drug in itself. Using both made him happy. He reminded himself, once again, that he wasn't hurting anymore. He was not the bad guy here. Everyone was consenting. Everyone knew what this was, even if that knowing was transient. *I am not the problem. I am not the solution. I am only a witness.* The speech was well-worn and play-acted; in six hours, the smell of drywall in his apartment, a song on the radio, and he knew he'd long for something more than convictions. He'd need a body. He'd need the primal scene to forget about what he'd seen.

"Hey, Bill?"

Bill Neilson glanced up from his desk. His thick-rimmed glasses framed his blue eyes and obscured some of the crow's feet that had started to gather. His mouth drooped slightly on his left side, revealing the only sign that Bill had had a stroke a year earlier, which made him switch from active duty to mostly desk work. The stroke had been small and inconsequential in the grand scheme of things— Bill was still fit, still healthy, and looked good for fifty-seven—but its effect radiated outward into the department. People often talked softer around Bill now, as if he'd aged ten years overnight. Bill's hard expression turned friendly when he realized Absalom was not there to patronize him but ask his opinion.

"Please sit." Bill gestured to a spot in front of his desk and pushed aside his own paperwork. "This about the string of burglaries in the student area?"

Absalom nodded. He described the latest house to be hit as a student hangout, smack in the middle of the downtown area that was ideal for university students away from home for the first time; the cheapest grocery stores, fast food places, a community centre, and laundromats were all within walking distance. The houses in this area, due to frequent turnover of tenants, also had piss-poor locks and zero security. It was a sitting duck; all the houses had been. "And yet nothing was taken. Just like the last cases. The only thing that's different here is that each and every single electronic was smashed."

"Smashed?"

"Yeah. It looks as if the perp had punched through any kind of screen he could find." Absalom withdrew a photo from the file he had with him. A computer was littered with several striated cracks. Bill glanced at it and then asked for the next one, where a laptop had been folded in half until it broke.

"Someone does not like Apple products."

"But it's not just those. He also ripped out appliances. Threw the microwave out the window. He utterly destroyed the house, but all his rage seemed to be fixated on anything that plugged in."

"That was a joke, Absalom. Don't worry."

Absalom nodded as he forced a laugh. How could he be this edgy already, considering what he'd done not fifteen minutes ago? His lip curled in disgust, something Bill didn't see as he scanned through more photos. Bill examined the image of the cords that had been ripped out of the walls and an outlet that bore a singed mark.

"Some cords were even knotted up," Absalom said, gesturing to the next photo. "It looks like maybe nautical stuff."

Bill tilted his head as he examined and then said, "No. Not nautical. Boy Scout stuff. Very basic—but how many kids are in Boy Scouts nowadays? Either way, this is strange. You think it was the same guy doing the cat stuff?"

"Yeah, but he's not a psychopath."

"Are you sure? A lot of people use electrical cord to bind someone. I saw a case in the seventies of a murder—one of the rare cases I did—where the person was bound with electrical cord and the outlets looked like this. Killer had ripped them from the wall in a frenzy. Bad case."

"No…the people are never home for this guy. So many of the calls we're getting are hard to place in a timeline because the students have been gone since April or May, one of them even gone since January, and they're only realizing now that something's amiss. If they do come while he's there, he never harms them."

"Wait. You think he's stayed in the houses when people have arrived?"

Absalom nodded. He gestured to a photo that he'd placed in the back of the file, mostly because it set his teeth on edge. Even more than the dead and eviscerated cat photo. The image was only of a coffee can in a closet. Bill raised his eyebrows, uncomprehending.

"He stayed in the closet long enough to need to go to the bathroom."

"Oh." Bill made another face, half-amused and half-disgusted. "I guess the guy doesn't like Tim Hortons coffee, either. Tastes like dust to me."

"Be serious, please." Absalom sighed. Maybe it wasn't just Becca getting under his skin. Or maybe she was a symptom of this case itself. Absalom was taking this so seriously, but he had no idea why. It wasn't like he doubted his skill as a cop. The rest of his cases this week had been easy, cut and dried, and he'd excelled at them. Made a couple of arrests and tracked a couple of stolen credit cards. But the house, with nothing stolen, and a man who stayed in a closet so long he had to piss…it bothered him. What was he trying to do? And if Bill had no concrete answer other than jokes, who were they both?

Absalom glanced at his phone. No messages from Becca. *Obviously.* But Sandra said she was coming in soon. "I'm asking you as a friend, Bill—but also as a colleague with way more experience on this force. So, please be serious or Sandra will be pissed I'm even sharing these. She gets really territorial."

Bill put up his hands in acquiescence. "Fine, fine. I do appreciate you asking a senior party like me."

"Thank you. Now have you ever seen anything like this before?"

"Pissing in coffee cans? And breaking shit? Yeah. It's called teenage rebellion."

"This person isn't young or rebellious. We would have had some graffiti or at least some mischief around the houses before or afterwards. We found nothing. Not even crank calls or egging."

"Do kids still egg? Or is it all cyberbullying now?"

"There is no cyber component. In fact, it is decidedly anti-cyber. Almost nihilistic." Absalom held up the first image of the smashed screen. "Why smash what you could sell? The computers and electronics seem to be the targets."

"So, he hates the NSA? Or rather, the Communications Security Establishment? Ugh, it sounds so much cooler in the U.S. But I can understand hating both," Bill said. "I want to smash my phone most days, especially when my wife uploads pictures of me to Facebook. But this seems extreme for someone with a bad selfie. There's more meaning and intent to it, even if it looks like chaos on the surface. So, I see the cat and I see the cords, and I think sexual homicide. But..."

"There are no bodies. Not a single one. No account of assaults near the houses, either, which is even stranger since it's a student town. One of the places was a frat house, too. Yet there's nothing."

"It's summer," Bill said. "Not that rape stops in the summer, of course, but it just means that students aren't there to be targeted. This guy must have started in season, like you say. May or April, just when the town goes ghost. If he was here before then, he was a ghost."

"Right. Yeah." Absalom sighed. Bill was telling him what he already knew. This consult was even more depressing than when he'd walked into sex crimes and asked for the records of assaults in the past three months. There had been some, of course, but they were in different areas. He'd only needed to skim the files before he put them away and walked out. Dianna

Martin, the main detective working those cases, would have been better to consult with than going in on his own. She was up to date on all the literature, all the crime stats, and motives. She wouldn't reference a 1970s case; she wouldn't crack jokes. But Dianna had once come up on his dating app, looking for a way to also not spend a night alone. Absalom didn't want those worlds to collide, any more than they already had, especially when he always wanted to swipe right.

So, what did he have then? Bad jokes. Baffling stats. Zero motivation, a backlog of unnecessary property damages, and a coffee can of piss. "I think I'm stumped," Absalom said, shame tinting his voice.

"Pass it off then." Bill dropped the photos on the desk with a casual shrug. "It's not a robbery anymore. It's something else. Property crime. Petty crimes. Mischief. Maybe even hate crimes, who knows?"

"But he broke in. So, it's—"

"So, it's either your problem, or it's not." Bill leaned back over his desk, effectively ending the conversation with his body language. "I can't help you. And you can only help yourself by solving it or giving it up. Or waiting, maybe. Some criminals are slow learners. Slow burns, just testing their limits. He'll steal something eventually, and you'll get to trace that serial number, and it'll all fall into place."

"But that's the thing—I don't want him to escalate. Escalation could mean that he hurts someone for real, rather than a stray cat."

"I thought you said you didn't think he was a psychopath."

"I don't." Absalom held his tongue. He thought about handing it over. Declaring it something else and moving on. But it bothered him. There was something hidden in these crime scenes, a clue he had not yet seen, and he wanted to know it. Just because everyone else was out of ideas when it wasn't a drug dealer, insurance scammer, student, or a psychopath didn't mean that those were the only options. It just meant it was going to be harder to find.

A long time ago, maybe even in one of the books he'd read by Kerri, a haunted house was described like a living organism. Haunting was a symptom of sickness. The house needed to be brought back into wellness through tender gestures—cleaning, removing cursed objects—or through extreme means like an exorcism, but an exorcism was like an amputation. You removed something from the house; you crippled it to save it. Absalom looked at the burglar's presence in a similar way. He was haunting them, making them ill, but he wasn't a criminal. He was... homeless. Vagrant. Lost and scared. They didn't need to amputate to solve it. They needed smaller gestures, kinder ones. He was sure of it.

And he didn't trust anyone else in this force to give those small gestures.

"I'll keep it. I have to figure it out. It's there. It's just...."

"I appreciate that. You're a good detective. But don't worry if you don't solve it. We all have cases like that."

Bill wasn't talking about the bottom drawer crime, the ones that were cold but still lingered in a cop's imagination long after was healthy. There really were no cases like that in his unit. Nothing too horrific happened here. In Scarborough, yes, there would have been back drawer cases. Cops with harrowing stories, ones that were catalogued as *Before Bernardo* and *After Bernardo*, as if his home-grown violence was a way to track time. So, Absalom had moved. He didn't want to deal with that way of keeping order. But what if he was turning some vagrant into the sun itself, so he could run after and catch him?

Absalom shrugged off the thought. Bill mirrored his shrug. He repeated his words from before as if they were a chant. "Give him time. Time is all we have now, anyway."

CHAPTER EIGHT

Conversation between Mona and Kerri unfolded in bits and pieces over coffee. Each time Kerri came by Mona's booth after their more formal introduction, she asked her about her reading, her dissertation plans, or how she was feeling. A day passed, and then another, before Mona finally confessed to what she'd been holding on to for so long.

The heat of the summer was already rolling on in thick waves. The bus stank of humans condensed to their most basic urges, coupled with dirt and rotting plant matter. Mona tried not to breathe as she headed towards the back of the bus; she only succeeded in stepping into an invisible cloud reeking of Axe Body Spray.

Time stopped and then rolled backwards. Summer became winter. Ontario became Quebec. Mona's mouth tasted of the vanilla coffee she bought on the McGill campus whenever she taught

Renaissance poetry. Then Gabriel was there, taking her by the arm. He walked her across campus; her boots squeaked on the tile floor, then rolled over the crunching of salt on the pavement. Everything was so loud, yet so silent. No one saw them on campus. No one was looking. She wanted to scream, but her breath was gone. Language was gone. At some point, when they passed the library, Damien had looked up from the front desk. He had seen them and realized what was going on.

Between that moment and the eventual standoff, Mona and Gabriel had been in an elevator together. The Francophone song was too loud in her ears, the lyrics so trivial in comparison to what she was dealing with. Gabriel's fingers dug into her skin. She would bruise. She would have the pinpoint marks on her arms for a week and a half. Purple to green to yellow. Her nostrils flared. The gun pressed to her ribs. The elevator made Gabriel's scent so much stronger. Axe masked the body odour, astringent with inchoate fear. She remembered thinking, *"Why on earth is he afraid? He's the one with the gun!"* before the elevator dinged open.

The bus dinged. Last stop.

Mona swallowed. Her throat constricted—but she no longer tasted vanilla. The heat of summer beaded sweat on her forehead. There were trees, green trees, and the diner sign called to her even in broad daylight. She was in Peterborough, Ontario. She was not in Montreal. She scanned the bus, though she knew deep down that Gabriel would not be there.

Coupled with her lack of sleep, Mona nearly dropped to her knees as soon as she stepped off. In gratitude, in exhaustion—both, everything, nothing. She was awash with emotions and frantic energy, as if she had to relive all the moments between now and her interaction with Gabriel almost three years ago in a single blink. Her heart raced, eyes blurred. But she was determined, steadfast. If she could make her way into the diner, then she was safe. She counted each step like a children's game, going so slow and yet on fast-forward. She thought of the first moving picture show, the one with a jockey on a horse as it ran. The long legs were bulky, jagged. Running and running on an endless loop, always in silence.

When she made her way to the booth, she let out a breath. The primary colours in the menu rooted her in place. When Kerri came by with coffee, Mona shuddered.

"What's wrong?"

"I think I'm having a flashback." Mona placed her palm flat on the table to keep herself anchored here. "I keep dipping in and out."

Kerri set down the coffeepot she held. She hunched down so she could be eye level with Mona. Mona met Kerri's face, recognizing something she hadn't seen before. Desire, yes, but also understanding. Sympathy that couldn't be found on a greeting card. Kerri's thin lips were firm, hard.

"Tell me the day today," she said.

"Monday."

"Tell me the *date*," she followed up, more insistent.

"Uh." Mona blinked. She thought February 21 but soon corrected herself. "June 21. Right?"

"Right. The longest day of the year."

Mona let out a low laugh. "Is that comforting? I don't know anymore."

"It can be. I think you're fine." Kerri rose back to a standing position. She picked up her coffeepot but fidgeted her thumb around the edge. "Do you want to tell me what you thought was happening, though?"

Mona blinked once, then again. "Nothing. I mean, nothing that was real."

"Well, you can still tell me. I can listen." Kerri gestured to the booth, a silent question. Mona nodded. As Kerri slid in, she added, "You'd be surprised at what my imagination can handle. I write horror novels for a living. You can't really scare me."

"You do?"

"Well, perhaps for a living is stretching it. I write them. Some people read them."

"I should read them." Mona noticed the plural in her mouth. *Them*. More than one novel. More than one idea of the horrifying. Kerri didn't answer. She sat across and waited, her face betraying no emotion other than utter presence.

"I...I suppose it's all like Kitty Genovese. I keep having dreams where I'm wandering alone in a city and a man attacks me. People see him do it, but no one stops it. I keep waking up with a pain in my chest, like I'm being suffocated. I know Kitty Genovese was stabbed, not strangled, but it's the easiest thing to compare it to. I keep feeling like I'm Kitty Genovese, and no one will save me in a city full of people. That's what I was thinking about when I came in."

Mona wondered if she should just stop obfuscating and confess the reality rather than the metaphor. *Gabriel was a student, he attacked me, and in spite of my ex-boyfriend, Damien, seeing it all and calling the police, I still feel like no one saw at all. I still feel like I'm alone in that elevator and the door will never open on the other side.* Instead, Mona translated her confession into French. She remained silent.

Kerri shifted, leaning forward. "In your dreams, can you move?"

"What do you mean? Like can I run away in the dream?"

"Is there any point in the dream where you know it's not real? That you're dreaming? And you try to wake up?"

Mona nodded with her mouth slightly agape.

The dream she'd had last night had been like all the others—except that, when she remembered Kitty wasn't strangled and that none of this was real, she had tried to wake herself up, only to feel nailed to the bed. She was aware she was dreaming, and the veil that separated her consciousness from being fully conscious had been punctured but not swept away. She wanted to move but couldn't. She wanted to stop feeling strangled, but she had to endure. When she explained this to Kerri, she nodded.

"It sounds like a Night Mare."

"Well, yeah. I've been having nightmares forever, though. This is far worse than anything I've had in the past."

"No, a Night *Mare*," Kerri said, giving space between the words. "It's where the term nightmare originated, but it's also a separate condition with its own kind of folklore. We'd call it sleep paralysis now. It's when you want to wake up, but you're literally paralyzed to do it. In other times, before sleep labs and psychological journals and WebMD, people said there were mares that sat on your chest and held you down whenever you were having a particularly bad dream. Mares were like little tiny demons—all your bad thoughts and feelings personified and made man-ifest. Sometimes, it feels like drowning, rather than a pressure or constriction. Other times, it just feels like there's a demon watching you, but you can't find him or do anything about it."

"What...about the flashbacks during the day?"

"These types of dreams often happen after extreme exhaustion. Your REM cycles go wonky, make you sleep deeper and stronger, and be unable to wake up. And because the sleep itself is traumatic, it often means you're still exhausted. Kind of like your body shooting itself in the foot. So, it's my guess that the dream world will bleed into the waking one, especially if you're prone to nightmares."

Mona looked down. Her hand was still pressed against the table, fingers awkwardly splayed, to ground herself here. She removed it and folded it in her lap. Her face was hot. Now that she had been so thoroughly seen, she wanted to go back to invisibility.

"Am I speaking out of turn?"

"No," Mona said. "How do you even know this?"

"It may have happened to me a handful of times, especially when I was a kid. I researched it recently for a story."

"Oh. That's...probably a good way to deal with it."

"Write what you know, I guess." Kerri rolled her eyes at the platitude. Mona always hated that adage, but she supposed she was being a hypocrite. Her latest research project had been a thinly veiled confession. At least Kerri knew she was dressing up her sleep disorder, however temporary, in monster's clothing. She seemed to be doing a pretty good job of it.

When pressed for details about her publication, Kerri pulled out her phone and did a quick Google search. She extended her device across the table, displaying an author's page on Goodreads for K.T. Stellar. The black and white photo was of a younger-looking Kerri with straight hair and a dark shade of lipstick. If she had not already memorized the sharp angular face and flat cheekbones, Mona wouldn't have glanced twice at the image.

"Look at the third book down," Kerri instructed.

The third book was titled *The Wendigo Forest*. The cover had three kids, all girls with tomboy leanings, sitting around a campfire with a shadowy figure lurking to the side. The description made Mona's skin tighten.

Laney, Kara, and Dionne go into the woods for their Girl Guides' retreat. After a near-drowning in the river, Dionne is rushed to the hospital while the other two girls finish their camping trip. While under the doctor's care, Dionne's dreams start to bleed into her reality. A small creature with red eyes sits on her chest and tells her she's still underwater, and the only way to save herself and her friends is to get The Old Lady of the Woods to destroy the Wendigo before he comes out of hibernation.

"It's basically a story about how nightmares

blur to real life," Kerri said, "and how nightmares tend to affect those who are liminal in some way. Do you know what liminal means?"

"Those who are in between."

"Right. Perfect. In this case, each girl is on the cusp of puberty and therefore needs to complete a ritual of rebirth before they become women and can leave the no-man's location of childhood behind. Until they do, they will be underwater, trapped, or stuck in some way. I suppose I was trying to figure out why I had nightmares as a kid. I made up this entire mythology about it before I realized that other people felt the same thing. I thought I was alone in my sleep paralysis, so I tried to make these three girls just like me. As it turned out, though, I was never alone." Kerri smiled. "Research is a good thing."

"You know, I was once of the same mind." Mona smiled weakly before handing the phone back to Kerri. "How do the girls stop being liminal? How do they beat it?"

"They bleed." Kerri laughed. "But the blood attracts the Wendigo, who wants to eat them alive. You know, it's kind of like *Are You There God? It's Me, Margaret.* but in a horror landscape. And at the end, Lana figures out a way to bleed that's not menstruation, so she survives. But I don't think that should be the takeaway here. You don't need to bleed for your nightmares to go away."

"I'm about willing to try anything at this point."

"Well, I think the first step is to realize you're not alone. People have been having bad dreams since the dawn of time. It's so common it already has a mythology to it."

"You mean the demon mare that sits on my chest? Or leaves bruises on my arms?"

"Yes, but there are other creatures, too. Do you have Netflix? Because there's a good documentary on sleep paralysis that describes all these creatures and myths in detail. There are a lot of testimonials from others, too, so you won't need to feel alone. It's a really good watch."

"I do. But I don't know if I should watch it. Though I suppose it can't be worse than the dream itself."

"It's not. Trust me on that." Kerri paused, as if she wasn't sure she wanted to reveal her next line. When she spoke, her voice was different. It was no longer the homey-twang she used to greet customers or even the sympathetic friend tone she used when asking the date. It was a sturdy kind, with the heavy hint of an accent over certain vowels. "If things ever get too difficult, like you're on a bus again and think you're dreaming, don't fight it. Just let the fear wash over you. It's what I do when I write. Things can seem utterly terrifying, but our mind is what makes it so. Just wait. Just breathe. Let the fear wash over you.

Then the paralysis melts away, too."

"That's…good advice. I know it is. It's just hard to hear."

"What if I watched the movie with you? Maybe it would be easier that way."

Mona considered it. Kerri's voice had returned to a neutral tone. A personal voice, but not the private one she apparently used when she spoke to herself. Mona wanted to be around to hear that other, secret tone again. Even if it was chatter, even if it was only through the paper-thin walls of her apartment as she wrote spooky stories. Mona wanted to trace the vowel sounds with her tongue, coaxing them out of Kerri's mouth. Mona wanted moans rather than screams. She thought of Kerri's gaze on her, the cruise that covered her so thoroughly it may as well have been Kerri's hands. She wanted Kerri next to her on a couch, comforting her if the red of the Netflix screen suddenly reminded her too much of Damien's blood.

"Okay." Mona nodded. "I'd be willing to try the movie with you there, too."

"At your place?" Though a question, Kerri left no ambiguity in her tone. They would be going to Mona's.

"Sure. It's Monday now. Are you free…?"

"Saturday."

Again, not a question. It was the only answer. "Saturday."

"Perfect." Kerri suggested a time, Mona gave her the address to her building, and they exchanged numbers. Kerri rose with her coffeepot in hand, a smile on her lips. "It's a date."

CHAPTER NINE

So, tell me about your latest book." Stuart Browne held the microphone close to Kerri's mouth without being invasive. As he leaned close to listen, his cane shifted to the side of his chair and made the flames that ran up and down it glow orange.

"Well, *Dante Under Ice* is a dystopian horror novel, one of the first I've written of that kind. It's about Mickey Alan and his wife, Starla, who are forced to confront a pack of creatures that live under the ice. When it starts to melt in a too-early spring thaw, the creatures are released. They flee into the woods where their problems only begin to grow, especially as they realize they're headed into a parallel version of Dante's underworld."

"Fascinating. I think that's a good point to stop the summary since we're attentive to spoilers here." Stuart laughed lightheartedly.

In the briefing material for the interview, several things had been outlined for Kerri—one, of course, being no spoilers, either for her work or other media. Some things that were popular or old, like Dante's original text, could be spoiled, but it was best to leave some gaps that the listeners could then fill in for themselves. The interview would not be filmed, which made Kerri feel instantly at ease, and let her get away with no makeup for the day. Stuart's show about Canadian speculative fiction called *Can 9 From Outer Space* was primarily run out of the local university radio station. After the first broadcast over Peterborough airwaves, the interview would then be condensed into a podcast for his website, which had a minor—but dedicated—following. Stuart was an ebullient presence, one that made her feel comfortable right away with his casual laughs and attentive listening. She wasn't shocked that his podcast did well to those outside Canada since his enthusiasm for his material, even the most obscure, was evident and engaging to even an outsider.

"But do tell me," he went on, "why have you avoided dystopian up until this time?"

With a smile, Kerri went into her still rough explanation about real-life horror versus fantasy horror that she'd shared with Roy and others at the diner. Ever since the impromptu release party, Roy had been telling her that her insights were far more than standard "writer's nonsense"; she was actually making interesting points, and they were wasted on him.

Kerri had been so secretive for so long about this part of her life, it was a strange concept to come out of her shell like this. She'd contacted her publisher's PR person about doing more interviews or even promo posts somewhere, and *Can 9 From Outer Space* had been mentioned off the bat. When she emailed Stuart, he was more than willing to listen. He'd actually reviewed one of her earlier books on his show, and a quote from that had been put on the back of *Dante Under Ice*.

"Very cool," he said. "I love the differences between fantasy and the real. We want monsters to be fake since not only does it make the horror easier to handle, it also allows for people who are often represented as monstrous to have some humanity."

"Right. I totally see that all the time. Mental illness—especially in horror fiction—is its own plot twist. And I hate that."

"Exactly. Disability too!" Stuart held up his cane and tapped it against the microphone. "Minorities in your work are not show pieces but fully fleshed-out characters with a different lens to view and understand the world."

"Yes! Starla is actually bisexual in the story—which I don't think is a spoiler, right?"

Stuart laughed. "No, no. Identity is not a big reveal."

"Precisely, so she's bisexual, and that actually

helps her to understand the Dante influence since she read it in college with an ex-girlfriend, who she ends up referring to as 'my Beatrice' during the novel, since she was the one that got away who she feels some regret towards. There's more to it, but you know, that's the idea."

"Yes, that's a good place to stop. I feel like that gives the listeners a good sense of *Dante Under Ice*. It's not just in that novel where you masterfully handle different identities. It's been a fairly standard thing in your work, especially the first book."

Kerri closed her eyes, wincing. "Oh, that was not a good book. I don't want to give spoilers, but it only sold a few copies anyway and is now long out of print. But it's exactly where I learned my lessons about monsters. It was a mystery story, and I wanted to give the end a believable twist. Something that was real, quotidian—but it only made the twist so obvious. And boring. Readers want ice giants, strange Wendigo creatures, and haunted houses because it stretches their imagination. It makes them think. The murderer next door, though? That's real. That's boring because it has happened before. Even in Canada."

"Well, I liked it. But I understand the hesitancy, so let's move on. And talk about some haunted houses."

Kerri let out a breath, utterly relieved. She could easily talk about her research into the paranormal community and Canada's legacy of haunted places. She could even bring up the Czech lore her stepmother had told her about ghosts without giving too much of herself, or her story, away. Stuart was more than willing to keep talking, asking interesting questions, and then situating her answers into a larger dialogue about Canadian speculative fiction and Southern Ontario Gothic. Kerri was amazed, quite frankly, because she had never considered her work to be part of anything other than a pulp mill. She was a next-generation Lovecraft or Poe, selling stories on the down low, and maybe hoping for recognition one day. The thought that even minor recognition from an indie podcast could happen now made her happy—as much as it scared her.

In spite of Stuart's radio station being a twenty-minute bus ride from her apartment in Peterborough, she had never met him before. She had never met anyone from the spec fic community, ever. The fact that Stuart was a leading figure in the small, tight-knit scene and queer like her (his husband, Raphael, had driven Stuart to the radio station) and that he actively liked and promoted her books meant she could envision herself as part of something larger than herself. She'd never been part of any community before. Not really—not even the LGBT community. Knowing she was gay and acting on it was just like her writing career. Something she did, she enjoyed, and didn't stress about—but something she did alone. Kerri had girlfriends, flings, and hookups, but it wasn't a community. She'd written stories, novels, and spooky scenarios, but it wasn't a career.

Now both of these things were changing. Maybe with Stuart, she could be part of the Southern Ontario Gothic or whatever he called it—and with Mona, she could have something more, too. Their date was tonight, after the interview and "spooky photoshoot" that Stuart wanted to take to add to his website. Kerri tried not to think about it too much. She liked Mona too much to worry about how things would go. Part of the reason she scheduled the interview with Stuart for this afternoon was to keep her mind off it.

She focused more intently on Stuart and his cherubic face, which seemed to light up with every detail Kerri provided. After a handful of questions about her queer literary heroes where she had ranted for fifteen minutes about how she adored Shirley Jackson and Flannery O'Connor—queer or not—Kerri forgot she was being interviewed. It was like talking to a friend.

And she was happy she came.

"You know what all this reminds me of?" Kerri said, after she and Stuart had laughed at a random Stephen King reference. "When I was a kid, my brother, Lee, and I would race each other up the stairs in our basement. Really common, right? We all think hands are going to grab us. But the moment we saw *Home Alone*—quite late in our lives, mind you—and Kevin was afraid of his furnace, we were utterly petrified. We had a furnace. It was something to be afraid of? We better be afraid. The moment the monster became a real object, we didn't want to go into the basement. The moment it was just us being silly and running, we were good."

"And yet another reason the fantasy horror is better than the reality!" Stuart said. "Ah, this has been great, K.T. One last question before we finish up."

"Of course," Kerri said, her voice feeling strained. Last questions were always doozies. She didn't want to be caught off-guard, especially after having such a good time. When Stuart only asked about what monster or evil villain she'd like to live as for a day, though, Kerri let out a low breath.

"That's easy: Evil-Lyn from *Masters of the Universe*."

Stuart let out a booming laugh. The two of them hummed the theme song from the 1980s TV show, before Stuart wrapped up the interview with standard details, a shoutout to some people from his Patreon account, and then a sign-off. As soon as he shut off the mic, Kerri grinned uneasily.

"That was okay, right?"

"Oh, my goodness, yes!" Stuart said. "And worth the nearly six years it's taken me to get you in the chair."

Before Kerri could make up another excuse, Stuart used his cane to anchor himself as he stood. "I think it's time for photos now, don't you think? I'm pretty sure Raph just pulled up."

Kerri could already hear *The Monster Mash* booming out of Raphael's car. From here, Stuart explained that he'd most likely take them to an abandoned building—or a graveyard—to have the right amount of "spooky" for the website. There was a quota to meet, she understood. A totally campy quota—but if this was what it was like to be a part of something, Kerri wanted every last cliché, fake cobweb, corny song, and moody, brooding poses.

It was so much better than the alternative.

⊱⊱⊱⊱⊰

When the photo shoot was complete, it was nearly five. Kerri had plans to meet with Mona at seven, which left a very small window for Kerri to get ready. Raphael had offered to drive Kerri home, while blasting *Thriller* by Michael Jackson, of course; though Kerri took him up on the offer, she directed him to the strip mall around the corner from her apartment building. She claimed it was to get some wine for her date tonight, but her heart was visibly calmed when Raphael's car was gone by the time she emerged from the liquor store.

A pang of guilt rushed over her. In spite of the good time she had, she was still treating Stuart and Raphael like any other strangers. What happened to her hopes of community? Of brotherhood? Stuart and Raphael were only a couple years older than her, so they really were like brothers in some way. They shared a generation. A culture. A pool of references that—like her *Home Alone* association with Lee—she'd come to rather late in life, but that still made them all crack up every five minutes with another joke. They should have been the safest people to share her life with, yet she put up a roadblock.

It's not your life, she chastised herself. *It's your apartment. And that's always a smart thing to keep secret.*

Whatever anxiety remained was soon displaced when she entered her front foyer and found a stack of letters in her mailbox. Two bore her full name—Kerrilyn-Rose Reznik—while the other had her casual moniker of Kerri in the address label. The two with the full name were from her father.

She tried to remember the last time she wrote him. Was it two or four letters ago? The numbers mattered; she had long ago come up with a mathematical formula to decipher whether it was appropriate to write him back. He would always write her more than she would ever want to write him, but there was a certain threshold where his letters went from being benign to belligerent and cryptic if she didn't write for a certain period of time. In her one-bedroom apartment, she checked her desk drawer. Including the two most recent ones, she was now at six letters from her father.

"Shit."

She was over the limit. The most recent ones from her father were thicker, too—meaning he'd gone on for a couple of pages, meaning that he was slipping into his cryptic ramblings. Kerri sighed. She would have to write her father tomorrow, which meant she'd have to read what he wrote, too. She usually liked to drink whiskey while doing it all at once, then burn them in a trash can, and then write her one letter back. It wasn't the greatest system, but it kept her sane.

And safe.

She glanced at the other letters in her drawer. The one from the diner still bothered her. It had been addressed to her (Kerri Reznik), with no return address, and it only contained a newspaper story from Montreal. The clipping had been in French, but Kerri knew enough to translate it. A technology company's CEO had kept microphones and cameras all around the office, including a bathroom. The article was about the investigation (all started when someone phoned in a bomb threat that turned out to be fake) and subsequent lawsuits the women at the tech company were filing for sexual misconduct. No other useful information was given due to privacy concerns—and due to lack of completion. The article had seemed done, but it was missing a bottom paragraph. When she'd fed the information into Google, the final paragraph wasn't revealing in any way. The back of the newspaper clipping had been about sales tax, and that article had fit fully into the space permitted. Perhaps that had been the intended message—why, she had no idea—but it still didn't sit right with her.

Who had done this, too, was another problem she didn't know how to approach.

Several ideas came to her at once. Could her father have found her work address? And if he had, did that mean he was sending people to deliver shit to her? What about a customer who stared at her too long? Had he known her father and his circle of friends? Was he going to finish what he never did? Anxiety clenched at her stomach. Her fingertips felt like ice. All interactions she'd had in the past two weeks came back to her; all became suspicious. She closed her eyes and breathed heavily.

Let the fear wash over you. She repeated it once. Twice. She waited until her heart rate returned to normal. *It's been a shitty day,* she reminded herself. Any day hearing from her father was shitty.

She drew her attention to the two new letters she'd received. One was from Ashley Mellon—a name that instantly put a smile on her face. Her old editor—

and one of her first girlfriends. The two had met when she was assigned Kerri's first novel and quickly fell into long phone conversations about semicolons that turned into even longer coffee chats once a week when she drove up from Kingston. By the time the book tanked and the publisher folded a year later, their relationship had fizzled out—but a friendship remained. Ashley's brother had owned the press, and—according to the letter which Kerri now read voraciously—had quickly moved on to something else after his first business empire failed.

He actually owns a Tim Hortons franchise now, she wrote. *Which can be a bit of a horror show at times, so I guess he's finally found his calling, or whatever. But I digress—I'm writing you like we're in a time before the internet because I received mail for you a couple weeks ago. Weird, right? The press has been dead for years. But apparently, someone is still reading that first book, and because Michael never closed out his PO box, I got your lovely fan letter from him the last time I saw him. So, enjoy your adoring fan, however belated their love may be.*

Kerri ripped open the enclosed envelope with shaking fingers. Any other author would have been excited, but Kerri only felt as if her skin had been pulled too tight. She swallowed and tasted a familiar patina of blood, as if her mouth had been made into a synaesthesic memory. Inside were several pages from her first novel, along with the front and back cover. Maybe someone just wanted her signature, she considered, though it would have been odd to rip apart a book to get it signed. When she flipped through the novel pages, she realized many of them had been marked up. Whole sections and words were blacked out. She held the pages out in front of her, trying to focus on the centre as if it was a magic eye painting. Then she realized it spelled her name. Not K.T. Stellar—but Kerrilyn-Rose Reznik. The only words that remained were her own identity, as if it had been hidden there all along, and it took some strange fan to carve out who she really was.

But what was the point of that? What was the point in mailing the publisher—now dead—to show the author a cypher of her name? What did that *do*? She tore the pages in half and dumped them in her garbage. This was dumb. Stupid. She added Ashley's letter, as well, already regretting opening it. And why did she even bother to keep the tech company article, too? She didn't need to read about any more pervs. She was in the process of adding it to the refuse pile when she saw the back cover of her book. There was no photo, but in its place were two large X's carved into the paper. *As if...as if...someone was trying to cross me out.*

Kerri shuddered. She looked at her father's letters with hate in her eyes. Her rage boiled over.

She wished he was dead. She thought it so hard she wondered if he felt it like a wound in his skin—and hoped he did. Though her hatred was not an unfamiliar feeling, she'd long since thought she'd put it to bed. She based her psychopath character in that first book on him, after all. The murderer next door. She'd killed his proxy character at the end—in self-defense, obviously, lest her leading protagonist seem to enjoy it too much—and then she thought she'd walked away from her intense feelings. She had her own resolution in fiction, where instead of her father going to prison for murdering her stepmother, he actually paid for it with his life. It was so much better than the alternative. So much better than his actual bullshit incarceration where he could still send her letter after letter after letter to beg for forgiveness or absolution. He didn't get that. No one ever did.

Kerri tossed his letters inside the trash without a second thought. She tied the bag and took it directly to her garbage, shoving it down the chute with delight. She was breathing hard, still shaking when she returned to her apartment.

She caught sight of the framed photo on her desk. She and Lee were sixteen years old. They posed on the front step of their grandmother's house, thin smiles on their faces, and wearing clothing that was oversized for both of them. They'd just come back from watching a movie at a mall, a normal activity for most sixteen-year-olds, but something that still felt like a huge indulgence for them after a decade of homeschooling and a media ban that their father had put in place. For years after his incarceration, it seemed that all she and Lee did was watch movies. And listen to music. And talk about their time together, in hushed voices. Kerri remembered the day the photo was taken well—her goth look was still new then, still something she was testing out—and while she'd been happy with their newfound freedom, Lee still had a hard time. If she looked close enough, she could see the lingering shadows in his visions, the darker things he still hadn't made his own peace with yet. Kerri wanted to fall into the memory of that day, of a time with Lee where their hatred of their father bonded them together rather than pulled them apart, but she couldn't.

She had a date to get ready for. As she changed and did her makeup, she thought of Stuart's laugh and Raphael's obsession with oldies. The cake Roy had bought for her and the bottle of wine she and Mona would share. Even Ashley's message had been a nice reprieve, if she didn't read all of it. Her day had not been shitty. Her life had not been shitty.

Everything was so much better now than the alternative.

CHAPTER TEN

Mona woke to an email from Dr. Conlin. She combed her hand through her hair, tugging a bit too forcefully as she did. The subject heading would have been benign from anyone else— Project Update—but Mona heard it in his voice. She regretted getting email alerts on her phone. It meant she had to answer it now because it was *there*, and the unknown quotient of it would make her mind race with what-ifs while her stomach acid roiled. Though she had set her alarm to give her enough time to get ready for her date with Kerri before she headed down for a nap, she shut it off when she got the email, and now, time was not her concern.

So, when her buzzer sounded, and Mona was still in wrinkled clothing and her hair was askew from her stressed-induced tugs, she should not have been surprised. She'd chosen to look at the email rather than get ready. She'd chosen her neurosis over her personal life, and really, how was that any different than any other day? Mona thought tonight was going to be special; it was why she'd wanted to have a nap, so she could actually be alert for the movie and Kerri. How did men still get in the way, even when she dated women? Mona thought of her mother, her initial coming out, and the bastardized French terms they'd fought over. There was no "queer" in French; it was *homosexuale, lesbienne,* or *bisexuele.* But Mona had wanted to present her life choices to her mother as distinct choices, not just as a desire for women and men, but something holistic, a way of life. Instead, her mother could only grasp the French and reminded Mona that she was pretty. *Even if you don't want men, they will still look at you. Les hommes seront toujours là. Men will always be there.*

The buzzer sounded again.

Mona swallowed hard as she rose from her desk. She avoided catching her gaze in her mirrors, not wanting to confront her red cheeks and shame.

"Hello?"

"Hey. It's Kerri."

"I'm sorry. I'll let you in, but can I have two minutes? Time got away from me."

"Of course."

Mona pushed the buzzer to let Kerri inside but hoped that she'd take more than ten minutes to get up the stairs to her apartment. Mona darted around her place, changing clothing, brushing her hair, and adding lipstick really quick so she didn't seem washed out. She was in the middle of trying to disguise how many dirty dishes she had in her sink when there was a knock at the door.

"Uh. I will—"

"I can go for a walk around the block, if need be," Kerri said from behind the door. "Or we can reschedule."

"No, no. This is happening."

Mona wiped her hands on a tea towel before walking to the door. She opened it right away, without looking through the peephole. It was only after the door was open that she realized she hadn't done that in over six months. She always checked, even when she knew who was behind because it might be more than just them. Her hands shook—but then steadied as she took in Kerri.

Without her diner uniform and nametag, she stood out more than before. Her red hair was brighter and flecked with natural bronze highlights, her features sharper. Her lips were painted in a dark red shade, one that matched the burgundy top she had on. She wore jeans that hugged her hips, making Mona feel better that she'd only slipped on jeans and a V-neck black shirt herself.

"I brought wine." Kerri held up a bottle by the neck. "If that helps at all?"

"Yes, it definitely does. Especially after the email I just got."

After pouring two glasses and sipping during small talk around Mona's kitchen island, Kerri finally took the bait. "So, tell me about your email."

Mona ran a hand through her hair again. She bit her lip as she gave a dry laugh. "My supervisor wants me to run a battery of experiments for him. Not out of the question, honestly. I've been his RA for some time, usually just inputting the data he's already given me. It just feels strange that he'd email me on a Saturday about this."

"Some academics have no work-life balance. Or so I've heard."

"Yeah, I know. I shouldn't even be checking email today, either. I wish I didn't. The whole thing just feels strange."

"The experiments… Are they on human or animal subjects?"

"Human." Mona took a sip of her wine. She watched its legs go down the side of the glass. "It's all aboveboard stuff. The Ethics committee has approved it. Dr. Conlin and another academic have already done this kind of experiment before, but they want to run it again. So, he needs people to run it, and he's chosen me and his other RAs for this round. It's…a compliment. He likes my work. And this is not like Milgram shocking people. You know that guy?"

Kerri nodded.

"Figured you would. What else do you research for your stories?" Mona tried to make the remark sound flirtatious, but it sounded nervous. She took another drink, hoping to loosen up and not be so upset over this.

"So, is it the human subjects that bother you or the fact that you have to run the experiment on human subjects?"

"Yes. Both." Mona shrugged. "He's...also been giving me the creeps for the past little while."

"The creeps?"

"Rumours in the department. Nothing bad has happened."

"Rumours always come from somewhere, though."

Mona nodded. She wanted Kerri to go on, to explain the folkloric history of office gossip in the same way she'd done for nightmares, but she was silent. And Mona felt like she'd revealed too much, especially when no actual danger had presented itself. Only the memory, an echo of danger. "It's fine. I mean...I'm in the process of changing supervisors, but I have to wait until someone's free. So for now, I guess I'm stuck running an ownership experiment."

"Ownership?"

"Yeah. Creepy, right?" With another sip of her wine, she explained the basics of Dr. Roger Conlin's work. "It's what I've been reading in those journals. I even had to write a quasi-reasonable dissertation proposal on the same topic—one that I'll never do anyway because I'm going to jump ship to a new supervisor in a couple months. But I don't want him to know, so…I guess I'm giving up my afternoon naps for experiments."

"That sucks," Kerri said. "But it sounds like you have an exit plan."

"I do. I try to not take on work unless I know how to finish it, you know?"

"I do that with stories," Kerri said with a smile. "And with places, too. Like when I was wandering around your building, I found the fire escape. I felt better when I did. Not that I think this is a bad place to be or that I need an exit strategy, but it's a habit."

A pang of recognition struck Mona. She wanted to show Kerri the baseball bat under her bed, the pepper spray in her purse, and the books on her shelves about stalking and sexual assault. After being caught off-guard once, it wasn't going to happen again. If men were going to get in the way, she was going to find her own way out. Kerri seemed to understand this hard-earned reflex, at least on the surface, and Mona desperately wanted to ask what she was afraid of. Instead, she replaced her curiosity with wine.

"So, if you know the research as well as you can," Kerri asked, "and it's been approved by an ethics board, then what about the study he's running is strange?"

"Just a feeling," Mona said. "Which I know is oh so academic."

"Just let it wash over you, remember? Read the email again. Don't fight the fear. And maybe you'll figure out why it scared you."

"Right now?"

"Why not? May as well."

After a second, Mona picked up her phone. She went back to the student inbox and braced herself. She took two deep breaths before reading the email again. Her anxiety seemed to pin her in place, like sleep paralysis, before she finally felt nothing. *Void.* It wasn't good or bad but a fog that made things unclear. Then she saw it in the email for what it was: a series of sentences that were all oriented towards the same goal: getting her on board with his study and making sure that certain gaps were filled in when finding subjects.

"*Special attention should be paid to twins,*" Mona read aloud. "That's it. It's like he's gathering—collecting, almost—a very specific type of person for his experiments. Makes it feel as if they're no more than meat. *Special attention.* Feels gross."

"I'll give you that. A bit Mengele." Kerri sipped her drink. "Why twins, do you think?"

"Perhaps he thinks, since twins share so many

things like DNA or a birthdate, they'll have a different relationship to owning something. I have no idea sometimes. So many of these studies seem to take a platitude or an assumption and find ways to prove it." Mona furrowed her brow. "Where am I even supposed to find twins for his experiment? I don't know any. I can't just put that on a flier for his work, can I? It seems creepy. Besides, don't they run in families?"

"They also tend to happen in older mothers. It's like your ovaries are going through a going-out-of-business sale, and they release multiple eggs more than once. That's for fraternal twins, though. Not identical. So, maybe it won't matter so much."

Mona scanned the email, trying to see if there were any further instructions. "It seems like he wants both."

"I'm a twin then," Kerri said. "Fraternal. I have a brother. Our mother was in her forties when she had us."

Mona tilted her head as she examined Kerri, trying to put her features on a male equivalent. It was difficult, though; Kerri was small to begin with, and right now, she was utterly beautiful. Mona didn't want to imagine that someone else sharing the same sharp nose and red hair could be walking around, especially as a man.

"That's interesting," Mona said. "I. Uh...."

"You're thinking about research. And me in

that research."

Mona looked down, nodding mutely.

"I brought it up, so it's okay to ask me."

Mona remained mute, still unsure what to exactly ask about. Though Dr. Conlin had attached the experiment protocol, she hadn't read the attachment, too focused on the way his words got under her skin. She thought of the reports he'd published and all their linguistic ambivalences. Nothing quite worked. "Perhaps this is because I speak French and English, but I think when he's talking about ownership, especially in relation to people, he means something else. There's a misfire or mistranslation going on."

"Oh?" Kerri asked, seeming genuinely interested. "I'm bilingual a bit, too, so I may understand."

Even more questions bloomed to the top of Mona's consciousness. Kerri must have seen the interest in her eyes because she instantly provided, "Czech. Now go on."

"Well, ownership is something that's part of capitalism. We critique it, but it's hard to escape in our current situation. Studying that kind of ownership would be like studying economics—but that's not always the case. In some of these studies, what the people are talking about is belonging, not ownership. They're similar. But one we can't escape, while another we don't always want to escape."

"We want to belong to someone?"

"Yes, I think so." Mona fought the urge to run a hand through her hair. She suddenly felt far too vulnerable. The wine made her skin flush, and the lack of sleep made her woozy. But each time she caught Kerri's gaze, she felt anchored in place.

After a moment of consideration, Kerri nodded. "I can see that. Belonging is like community. And twins would be an even better asset when studying belonging like that because for a time, I do think it's like you belong to someone else. I mean, Lee was around for my entire life. We shared so much and have so many inside jokes. Even though he looks nothing like me, we used to pretend to be mirrors of each other and mimic the other's movement. We'd practice together and then freak people out by mirroring their motions at the same time." Kerri smiled, but it soon disappeared as if she remembered something painful. Mona couldn't help but notice the shifting past tense in Kerri's words. Her pained expression was gone in a moment as she brushed it away with a strand of her hair. "I heard somewhere that your siblings are always the ones who know you the best. Not only do they see you grow up, but they witness the zaniness of life alongside you. Twins even more so because there's only a minute between us."

"I'm an only child," Mona said. "But what you're saying makes a lot of sense. Are you close with your family, other than Lee?"

Though Kerri smiled, it seemed forced and painful. "No. Not anymore. My mother actually had some pretty severe complications when she gave birth to us. She died not long after."

"I'm sorry. I shouldn't have asked."

"I offered."

Kerri's body was rigid, strong. Mona wondered if she was reciting the same piece of advice that she had once given her inside her own mind. *Let the fear wash over you.* Mona took a breath and set her phone down, powering it off in the process. The moment the screen went black and revealed her own face, she felt instantly better.

"I'm sorry. I feel as if I've completely stolen this moment. Let's start again, okay? I should have shut off my phone two hours ago and not had this happen. I shouldn't have let my emails go to my phone."

"While I agree that having no emails on your phone is good…you were fine. This was interesting." Kerri smiled before she gestured to the door. "But if you want, I can go back down and buzz in again. You know, to truly start over."

Mona loved the idea. It was so simple—just pretend. Start over like nothing had ever happened and no bad blood had been stirred. It was like moving to Ontario and wiping all her social media clean. For a while, Mona could become anything she wanted. She had still become a neurotic with nightmares, working for a possible lecherous man who fetishized twins, as if her life was going to repeat itself endlessly—but she had at least done the action of trying again. Maybe her relationship with Kerri could get off on the right foot, if they tried together.

Kerri set down her wine and walked out of the apartment. Mona waited in her place, adjusting her hair and adding another touch-up of lipstick, before the buzzer sounded again.

"Hello?"

"Hi, it's Kerri. I think we have a date."

"Yeah, we do. Come on up."

CHAPTER ELEVEN

After a couple more drinks and light appetizers, Mona had a confession. "I have no TV, so we'll have to watch *The Nightmare* on my laptop, which is in my hybrid bedroom-office."

Mona gestured from her kitchen to the hallway. Her apartment was remarkably narrow; once she opened her bedroom door, she could see everything from the head of the bed. She'd leased the apartment after taking a virtual tour, and she realized the many benefits of seeing everything at once. This design meant that her kitchen island acted as the dining room, and her living room was nonexistent. Mona had purchased a chair from a thrift store and put it in one corner, facing a bookshelf with an end table that was now stacked high with psychological journals and old Renaissance poetry tomes. From day one of the apartment, when all she had was a mattress and milk crates, her office had been her bedroom—which meant the only place to sit and watch a movie was her bed. Though Mona could move her apartment around a bit to make a better viewing station, she didn't want to. Her confession had been part titillation and part testing. She wanted to know whether or not this was a date in the conventional sense, or if Kerri was one of those oblivious straight women who had no idea the power of their words or teasing actions.

Kerri assessed the apartment with a quick gaze. When Mona walked two steps towards her bedroom, Kerri also followed. Mona's bed was tightly made, all hospital corners done by rote impulse in her mad dash to get ready. Her desk was clean of debris, and her computer blue lights flickered while the machine hummed.

"I can get more pillows if you want," Mona said. "And we can sit on the floor."

"Nah, this is okay." Kerri flashed a careful grin. "Kind of like sleepovers as a kid, right?"

Mona's body panged with desire and frustration. Kerri's words could mean so many different things— but her grin communicated that they were on the same page. As Mona set up the film on Netflix, Kerri brought in the wine and added more to their glasses. The still image Netflix used for the movie made all of Mona's previous frustrations disappear. A pillow was torn in two, and a half-beast creature looked out from the frame. Mona's palms sweat beneath the mouse as she queued it up.

"Here. Drink." Kerri handed her another glass of wine. "And remember…"

"Let the fear wash over you. Yeah, yeah. I'll try."

"I was going to say, you can hold my hand if it's too scary, but yeah. That works, too."

Mona wanted to kiss Kerri so much in that moment. Her smile was playful, teasing…but Mona did not have time to dwell. *The Nightmare* was about to begin.

The film used the same interview and voice-over techniques common in the documentary genre, where people spoke in detail about their experiences with sleep paralysis, but the movie made no explanation of its cause. Instead, it acted out the dreams. Sometimes funny, but mostly horrifying, the film took the mares, the hags, and the monsters so common in these nightmares and let them run wild.

Mona found it comforting. It reminded her of being in her first-year psych class with a casual boyfriend and the week and a half period where he'd tried to write down his dreams. When he came back with nothing that made sense in a dream dictionary he'd bought online, he brought his findings to his TA along with Freud's *The Interpretation of Dreams*. The TA had been a late-in-life graduate student, utterly disgruntled, and wanted nothing to do with this. Freud was anarchic and useless now; his theories were far more about stories than science.

"And besides," the TA had added. "Your dreams are always boring. The only thing worse than reciting your own dreams to yourself is hearing someone else's. Please never bring them to me again."

At the time, Mona thought it was funny and deliberately decided to joint major in English and psychology because of this conversation. Now, though, she wondered how long it would take her to turn into the same disgruntled TA. Or was she there already, but without a class to lash out at?

When she'd made her academic move, she wanted to believe that the only difference between having an English PhD and a psych PhD was that one specialized in fake things, and one studied real things. She thought her work in psych would be the basis for case studies, that it would develop more insights on Kitty Genovese and the urban city. But instead, it was nothing but turning people into numbers, charts, and figures. It was about ownership. All the poetic quality of dreams, no matter how horrible, was turned into a bunch of lines on a graph and REM cycles. It wasn't that Mona didn't want or respect the science; she did. But she wanted balance. She wanted a life. Instead, her phone buzzed and buzzed and buzzed with either more emails from Dr. Conlin—or Carmen, telling her about her own human experiments.

"Are you okay?" Kerri asked about forty minutes

into the film. One of the main dream monsters had been introduced called The Shadow People, and they were now showing the same paintings that Kerri had mentioned about Night Mares.

"Yeah, I'm fine. It's not too scary. Interesting, really."

"That's good. But you're fidgeting."

"Oh. Sorry."

Mona shifted to one side and removed her phone from her pocket. It was still turned off. She could have sworn she felt it buzz in her pocket. She swallowed down the urgency to look and see just in case something had been sent but discarded the phone on the floor.

On her computer screen, the voice-over made the startling revelation that each one of these dream figures—The Shadow People, the Mare, the Hag—were in people's dreams who had never met one another. It was as if they all shared a similar imagination or that their consciousness was linked through the same dreaming world they could remove themselves from.

"Shit," Mona said. She reached around and gripped her neck, feeling a sudden pinching sensation.

Kerri placed a hand over Mona's other one. "You see any of these guys when you're having a nightmare?"

"The Shadow People, yeah. The last one I had..."

Mona shook her head. "You don't want to hear about it. At least, not right now with the movie playing."

"We could always pause the movie."

Kerri's gaze betrayed her desire. She wanted to stop the movie for Mona, yes, and maybe for more. When Mona flicked the space bar to pause, she spoke about her dream in hurried, clipped sentences.

"It's like the same Kitty Genovese ones from before. Except that now I was her. I was walking to her apartment in Kew Gardens, even though I've never been to New York City. Each time I looked behind me, a shadow moved away. I tried to look behind me at least eight times, but they kept disappearing, as if I was the sun. And then, well, you know the rest."

Kerri nodded. "When exactly do you wake up?"

"Right at the end. I...I'm pretty sure I died in the dream. I remember wanting to wake up, and when I couldn't because of the paralysis, I thought I was dead." Mona tilted her head, examining the paused computer screen. "You know, I think I may have seen the hag then. An older woman who was there, looking at me, like she was supposed to lead me to the other side, but I couldn't move."

"I'm sorry."

"It's fine. It's making a lot more sense now. It's good I'm not alone..." Mona flinched when her phone buzzed and rattled against the floor. She cursed under her breath, wondering how and when she'd turned it on.

"Sorry, sorry. Let me..." Mona turned the phone off once again—holding the button down extra long—before turning back to Kerri. She was about to apologize again when Kerri closed the distance between them with a kiss.

Kerri's lips were soft and tentative at first, a kiss given to a wounded creature to heal them at the end of a fairy tale. When Mona's hand reached for her leg and gripped hard, Kerri moved in for more. The bed shifted with each movement, making their bodies rush together in an even deeper embrace. Kerri's hand grasped the back of Mona's neck, holding her closer. Anxiety became desire and elation. Mona held Kerri's thigh tighter before slipping her legs apart and leaning her down onto the bed. Kerri moaned softly, her body easily pliant. Mona's heart thudded so loudly in her ears it felt like she was under water. She remembered Kerri's words about drowning in dreams, about her Wendigo book, and felt goose bumps cascade over her body. Arousal percolated inside of her, pinching and biting as her skin felt too tight.

When Mona opened her eyes for a brief movement, it was only to find the edge of Kerri's shirt and touch her pale skin underneath. What she once thought was a mole or freckle suddenly moved against her thumb. Mona's eyes stayed open, a sudden feeling of disjointedness and unreality descending around her. Another mole moved, cascading in Mona's vision.

No, she begged. *Don't be a dream, don't be a dream.*

Mona hadn't had a sex dream in at least a decade, not since her first month at university, and she realized how much she wanted to sleep with her English TA named Natalie. But this was real. Mona was real, and so was Kerri. She felt another pinch against her arm; Mona looked down with enough time to watch as a bug ran from her elbow to Kerri's stomach and then against the bed—where two more bugs were already there and waiting.

Mona leapt up from the sheets. Kerri remained in place, her face hot and brows furrowed in confusion. *No, pain.* The rejection was hard and etched onto her face. Mona could only focus on the bugs that were now skittering up her mauve comforter and towards her pillows.

"Bugs. Kerri. I'm sorry. There are bugs on my bed."

Kerri glanced down and then leapt to her feat. "Shit. Those are bedbugs."

Mona groaned. When she felt another pinch on the back of her neck, she wriggled and screamed as she saw two more bugs fall from her hair. God, she was covered in them. It felt like half her body was now bugs; every itch was suspect, every one of her own moles now a traitor against her skin. She had no idea what to do. She could barely contain her sudden fear and disgust until Kerri grasped her hands again.

"They're gone. You got them out."

Mona glanced to her carpet, where Kerri had smashed the two bugs into the floor. Red blood spilled out from the crushed bodies. Mona let out another despairing groan.

"I'm so sorry. I had no idea. If I had, I wouldn't have…"

"Hey. It's okay. I know. This stuff happens." Kerri shrugged as she gestured towards the bed. "Do you mind if I lift up your sheets to see what you have here?"

"Go for it."

After Kerri pulled back the comforter and found nothing, she tackled the sheets. Two more bugs emerged from the corner.

"Jesus. I just made the bed before you came and saw nothing."

"They hide really well during the day. They come out at night, and they wait until you're asleep— or motionless. You have any bites? Maybe around your legs or ankles?"

"No."

"You sure? They may look like shaving stubble. Or even allergies, something easy to dismiss. If there are three in a row, that's them. Breakfast, lunch, and dinner." Kerri let out a low chuckle.

Mona's eyes widened. She'd shaved earlier that day and was shocked to see so many ingrown hairs. She lifted up her ankle and examined the marks. Sure enough, three in a row.

"Shit. I'm so sorry. I shouldn't have invited you over. This is—"

"It's bad, yeah. But again, you didn't know."

"But I should have. Jesus. No wonder I can't sleep!" Mona ran a hand through her hair, wondering just how long this had been going on. Was this the entire reason she was having bad dreams? Why her sleep schedule had been reversed? Her skin often felt too tight in the midst of a nightmare—but maybe she was just being eaten alive. "God. This could be the entire root of the problem."

"Maybe. But the bugs don't make you see the old hag."

Mona nodded. Even if these weren't making her life great, Mona knew it was far too premature to start blaming them for everything, especially when she did know the real cause. "*D'accord*. Okay. But...what do I do now? It's nearly midnight. I can't call my super."

"But you do have a freezer and a laundromat close by." When Mona furrowed her brows, Kerri went on. "The only way to kill these guys—other than an exterminator—is extreme heat or cold. So, a freezer and a dryer are your best friends right now. Unless you have a steam cleaner."

"I have an iron."

Kerri laughed. "Nah, not efficient. But sleep with it by your bed if it makes you feel better. In addition to the baseball bat." Kerri gestured to the corner of the room where Mona's just-in-case bat was leaned in a corner. "Anyway, your landlord will take care of this—but in the meantime, you can blast your sheets and your clothing. Check everything in the apartment. It's going to be frustrating to get rid of them, but it's possible."

"You've had them before, I take it?"

Kerri nodded with wide eyes. "First apartment I lived in by myself. I was so scared—then I was just pissed. But hey, I survived and then I turned them into villains in my next book. They were space bugs, meant to latch on to the bedbugs and take over, but it did the trick. Take that, bugs."

Mona had to laugh as Kerri gave her bed, and the bugs that were in it, the finger. When their gazes met again, all fear and disgust passed away; it was only desire. That kiss had been so nice and so promising. The space between their bodies lingered like another entity, a shadow of potential cut too short.

"I'm…I'm sorry I fucked up our date."

"Again, it's okay. We can try again some other time and pick up right where we left off. Right?"

"Definitely." When Mona bit her lip, she still

tasted Kerri. Tension released from her body until she saw another bug scurry across her bed.

"Until then, though... Do you mind if I tag along to the laundromat with you? I think I'd like to prevent all cross-contamination in my place, which means changing clothing and cleaning here."

"Sure, of course." Mona was relieved to have Kerri by her side as she dealt with the invasion. Even if it wasn't the best first date, it was something to look back on and laugh at, rather than be terrified of, she hoped.

After a quick assessment of Kerri's size, Mona ventured to her closet and dug through some of her clothing that would fit her—without, hopefully, having to come into contact with the bugs. It felt like an insane prospect to clean the place without making the matter worse, but Kerri had good methods she had already tested out. By picking the clean outfits they would wear after gathering up and checking the apartment and putting those in the freezer, they doubled their chance of not taking too many of the creepy-crawlies with them. By having two outfits, one of which would remain sealed in a plastic bag, they could also change at the laundromat.

"You should seal up all your books and papers, too," Kerri said. "The bugs mostly like beds and chairs, where people are, but I've seen them crawl into book spines. It's partly why I just don't bother to keep my author's copies anymore. Too many places for them to hide."

Mona did as she was told, though she didn't exactly want to seal up Dr. Conlin's journals. She'd rather they be infested. They talked aimlessly as they worked, Kerri doing most of the linens and Mona taking orders on sealing items. The movie remained paused and static on her laptop until Kerri asked to put on music. When she found a station that played 1980s hits, the experience of cleaning started to seem downright pleasant.

An hour later, Mona had bagged up all the items that needed to be cleaned at the laundromat around the corner. It was nearly two in the morning, but the place was open twenty-four hours to cater to the student crowd. Mona stacked the two large garbage bags by her front door while Kerri did one last walk-through.

"What is the assessment, Doc?" Mona asked. "Should I move out?"

"You should call your landlord because these are probably part of the building or another apartment. And don't let him bully you into thinking you brought them in. The fact is, no one can ever tell where they come from, and it's still his responsibility to fix it." Kerri folded her arms over her chest. She was decked out in a hoodie that didn't fit her and a T-shirt that had been Damien's. Mona looked at it listlessly before Kerri went on. "But it seems to be mostly concentrated in your bed and bedroom. Chances are, you've actually had them for a while, but your sleep paralysis and insomnia made it hard to tell. I don't see any in the living room area, but you know, be careful."

"Thank you—honestly. I don't know what I would have done without you tonight."

"You would have survived. It's actually striking how much we can endure when we get right down to it."

Mona was struck. Kerri's eyes were glassy, as if she spoke from an experience beyond bedbugs, but something from another time. Mona was overcome by just how much she wanted Kerri to speak, to give voice to whatever trauma lay hidden because it would mean that survival—not fear, not shame, not guilt—was the end goal in something traumatic. Even in little traumas, like a bug bite in three simple marks, the point was to move on.

"You ready?" Kerri asked, moments later, not allowing the revelation to linger.

Mona grabbed the bags with one hand and Kerri's with the other. "Let's go."

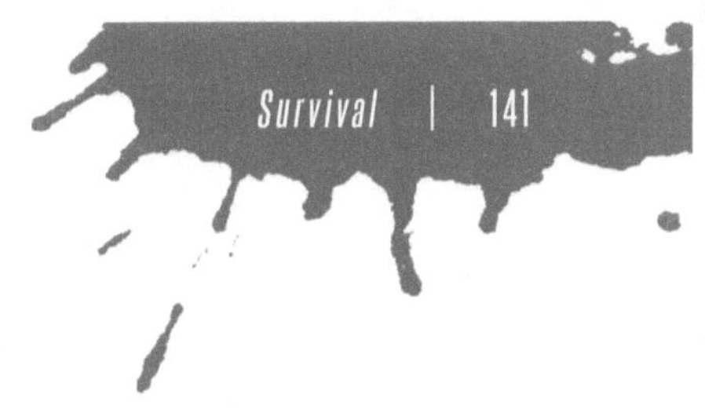

CHAPTER TWELVE

Even under the fluorescent lights of the laundromat, Kerri found Mona utterly beautiful. It didn't seem fair, really. Mona's home life had been turned upside down because of a bedbug invasion; she was sleep deprived and dealing with vivid nightmares; she was still flushed from the wine and making out; and she had been running late today because of an invasive email from her supervisor. Yet she didn't seem haggard or disheveled in the least. The sweatpants she wore had white paint stains over the knee, and her shirt was at least two sizes too big for her, like Kerri's was. Yet while Kerri felt short and awkward in the backup clothing, Mona seemed as if she had wandered out of a photo shoot for shabby chique. Her long dark hair was pulled back in a messy bun, making the look even more magazine spread-worthy.

While Mona set to work sorting the materials,

Kerri broke a twenty at the change machine. The two of them worked together extraordinarily well, mostly because Mona was more than content to take a backseat to Kerri's administrations. And Kerri was more than content to be in control, at least in this aspect. As she gathered quarters and loonies into her cupped palms, she thought about where her hands had been only hours ago. She may have been in control now, but Mona had been the one guiding them at that moment. Kerri shuddered. There was such a delicate push-and-pull between them, something that was so sensitive and fragile, the only thing Kerri could think of to compare it to was a tulip petal in the heat of summer.

Maybe it was a good thing the bugs had disrupted them. Kerri could feel herself slipping so far into Mona's body and her delicate, easy beauty that it would mean slipping into Mona's world. Before any of that could happen, Kerri had some definite questions.

While Kerri had helped clean Mona's bedroom, she also unearthed Mona's separate life. It wasn't as invasive as reading someone's diary; Mona's double life was in quotidian details, like the baseball bat in the corner of a room, the easy access to a landline phone, even though no one had those anymore, and the older clothing from a boyfriend—not a girlfriend—marked with paint and French phrases. Artefacts from another time, another place, and a different version of Mona. Though Kerri knew Mona spoke French, the shirts they wore now had French culture on them that Kerri couldn't comprehend. When Kerri first tried to find Mona on social media and came up with a big fat nothing, she assumed it was to do with the same French discrepancy. Being Quebeçois was so different than being from Ontario—so maybe there was something else that French students used to stay in touch online. While that could still be the case, Kerri was sure now more than ever before that Mona wasn't on social media at all, French or English. Not even her university profile had been filled in for Trent. And though Mona was a graduate student, she made absolutely zero mention of teaching.

It became very clear to Kerri, especially as they walked the streets of Peterborough at night, that Mona did not want to be found. It wasn't just that she was beautiful and people invaded her space because of it—she had been catcalled on the way over to the laundromat, in sweatpants and baggy T-shirts—there was something more to her fear of public space. She looked around every corner from every angle before crossing the street and braced herself for impact, as if each car would mow her down. Mona was running from someone or something, and Kerri desperately wanted to know who that was before she read too much of her own experience into Mona's traumatic edges.

"Hey, Kerri." Mona gestured to a bulletin board across from their seats in the waiting area. All the machines with their items had been started. "Is that you?"

Kerri squinted in confusion until her author photo came into clearer view. *Can 9 From Outer Space* was printed below in B-movie font. She let out a low laugh, baulking a bit. "Yeah, that's me. It's for a radio interview I did."

"That's so cool." Mona squinted, too, as if to make out the station number. Kerri offered up the information freely, telling Mona about meeting Stuart that afternoon, his oldies-loving husband, Raphael, and how well the time had gone. Kerri was impressed that the two of them had gotten the posters up so fast, though perhaps they already had them made well in advance of the interview, so the right amount of publicity could be generated.

"That sounds like a blast. I can't wait to listen... even if I have to buy a second-hand radio to hear it. Or rent a car for the radio."

"It'll be a podcast, too."

Mona let out a visible sigh. "Excellent. I can listen that way. I really think that's cool, though. I can't believe you didn't mention it before."

Kerri shrugged. The idea of generating any kind of publicity was still anathema to her. Like Mona, she supposed, she had tried to wipe her presence from social media—except that, when her father was arrested, there was no such thing as Twitter or Facebook. So, she'd tried to wipe herself out of the public sphere entirely.

It had more or less worked.

A decade after his arrest, when she started to write and wanted her stories to live somewhere else other than her desk drawer, she wrote under a pen name. And she'd been adamant that her photo not be on the book. Her publisher had wanted it there—*people want to connect with authors, especially in a violent genre; it humanizes you; your face is a selling point*—but she had refused. She made them write it into her contract. And when the novel bombed six months later, her publisher had an easy excuse as to why. Kerri—or K.T. Stellar—was unreachable. When the publisher folded a year later, it made their claims somewhat baseless, but their criticisms and her utter failure had gotten under her skin. When she signed with the next publisher, she relented. A photo was taken. She'd tried to disguise herself a bit—straight hair, different mannerisms—but it was still her. Sometimes, the thought that her photo was on a book, making her easy to find, made her want to stop writing. When nothing happened but success (or at least, marginal success to keep food in her fridge if she also had a second job at the diner), her fear had subsided. She still hadn't known what had allowed her some kind of success—her writing style, her real horror versus fantasy horror subject matter, or the fact that K.T. Stellar now had a face.

Either way, the photo on the back cover hadn't led to ruin like she thought. And well over ten years after her father's arrest, her fears of persecution didn't seem as valid. So, she had created an author Facebook page and sometimes used social media for book promotion, but she was relatively low-key. She would always be low-key in this regard—but that didn't stop Stuart or Raphael from plastering her image around. She told herself that was good, that it was okay. She had to be more present, right? But it also occurred to her that she was still hiding herself as a person. She was secretive without even meaning to be, keeping her book releases to herself until the very last days and not even mentioning her interview to Mona when it had happened hours before. She could try to write it off as not wanting to be a braggadocio or smug—or even pin it on Mona's monopolizing the time with her email issue—but that wasn't it. She was scared of being seen as Kerri Reznik, and not just as K.T. Stellar.

And especially as Kerrilyn-Rose Reznik.

When she realized Mona was still staring at her with her big brown eyes and small mouth, Kerri wanted to kiss her again. Kissing her and falling into bed with her was easy. As much as she wanted to know what was in Mona's world, Kerri knew she'd have to share her own.

So, she had to start somewhere.

"I guess I don't always think people will want to hear about horror novels. It's not everyone's favourite genre. Sometimes, it can be pretty gruesome."

Mona laughed. "You do realize we were watching a documentary called *The Nightmare* while being bitten alive by bugs, right? And the first conversation we had was about Kitty Genovese, a murdered woman who I keep dreaming about. I don't think your horror novels will scare me. In fact, I think it might be nice."

"Ah, but there is a difference between real horror and fantasy horror."

When Mona gave her a quizzical look, Kerri expanded. She worked her way through her novels, her writing process, and even the asinine interview questions she'd shunned in the past, like her inspiration and whether or not she had a Pinterest board full of character faces. Mona listened and asked the right amount of follow-up questions and gasped at all the right nuances. She even vowed to buy Kerri's most recent dystopian one because it sounded "so fascinating and moving" to Mona, especially as she explained the Dante connection.

Mona's attention only drifted when she rose to switch clothing from the washer to the dryer. She slotted in some coins as Kerri rolled the base of her palms against her jeans. "What made you write dystopian, though, if you've never done it before? What did you draw on?"

Kerri swallowed. The dreaded question from Stuart's interview. She knew the answer she could give, but she decided, for once in her damn life, to be honest to someone who wasn't her family. "I wrote it because it dealt with something I was always afraid of and wanted to move past. Like the bedbugs and the girls trapped in the forest, I wanted to let the fear wash over me by creating a monster out of it, so I could beat it at the end."

"I thought you didn't want to talk about the horror of real life, though."

"I don't. So, it has to be a metaphor. And in this case, it's a metaphor for my dad. He was a survivalist. He always thought the world would end. He prepared us for it regularly, religiously."

Mona turned from the dryer, leaning against it as she recognized the gravity of the statement. "You and your twin?"

"Lee, yes. We were his only kids, and he wanted us to be prepared for the apocalypse. We had drills. We went through all the lessons in a survivalist tome he gave to each one of us. We learned to tie knots, start fires, smoke signals…you name it. It was intense. And oddly rewarding. I mean—I could have never handled my bedbugs or anything else in my life without his drills. I can change a tire without blinking, in the middle of a rainstorm, because it's hardly the hardest thing I've ever done. He prepared me for so much, but…it was all based on the idea that we didn't have long on this earth. That we were going to die."

"Jesus. I'm so sorry."

Kerri shrugged. Her palms were drenched with sweat. She ran them over her legs again to dry them off. "So, I wanted to write in a genre that embraced the idea of survival skills. I wanted to take the idea that the world really was going to end and give it some credence. What would I do? Or what would my protagonists do when faced with this? And so, a dystopian novel about getting out of the underworld. *Dante Under Ice.*"

"Huh. I still want to read it. And I'll buy it. I know you said I could just get the e-book from you, but there's something to be said for physicality. I'll order it as soon as this nonsense is over." Mona gestured to the laundromat around them.

"Thanks. I appreciate it." Kerri didn't care about the royalty that would come in from the purchase, but the thought that Mona would buy her book to touch her book made her quiver again. *There, I've shared. And now when Mona touches the book and reads about the murders Mickey commits on the pages, she won't run away scared because I've sort of told the truth.* Kerri bit her lip, hoping this was true.

When Mona rejoined Kerri on the bench, a silence spread between them. The night was reaching its end, the sound of morning birds loud even in the white noise of the laundromat. The sounds of summer, no matter what city she lived in, always reminded Kerri of the woods where her father took them. Everything had been so quiet there, making every last tiny sound magnified. The cicadas, the animals crunching twigs, the grass in the wind. All of it had a sound. All of it had a smell. The only thing keeping the ashen scent of meat and gunshot away from Kerri's mind was the chemically rich laundry detergent aroma and Mona's slight scent of cherries. Kerri glanced at the dryer; only a half hour left. Even if they had to restart the machine to make sure it got hot enough to kill any remaining bugs, it only allotted them another hour or two at most together.

"What did you do before this?" Kerri asked, trying to be as neutral as possible. "You know, before Trent?"

"At my old school? I was in English. Studying poetry...translation actually." Mona went to run a hand through her hair but was stopped by her messy bun. "I was looking at the ambiguity between certain translations and the interpretations between French to English. During the sixteenth century, here was a group of French Renaissance poets called *La Pléiade*, after the constellation—"

"The seven sisters in the sky," Kerri said. "My dad taught me how to stargaze, too."

"Well. That's…good. Their name was also a reference to a group of Alexandrian poets. Seven people all creating things together. Studying it was a blast for a time, especially since Canadians love groups of seven. But…it didn't work out. Still have the books, though. Still like them."

"And when you do change supervisors, will you go back to Kitty Genovese? Or would you try again with the seven poets?"

"I—I don't know. Hard to think that far ahead. Everything, no matter the discipline, feels like Freud's *Interpretation of Dreams*, except that I can't cite the work of Freud anymore. Or Jung, for that matter. Which means I'm attempting to translate something that there is no word for in my current language, or I'm hearing a language that had no written records. I'm lost without a fucking map, waiting until I can move on."

"Poetic." Kerri then reconsidered. "Ironic."

"Sorry. I think I'm just pissed. I'm tired all the time. I want things to be easier, but it keeps exploding into something I didn't want."

"Do you regret moving?"

"Not at all. I feel safer here, in spite of everything with Dr. Conlin. But I still feel as if I'm waiting and waiting for something that won't come in. Like

Godot."

When Kerri nodded, understanding the reference, Mona seemed relieved. Kerri moved closer to her, right on the edge of her seat so their knees touched. "Why don't you teach here?"

"Hmm?"

"Don't graduate students teach? I always thought so."

"They usually do, yes. But I opted for an RA position instead. Data entry. And now, running experiments." Mona rolled her eyes. She seemed to want to grab her phone but realized she left it at her apartment. "Teaching doesn't exactly thrill me anymore."

Kerri nodded. A second passed, then another. Mona broke the edgy silence to share a couple of stories from her officemate Carmen about the classes she taught and how it was all mostly computer-run anyway since all the tests were multiple choice. Kerri wanted to know more about Montreal and what had happened, but she was starting to feel lost in a similar translation. The word she needed was gone from her lexicon. There was no way to approach the topic without pounding down a door, something that any culture and any language would understand.

"Mona," Kerri asked.

Mona was standing again, watching her sheets roll around and around. She turned and looked at

Kerri from the side of her eye.

"Why are you here?"

"With you?"

"In Peterborough. In this school. Why here of all the places out there?"

Again, Mona gave some half-cocked reason. Best apartment, only department that would take her previous credits. But Kerri pressed again. "Mona, what are you running from?"

Mona turned away. She stared at the machine going around and around. Kerri wondered how long they could both watch the same fixed point before it failed to have any meaning, before quiet could turn them into strangers again. Kerri felt the threat of her confession on the top of her skin like a film from an algae-filled lake. Her face on the bulletin board seemed like too much, especially when it was right next to a LOST CAT sign that seemed to look exactly like the one that had been eviscerated on a vine. She clenched her jaw, ready to leave, when Mona finally answered.

"It's a long story."

"And you think we don't have time?"

The machine buzzed. Mona opened it and felt the sheets. Dry. Warm. "I will tell you." She pulled the sheet out in one long stretch. Kerri rose to grasp the other end. Mona's eyes were evasive, but the pair worked together in sync to fold each sheet.

"I will tell you," she repeated. "But I need some time to process some things. I need more sleep. I need...to know you won't run away."

Kerri laughed. "I think you underestimate me."

Mona met her gaze. They looked at the sheets and the garbage bag full of clothing that they were going to have to change into once again to prevent cross-contamination of bedbugs.

"Maybe you're right. I was afraid you didn't actually like me earlier. That we were just going to watch a movie and gab. Which was fine. Just not what I wanted."

They were quiet as mutual want spread between them. Kerri wanted to say that, *no, don't worry, I want you in more ways than you can imagine*, but she held her tongue. She said instead, "You know, at one point, I wanted to write romances."

"Oh, yeah?"

"It's always been a battle between romance—rather love and fear. I figure everyone has felt those two emotions before."

"And fear won out?"

"It did. For now, anyway, I think it's the quickest vehicle for me to get what I want. I need to create the monsters to fight them."

"I understand."

"I know you do. I think...that's why I do want to see you again."

Mona smiled, just barely, and then nodded. "Another night, we'll talk again. About this. About something more. But right now..."

Their gazes both fell on the plexiglass windows. The sun poked its head out from the east, snaking through the trees. Businesses around them started to hum to life. Delivery trucks and moving vans beeped in succession. Two people entered the laundromat and took up machines. Whatever moment they had was now gone.

Another time would have to be enough.

Kerri and Mona took turns changing clothing in the cramped bathroom at the laundromat. When they were both composed again, the morning was bright. Kerri walked Mona to her apartment complex under a blue sky, the birds only as loud as she let them be.

"You going to be okay to get home?" Mona asked.

Kerri nodded. With a quick kiss on the cheek, she turned away. Something bitter was still left on her tongue, unspoken and unquestioned. From the corner of her eye, she thought she saw one of The Shadow People from a nightmare—but she dismissed it. She was so tired of chasing things that went bump in the night.

CHAPTER THIRTEEN

Absalom was thinking of her again.

Maybe it was the fact that the burglary call came in from a basement apartment on Barnardo Street, just around the corner from Parkhill. So, he was already thinking of Paul Bernardo and the legacy he left over Scarborough. Each time Absalom wrote the address on the paperwork, each time he called in any detail or went over the woman's statements, the street name hung in his vision. It was a silent scream, pure Edvard Munch, twisted and contorted. BAR-NARDO in all caps, a persistent wound, a sketch of the Scarborough rapist on telephone poles when he was five or six. He always thought the posters were so high; he had to look up to see them. Then when Bernardo was caught, and his photo was plastered on newspapers, young Absalom could stare at Bernardo's face straight on in the newsstands. He looked so ordinary. Like someone Absalom could have seen on the subway or his mother could have helped at work.

His mind reeled as he wondered how much truth there was to that. Had his mother met Bernardo? It was entirely possible. She met everyone as a cashier at a grocery store, and then as a cleaning lady, since everyone needed food and then to be cleaned up. Even Paul Bernardo, the Scarborough Rapist, and his deceptive wife, Karla Holmolka. They were not monsters but humans who did monstrous things to teenage girls while also needing to make dinner every night. It was very possible that Absalom's mother had told Karla what a beautiful dress she had on or that Paul's taste in potato chips on the conveyor belt was the same as her own. Entirely possible, indeed, it was probable.

But what did you do with that information? And why bother thinking about all this nonsense, when Absalom was really just trying to avoid his own Jane Doe—so eerily like one of Bernardo's—who captivated his own memory? He was obsessed with his own near-victim, not the legacy of one of Canada's most famous serial killers.

So, Absalom cleared his throat. He cleared his mind. He asked the burglary victim to start again, though it pained him to do so. She'd obviously been crying well before he showed up. Her eyelids were red-rimmed, and her voice sounded as if she had been held underwater. Each word trembled; each item that she reported as smashed or ripped apart or otherwise broken from her rented room was also tainted with sadness.

A sadness that was so familiar. A face that was so familiar. If not for the impossibility of this woman now being the same as the one Absalom had seen at fourteen, he would have sworn they were the same person. A doppelganger Jane Doe. A ghost.

A chill passed through him. *No, not a ghost.* The woman he'd seen at fourteen, stumbling out of the woods in the early dawn hours while he'd been on a run, had been alive. She was not dead, though she was bleeding. She'd been sobbing, too.

Absalom tried to focus on the woman—here and now named Tanya Winters—and not his shitty fucking experience. He did not want to look at his past, examine it with the alacrity of a shrink or even a damn detective. Both were pointless.

Yet she came back, again and again, in his mind. Jane Doe. Victim without a name. Her, her, her, the woman he saw at fourteen, dress torn and breast revealed like an Amazon warrior, sobbing in the bushes that she'd been attacked. And because he thought of her, it meant he also thought of himself, scared shitless at fourteen, seeing a breast for the first time in real life, and wanting to throw up. He'd not said a single word to her. He only turned around and ran away, terrified, back up the mountain.

Absalom's Jane Doe was the woman he could have helped but didn't. She was the woman he should have helped but didn't.

And so, she was the woman who made him feel like an utter coward. Close enough to understand Bernardo's hidden life without actually being him. Close enough, in some way, to be more like Karla, a witness in the background who did absolutely nothing to stop it.

When Absalom finally confessed to what he'd seen that morning, it was seventeen hours later. His mother was still at work, on her break, and had called to check in with him. He didn't even say hi before he spilled the story. *I saw a woman. She was hurt. She was...*He expected his mother to yell. She'd raised him better than that. She'd raised him to help people when they were down. When his family had driven to Florida when he was eight years old, they'd stopped to help a woman change her tires in the middle of Savannah, Georgia. She'd been so grateful to his father—who, admittedly, did all the work—that she'd bought them lunch at a local truck stop. *It has the best hush puppies. Trust me. It's the least I can do.* So, trust her they did. Each time Absalom saw someone in distress, he thought of her sweet, Southern voice. *Trust me.* He had to trust the world; he had to help people. If it wasn't already the social contract, then it was his family contract.

He waited on the other line for his mother to yell at him. Ground him. Instead, she told him he made the right choice.

"That woman was having a hard time. You would have only made it worse for the both of you."

"But she was in danger."

"No, Abby, she was coming out of danger. Those are different things. What happened to her already happened to her. There was nothing you could have done. No time you could have turned back. Nothing could be done by you without causing problems for the both of you."

The heavy silence in his mother's voice made her intentions clear. He would have been put in danger by helping, by tangling his personal life with a stranger who was not like him, not like them. The woman sobbing in the bushes was petite and pretty and blonde. The woman on the side of the road in Savannah was black, elegant, and wearing a nurse's uniform. Someone just like them.

The trust Absalom had once had in the world broke in that moment. Though there were many things that had occurred to signal he wasn't a child anymore, he knew that that morning, and then seventeen hours later, he had fully left that realm behind. He was an adult now, with an adult body, and he had to get used to that. Part of being an adult was understanding where one's limitations were, along with the history of a body—but also a place in time. Scarborough was no longer a location he wanted to live in. It was a minefield of dangerous bodies and predilections. It was a place full of decay.

"I know they're just things," Tanya Winters said, her voice catching. She gestured to the torn drapes and smashed computer in her bedroom. "But it's so strange. Someone has been in my bed. There is dirt everywhere. In the sheets. Look."

She walked to her bed, and because Absalom was desperate for distraction, he followed her to examine the dirt for himself. He would have guessed that her bedroom used to be a nursery or children's playroom for the first people who owned the house; the person who flipped it barely removed the pale blue wallpaper that cried out IT'S A BOY with its shade. Tanya's bed was unmade, the sheets twisted, though their dark colour made it difficult to see if there was dirt at all. Absalom was about to nod for the sake of it, when finally he saw the caked mud in a corner. A footprint, almost, as if the man had stood in the corner of the bed.

Absalom looked up. He tried to follow where the man's gaze would have gone if he had stood in this position—and he found a misplaced ceiling tile. After asking Tanya if she'd been the one to disturb it and confirming that she hadn't, Absalom made a note to ask the techs to dust for prints here along with their standard surfaces. Maybe they would get a hit—and for once, there would be a definite likelihood that it belonged to the robber, rather than a random renter, transient student, or one of their friends.

"That's a good catch," he told her. He walked with her back to the living area of the basement apartment, away from the main focus point of her smashed possessions. Each time she talked about her computer, she trembled again.

Latent rage flickered underneath Absalom's skin. He wanted to tell Tanya that it was *just* a fucking computer, and she needed to realize how lucky she was, but he held back. A trauma was a trauma was a trauma, wasn't it? There'd been a new bulletin updating their police department's protocol on sexual assault reporting lately, and most of it boiled down to that tautology. *There is no such thing as Oppression Olympics. A rape is a rape is a rape. Report everything.* Absalom had listened along quietly, then put the pamphlet in his desk and tried to forget about it.

He tried to forget about her. Her. Jane Doe.

He focused on Tanya again. And he even started to sympathize with her. Someone had come into her personal space and treated it like garbage; he'd actively destroyed her property for no discernable reason other than it was hers, and he'd stomped around in her bed while doing so. It wasn't like a bodily violation—no, not at all—but it was definitely a boundary violation. Houses with locked doors were always, even at the best of times, an illusion of safety. In a city so full of students like Peterborough, this was even more the case. If someone wanted inside… they would get inside.

And someone had wanted inside here. All Absalom had to do was figure out why.

"Have you been away for long periods of time?" he asked.

"No! That's the odd thing. I've recently gone back to school, but it's all online. I never leave—the moment I do, just for a birthday party in town, this happens. I was gone for three hours. And…."

Tanya's voice cracked. She mumbled about how she needed a term paper that was on her computer. It was the only way to get her degree. And because she wasn't insured, there may not be another chance to replace it. Absalom almost wished the laptop had been stolen, so he could present the idea of hope in its return. He wanted to comfort her in some way, but he refused to divert from his standard interview questions for too long.

He spotted Sandra through the basement window. She'd volunteered to check the other unit in the house to see if anything was disturbed. When she gave him a thumbs-down signal and a nod, Absalom was able to figure out how the burglar had gotten in and done so much damage in a short period of time: He was in the other unit. When Tanya left for a birthday party, he saw his opportunity. Then he booked it.

This was the closest they'd come to catching him.

Absalom's heart pounded in excitement. He gathered more intel about Tanya's standard schedule, her movements, if she noticed anything in the other apartment. He and Sandra would have to notify that rental unit, as well, taking up the rest of their day, but he felt it as progress and less of a burden.

"Anything else missing?" Absalom asked as the interview drew to a close. She was in the middle of writing down most of her statement while he did another walk-through.

She shook her head but soon doubled back. Her face went pale. Absalom readied a speech about drugs and how he didn't care what she had, but it was good to tell him so he could get a sense of the burglar, but it never reached his lips. Tanya darted to the foot of her bed, peeled back her covers, and reached under the mattress. *Not exactly a drug spot....*

"I didn't think to look here when I got home. I was so upset about the mud, the computer, the drapes, but..."

She gasped as her hand felt for something that wasn't there. She got down on her hands and knees, now looking under the bed itself. She finally pulled out a box that was completely empty. Absalom anticipated a passport, birth certificate, cash as its former contents. The cash was a write-off, and the other items could be found, but they also posed the rather delicate issue of identity theft. He turned over a page on his paper and readied himself for a call to the cybercrimes and fraud unit. At least, once again, this was some kind of progress.

"I can put you in touch with someone who deals with this issue. Don't worry. We can get back any kind of ID you may have stored."

"No," she said, wiping her eyes. "You don't understand."

"Okay. What's missing then?"

"This is...This is the scary thing. That was the box for my gun."

CHAPTER FOURTEEN

One of the appeals of Trent—other than it being the only graduate institution that allowed Mona to make a degree transfer—was its beautiful campus. The Otonabee River ran right through the university, dividing it into the east and west campuses. In the fall, the woods that surrounded both sides were all pale oranges, reds, and yellows, an Emily Carr painting come to life. In all the photos online, she could imagine herself reading poetry in the woods that lingered close by or on the edge of the river—even though she wasn't going to be studying poetry anymore. So much of her life had been devoid of beauty for so long, even if her nightmares persisted in a new place, she'd hoped the landscape itself would help her out of it.

It didn't. Instead, Mona felt like she was being swallowed whole.

Though the Psychology Department was behind

Otonabee College, the river was not visible. The foliage was hidden behind walls. And the experimentation area—the one where she'd be spending the bulk of her time with Dr. Conlin's study on ownership—was in a brick basement that seemed to absorb all sounds, and Mona feared, all people, as well. In her mind, the building morphed into a subterranean creature, hungry and waiting for bodies to run through data sets and heed to experimenters' instructions.

Each time Mona stepped down the staircase with brass railings, the squeaks of her shoes became muted as they hit the thick brick walls; all motion underground became whispers and echoes that blended into a low rumbling. Impossible to hear if anyone was coming or going. Mona became obsessed with visual cues; she constantly paced the hallways whenever she believed she was alone to, in fact, make sure she was alone. More often than not, the two other experimenters running the study with her, Joyce and Lisa, were around. They didn't seem to be as spooked by the building's acoustics as she was, though, easily falling into their roles.

The Saturday after the bedbugs scare, Dr. Conlin had brought Mona, Lisa, and Joyce in for training. Dr. Conlin had lingered far too close as he went through the typical experiment procedure, emphasizing all the wrong words until they sounded more like personal commands. When Joyce and Lisa saw no issue with his movements or mannerisms, Mona figured it was just the basement itself distorting him. Her apartment was being fumigated during the training, so even when Mona wanted to leave and go home, it was impossible. While Joyce and Lisa caught the bus, Mona went to her office to sleep. She caught a few hours, blissfully blank, and then made her way to the diner.

Dr. Conlin spotted her before she'd even left the parking lot. "Burning the midnight oil?"

Mona nearly jumped out of her skin. Dr. Conlin's car was a dark four-door sedan. Utterly indistinct. Mona became fixated on how little she knew about cars, unable to report what vehicle this was if she had to. "No, no. Just working late."

"I hear that. Conference coming up. Gotta be ready." He glanced around. Shadows danced across his face. "Can I give you a ride? The buses have stopped running."

Mona shook her head. She was walking to the diner, anyway. When she left the lot and a bus passed her on the way to campus, her heart seized. They were still running. Had he not known or deliberately lied? She didn't know.

As training went on for another day and Mona spent one last night out of her apartment, she was presented with more situations like this. Moments where she asked questions where the answers could be benign or sinister. Questions that Lisa or Joyce didn't seem to be asking.

When she arrived at the diner the second night, she looked into Joyce and Lisa some more. Both were type-A personalities, that much had been obvious during training. They were gung-ho about every last detail and dying for Dr. Conlin's attention, often asking him follow-up questions that pertained directly to his research outside of the experiment. On the department website, Mona discovered that Joyce had been published in one of the same journals that Conlin had been in; Lisa had been published in two. Both were supervised by Dr. Conlin, and both, as it turned out, were working on projects with ownership as their main theme.

When Mona told Carmen this over texts, her response had been, "It's a harem." When she told Kerri, though, her response was more tempered. "It's hard to be a female scientist. Maybe he's actually doing the good thing and paying the respect and awards forward? It's hard enough being a female author in a male-dominated genre like horror. So much changed for me when a male reviewer liked one of my books. Now, maybe it was a good book on its own merits— like these women are good scientists on their own. But the world does change when someone with clout says you're good, you know?"

Mona considered this. The department website

listed grants professors had obtained, and if a student was also assisting in research, their names became associated with the grant, as well. Which then made it easier for them to succeed in the future. Dr. Conlin had a lot of grants. So, why wouldn't he want to give a lot of students the benefits of that?

"But you know," Kerri soon added, "if you're getting a gut feeling about this, then trust that."

"That's the thing. I don't know if my gut is good anymore. I've been so wrong about so many things."

"Not everything, though."

Kerri slipped a hand over Mona's. When a flash of desire passed between them, Mona's world righted itself. The sensation lasted for only fifteen minutes, before Kerri had to jet and help some customers, but it was enough to get through the training exercises.

They still had yet to plan another date together; Kerri was always busy at the diner, and Mona was going to be submerged in the subterranean hell for the next month and a half. From training to preliminary trials and then to full-on experiments with useable data, Mona would be occupied until the end of the summer semester, most likely. Kerri assured her, over sporadic text messages, that they would find the time to be together again in between that time period. Until that date emerged, quick jaunts to the diner for dinner or a hello would have to sustain them both.

Most of the people who came for the experiment

were students desperate for cash. Others had read the bulletin and been intrigued. A handful of others seemed to wander into the basement accidentally and were swept up into the commotion. No one was barred, but others—like twins, like business owners, and people from other countries—were preferred. After a participant went through the first questionnaire, Mona (or Lisa or Joyce) would give the participant ten dollars and a yes or no slip that would bring them back for the next round, where the real experimentation would begin. The first round acted as a filter to weed out those who were just doing it for the cash alone. If anyone answered a question randomly, for instance, they were paid but ultimately dismissed. The ones who made it to the second round would then listen to a set of scenarios dealing with humans, aliens, families, and then twins; they would then be given a new set of questions to answer about the story they just heard. Though disguised as reader comprehension questions, they all dealt with a variety of interpretations on ownership, like "Who has a right to the book from the first story?" or "Who owns the house from the second?" From there, the data would be culled. Eventually, Dr. Conlin would turn it into a paper, and they would be credited. A line for the CV, an acknowledgment in a professional journal, and of course, grant money for their own time.

All easy, all fine. Two weeks passed. Mona

started to believe Kerri's interpretation of events. Dr. Conlin needed people to run these experiments—there was *so* much work to do—and he was doing a good thing by selecting women in a typically all-male field, especially since Joyce and Lisa were super qualified. The more Mona read the fourth scenario, the one with aliens, though, the more her lingering doubts returned. The aliens were supposed to stand in for humans, that much was obvious in the story itself. In the questions afterward, the participant was asked if it was okay to own an alien—i.e. is it okay to own a human? It was designed to be provocative and elicit data for Dr. Conlin to use.

But she hated it. It made her feel, all over again, like she was being swallowed.

Mona and Joyce were given the job of recording the stories beforehand so the experimenters could listen to them before the question period. Mona's voice betrayed her feelings with a slight quaver for that question. It was barely noticeable to strangers—but Mona wondered if Dr. Conlin heard it, liked it, and wanted it to be there. Joyce may have also had a hard time with the word problems, but if she did, she didn't show it. In spite of working in such close quarters with both women, Mona had barely gotten to know them. Each and every day became a haze of strangers and data, grilled cheese sandwiches to go, and sleeping whenever she could.

After running the preliminary set of questions, Mona was shocked to find only a handful of people who could move on to the second round. Even the identical twins who had shown up didn't make it past the first set because they had answered randomly. Mona's frustration grew with each passing day, especially as the empty chambers of the psychology wing seemed to want to devour her.

So, when Kerri showed up during the last day for the preliminary screening, Mona was relieved.

"Oh, thank God, you're here!"

Mona closed the distance between their bodies instantly, wrapping Kerri in a tight hug. Though Joyce and Lisa were in their own experimenter rooms close by and could easily see the previous relationship between experimenter and subject, Mona didn't care. In theory, there was supposed to be distance. But in theory, people—or aliens—weren't supposed to be owned, so Mona delighted in bending the rules.

Kerri wore a black V-neck shirt and black pants, which made her pale skin stand out. Her hair was tied back in a ponytail, as if she was about to head to the diner. She hugged Mona back just as fiercely, her palm lingering on the small of Mona's back a beat longer than was necessary.

"Of course I'm here. I won't be able to stay long, but I hear being a twin is an asset."

Mona laughed. "Don't remind me. But you're

right—this part won't take long. And you'll get ten dollars."

"Oh, then please make my day."

Mona guided Kerri into the windowless examination room. Consent forms were stacked high on a table, along with pens emblazoned with the Trent Psychology Department and school logo. A blue computer screen blinked to life once Mona took a seat across from Kerri. Mona held an iPad with the questions she would ask Kerri, and then fill in for her data set, while Kerri watched the screen above her head.

"I know it feels completely Big Brother-like," Mona said, explaining the blue screen. "But we're not using that screen for this part. Just the iPad. After the form, of course."

"Naturally."

Kerri filled out the form rather quickly, though she then went back to her name slot. "Kerri is technically a nickname. Do you need the full version?"

"Yeah. Sorry."

Kerri shrugged. When Mona took the form back, she smiled at what it revealed. *Kerrilyn-Rose*. Pretty. She would have commented on it more, asking about family associations, except that Kerri was fidgeting with her hands. The room was getting to her, and Mona couldn't blame her.

All hint of a previous relationship disappeared as Mona went through the statements. Even Kerri fell easily into the role of subject as she answered, only pausing briefly between certain harder questions. By the time they reached the end and Mona asked if Kerri had guessed randomly at all, an hour had passed.

"No, no random answers."

"Thank God," Mona said. The smile on her face felt robotic and strained after such a long interview—but Kerri mirrored her expression easily. Her back loosened, and she took a breath.

"Is that it? I did good?"

"You did great. Thank you so much." After clicking save on the final question, Mona raised her hands in the air in mock cheer. "You have completed the first round. Congratulations! Come and gather your ten whole Canadian dollars."

With a laugh, Kerri rose and walked by Mona's side of the table. Mona filled out the receipt and gave Kerri the cash from her storehouse. With a smile, Kerri tucked it away.

"I have to admit…This was a lot more intense than I expected. Do you have another person to see right away or can I recoup in here?"

"You can recoup. I think I need to, as well."

Kerri touched Mona's elbow, tracing along her arm until their fingers met. Their hands intertwined as the distance between their faces disappeared. Mona tasted honey on Kerri's mouth, as if she had stopped for coffee and used a honey stick rather than sugar before coming by. The quotidian detail of Kerri's life—like her full name—made Mona want so much more from her. Mona kissed Kerri harder, and slightly faster, as if to make up for all the time between them. Kerri opened her mouth wider, allowing for Mona to take and take and take what she wanted. Kerri leaned on the table, moans mixing with panted breath as she did. She squeezed Mona's hand harder.

Then, as quickly as the kiss began, it stopped. Mona rested her head on Kerri's shoulder with a sigh.

"This place is getting to you, huh?" Kerri asked, rubbing a hand down Mona's back.

"I just hate it here. It's dark and cramped, and I hate doing experiments."

"Shh. It's almost over."

"Still another round. And that's the worst. It's—" Mona bit her lip, realizing now that she couldn't even complain about the alien scenario because Kerri was going to progress to the next stage. "Shit. We can't be doing this."

"I'm not letting go of you."

"Okay, but...I should let someone else do the next interview."

Though Kerri's lips pressed together in a disappointed frown, she nodded. She went to kiss Mona again, but Mona's passion had been vanquished by details. She still held on to Kerri, but the experiments bothered her.

"Think of it this way," Kerri said when Mona complained—without really saying anything about the job itself—after their failed kiss. "No one is forcing this experiment. Everyone here is a volunteer."

"I don't quite know about that. We say that to make us all feel better—and we compensate them—but how often do people volunteer for experiments without being desperate? Still seems like exploitation."

"Well, in my case, I don't feel exploited. I'm glad I came."

"I am, too."

A casual smile turned into another kiss, this one more out of comfort. Mona felt touch-starved and wanted to hold Kerri as long as she could. So, they lingered in each other's arms until a loud knock ruined the mood. Mona jumped, but Kerri only giggled. She pulled Mona's hands to her mouth and kissed them.

"I think that's my cue to go. You're doing a good job, okay? And we will hang out soon."

"Very soon. This is quite unfair that I have to see you in laboratory conditions."

"Very unfair."

All that had once been difficult between them seemed to vanish. If not for the lines around Kerri's mouth that signalled stress and the same marks around Mona's eyes, she would have thought that the bedbug interlude had been a waking nightmare.

It was real, though, and it contained secrets into both of their worlds. Kerri wanted to know what had happened with Mona's past in so many words. And Mona wanted to tell her. She just...wanted to do it after this nonsense was done—or at least the first stage of it.

When a knock sounded again, this time more forceful, they drew their lingering goodbyes to a close. Kerri promised to text, and Mona promised to read it before bed—and sleep through the night. The last part was a gamble, but Mona wanted to pretend with Kerri a little while longer. When they opened the door, no one was around. Mona wondered if the knocks had been the muffled sound of her heartbeat in the psychology beast—but Kerri had heard it, too.

"Odd," she said. "But maybe Joyce needs a new tape or battery."

"Maybe. But this means you can walk me out."

Mona couldn't say no. She walked Kerri down the brick hallways, hands touching. Mona even walked her up the stairs and into the hallway, in hopes of catching a glimpse of sunlight against Kerri's red hair. The world was not a bad place, she reminded herself. With another hug from Kerri, she really started to believe it.

With a sigh, Mona went back into the basement. She turned a corner to her experimentation room and came face to face with The Shadow Man.

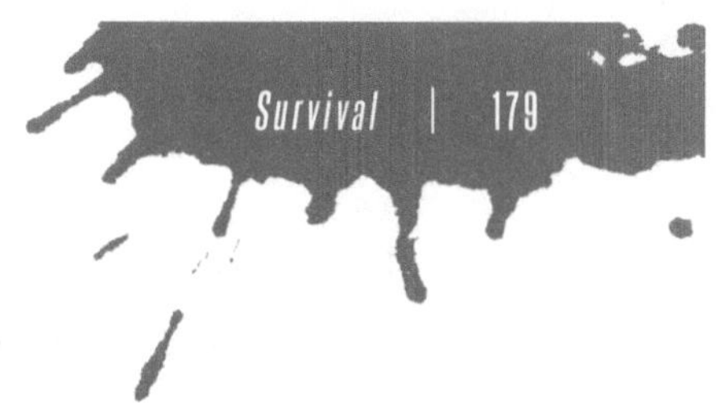

CHAPTER FIFTEEN

As quickly as Mona saw The Shadow Man, he was gone.

Mona blinked several times. She willed her heart rate to slow. No way had she seen what she saw. The Shadow Men were only in dreams. Nightmares. She was *awake, awake, awake.* She had just kissed Kerri. That had been real. She ran her fingers over her lips as she glanced up the stairs. Kerri was nowhere to be seen; neither were any other possible participants in the study. Joyce and Lisa were most likely in their experimentation rooms. And Dr. Conlin hadn't been to see them in days, trusting their occasional report as a valid enough status update.

The building was getting to her—that was all. It swallowed all the daylight, along with the sounds, and made shadow people drift across her vision. This was nothing, a trick of stress and light. Mona walked down the hallway and stopped in the bathroom. She washed her hands and straightened herself. Her lips seemed bruised, though not much kissing had actually occurred. Was her skin that sensitive now? Red patches radiated up her neck, though Kerri hadn't even touched her there. Her skin was already anticipating marks—like an attack? The light buzzed and flickered. The marks disappeared. She made herself breathe in and out several times.

When she stepped out again, the hallway was now completely dark. Someone had shut off the light.

"Joyce?" she called.

No answer.

"Lisa? Dr. Conlin?"

She took two steps forward. Nothing, which was both good and bad. She used her instinct to guide her towards her examination room, reaching into her pockets for the keys. She cursed when she realized she left them in her bag, opting to walk Kerri out without even thinking of the need to get back inside. She walked slowly, tentatively down the hallway until she reached Lisa's experimentation room. No answer when she knocked. She tried the knob. Locked.

"Shit."

She walked to Joyce's office and knocked. Same lack of response. She turned around to walk back up the stairs, in hopes of finding a janitor or someone who could let her inside. She turned the corner and nearly ran directly into the chest of a tall man.

Mona opened her mouth, but no sound came out. The man was at least six-foot-two, with broad shoulders and a stiff body. Running into him had been like hitting a wall, knocking all the air out of her. His hair was dark, and he wore all black, save for a green jacket that had a stitched-in patch with a fire in the centre of it. Mona didn't recognize the symbol. Or his face. But she suspected, deep inside, that this was her shadow man from before.

The man smiled wide—his grin almost boorish—when he saw her.

"I'm sorry," he said. His voice was slightly accented. He reached his hands out to brace Mona, but soon put his palms down when she flinched. "I didn't mean to scare you."

"What exactly did you mean to do?"

The man tilted his head, blinking back the harshness of Mona's words. His face softened. "I'm sorry. I got lost down here. I'm looking for the experiment."

He held up one of the tear-away information sheets Lisa had been tasked with putting up across campus. Though he seemed too big to be a student, there was a youthful quality about his smile. Though his presence had shaken Mona to her core, it was clear this kid had been wandering around in the basement not to frighten her, but to make ten bucks.

Mona put a hand on her chest. "Oh. *Oh.* I'm

sorry. This place is a bit of a maze. I just lost my keys and was about to find someone to let me in."

She tried Joyce's knob again, and to her surprise, found it open. Mona wondered if hers or Lisa's room had ever been locked, and her reluctance to be here was changing her environment. The thought frightened her deeply. She wondered if, like her mother had suggested on the phone, she needed to go to a sleep clinic and solve her *petite problème* once and for all.

She pushed the thought away. Another hour here with this new participant and maybe she would be able to find a maintenance person to let her in her room. If it was still locked. Then she could just go *home*. She waved the man inside and gestured to the consent forms. Joyce's room was exactly like her own, but inverted, the blue screen on the other side.

"Please take a seat and fill out the consent form. Then I'll begin the first battery of questions, and you can get paid."

The man looked at the forms with a raised brow. He took the pen and wrote in his answers quickly, before sliding it to her. The name Mickey Alan stared back at her.

"Do you mind filling out your full name?"

"What do you mean?"

She glanced up from her iPad. The man's eyes had turned stormy. Goose bumps prickled on the back of her neck. "Is Mickey a nickname? Short for

Michael, maybe?"

"Yes, that is correct. Mickey stands for Michael, like the angel of the Lord. But that's too ostentatious for me, as a mere mortal, so I go by Mickey. But not like the mouse. Never like the mouse." He smiled, his eyes no longer stormy. The change had been so abrupt Mona wasn't sure if she had witnessed it.

"Oh. *D'accord.* I will make a note for our records but call you Mickey during the test. Sound okay?"

He nodded with another smile. She gave him the basic rundown of the test, all of which he nodded to. In spite of the outburst about his name, he ended up being a rather easy person to work with; he answered each question methodically and seemed to be thinking, rather than giving random answers like other participants. When it got to one of the early alien questions—not the full word problem, but a preliminary scan to see if they needed to weed out anyone—his response changed. His eyes turned stormy once again as his brow arched. He almost seemed to be a statue, his breathing so shallow it seemed gone.

"Are you okay, Mickey?"

"Why are you asking?"

"We can skip that question. You always have a right to skip."

Though that wasn't entirely true—in theory, this would count as a random answer and disqualify him from later study—she moved on to the next question. Mickey smiled again and answered, but there was a lingering tension in the room. Something had been broken, a thin veil of fantasy now removed. He no longer thought long and hard about his answers. His voice was short and clipped.

Mona read them faster and faster. By the time they reached the end of the questionnaire, the air in the room seemed thick. Mickey was still smiling, but he also seemed to be calculating. Mona repeated her speech about the second wave of testing as she filled out his receipt, declaring his job now done. She reached into the money bag to grab his cash just as he stood. She couldn't help but flinch again. Maybe he was desperate, rather than dangerous, and just wanted the money. She'd give up the cash bag no problem. There was no fight left in her for something as trivial as a couple hundred dollars—especially when she knew Dr. Conlin's grants were in the hundreds of thousands. She waited and waited, but Mickey did nothing.

So, she finally extended the ten-dollar bill. He took the money from her with a mumbled thank-you. "When will I know the results? For the second wave of the experiment?"

"We'll be in contact with you."

He mumbled another thank-you, gave another smile, and then left. Mona waited with her back pressed against the door. She barely breathed as she strained to hear his steps. But the noise was void. It was swallowed whole.

Mona walked over to the stack of consent forms. She changed the name to Michael "Mickey" Alan. She realized the contact information he gave was bogus for a street that she knew didn't exist in Peterborough. Maybe anywhere. Even if she wanted him to go to the next round, he would not. She was relieved and tucked away the form in Lisa's documents. If she had any questions, she could deal with them later.

When Mona stepped back in the hallway, almost an hour had passed. She peered around the corner, the dark hallway now alight. Her stomach sank as she set eyes on her experiment room. The door was open. Only by a crack, but it was clear as day. She pushed the door open the rest of the way, dreading what she'd find.

But nothing was touched; the iPad and all technical equipment were still there, along with the bag of money. Her purse, her keys, and all her books. If the room had ever been locked, it was now no longer so. Which meant that Mona was *definitely* going crazy, and she should listen to her mother's advice and get herself to a sleep study, or someone was decidedly fucking with her. Whether that was Mickey, another random stranger, a shadow person, one of the other participants—or Dr. Conlin himself—was anyone's guess. Everyone was a suspect, which meant, of course, that no one was a suspect.

Mona clutched her keys so hard in her hand she was shocked that she didn't break the skin. The blue screen in the room haunted her, taunted her. She was overcome by how much she didn't want to be here. Down to her bones, every last hair follicle, her body rebelled.

"I can't do this."

She shut off the computer, left a note for Dr. Conlin that she had a family emergency, and redirected her second-stage people to Joyce and Lisa. She was not coming in next week, if ever again. She ran all the way up the stairs, never once looking back.

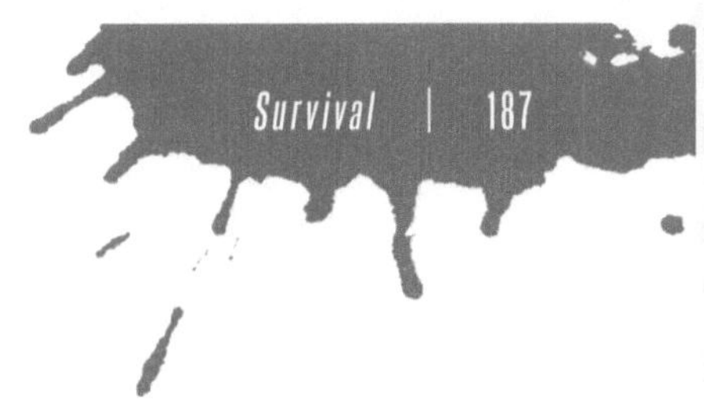

CHAPTER SIXTEEN

Absalom knew exactly what would happen the moment he logged on to his old laptop. The silver colour of the device, along with the stickers from Canadian punk bands that never broke it big, triggered a chain reaction. He'd open a photo folder filled with pictures of his family, like he and his half-brother at all these old concerts, and stay there a while. This was why he kept the laptop, after all— for the old memories. It wasn't because he needed the device to be a conduit of his unrelenting desire. If he touched the laptop, it was like he gave himself permission. Soon enough, he'd open the browser. Go incognito. He'd go to a porn site, a chat room, or a Craigslist thread. Like divination, he'd take all these random objects and project it into a destined future, where he was online and looking for sex, and then finding it.

It all just happened so fast.

This time, she was blonde. He usually avoided blond women. He preferred darker features, be it skin or eyes or the clothing that they wore. Blonde reminded him of high school, of cheerleaders and prom queens, a preppy life he never got to live. Blond women reminded him of Jane Doe. Of her.

Tonight, that was what he wanted. She appeared in his chat window and sent him a photo. Her face was cherubic, caked in makeup, as if to hide scars or cystic acne. She was gorgeous, though. Small body, average breasts, and available. That last part was important.

That last part was what got him to her apartment, a shitty one-bedroom in the worst part of the city. She asked to see his badge before she let him inside.

"You know I'm a cop?" he said.

"Oink oink. I like bacon."

He almost left. He thought he'd wiped all traces of his personality from the profiles. Online, he was a nameless, faceless entity—though not entirely. He was a distinctly black man online, or rather, a black body. He was used to being fetishized on hook-up sites for his skin colour. It was part of the appeal, in a way, to be boiled down to his most basic parts and trade in it frequently. But the cop part—that was new. He wasn't sure if he liked it.

Once the disgust passed and she revealed it had been the way he carried himself from his car to her apartment, "a weaver stance of a walk," he started to grow used to the idea. He wondered just how much more sex he could get if he traded on his occupation.

He wondered why he hadn't been doing this all along.

He tangled his hands in her hair as she got on her knees. He gripped her hard, tugging more than was probably comfortable. She seemed to like it more, though. When they moved from the floor to the bed, he lost himself in the visuals of his hands over her small waist. Cupping her breasts almost entirely, swallowing up her most delicate parts in a single touch. He lost himself, then found himself, over and over again. When she called him names, ones more to do with his cop status and begged to be arrested, it was a cheap thrill. A stereotype. But it meant, once again, that he was faceless. He wasn't his memories anymore, even if what was occurring also blurred the edges of that memory.

"Say you need help," Absalom said during the second wave of their interaction. She leaned against her bed, her back arched.

"What?"

"Say you need help," he said again. "And then beg me for it."

She did it without question or qualm. Absalom entered her with more force than he meant to—but again, she seemed to like it. She begged him for help. She begged him for release. And when it was over, she said it was good.

"We should do this again," she said, slipping him her number. "Oink, oink."

He swallowed hard as he took the slip of paper. In his car, on the way back to his place, he let it flutter out the window.

And then he went online again.

⁂

It was the gun, Absalom was sure of it. The gun being missing from the last crime scene bothered him, and this was why he had to drown himself in sex. He just didn't want to think about it. So, he went online to forget, entered a seemingly endless loop of sex and sex until he could do nothing *but* think about the gun. In a bed with another stranger, her head bobbing up and down, the gun filtered to the front of his mind, like an exit sign on the highway he should have taken.

He got soft. He went home. He stared at the un-closable cases once again.

It wasn't just that this burglar now had a weapon that could be used in a deadly standoff or that the gun Tanya Winters had wasn't registered and purchased illegally, so it couldn't be traced with any validity. It was that the MO of the robber who wasn't a robber was no longer a valid supposition. He was no longer a strange man squatting in student-run housing, eating their food and pissing in coffee cans before he smashed their electronics and left. He was now an actual thief of an item that had a definite criminal component. He could become violent. With a gun, it was far more likely he would become violent. Everything Absalom wanted to believe about him was now in ruins, giving him yet another existential crisis.

After hours of staring at the lack of results from the Winters' case—the fingerprints hadn't panned out, either—Absalom wondered if he was missing something. Not all the information was here. If the type of burglary was changing, then maybe the type of house he robbed would also change. So, when a radio call came in for a disturbance at an abandoned house off the Otonabee River, Absalom said he and Sandra would take it right away.

Sandra shot him a cold stare as soon as he turned the car around. They'd been heading to the diner to complete paperwork for the night. No way was that going to get done before the end of their shift now. Sandra let him know just how she felt about that with a sustained glare.

"Don't look at me in that tone of voice," Absalom said, trying to be playful.

"Oh, I can look at you in whatever tone I want. You are parting me from my fucking sandwich."

"We can get one to go."

"No, no. It's not about the food. It's because

you're playing super-cop and trying to link all your damn open cases so much that you're just grabbing anything that's open and hoping it will stick. You're a giant spider, Anansi, but you're spinning too many webs. You're just going to trick yourself."

Absalom had to laugh. He'd been the one to tell her about the trickster spider figure during their first week on the job together. He'd used it to elucidate an accidental drug bust they'd made during an incidental call; the dealer had been spinning so many lies he walked right into an accidental confession to avoid saying something else. Now Sandra repeated the folk wisdom as if she'd been the one to say it to him, rather than his grandmother when he was a kid. Sandra did that, though. She heard ideas and internalized them so quickly that whenever she spoke about them, they sounded as if they were hers. He let the reference go, taking it as a compliment, and tried to focus on the matter at hand.

"I'm not trying to link *all* my cases. But a disturbance is a disturbance is a disturbance. Someone needs to look into it."

"*Please.* Disturbance is your pre-crime report. Disturbance leads to a burglary, yeah? Which then leads to sexual assault. Isn't that how it goes? According to Miss Kerri, anyway."

Absalom rolled his eyes. Ever since he repeated what Kerri had said about the theft of lingerie, Sandra wouldn't let go the simple mathematics she had tried to present. He was relieved he hadn't let Sandra know he was still consulting with Kerri, especially when the cat had shown up.

"Ah, you're quiet. I've offended your girlfriend."

"No." Absalom's anger was clear in his clipped words. "You haven't. Because that statement is wrong."

"Ah. Well, at least you can admit when you're wrong."

"DeVos," Absalom said. "What exactly is so wrong with the formula she presented? A disturbance often does indicate someone casing the joint, which would then mean a burglary is next."

"Or some high school kids looking around. People aren't numbers."

"But behaviour can be."

"Well, people are stupid. They disturb things. Take things. It doesn't have to mean anything more, other than that we need to stop it."

"So, we are going to stop it," Absalom said. Though he wanted to defend his position—and by proxy, Kerri's—he knew arguing like this would lead nowhere. He was the one driving, so they were going to check out the disturbance. That was what mattered. "Besides, if you're right, this should only take two minutes, and I'll buy you a sandwich when we're done. I have a feeling you're more hangry than angry."

"You know, maybe."

The abandoned building was lit by a streetlamp on the corner. Absalom wondered if it was worth passing another bylaw to get more in this area to prevent crime but shelved that thought for now. He told Sandra to go around the back while he took the front. The door was propped open with a cinder block, allowing him easy access to the inside. His flashlight scattered the bugs that had made their home here and illuminated the safe places to put his feet. There were no needles—thank God—but a lot of broken beer bottles. Amber light cascaded around him, presenting an eerie version of disco light. It reminded him of a club he'd been to earlier in the week, one where he'd found another blonde in a bathroom. He pushed the thought away. When he found a broken cellphone, snapped in half at the folding point, among the glass, Absalom wondered if he really was on to something.

He walked farther into the house, finding old chairs and a desk. One of the drawers had been pulled open and pages scattered on the floor. They were still bone white, not covered by dirt or yellowed in the sun. Absalom tried to read the pages, but several paragraphs had been redacted, save for a couple of words. Chicken scrawl littered the margins of other pages, as if someone was trying to crack a cypher-code. He shrugged and walked into another room, still finding nothing of consequence. The next room had a couple of pillows and an old blanket in a corner. What seemed to be the body of a squirrel, now growing foul with decay, sat next to another stack of books.

Absalom was about to turn around and meet up with Sandra when his flashlight caught the title of one of the books. *Dante Under Ice*. Kerri's latest book. He hadn't had a chance to read it yet, but he remembered seeing a copy around the diner. What on earth was it doing in a house like this? She was a popular author for her niche from what he could tell, but her books weren't exactly in stores. She'd explained to him one night about print on demand and the rise of genre publishing using it, promoting most of her work through e-book sales. It made no sense to him, but it clarified why she was still selling coffee when she'd apparently penned more than eight novels. He was about to pick it up when a thud sounded from behind him. The sound was like metal and rocks, someone throwing something against a window or from a window. Absalom strode towards the sound, his flashlight leading the way.

Nothing.

He made his way back through the rooms he'd examined and caught sight of a coffee can he'd bypassed before. It was now knocked over, liquid spilling out of it. He beamed at his discovery while also gagging at the smell of fetid urine. This *had to* be the same guy. He was now squatting in an actual abandoned house, and a raccoon or a possum had knocked over the evidence. Absalom was sure the man wasn't here anymore since he saw no footprints in the dirt. Only tiny paw prints.

He left the building to tell Sandra. He even took her back inside the building to see. She confirmed that she'd found no one on the premises, either. Any evidence of an actual disturbance was maybe a day or two old now. She reminded him of that fact. "If he has been here, we know he's long gone. Whoever called this in was reporting a raccoon. Waste of time."

"Not a waste," Absalom insisted. "We know he's been here. We know it's the same guy."

"Great, so we get the whereabouts of the coffee-pisser bandit. But no one owns this building. It went into foreclosure years ago, and the bank took the losses."

"So?"

"So…How can you steal something no one owns?"

Absalom didn't answer. He had been asking himself that question for months and months, but now it was Sandra's quandary. Except she used it to justify not investigating, rather than asking it to probe for a deeper understanding. In spite of the fact that this was the closest they'd come to tracking the burglar, it still didn't take them anywhere. No one did own this house. The gun wasn't here. And maybe he didn't even take that gun. Maybe Tanya Winters's boyfriend did. Her landlord. Someone else. It was time to stop searching for clues in nothing, stop trying to spin a web that would only get himself into trouble. He was catching too many things, both here and online, ensuring that whenever he did stumble on to the right person, he would be too blinded by minutia to see them.

"Okay. Fine. We've cleared this disturbance. We're done. I'll call it in, and we can go get you a sandwich."

"Thank you. All I ever wanted."

Absalom scanned the area one last time before shutting off his flashlight. He hoped, for once, that Sandra was right. As he drove away from the house, he thought he saw a shadow figure in the window. But it must have been his imagination playing tricks on him.

CHAPTER SEVENTEEN

Mona's landline phone rang. She was so used to keeping her cell on vibrate that the jangling sound of the ring struck fear into her. She'd been dozing on the lone chair in her apartment. She'd been sleeping a lot lately—but anywhere other than her bed. Though her apartment had been "cleared" by her landlord, she knew from Kerri and her obsessive Wikipedia searches that a bedbug's lifecycle was twenty-one days. If there had been eggs in her room and they had survived the noxious gas the exterminators used, she had twenty-one days until she'd know about it for sure.

Until then, she was still hesitant to sleep in her bed. Getting only three hours of sleep here and there had worked for a while. It made the dreams stay away. She'd gone a week and a half without feeling paralyzed. She'd treated it as a miracle.

Then she thought she was seeing The Shadow

People in the daytime. She was imagining locked doors. So, she'd finally scheduled a therapy appointment at a sleep clinic, recommended to her through the counselling services at the school.

The phone continued to ring. Mona hovered her hand over the receiver until she felt the vibrations tighten her skin. She didn't know why she was so afraid of this. It wasn't like she'd never gone to therapy before. It was pretty much all she did her first year away at McGill, especially when she had a hard time coming out to her parents and dealt with a bad breakup. Then, after Gabriel, it was a no-brainer to go to therapy again. She did a few sessions, spoke her feelings, and then bled herself dry with other inane confessions. None of it was her fault. She did all the right things. *Blah, blah, blah.* Diagnosis and conditions all blurred together like some alphabet soup: CBT for her PTSD, according to the DSM-V.

None of it seemed to really help.

When her therapists wanted to medicate her, she withdrew. If there was nothing wrong with her, then why did she need to take pills? If this was all Gabriel's fault, anyway, and she was absolved of her role, then why was she the one who had to suffer? When no one had good answers to her questions, she'd picked up her stuff and moved in an attempt to find the answer for herself.

All of it seemed too obvious now. She wasn't

afraid of therapy or even this sleep clinic. She was afraid of getting there and realizing that there actually was something wrong with her. That she'd brought this on herself in some way, given Gabriel all the wrong signals, and handled herself in all the wrong ways. *You are pretty, Mona.* Was this the cost of forgetting herself and her body? She swallowed hard. Everything about herself and her motivations seemed so utterly transparent. Would it be this obvious to a sleep doctor, too? Would he take one look inside her consciousness and realize she was actually a black hole of feeling? All prettiness but with no responsibility?

The phone continued to ring.

And ring.

And ring.

Finally, Mona picked it up.

"Hello?" she asked. A click-click-click sounded. There was no dial tone but also no voice. She repeated, "Hello?"

Still nothing but a click-click-click. She was about to hang up, thinking she'd just missed the clinic calling her, when heavy breathing sounded. Deep breathing. Like someone had been running. The panting was so close to her ear that the receiver became a mouth in her mind. And the phone wanted to bite her, consume her.

She hung up. She unplugged the phone.

She was not going to any sleep clinic anymore.

She tore back into her bedroom and stripped the sheets. No bugs, no nothing. She put the sheets back on, however haphazardly, and checked the fridge countdown. Day twenty. She was almost out of the woods. Maybe all the nonsense she was seeing during the day had been a side effect of the bugs. Maybe the noxious gas was affecting her in a more delayed way. She'd almost convinced herself of that entirely as she crawled into bed again. She fell asleep within moments, her last thoughts before drifting off: *See? I don't need anyone's help.*

Kerri was in the dream.

She and Mona walked down a city street at night. The landscape was a mash-up of Montreal and New York City, yet in the dream world, Mona knew it was supposed to be Peterborough. A bright light shone behind them, fluorescent and pulsating like the laundromat. A 1980s song from their cleanup hummed in the background as their hands connected. Kerri pulled Mona off to the side, down an alleyway, where they kissed. Everything tinted red with desire.

She pushed Kerri into the apartment building, smiles on their faces. They laughed as they walked up the apartment stairs towards a bedroom, hoping to finish what they'd started. Mona was sticking keys in her door—the jangle so utterly loud—when a deep pressing sense of dread returned. Up until this moment, she had felt downright safe in her own consciousness. Her belly was filled with warmth that spread to her thighs.

All of that was gone. Kerri laughed and spoke easily, until the dread, like a cloud of smoke, spread to her, too. The freckles on her face seemed to melt off and become a pile of glass at her feet. An emergency light flicked on in the apartment hallway. A man stepped out from the shadows, holding an ax from the emergency fire prevention area above his head.

Mona turned over in bed. Gradually, then suddenly, the fear came back and then it went away. When Mona was an undergrad, she read *The Sun Also Rises* where Hemingway describes going broke as gradually, then suddenly. When she was still seeing therapists after Gabriel, she'd read *Prozac Nation* where Elizabeth Wurtzel had said the same thing about depression. Gradually, then suddenly. Could her nightmares fall on the same continuum, go from Shadow People and beasts sitting on her chest to dreams that merely nudged her awake with a pleasant feeling between her legs? If so, could they go back to dangerous images just as quickly?

Kerri remained motionless under the man's ax. His outline remained static while Mona struggled with her keys. The door would not open. She panicked. She started to cry.

Meanwhile, Kerri spoke. Her words were muted, but Mona knew what she was saying.

Let the fear wash over you. Let the fear wash over you.

Mona got the key in the door. She opened her apartment to a flash of red. She tried to turn back to see Kerri, but she'd been jolted awake.

A low thudding continued to sound. Mona rubbed her forehead. Light spilled in from her bedroom window, illuminating the now bare mattress and the sheets she'd twisted into knots. A nap had turned into a longer dream. She examined her legs, found no bug bites. The thudding continued before she realized it was her cellphone.

She walked across her apartment as her iPhone buzzed with a voicemail message. Seven missed calls stared back at her, along with one voicemail and two text messages from Carmen.

"Sweetie pie," Carmen's first message began. "I hope you're sleeping right now because this is some creepy bullshit over here. I thought Roger was being an ass and going through your files—but it turns out our office has been broken into. So, yeah, you better get down here when you can so you can tell them what's missing."

The second message simply read: "Oh, my Lord! This detective is beautiful. And his partner is pretty butch, so maybe you'll find something you like, too. I'll see you when I see you."

"Shit. Shit. Shit."

In spite of Carmen's lackadaisical attitude, Mona could sense her fear. She only reverted to extreme flirting when she was uncomfortable; she also only tried to set people up when she was feeling helpless. Mona didn't need to listen to the voicemail to know it was Carmen once again. When Dr. Conlin's name also appeared in her missed call log, her stomach sank. She'd bailed on his experiments and still hadn't faced him. And now she didn't even have the sleep clinic to use as an excuse. She could lie, but she didn't trust her words anymore.

One thing at a time, she told herself. *Gradually, then suddenly.* Mona checked her entire body for bites or sores as she got dressed. She found nothing. She searched for more bedbugs around her mattress and laundry basket. The chair she'd taken to sleeping in during the day. All gone. No more. She marked the twenty-first day off her fridge calendar with a sigh. *One invasion to another.*

She closed her eyes, savouring the last image of Kerri from her dream—before the ax, before the fear—then she left for her office.

CHAPTER EIGHTEEN

Brace yourself for a throwback. It's kind of like a Tears for Fears video in there." Carmen was already talking a mile a minute. The moment Mona told her she was on the bus on the way over, Carmen's texts had quadrupled. Now, as Mona stepped off the bus and into a quick hug, Carmen didn't slow her pace, though her voice was rough and deep around its edges, as if she'd been talking a lot.

"Tears for Fears?" Mona asked. "Were you even alive for that?"

Carmen nudged Mona. "Admittedly, no, but I did go to a lot of eighties dance parties in my youth. And it's in the 'Head Over Heels' video where they walk into a library and make it rain with index cards, right?" When Mona nodded, Carmen went on. "Well, I think our perp also drew inspiration. It kind of looks like that in our office. And all the other offices on our floor. Just fuckin' ransacked. Paper everywhere."

"All the offices? Not just ours?"

"Yeah! I thought you were reading those texts. Well, anyway, I might have confused you because I *thought* it was just us at first and freaked out. Called security, asked for a personal escort because who knows if this guy's still in the building, right? Then I saw Joyce and Lisa freaking out around the corner because their office had also been gone through—but they discovered it when the experimentation room was trashed. The security guard's phone was nonstop after that because people started to check their own place and boom. Paper shower. Still don't have that personal escort, though, so I'm glad you're here."

"Right back at you."

"Teamwork." Carmen smiled. "Let's work through this trauma together."

Carmen held the door open for Mona as they headed into the ornate building on Otonabee campus where their psychology offices were, along with the Anthropology Department and the basement experimentation rooms. There were also large meeting areas and classrooms in this building, but since they were not targeted, none of the morning classes had been aware something had gone on. Though the burglar had apparently trashed several rooms, he'd closed the door after each one. His destruction had been invisible until grad students—already notorious for skipping early meetings—finally realized something had occurred and started to call it in.

Mona rested somewhat easier knowing that their office was not the only place hit; they barely needed to get around the corner before the chaos became obvious. Psych graduate students she'd seen during class—then never again—spoke in angry voices to security guards, while other graduate students and supervising professors attempted to gather up data charts and were pushed away by plainclothes detectives. Mona scanned the crowd for Dr. Conlin, but he either wasn't in any of the burgled offices or he was in another part of the school.

"I think at one point," Carmen said, still explaining what she'd already texted Mona with in a clipped voice, "they may have sealed the department thinking the guy was still in the building. But he was most likely long gone."

"What was taken?" Mona asked.

"I have no idea. Nothing of mine. But like I said, it's hard to see anything in there but paper."

Mona peered into an ajar office door where a black detective was interviewing another graduate student in the middle of what looked like a ticker-tape parade. Every single exam booklet seemed to be tossed on the floor, along with photocopier paper. Every single book seemed to have been yanked off the wall, as well, pages fanned out, and then left in a pile on the floor—almost as if the robber expected one of the books to be a fake one, a plant that kept money inside of it.

"Some of the anthropology offices had their computers smashed. And the creepy blue screen ones in the experimentation rooms are now duds. Only the iPads were safe since they were locked up."

Mona tilted her head. "So, the robber misses a gigantic sign that there's something valuable but smashes everything else? Like with a baseball bat?"

"Or a fist. Looks like someone literally punched a screen."

"Ouch." Mona made a face. "But not stolen? Nothing at *all* is missing? I find that hard to believe."

"It is. And maybe something has been taken, but I can't yet see it under this mess. But apparently, according to Joyce and Lisa, not even the cash reserve bags were touched."

"Well, that's good for Dr. Conlin, I guess."

"Don't worry," Carmen said. "He's not here. Joyce and Lisa said they had a hard time reaching him. They also seemed really mad when I brought you up."

Mona didn't answer. She stared straight down the hallway, where their offices were located second from the end. She tried to walk faster, but balled-up paper and people had migrated into her way. She really did start to feel as if she was in the middle of that stupid Tears for Fears video. Carmen was able to easily catch up to her.

"I know there's a story here you're not telling me," Carmen said.

"Yep."

"Well...I will ask at another time."

"Thank you." When Mona met Carmen's gaze, she saw genuine understanding there. The moment quickly passed, though, as she gestured to their office. "So, let's check it out."

Mona gasped right away. She was prepared for the rain of paper from the other offices, along with the book toss, but her desk somehow seemed worse. It was always going to seem worse when it was your own stuff, she knew from reading those damn ownership articles, but she was sure that it was actually, objectively worse on her side of the office. Instead of her papers being tossed, they were shredded. A pile of paperwork had been ripped into several sections on top of her desk, almost as if there was going to be a campfire, and her psychology reports were kindling. From the thick black lines on some of the pieces, she knew these were her completed consent forms for the experiment trials. All her work was now gone—and so was the motivation to fix it.

"Oh. That detective is coming. The cute one. Tell me you got that message, at least."

Mona barely nodded. Thudding footsteps down the hall were from the black plainclothes detective she'd seen briefly.

"Hi again. Is this your officemate?" he asked Carmen.

After she nodded, he extended his hand to Mona. Carmen had been right; his six-foot-three frame gave him a marked elegance, and his booming voice as he introduced himself as Detective Absalom Lincoln was quixotic. His hands were soft, as if he used lotion, and his grip was firm. He made her feel safe just by being there.

"We're still processing the scene, but are you able to tell me what you think could be missing from your desk?"

"Um. Well. It's hard to see under the mess." Her voice was flat, defeated. She put a hand to her forehead, emotion overwhelming her as she saw the torn-up consent forms again. What did those reports matter? She didn't want to do them anyway. Maybe this burglar had given her the perfect official resignation.

Or maybe Dr. Conlin would think she did this to spite him. The thought was enough to sober her emotions. She needed to cooperate fully to shift all suspicion from herself. "Can I step closer, though? I'd like to open some desk drawers."

"Let me open them under your direction. But yes, come in."

Mona tried not to step on paper to maintain the scene, but it was difficult. She scanned the sheets on the floor that weren't torn. Some were notes from older classes—hers or Carmen's, she wasn't quite sure. Some were pages from the books from other rooms. She and Carmen never had an extensive shelf collection here, and she was relieved. The thought of her poetry collections torn up or her books on Kitty Genovese made her far sadder than it should have. The two medical journals that Carmen had on her desk were torn in half, mere obstacles he'd tackled successfully.

With her direction, Detective Lincoln opened each one of her desk drawers. An ink stain covered the bottom of the top one after a pen had burst. All her office supplies were unorganized but still there. She was about to shrug when her bottom drawer seemed strange.

"What is it?"

"I...I think something's been added." Mona gestured to the bottom one. "It looks off-kilter, as if something heavy is inside. Or he slammed it too hard."

Using a latex-gloved hand, and probably far more caution than was necessary, Detective Lincoln opened the desk drawer. The crunching metal sound signalled it had merely been off-kilter. Blank consent forms littered the bottom. Mona was about to tell him this was a false alarm when she saw the worn edge of a newspaper.

"What's that?" Mona asked. "I don't read any paper."

"Not even the school one?" Detective Lincoln asked. "Just one time—maybe even using it as an umbrella or something?"

The scenario he described was so picturesque, something from a 1950s detective movie, rather than a modern-day robbery. She shook her head.

"Okay, well, maybe it was left by our guy. He'd put up newspaper over some of the other office windows. Mostly the student paper since it was free, I guess."

When Detective Lincoln pulled out the corner, the distinctive blue font of the *Toronto Star* was visible. The paper was yellowed, weathered as if it had been saved for quite some time. There was no discernable date, and the article itself didn't seem to be complete as it was torn in half along a seam. A headline about a murdered woman and Etobicoke native named Layla Hunter was all Mona could make out, along with a photo that showed a worn-down blond woman smiling for the camera at a hunting trip with two kids. Their faces had been blurred out deliberately by the paper.

Detective Lincoln asked once again if she or Carmen had a subscription. Both shook their heads. Carmen stood next to Mona, their shoulders brushing. Mona wished it wasn't weird to hold a friend's hand; she longed for a hug. For some kind of contact.

"Did you maybe know Layla Hunter?" Detective Lincoln asked. "Or Maria Black, the author of this piece?"

Again, she and Carmen shook their heads. Carmen even went through her phone, double-checking some of her friend's birth names against the previous headline, in case one of them had once gone by Maria. She came back with nothing. Not even anyone with the last name of Hunter or Black, as common as those were.

Though Detective Lincoln seemed disappointed in the lack of connection, he merely took the paper and added it to an evidence bag, sure it meant something. The more they dug through the drawer, the more newspaper stories they found. All but one article was about Layla Hunter and her murder; the outlier had been a magazine story about an internet virus that was attacking people's computers through malware from about 2008. Mona had no idea what any of this meant, but she was deeply concerned. A second photo of Layla, one from her school days in the 1970s, looked a startling amount like Kitty Genovese. Layla had longer hair, bangs that framed her heart-shaped face, but there was something about her slightly open-mouthed stare that was just like Kitty Genovese's mug shot. Though there was absolutely no indication that Mona had been the target, she couldn't help but feel as if she was. As far as she could tell, there were no cryptic news articles in any of the other offices. The student paper was incidental; the burglar used newsprint for privacy curtains to do his work. *This,* though—this was a culled collection. A veritable scrapbook of memories, all of them horrific.

And it was in her desk drawer. A gift from a stranger.

When Detective Lincoln read out an underlined passage from one of the murder articles that said Layla Hunter had been murdered with an ax, Mona flashed to her dream. The glinting blade above Kerri's head.

"I...I think I have to go. I have to go." Mona turned to Carmen and grasped her arm openly. "I need to go."

"Oh, whoa. Okay." Carmen placed a hand on the small of Mona's back, quickly stepping into a protector role as Mona's knees buckled. Mona had never appeared this vulnerable to Carmen—they'd always kept a pleasant but healthy distance, and even her reservations about Dr. Conlin had been communicated in code words and whispers—but Mona was relieved that Carmen was rising to the occasion. Her grip on Mona's arm was strong, firm. Comforting. Her knees returned to normal, but her stomach was still queasy.

"She can go, right? You don't need us anymore?" Carmen asked the detective.

Though his mouth pursed, he nodded. "We'll be here a while sorting through this. We have fingerprint techs coming in. There's a lot to gather. Maybe we'll get the right one this time, and we can finally run the results."

Mona swallowed. The way Detective Lincoln spoke, it was as if he'd gathered prints before on this perp in particular. As if there were multiple cases. He'd been speaking of the university robbery as one solid unit in all other parts of their conversation, even if a lot of rooms and departments were hit. His questions were also directed, probing, as if he was searching for something in particular. Mona flashed to all of them, all over again, and wondered if she'd said the right things. Her mouth opened, frozen like Kitty's without sound, until Carmen tugged her into the hallway and back out into the light.

❧❧❧❧❧

Carmen and Mona needed to walk halfway across campus to find a decent coffee shop that was open during the summer schedule. They were both red-faced with sweat-matted hair by the time they arrived, but it had been worth the trek. The summer schedule usually left the campus barren of people, save for graduate students and still-working profs. The break-in had changed that dynamic in the

Psychology Department, obviously, and some kind of serene order needed to be restored. Carmen insisted that Mona sit on a bench outside the café as she went inside to get them their drinks. In the moments she was alone, Mona's thoughts flitted back to Kerri. She read old messages Kerri had sent the night before—about going on a trip together since she finally had time off—and Mona's heart hurt. Why did something always get in the way? She didn't want to leave campus now, let alone go on a trip. Mona wrote and then deleted two texts to Kerri by the time Carmen came out with a large order of coffee.

"Filled with an inordinate amount of sugar and cream, you menace."

Mona mumbled a small thank-you. Carmen sipped her own drink, eyeing Mona in a not-so-casual way. The wind whistled around them; the sound of chatter and birds was calming before Carmen finally broke under the silence. "So. Put my mind at ease. You didn't do this, right? As a way to get back at Roger or something?"

"What? Of course not."

"Mm-hmm. But you feel responsible for something, that's for sure."

Mona knew her deflection would be less than stellar. And she knew the suspicion was valid, too. She sipped her coffee again, wondering how exactly to unpack everything that had happened. It was simultaneously too much or not enough. She spoke of the training, the emphasis on the wrong words, the bus stop lie, and then the fact that Dr. Conlin had been calling her pretty consistently since last night.

"Part of that is the break-in, I know it is," she said. "And another part is asking why on earth I've quit. He needs my work. Legitimately."

"Uh-huh." Carmen pursed her lips, her manicured brows furrowed. "You ever wonder if one of his former victims did this?"

"Former victims? You have proof of his misconduct now?"

"Not like, you know, legal proof. A lot of good that does, though. Just look at Jian Ghomeshi." Carmen huffed at her mention of the former radio giant who was vanquished by rape accusations, many of which had documented proof of violence, but never earned him a conviction. Carmen had watched the trial religiously and nearly changed her entire MA to talk about the case when he was acquitted. "But I went to a conference a couple weeks ago with someone who graduated from here. She knew of Roger and all his, um, little troubles."

"Wait. So, she actually experienced something? She can—"

"Not precisely. She just told me that he has office parties every Christmas, and he can drink too much."

Mona had to laugh. Wasn't drinking too much the very point of Christmas? She already knew he had office parties. She'd been invited to them—along with everyone else in their class—but she'd not gone. Not because she was afraid, but because the beginning of winter always made her sad. It reminded her of the ice in Montreal and *La Nuit Blanche.*

Yet Carmen kept insisting. Roger Conlin's former student got the heebie-jeebies anytime they were alone. She hated working in the experimentation rooms. "Said they made her feel icky."

"I feel icky."

"See?"

"I feel icky all the time, Carmen. I feel icky sitting here right now because I remember that someone walked through my shit. I remember someone tore up my stuff. I remember…" Mona sighed. She ran a hand through her hair, not wanting to rehash Gabriel. "I remember I'm not sleeping. And yeah, I feel icky around Dr. Conlin, too. But I don't know anymore where my own shit ends and his shit starts. I feel like I can't see anything clearly anymore. The only thing that doesn't make me feel icky is Kerri, but even then, the ickiness just surrounds us."

"Kerri?"

Mona blinked. She could have sworn she'd told Carmen about the woman at the diner. And maybe she had, but since Kerri wasn't wrapped up in the whole

Dr. Conlin affair, she was easy to forget. Mona didn't want to forget, so she willingly took the bait and updated Carmen with everything that had happened between the two of them. She talked about the date at the laundromat, her bedbug scare that hadn't actually driven Kerri away, her red hair and cute laugh, and of course, her writing career.

"Oh. I love her already," Carmen said. "A writer-artist type? How cool."

"She'd probably deny the artist label since she writes horror and pulp stuff, but I think it's cool. I haven't read anything yet, but I did order her latest book. Wait. Did you see a package in our office?"

Carmen shook her head. "Could be buried under a mountain of stuff, but no, definitely no Amazon package."

"I got an email a day ago telling me it had arrived. Maybe it's in the department mailroom."

"Or maybe it got lost in the shuffle. Could be. I'm sure if you explain it to Amazon, they'll send you a new one. They certainly have enough money to spare. And then if it does turn up, you can give me the extra copy so I can read it. I'd like a nice, easy spook that has nothing to do with breaking and entering, sexual harassment in the workplace, or transphobia."

"Same."

Carmen soon veered the conversation back to lighter topics—like her upcoming party for her MA graduation and the guy she was interested in—but Mona soon drifted back to the burglary. Why would someone take her Amazon book? She didn't think she'd seen it shredded in the piles of others, so did the perp want to read a horror novel? She imagined a Shadow Man hulking around in her office, finding the book and then finding some kind of camaraderie with it. A nightmare for a nightmare. Then she remembered Mickey, who she thought was a Shadow Man but who had turned out to be strange. *Really strange.* Maybe strange enough to break into offices, so he could tear them apart?

"Carmen," Mona said. She placed a hand on her arm, interrupting her. "I'm so sorry—I want to hear all about this in a bit—but I have to tell Detective Lincoln something I totally forgot."

Carmen feigned a sigh but flicked her hand easily. "Go ahead and catch detective sexy. I'll be right here."

Forensic techs with yellow booties on their feet were in the midst of processing the broken-into rooms when Mona arrived. The insistent chatter had come down to a dull roar; almost no graduate students were left, now defeated in saving any of their research. When Mona finally spotted Detective Lincoln in the crowd of new techs, he was talking to Dr. Conlin. She froze in the hallway, but it was too late. Dr. Conlin raised a hand to Mona. Detective Lincoln turned around. Their gazes met; he seemed to understand the gravity of what was going on. He left his position with Dr. Conlin and spoke to her directly.

"Mona, right? Did you remember something?"

She explained about the man who had come in for one of the experiments, all within earshot of Dr. Conlin. He remained a step behind Detective Lincoln to present the illusion of privacy but kept his ears peeled. His arms were folded across his chest, as if trying to contain his kinetic energy and reaction to her story of the large hulking man she'd interviewed. She wondered, albeit briefly, if she had done something wrong. Should she have reported him?

"This could be nothing," Mona said. "A strange kid that I don't want to get in trouble."

"Everything seems like nothing until it means something." Detective Lincoln continued to write down all the details she gave him, right down to the patch of fire on his jacket. "Do you remember anything else about him? The name is good, but it's most likely a fake."

"Definitely, especially since he gave no proper address or contact information." Mona thought. She could see his green eyes so clearly, along with the sharp outline of nose and jawline. Yet words escaped her. He was so familiar, yet so hard to describe. "Maybe if I could speak to a sketch artist. I don't know the terminology for faces. I feel like I'm translating a memory from another language."

"That's an idea. Those tend to take a while, though. I want to run the prints again to see if we're lucky. And if we're not, then I'll make a call."

"I think that's probably the right move," Dr. Conlin said. "If you don't mind me saying so. As weird as this kid was, sometimes kids are weird. I was weird growing up. I lurked around psychology buildings. But I never burgled anything."

Though Detective Lincoln nodded along, he didn't seem convinced. How many other people could there really be? If it wasn't this guy, not only did that make the world so much more complicated than she wanted to believe, but it meant that it could be someone from her past. Someone like Gabriel? She swallowed back that thought. It was impossible. Utterly impossible.

Unless...

"There was also a book," Mona said. "It may be nothing, again, but I think I had a package here from Amazon that's no longer here. So, it could be stolen."

"That's good. Thank you." With another few kind words, Detective Lincoln excused himself to talk with the techs and his partner. Mona was about to turn away and go back to Carmen when Dr. Conlin put a hand on her arm. It was a ginger touch, soft and almost caring.

"Are you taking this okay?"

Mona didn't know how to answer. "My office's been broken into. So, that's not fun."

Dr. Conlin folded his arms across his chest again. "Not at all. But if you're worried about the work that was destroyed, don't be."

"Really? I mean—thanks—but it's going to set you back for a long time. Especially since Joyce and Lisa were also hit."

"And the experimentation rooms," he added. "So, yeah, all the preliminary findings have been shredded. So, even if we had computer backups on the iPads, the consent forms are gone. We have to start from scratch."

Mona wanted to say another kind platitude, but Dr. Conlin didn't seem to need it. His nonchalant stance suddenly bloomed into utter delight. A Cheshire cat-like grin poked out from his greying beard. He bounced on the balls of his feat, almost joyful.

"You should appreciate this, too. The irony of it."

"I should?"

"Yeah, the former English major in you. Research on ownership was destroyed? Amazing. This is so wonderfully poetic I'm inclined to write a paper on it and get it published. I don't exactly know where, but I suppose I could depend on you for that."

Mona tried to feign a smile. Ever since she had

resigned herself from running experiments, she knew she'd still have to do some kind of work for him. Maybe not the lucrative stuff that got her a line on her CV or an acknowledgment in a journal, but the stuff she was doing before. Maybe even editing, proofing—English major things, as he would put it. She was dependent on some kind of RA work from him for funding—at least, until she left. The summer semester was nearly over. Carmen was nearly done. Mona wouldn't need to depend on Dr. Roger Conlin much longer.

So, she'd ignored all emails and phone calls about this situation. Not answering an email was so much easier than just speaking to someone in front of you, though. She had to smile now and nod and pretend to be enthusiastic about the irony in her work being destroyed and that she still depended on him to live. Every last part of her body felt violated—from the robbery, from Carmen's ideas about Dr. Conlin—yet no one had touched her. Dr. Conlin may have never touched anyone at all. There was no proof. There was only rumour and conjecture, a parade of shredded papers and gobbled-up words. The feeling grew in her stomach, making her queasy.

"So, what do you think?" Dr. Conlin asked. "Maybe we can shed light on this situation. Perhaps try to figure out the root of the anger that could make someone destroy work on ownership—as if his feelings of anger trumped our right to research."

"I thought you said that guy could just be a weird student."

Dr. Conlin shrugged. "Or something like that. It doesn't matter who actually did do it. We're just all playing detective."

"Why write the paper then, if it doesn't at least try to point to the truth?"

Dr. Conlin looked at her as if she was crazy. When Mona didn't budge, he uncrossed his arms so he could gesture as he explained, as if this was in one of his classes. "All truth depends on context. Our experiments weren't finding the true meaning of ownership, only ownership dependent on certain contexts. The aliens, for instance. If we think someone else is not like us, it gives us more credence to think we own them. Maybe. That was what we were testing for, in one of many contexts. Really, the same goes for that detective and his crew as they attempt to parse out motive here. Why did someone do these things? There is no truth, only what emerges around the clues. The same goes for you and your poetry translation. There is no ideal poem, carved out of stone—there are only constellations that we connect. Right?"

Mona felt exposed, found out. She had only published one article on poetry translation—on her beloved *La Pléiade* group—but it was clear now that he had found it and read it. He quoted it back at her.

"We all want to play detective here," he went on.

"Academics, especially, and academic psychologists even more. We're all looking for signs and symbols to tell a good story. The end result doesn't matter, though. That's why Freud was tossed out. He was all about the endings—Electra, Oedipus. They're all stories, and they're mostly tragedies. They tell us nothing about methodology, which is what we should be focusing on. And this methodology just got interesting. We had a participant steal ownership. I can write that. Someone, also wanting to play detective, will publish it. But will you proofread it? Give a talk on it with me?"

Mona didn't understand why he wanted her to read it. Why he wanted her to find his shitty grammar mistakes and passive voice. Why couldn't Joyce or Lisa? Even if they weren't former English majors, they still knew how to write. They were qualified and already published. But the answer was clearer now than ever before: He wanted her to play detective, too, to examine her life and her choices, and be rigorous with how she structured her thoughts. She could never study Kitty Genovese because that was too focused on the outcome, and the outcome was always a dead body.

"Sure," Mona said. There was no other answer she could give. She would proof his work, sure. But hopefully, she would also be gone well before he even finished the first draft.

"Excellent! Thank you so much. *Merci beaucoup*." He touched her arm again, gingerly like before. "I hope I can get a draft to you quite soon then. There's an upcoming showcase where I think this work would shine. We'll do the paper, test it out on an audience, and then revise for publication. Perfect."

"A showcase?"

"Yes. In a week or so at the school. Ah, this is perfect." Dr. Conlin rubbed his hands together in genuine enthusiasm. Mona merely felt crushed. She'd said yes to his proofing without quite fully grasping the nature of the "talk" he was speaking about. A talk as in a public talk. A lecture. He wanted them both to lecture—or worse, for her to be the public face of their research on ownership, which had now been stolen and destroyed at least once. She swallowed hard. She didn't bother to argue with his visions on their joint research. She hoped to wait out the rest of her time here, and then she could finally be free.

When they finally parted, he turned towards the other end of the hallways, bypassing the techs and other detectives as he did. Mona walked across campus, replaying their conversation at least twice, before she sat next to Carmen again. Carmen's coffee was long gone, while Mona's was cold and taking up her place on the bench. Carmen was typing frantically on her phone, her foot jiggling as she did.

"Perfect timing," Carmen said, rising to meet Mona. "I have to jet real soon. But you're invited to my party, you know."

"Thanks."

"Hey." Carmen touched her arm again. It was the exact spot where Dr. Conlin had touched her. Mona didn't know if it was better or worse to be grasped there again. "Are you okay?"

"Fine. Just ran into…"

"The man who shall not be named." Carmen sighed. "I know it's shitty, but things are going to turn around. I see it in your future."

Mona barely smiled. She hated the fact that, when she looked at Carmen now, she was trying to see her as a detective. Because Dr. Conlin was right. That was the very point of why she'd transferred from English literature to psychology; we were all just looking for signs and symbols to make sense of our lives. Carmen saw signs of hope and happiness for those she liked, while emphasizing the danger signs for those she disliked. In one of Carmen's stray texts about the break-in, she'd joked about how relieved she'd been that no one thought she'd done it. Mona had wondered why, but of course, the transphobia was obvious in the statement. In popular culture, in mystery novels especially, the trans person was the criminal. Buffalo Bill. Norman Bates. Gender transgression led to social transgression.

For once, though, Carmen was an innocent by-stander. She didn't do the break-in, and she wasn't in danger. So instead, she played the therapist-detective to Mona, acting as a confidant but also creating the problem she knew how to solve. Dr. Roger Conlin and his bad touch. But Carmen was touching her arm in the same place. If the end result didn't matter and the detective was about methodology, then how was Carmen any different than him?

Seeing it all so transparently should have been exciting, but Mona was deflated. She stepped away from Carmen's touch.

"Oh, sweetheart. You're going to be okay." Carmen stepped forward, and without permission, wrapped her arms around Mona. When Mona let out a sudden cry, Carmen hugged her tighter. She expected this. She saw all the signs and knew what would happen. In that moment, Mona leaned into her roles, and accepted the help. It seemed as if there was no escape.

"You ever think about what I offered before?"

"Hmm?"

"About the sleeping pills. I still got 'em. Maybe... maybe some rest will do your tired mind some good. You've been running on empty so long now."

Mona stared blankly into the wall as Carmen still hugged her. When their gazes met, though, she saw the answer to her own mystery so clearly. If she was now a detective of sleep, on nightmares and Shadow People, then this was her final clue.

"Yes," Mona said. "I think I'd like that a lot."

CHAPTER NINETEEN

Hey, Roy?"

Roy glanced up from the grill. Sweat beaded against his forehead, his cheeks red. It was after two p.m. on a Monday, their quietest time, and free of a staff meeting. Kerri had bused most of the tables and served hunter Jim his coffee with eggs. She had at least another twenty minutes to herself before he'd want a refill—so she stood in front of the kitchen, awkwardly touching the jagged scar against her elbow, one that wasn't visible against all the creases in her skin.

"You okay, Kerri?"

"Oh, yeah. I just... Would you like to come outside with me for a minute? It's probably cooler out there than in here."

After grabbing his pack of cigarettes, Kerri held the door for the two of them. Tara, a new waitress still in training, perked up at her station, ready to take over if need be.

"What's up?" Roy asked after lighting up. "You're doing that fidgety stance when you're nervous."

"I…what?" She folded her arms at her sides, completely immobile. "I do no such thing."

All Roy did for a few seconds was smile. Then he shook his head, dislodging some of his grey-blond bangs from his bandanna. "Never mind. What's up?"

Kerri took a deep breath. She repeated her mantra and felt her heart rate go down. "I was wondering if I could borrow your car."

"My baby?"

Their gazes both fell on Roy's Mazda, so rusted around the wheels that his regular spot in the diner parking lot had permanent red impressions. He'd driven the car since he first started working there two years ago, and not once had Kerri ever seen it break down. She trusted it far more than any car out there, even at a rental place.

"I can pay you. You can be my Hertz man. You know?"

"As long as you don't mistake me for O.J." He paused. "Is that reference out of date for you?"

She smiled and shook her head. "I may have been homeschooled a good chunk of my life and not had access to TV, but I assure you that I've since boned up on all my popular culture."

"Ah, well, you'll forgive me for thinking I'm an

old man when you're so young and vibrant. You're probably not even old enough to rent a car, are you?"

Kerri rolled her eyes. Though Roy flirted like this often, it was never for real. Not like some of the diner's regulars that she had to find new and interesting ways to let down easy and definitely not like Absalom when he first started showing up. His attempts at flirting with her had been so genuine, and Kerri had liked him so much as a friend, she had to tell him the real reason she was constantly "busy" on Friday nights: she was gay. Absalom had taken that well, casually brushing it aside and moving on, but she didn't exactly trust many of the other diners in the same way.

Roy, though, was different. He would understand reason. Kerri was about to lay out her plan once again, stating her case with finely researched points, but he'd already acquiesced. "Yeah. You can borrow it. We talkin' a day or two?"

"Two days, one night. I want to drive to IKEA and pick up a new bed." She was about to add more, explaining about Mona's bedbug situation and her own sudden urge to redecorate, but Roy waved his hand, smoke cascading, and cut her off.

"Then have at it. No payment necessary, save for the gas you wanna put in her, and if you fender bender someone, you pay it. But yeah, sure. Take my car and have fun with your lady friend."

"Oh, you see right through me."

"You're a very easy person to know."

Kerri was touched by his words. She wanted to tell him her full plan then, not just as an excuse to use his car, but as a way to share her excitement. Though Mona was the brainchild behind the idea—at least, through stray text messages when she complained about her lack of furniture for her place—Kerri had instantly been drawn to the plan. In the past, the two of them would have most likely just gone to a thrift store for a lamp or shelving units; the bedbugs had somewhat spooked Mona from ever doing that again, though. While Kerri insisted that they could have gotten in her building any number of ways, she wanted to be indulgent for a while. *Dante Under Ice* was selling moderately well (meaning Kerri's royalty cheque was higher than her conservative estimate), so she wanted to update her own apartment, too. She wanted to go shopping and find items that matched her décor—hell, to even *start* a décor. Kerri found herself looking through catalogues that showed up in her apartment complex foyer; she thought in colour pallets and swatches and wondered what she actually liked. Though she had lived in her current apartment for years, she had never considered it permanent. She was always month to month. Owning something more permanent made her feel chained.

Or so she thought. Being with Mona had made

her feel grounded. So, maybe new furniture for both of them would help.

Kerri didn't want to broadcast their relationship too much, though. As caring as Roy was, she'd always maintained a distance at her workplace. Out but not out. She never hid her affections, especially not with Mona, but she also never announced them. Yet apparently, she was transparent. *Lady friends.* She had to laugh.

"So, what gave me away?" Kerri asked. "My love of softball?"

Roy chuckled. He flicked his cigarette out on the sidewalk and ground it out. "No, no. You're very secretive, Kerri, and you manage to keep a lot of them. I get not wanting to broadcast the girlfriend around. Relationships are new and scary, and some people ain't as cool with the gay thing as others. But you keep secrets about your books, about your mail, about how you like your coffee."

"That's not a secret. It just changes."

"Uh-huh. Whatever it is, it shuts people out. But it also doesn't prevent them from knowing you."

Kerri glanced down, focusing on the embers and ashes from the cigarette. Roy was always smiling, even when he was serious like this—yet his words felt like a reprimand. She wanted to tell him he was wrong, but she knew he wasn't. She was always keeping secrets, holding the world so tightly inside of herself because it was the way she had stayed safe for so, so long.

"I'm getting better," she said instead. "I even did an interview. Like you said I should."

"I know. I listened to it a couple nights ago. And I found out you had a brother. I didn't even know that."

Kerri nodded. She wanted to explain that talking about Lee to *anyone* was difficult—but especially men who were nice to her, friendly with her—because it made her miss him even more. How could she even explain that she wanted to keep those memories safest of all because they were all she had left? And how could she forgive herself for thinking of him in past tense, when as far as she knew, he was still alive?

"I'm sorry," she said instead.

"Hey, don't apologize. Your life is your life. But I just figured that we were closer than that. And I wanted you to know, especially for your lady friend, that when you care about someone, knowing things about them and them knowing things about you isn't a burden. It's fun. Sharing is caring, as they say. I suppose I just hope you're talking to each other, you know? And not just about the daily specials."

Kerri nodded. She knew Roy was referring to, not the diner specials, but the quotidian details of life. She'd heard him talk about his wife, Nancy, and how, past a certain point, you fall into a pattern of checks and balances, well-worn phrases and sentiments. Part of the reason he had taken a job as a short-order cook so late in life was to change the narrative of his daily existence to keep their relationship strong. He didn't say it in so many words—"just wanted a changeup, you know? And we've been better for it"—but it was evident. It was so easy to let life as life take over and to remain in present tense. Kerri had wanted to stay in present tense for so long because the future was precarious and the past was painful. Letting the fear wash over her allowed to her stay put in the moment and appreciate the moment for what it was: here when she didn't think it ever could be.

But she was slowly learning that there was more to life than that. Beyond that. Like teal trim in a bathroom. Picture frames. And bookshelves where her author copies would maybe stay on the shelf a little longer this time around, before donating them to a library or the diner crowd.

"Anyway," Roy said after some time. "I don't want to lecture you. But I do want to meet your girl in a more formal setting. Maybe have a party, you know?"

His gaze lit up at his own suggestion. Kerri found it intoxicating now, rather than shameful.

"Like a book release party?"

"Yes! Now you're thinking."

"Maybe I'll even have it in my apartment, you know."

"And give me some warning so I can get a better cake."

"Obviously."

"Oh, my girl," Roy said, beaming. "This is a breakthrough. Feel like I'm on *Dr. Phil*. Feel like I am Dr. Phil."

"Now, now. Don't sully the mood entirely."

Roy chuckled. When a bus full of students pulled up to the stop and got out, Kerri and Roy knew they needed to get back to work. Roy held the door as Kerri surveyed the students inside, wondering if Mona was among them. Seeing nothing, she followed Roy back through the diner.

"You know what?" Kerri said, as Roy sank back on the grill. He raised his brow as a sign for her to continue. "I should tell you, in this nature of sharing. I'm...writing a new book. And I may even name a character after you. Pretty sure I have the perfect one."

Roy extended his hands in the air, his cheer louder than the bell for customers. By the time Kerri turned her attention to the influx of people, Absalom and Sandra joined the counter. She gave them a quick nod and attended to other tables before making her way with large cups of coffee.

"How goes it?"

"Busy," Sandra said. "Seven robberies in one day."

"Yikes."

Absalom nodded. His dark complexion seemed strained, as if he was entrenched in something far bigger than he could understand. "They're all in the same place. At the university. Seven separate offices, along with two computer areas."

Kerri tensed. "Oh, yeah? What part of the school?"

Absalom tilted his head, catching Kerri's faint interest. "I know someone in the psychology wing. Has anyone been hurt?"

"No, no. But we're just hoping this isn't a Unabomber situation. So far, no weapons or manifestos for that fact, but universities as targets freak me out." Absalom stopped when Sandra nudged him and shot him an intense glare. "But I can't exactly divulge personal information at this time about any psychology students."

Absalom's subsequent expression, coupled with the tone of his voice, communicated all Kerri needed to know. She completed the rest of her orders, topped up the coffees, and then stepped outside once again so she could check her phone. No messages from Mona. She sent her several quick texts to ask how she was and whether or not they were still on for their date later tonight.

Kerri bit her lip as she waited. All thoughts of IKEA and the trip to Toronto, where maybe the two of them could get dinner and have fun like a couple, disappeared. Panicked thoughts, ones filled with Mona's and her own past, swarmed her.

"I'm okay." Mona's message came in five agonizing minutes later. "But yeah, that was our department. Work shredded, computers broken, shit disturbed. I'm kind of upset about the whole thing."

"Can I do anything?"

As Kerri waited for a response, she kicked herself. She shouldn't ask. She should just *go*. Her suspicions were confirmed when Mona texted back a simple no.

"Are you sure?"

"No…" Mona said a minute later. "But I think I just need to be alone right now."

When Kerri tried to call, there was no response. She texted back a couple more words of encouragement but stopped when they weren't returned. This wasn't about her. She knew this wasn't about her—personally, at least. Mona had always been running from something, and now *something* had happened. Even if she was safe, it probably reminded her of all her darkness and nastiness. So, she wanted to retreat. It made perfect sense. It was what Kerri had been doing her entire life.

But I'm part of that nastiness, too. Kerri thought of Roy's words. She thought of her own past. She saw them as inextricably linked. Together, she and Mona were a mobius strip of trauma—circling, oscillating, and repeating together. They could not stop this dance until they embraced it. Until they embraced each other.

Kerri sighed. She watched as more people came into the diner. She still had four hours left in her shift, and then she could take Roy's car for a trip that obviously wasn't going to happen anymore. Or happen the way they'd planned. Kerri could *still* take a trip, though, and maybe face her own darkness.

Kerri trembled at the thought. She balled her hands into fists and took a deep breath. When she stepped into the diner again, her mind was made up.

Four hours from now, she was going to visit her father.

CHAPTER TWENTY

The drive to the Kingston correctional facility only took one hour and fourteen minutes. Kerri documented every last geographical ping on her phone, hoping that the twisting lines of green, yellow, and sometimes red (to indicate a traffic accident that set her back six minutes) could become the multicoloured version of the thread Ariadne had given to Theseus in Greek myth: It would lead her out of the labyrinth if she became lost and forgot why she was there.

The last time that Kerri had seen Amos Reznik was one month after his sentencing. She came to see him in hopes of putting his mythic image out of her mind. Even as a child, her father seemed far more part of her storybooks than real life. A Paul Bunyan in military fatigues, a giant standing six foot five inches, and of course, a Minotaur, who seemed to be all human until he opened his mouth and spoke of "The Redemption Arc." When she'd heard this as a kid, she thought he meant ark as a boat. It was a strange quirk about her father, a reference she didn't understand. It was only when she was older and she saw the words written in his survivalist literature that she understood he was talking about a story—a character arc, a plot arc. She'd felt a connection with him in that moment because it meant they were both writers.

For a time, she was in love with that idea. She'd write her own stories during homeschooling sessions their stepmother saw over while he penned his survivalist pamphlets. At night, they'd shared. Lee and Layla would listen, ask questions, and be the best captive audience. It was only when The Redemption Arc finally came to fruition that Kerri realized her father wasn't talking about fiction anymore. The edges had blurred. The fantasy was reality, and the world was ending.

When Amos was on trial, he still seemed mythic. A subdued giant, without the knives and guns and now medicated, but his dark beard still glowed like fire. He still seemed like the man she loved, in spite of knowing what he'd done. In spite of ruining everything and seeing it all laid out in stark exhibits. When he insisted on testifying on the stand, though his lawyer had protested, Amos had sealed his guilty verdict when he brought up the same Redemption

Arc. He'd spoken so eloquently, though, that Kerri was afraid he was still mighty. She needed to see him in prison clothing, behind glass, sentenced and locked away for at least twenty-five years to life, before she was sure he was truly subdued.

At sixteen, she waited by herself on the other side of the door. He came forward and sat down. His face was swollen with newly acquired weight. His voice was quiet as he picked up the phone. She'd let out a breath instead of a hello. The myth of her father was crumbling. He was still a giant, but now there were barriers around him to keep him in place. After an awkward conversation, she had moved on with her life.

She didn't hear from him again until she was eighteen. A forlorn birthday card arrived, which she promptly threw out. She moved. Nothing happened for another year, when another birthday card somehow showed up. She started to become more secretive about her address—but somehow, inevitably, he always found her. The letters started to grow in length and frequency, as if they were making up for his lack of presence. She moved three times in one year before the same damn letters with the Kingston numbers on them showed up. So, she gave up and stayed at her current place. He was going to send her letters. *Fine.* Sometimes, she would even read them. And she would even write back, if only to keep whatever force of his will contained and no longer at dangerous mythic levels.

But she never had to see him again. The longer she was away from him, the weaker his hold became. He could not physically make her come, even if he had insisted that she was on his approved guest list and that he was on medication now, and so things were different and he was normal.

Kerri had seen what "different" looked like. She had seen what "normal" Amos Reznik looked like, too. It didn't matter if he was on drugs or not, contained in a cage or not, Amos Reznik would never receive his own redemption arc in her eyes. He could find God (and probably had, at least once, so it looked better when he applied for parole) and be washed in the blood of the lamb, but he would never be forgiven by her. Time and distance had only made this fact clearer. He would always be the giant who killed her stepmother and kidnapped her and Lee when they were twelve years old. He would always be the man who ruined her life and the source of the scar on her elbow. She didn't have to forgive him or see him anymore.

Yet she found herself here.

Roy's words had blurred by the time she reached the prison. She wondered what kind of meaning she had interpreted in them to end up here. She knew she wasn't going to forgive her father. To forgive him was too simple, too reductive. But maybe seeing him in person would change something. Maybe it would make her less afraid of her mail and all the possibilities. She'd attempted to write her father out of her life by turning Mickey Alan from *Dante Under Ice* into an Amos proxy and by murdering him in the final pages.

For a couple of weeks, it had felt better. She drank whiskey and then sent the novel to her publisher. When she ran her fingers along the edge of her elbow, the scar had felt like plain skin. The wound that her father created in her life had subsided, eased. Maybe that was why she was here—not for him. Never for him. But for herself. She could write about her fear all she wanted, to let it wash over her, but it was always passive. To look him in the eye and turn away, unharmed, meant she was active. Meant she was strong.

It meant she was the last one standing, like Starla in the novel. A goddess, a warrior. She was the mighty one.

She'd forgotten to have a Starla figure the first time around, when she'd tried to write about Amos in the mystery genre. She needed Starla to bear witness to the murder but not commit it. Kerri was sure that had made all the difference. And certainly, the book was selling better than the failed mystery one ever had. Maybe whatever magic she'd worked had actually worked.

Kerri repeated all this to herself as she went through the protocol for visitors. He would still be behind glass, and they would use a phone to communicate. He didn't know she was coming, but the guard appeared with him almost right away, as if he had been waiting for her since she was sixteen.

All thoughts vacated her mind. His massive beard was now gone. His once dark ruddy hair, so much like her own, was white and curled close to his skull. *And there's no beard.* She repeated this fact over and over again. It changed his entire face shape. It made his smile wonky and unfamiliar, too jarring and misplaced.

He looked so much like Lee without a beard. He looked so much like someone she loved.

"Kerri?" His lips moved against the phone, but Kerri didn't hear. She hadn't picked up the receiver yet. He gestured to it in front of him. Kerri grasped it in her hand, hoping he didn't see how much she shook.

"Hi, Dad."

"Notice anything new?"

"Hard not to."

"It's been like this a while. But what's old is new for someone who hasn't seen it yet."

"I suppose so," Kerri said. *And I never want to see it again.*

Kerri closed her eyes in an extended blink. She wanted his beard back. She wanted to erase whatever familiarity had been conjured. Behind her eyes, she focused on Layla's body, sprawled out and prone, a hatchet in her back. Her father was a murderer. Lee was her saviour, her twin. They may have come from this man, they may not have ever really known their birth mother, but their father was not their family.

"How are you doing, Kerrilyn?" Amos asked. "Your last letter was a while ago. But I suppose if you're coming in now, that's a good thing, right?"

"Sort of," Kerri said. She suddenly became aware that her father's birthday was in the beginning of August. She usually wrote to him then. She started to tell him now that this was an early birthday present since she was going to go away for a while at the beginning of the month and wouldn't have a chance to correspond.

"That's very kind of you to come in now then. I don't have too much contact with anyone else."

"Don't you?"

He shook his head. Kerri waited, silent, probing. She wanted him to confess that he'd sent someone to terrorize her and Mona. To break into the university and destroy what beginning of a relationship she had. To leave creepy messages in her mailbox in an attempt to work his way back into her life. Even before the murder, his favourite weapon had always been words.

He'd grown obsessed with pamphlets at gun shows and traded them back and forth with other survivalists. He was a proficient letter writer; memories of the post office and their mailbox overflowing were some of Kerri's first. When the trade shows and pen pals weren't enough, Amos created his own literature. He was always a man of paper and carbon and ink. So, why wouldn't he pass off this weapon of choice to someone else? Why wouldn't he keep writing letters to other sad, paranoid men on the other side about the end of the world? She wouldn't have been shocked to find a fan club devoted to her father's Redemption Arc. It was catchy. It was poetic. It was compelling enough to murder for.

Kerri waited for him to confess all of this, but Amos said nothing. When she brought up mail, he talked about a fishing magazine he had ordered with commissary money and a rainbow trout that was hard to catch. Then he talked about the show *River Monsters* with Jeremy Wade, asking her if she'd ever seen it. Benign, boring conversation. If Kerri didn't know any better and hadn't shared so much of her youth with this man, she would be convinced he was a stranger. Or that he really was cured. Amos may have been on medication that made him bloated, and he may no longer have the same red hair or a beard, but Kerri couldn't be fooled.

"Have you had a cellmate get out recently?"

Kerri cut him off in the middle of his story, so she repeated the question. "Have you? Because I've been getting strange mail. That's sort of why I'm here."

Amos was quiet. She hoped it displayed guilt. Instead, his doe-eyed expression seemed hurt. "No, Kerrilyn. In one of my last letters, I mentioned I was put in solitary after a scuffle in the common room. It's how I got this scar."

He held up his elbow. Striations appeared against his pale skin, so similar to her own wound from youth. She looked away, anchoring herself in the present moment and not the final accident that gave her own markings. She breathed through her teeth. She had no idea he was in solitary. That he'd been attacked. She didn't care.

"What about before then? Did you share your cell with anyone?"

"Of course. But I never talked about you or Lee."

"Yeah, right," she mumbled under her breath and away from the phone. "But you wrote me letters. They could have seen my address."

"True."

"Great." Kerri cursed again, her phone away from her face. Her father was talking again, but she didn't care. She got what she needed. Someone who shared a cell with her father was sending her letters. Maybe he knew who she was because of her books, or maybe it was a random twist of fate. She didn't know—but she didn't have to know for sure. She was going to feel guilt regardless, like she shouldn't have put her photo up online or made a Facebook page.

Like she shouldn't have tried to outshine her father in her own writing.

"Why couldn't you have let me have this, Dad?" she asked, but it was away from the phone. Distressed and unable to parse out what she'd revealed, Amos tapped the glass where her phone was. She put it to her mouth again and said goodbye.

Kerri didn't wait for a response. She set the phone down on its cover and turned her back on her father. When the world didn't end, like he always told her it would, she considered it a small victory.

CHAPTER TWENTY-ONE

The next morning, Mona was in the kitchen making coffee before she realized she'd slept through the night. More than that, she had been dreaming—but without feeling. She'd moved through the cityscape in her dreams, the shadow killer on her tail, but there had been no pressure in her chest. No heart palpitations. No shooting awake or the need to vomit in fear. There had been no fear at all, in spite of the same landscape that had once haunted her. She simply rose from the bed, her dream just a dream.

It was like everything was normal again.

When Mona caught sight of the sleeping pills on her nightstand, she understood what happened. She'd taken the pills from Carmen with shame prickling her skin, never believing that she'd actually get to this point. But how many therapists had told her to just *relax*? To let medication help? If she was going to be irresponsible and not go to the sleep clinic, she may as well *try* Carmen's solution. So, she'd been lured to bed the night before with the promise of little anxiety as she shut her eyes. That had been precisely what she received. After swallowing one blue pill, her vision had tinted dark and she slotted herself into bed. She counted to five before she was gone.

And now it was morning.

Mona held the bottle in her hands, marvelling at medical science. Sleep itself had been once so elusive. The lack of it had made her entire world sepia-toned, dreary and dark, without realizing it had been off-coloured. Lack of sleep had been her new normal, blurring out the memory of what normal had once been, like she had forgotten what colour was. Now everything was better. Not neon or fluorescent—but back to regular hues. The bad things still happened in her mind—Kitty or she or Kerri were stalked—but the fear was gone.

Mona forgot about her coffee. She took another pill instead. Sleep came again, quickly and easily. The dreams came again, as well. Soft and amorphous, her consciousness rolled out like a cloud to a different world, but quintessentially her own. It was so comforting, after so long of nothing but darkness.

She had so much time to make up.

By the fifth pill, Mona lost all concept of time. She'd spent so long under that she was now thinking better when she awoke; she rose in a hazy state, commanded her body to pee, drink some water, eat. She slid a blue pill in between the sandwich meat before falling into another napping fit. The lucidity of her thoughts was no match against the lucidity of her dreams. Daily reality was easier to handle now that it was back in normal colour, but Mona didn't want to stay there. Once her conscious thoughts had repaired themselves, her unconscious ones started to, as well.

And she realized she could control her dreams.

Now, when Mona awoke into a dreamland city with twisted buildings and shadow men at every corner, she was fighting back. The bystander effect was displaced. Instead of Kitty Genovese running from Winston Moseley, Mona Ouellet emerged on the scene and swooped in to save her.

In the first iteration of the dream, it took Mona too long to realize she could stop it. She'd walked into the stairwell like she always had, but Kitty and Winston were already tangled together as an infinity loop of violence. *Too late.* The hollowness inside Mona when she realized she could have prevented this was worse than the feeling of being swallowed whole in the psychology wing. So, she swallowed another pill and tried again.

This time, she walked the street with her keys

between her fingers. She ran up to Winston Moseley before he reached the stairwell and stabbed him in the neck. His blood ran horizontal, defying gravity, as it shot out like a ribbon that then pulled her and Kitty's bodies together. They were not wounded. They had survived. Kitty kissed Mona in gratitude. Then she walked the rest of the flight of stairs.

The dream ended before Mona could see what was at the top of the stairs. She somehow knew it wasn't Mary Ann in the Kew Gardens apartments but the same apartment building where the ax man had been. She was in the middle of taking another pill, so she could follow Kitty and understand the rest of the story, when a loud thumping pulled her back into the conscious realm.

She let out a low moan as her sleep-coma faded. Her mouth was dry and smelled like mothballs. Her skin ached. She tried to turn over so she could blot out the light, but the sheets pulled tight against her body. All the sheets had been torn from the edge of the mattress. Coarse hair poked out of her legs, long and sharp against her skin. How long had she been here? She didn't know. It felt like months, but it could have only been hours.

The thumping did not stop. Mona struggled to overcome her drugged state. The sound was her door. Someone was knocking on her door. Frantically.

"I'm coming, I'm coming."

Mona stood and then had to sit again. It took her five minutes to walk to her door and another two minutes for the words coming out of Kerri's mouth to make sense.

"I've been calling you," Kerri said. Her blue eyes were sharp sapphires, glassy with fear. "You didn't pick up."

"I was asleep."

"For how long?" Kerri asked. "I've been calling you for two days, ever since the campus robbery. You never answered. And my last three went right to voicemail."

Mona blinked several times. Kerri's jaw was set tight, clearly clenched. Her hair seemed dishevelled, her clothing casual. How long had it been since they'd seen each other in person? How long had she really been asleep? Overwhelmed by her own emotions, yet clogged with sleep drugs, the only thing Mona could think to do was close the door instead of answering the hard questions about time. Kerri's arm blocked her attempt. Her voice was hinged and frantic when she spoke; it hit Mona in the centre of her forehead.

"What's going on? Are you drugged? Willingly?"

"They're prescription."

"And is it *your* prescription?" Kerri asked, sussing out the real problem like a pro.

Mona walked away from the door and into her bedroom. Kerri followed, sliding the lock in place after she stepped inside. The moment she entered Mona's bedroom, she made a face. The smell? The state of her laundry? For a moment, Mona remembered the slightly bitter raspberry odour of bedbugs and wondered if she should be frantically checking her bed again. But she didn't move. She had once been so anxious that relaxation seemed a threat. Now she was so drugged up and sleep-bloated that consciousness seemed like a wound.

There has to be a middle way. But she had no answer. If there had been a middle way, she would have taken it years ago, when Gabriel first showed up in her class and demanded everything from her. All Mona knew now were extremes. So, she may as well stay in the extreme where she could kill Winston Moseley with a flick of her keys, rather than the one where she was a silent victim all along.

Kerri walked right to the pills. She examined the label in a few quick blinks before she walked out of the bedroom towards the bathroom. Mona understood what was happening in a flash and scrambled from the bed. She grabbed Kerri's arm in slow motion, begging her not to flush them.

"Do you have any idea how strong these are? How serious this medication is?"

"They work."

"But you've clearly taken more than the prescribed dose."

"Please. Don't. I need them."

"Not this many. Give me one good reason why I shouldn't get rid of all of them before you do something stupid and harm yourself."

"Because it's the only way I can save Kitty Genovese. It's the only way I can dream again. I'm in control with these. And if I save Kitty, then I save myself."

"From who, Mona?"

When Mona didn't answer, Kerri set the pills on the bathroom counter. She grasped Mona's hands in her own, holding her closer. Some of Kerri's anger dissipated into a strong grip, which then turned into a comfortable stroking against Mona's bare arm. "Who are you running from?"

"Gabriel. I'm always running from Gabriel."

"He's not here," Kerri said. "Not here. I promise."

"He is."

Kerri took Mona by her hands into every last room of the apartment, examining every last crevice and surface, however improbable. When she pulled back the mirrored closet doors, she left them open with the mirror angled. Mona could see into her bedroom from the front hall, and she was shocked by how empty and sad it seemed. She was shocked by how empty and sad *she* looked, only wearing a tank top and short-shorts. Her hair was a mess. She probably smelled awful. But Kerri still looked at her with kindness and sympathy.

"There is no one here but me, Mona," Kerri said. "And I'm not here to hurt you."

"Prove it."

Kerri's gaze was hard, examining Mona for what felt like a long time, before she finally brought their mouths together in a kiss.

Mona gasped at the contact, which allowed for Kerri to kiss her deeper. Her hands moved to Mona's neck, keeping their focus on each other. Mona melted; she went from stone to sand in seconds. Kerri held her with the sturdiness she needed but also the passion she felt deep inside. Before she'd tried to bury her feelings with anxiety, with work, and now the pills, Mona's want for Kerri had kept her up at night. It had invaded her dreams, leaving her sheets soaked and her body aching for more. She wanted to fall into bed with her, not to forget the world, but to embrace it. Tangling with Kerri didn't feel like an escape from the trauma of her past, but meeting someone who had felt something similar. Mona didn't know how, but Kerri could see the trauma underneath as easily as an x-ray, but unlike a machine, she could also reflect it back.

Mona ran her fingers along Kerri's arm, down to her elbow. The first time they'd kissed, she'd felt the scar tissue there. It was star-shaped, like a bullet wound or a butterfly knife twisted out. Kerri flinched when she touched the area, but it was not as if a nerve had been hit, more like a memory had been. Mona wanted to touch the memory and touch the body it belonged to; she wanted to direct Kerri to the places on her own body that hurt the most.

Mona broke the kiss to slide her tank top off her body and toss it on the floor. Kerri cupped her small breasts almost instantly, as if to hold her in place. Mona slid one of Kerri's hands to her ribcage, right where Gabriel had pressed the gun into her body. At night, she'd sometimes run her hand over the same area—as if she was afraid it would disappear, as if she was afraid that him merely touching her skin in that act of violence had taken it from her. She was always surprised when that part of her skin was still there and that her ribs were still visible beneath. And she'd always been skeptical, checking again the next night and the next, just in case she'd been fooled. Now as Kerri cupped her hands over the same spot, she may not have known the history, but her hands helped solidify it. Mona saw her own body in full colour again; she saw Kerri's, too, and ran her hands along her waist, her neck, and then over her mouth as they kissed again.

Kerri continued to explore. From ribcage to navel to her thighs. Mona wore nothing underneath her short-shorts. Kerri must have felt the heat between her legs because she shuddered.

"Bedroom," Kerri mumbled. "Are you okay with that?"

Mona walked to her room and lay on the bed as the answer. A sense memory wanted to lie down and sleep; whatever was left in the pill made her ache with exhaustion. But Kerri between her thighs made her feel alive again. Kerri removed Mona's shorts, smelling and kissing her skin as she did. She removed her own top, her breasts spilling out of her bra. Kerri reached behind herself and unhooked it the rest of the way.

When their mouths met again, Mona's eyes closed. She could find every last place on Kerri with ease now. She knew how to unhook her pants and slide her jeans down her legs; she could run a finger along Kerri's folds and know where to touch to make Kerri's breath change. But there was a darkness to her actions that didn't feel right. It was too much like dreaming, too much like she was caught back in her lucid state of mind and someone would come by, ax in hand, and ruin it.

"Look at me," Kerri said.

Mona opened her eyes. Kerri stared at her, cheeks flushed and body rigid. Her breasts bounced as she panted, and the apex of her thighs was red thatched with hair. She was so pale, her hair so red like fire, that she seemed more like a dream again.

"This isn't a dream, right? I'm not sleeping?"

"No. Not at all." Kerri smiled. She looked behind her. Their gazes caught in the mirrored closet door. Kerri must have seen the fear and hesitation on Mona's face—not for their actions, but for her own sanity—and knew the mirror could be an anchor object. The mirror image, in some way, projected more truth. Their naked images, tangled together, broadcasted who they were better than names.

"Come."

Kerri guided their bodies into new positions. Kerri lay on the bed now, Mona on top, facing the mirror. Mona watched as Kerri's fingers traced a new cartography of her body, from nipple to navel to the folds of her vulva and what was hidden beneath. After a few strokes, Kerri moved so her kisses reached Mona's thighs, and her breath was hot against her skin.

"Don't close your eyes." Kerri touched Mona's petal-like skin and then pulled away. She repeated it, each action lingering longer the next time. Each time pleasure overwhelmed Mona, she wanted to shut her eyes and revel in the feeling. But then it felt more like dreaming. And she felt like she was slipping away. So, Kerri nudged her back into consciousness.

"Stay present, Mona. Stare at me. In the mirror. Look at me. Look at yourself. You have power in this."

Kerri punctuated some of her commands with touches. Mona shuddered. She struggled to watch as Kerri soon swapped her fingers for something more intimate. She stared and remembered Kerri's words. Pleasure washed over her. She saw her own face twist and contort. Bit her lip and sighed. Kerri's mouth moved against her; Kerri's red hair bounced in the mirror as she worked. A lattice pattern of pink hues, an imprint from their hands against each other, emerged as new terrain on Mona's body. Marks that Kerri had made, marks that Mona wanted to keep.

Mona stared. She negotiated her desires with her fears, and she watched as it all unfolded. She was in control now, as much as she could be, because this was her body. Many people had tried to take it, but it was hers. Even as Kerri made her melt, made her pant and moan and writhe, Mona was still herself. She could watch it all happen.

Her power was not a dream.

She kept her revelation on the tip of her mind, on the tip of her tongue, until Kerri's motions won out. When Mona came, it was the only time she looked away from the mirror. She looked down at Kerri in that moment, their gazes meeting. Not a dream. Not a dream at all. Kerri beneath her soon became Kerri in her arms, and she repeated all she needed until they were both spent.

❧ ❧ ❧ ❧

Mona didn't need sleep after sex, but Kerri did. Her exhaustion seemed to fall off her in waves, so Mona tucked her into bed and made coffee for herself. She charged her phone and cleaned her apartment as quietly as she could. She wanted to welcome the world again, after being gone for so long, even if it was only two days. Time still seemed to fold and constrict; it felt more like the day after Gabriel than three years later.

She was halfway through responding to emails—mostly from Carmen about her party—when she heard a small knock on the door. She looked out her peephole and saw nothing. Though apprehensive, she opened the door. A package from Amazon stood in front of the door. It was late in the evening, so out of the range of possibilities for a delivery—and when Kerri had come in, she mentioned no package. Mona's heart rate climbed. She wanted to believe it was Amazon making good on the missing book. But she knew, deep down, that was not what she was going to find.

She bent down closer to the package. There was no tape against it to keep it shut. On the side, where her address would have been had this been a real package, was a newspaper clipping from the McGill paper. It was old, dated almost six years ago. Gabriel Côte was the main writer.

Mona slammed the door. She turned around,

caught sight of her fearful expression in the mirror,
and started to cry.

CHAPTER TWENTY-TWO

Mona. Mona?"

Kerri's voice broke through Mona's flashback. Her panic crescendoed into vivid memory; her cries had become screams then whimpers as the Francophone song remained inside her head on an endless loop. The elevator's buttons went down, down, down. The gun was in her ribcage. Gabriel smelled like fear. The door was about to open, but Kerri brought her back. She was clad in only her bra and underwear, but she moved with the composure of someone in an Army general uniform. Her mouth was a moving machine part, calling Mona's name and then barking out muted commands.

"Mona, Mona. Pay attention. Answer me."

Kerri shook her shoulders. She snapped her fingers in front of Mona's face. There was no time for hugging or hand holding. When Mona gestured to the door from her spot crumbled on the floor, Kerri assessed the danger with a quick glance out the peephole. Seeing no one, she opened the door with the tactics of the police. Only when she was sure that everything was clear did she nudge the package before picking it up.

Mona shut her eyes. "Please be careful. It could be—"

"It's not a bomb. It's not a dead animal. It's not even that menacing. It's just my book."

Mona's chest tightened. Had she freaked out and imagined the whole thing? Was she now turning inanimate objects into frightening talismans? Kerri shut the apartment door and turned the deadbolt. She carried the packaging to Mona's bedroom, leading Mona there, as well. Kerri opened all the adjoining doors to the other rooms, so Mona could have a clear view of the entire apartment. When Mona saw the newspaper article along the side of the box, she shook her head.

"No, no, no. That's him. That's Gabriel."

Kerri examined the side of the box. She tilted it to Mona. "That's you."

"What?"

"That's your name. It's a French label, though."

Mona examined the side where she'd once seen the newspaper. Her name was clearly there, along with the French label for Amazon. Had she been shopping in French? She sometimes left her computer in French settings to feel more at home. Had she done that for Amazon and then her anxiety had twisted it to read something far more sinister? Mona wasn't sure what was better—Gabriel appearing to taunt her with his old writing from the student-run paper or merely creating Gabriel out of a handful of misplaced accents in her own name. It was like she'd never be free.

When Mona started to sob again, Kerri put a hand on her shoulder. She rubbed it back and forth before asking, "Who is your neighbour?"

"What? What do you mean?"

"Who is your neighbour?" Kerri repeated, her voice stark and far too businesslike considering what they had done the night before. "People around you probably heard the screaming. So, I want to be prepared with a story when someone comes by."

"No one is going to come by. An old lady lives across from me, half deaf, and the rest of the place has students. Either they're gone for the summer or they don't care."

Kerri seemed to doubt that no one would come. Mona could only think of the thirty-seven people who had heard Kitty Genovese. Several of them had called the cops; one even yelled out to Moseley to knock it off when he saw them from outside his window, but what good had that done? Even if one of the students reached for their cell and called in Mona's whimpering, there was no guarantee that anything would happen.

Seeming to reach the same conclusion, Kerri nodded. She set the box on Mona's desk and reached for her pants.

"Please don't leave."

"I'm not. We need to talk about this, though. Because even if that label is from Amazon, they clearly didn't deliver it. It just looks exactly like how my book would have been delivered. It's like it's been tampered with."

"It's...it's the package that was taken from my office during the university break-ins. But...how did he know where I lived? How could he have figured it out?"

For a moment, Mona didn't know who "he" was anymore. Was it the weird guy who had said his name was Mickey, who probably did do the university burglary? Or was Dr. Conlin right and that kid was just in the wrong place at the wrong time, and she wasn't going crazy because Gabriel had always been around and was locking all the doors on her? Was it paranoia if someone was actually out to get you? Was it really called a nightmare if it just repeated in real life?

Mona's thoughts were cascading again. Now dressed, Kerri put a hand on her shoulder before she opened the box. The inside had been painted red. The packing peanuts were shredded French newspapers, all familiar, and all student-run. Kerri picked up the book from inside, finding *Dante Under Ice* with its purple and black cover. When she turned it around for her author's photo on the back, her eyes had been x'd out.

"Oh, God." Mona turned away. This *had to* be Gabriel. He was here now, out of whatever jail or prison he had been in, and now he was hunting her and taking those she loved. Just like he'd done to Damien. "You have to leave. It's the only way to be safe. You have to go before he knows you're here."

"I'm not going anywhere." Kerri stared at her face on the back, her voice placid. She traced fingers around the x's over her eyes. They were heavily indented and white in colour, as if a knife had been used to peel back the original dark colours of the cover. When she opened the book, words in the first chapter had been blanked out, as if parts had been redacted.

"Is this a message?"

"No." Kerri closed the book cover and put it back in the box. "Don't get on the same level. Don't try to figure it out. You can't."

Mona bit her lip. She tried to nod, but she was shaking. When a creak sounded from inside her apartment, she nearly screamed again.

"Calm." Kerri put both hands on Mona's shoulders. "That's the apartment shifting. No one is here. I checked."

"Can you—"

"I'll check again. Then we will sit in the bedroom and see if anyone calls the police. And if they don't, then we will call the police, okay?" When Mona was silent, Kerri insisted again. "We're calling the police because this is a crime. It's menacing. Stalking. Whoever did this, it is not your fault. You're not alone. You did not bring this on yourself."

Mona looked down. Kerri squeezed her shoulder. She only spoke again when Mona finally nodded.

"Before we do that, I need you to tell me who Gabriel is. Please."

Gingerly, Mona nodded. Maybe with someone else around, it would be easier to not slip back into the memory as if it was happening right now. When she added words to it—even just in her head—she no longer let it become about emotion. Gabriel was a student. Gabriel loved Edmund Spenser. He barely spoke French but had grown up in Ottawa, then decided to go to McGill because a cousin had gone here. He never went by a nickname. He had a bad haircut. Used Axe Body Spray. Her mind had become a redacted story, the scenes not strung together in any proper order but only in necessary bursts she could never control.

She wanted to change that. While Kerri left the bedroom to check the apartment once again, Mona tried to think of her life as an outsider would have seen it. Soon enough, it became an act of translation, from memory to language, from French to English. Even the Francophone song that seemed like a jarring warning became a benign ballad about club life. By the time Kerri returned, Mona's breathing had righted itself.

"No one is here but us." Kerri sat next to her. "So, tell me now."

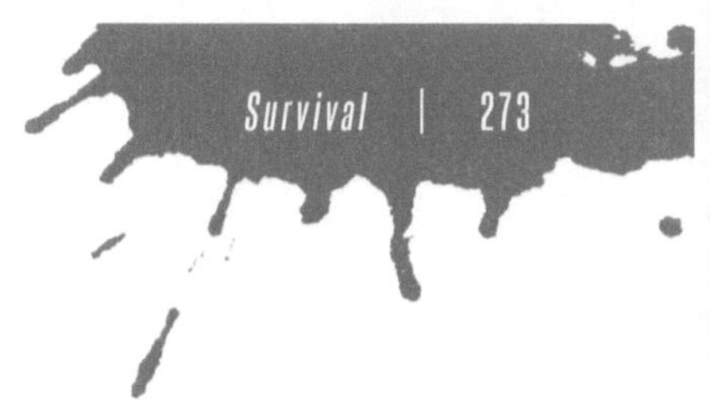

CHAPTER TWENTY-THREE

The first class I taught on my own was Renaissance poetry. I had been a TA up until that point, dealing only with one small section of the Introduction to English class. But by the time I was in my third year, I already had a publication in my specialized area, so they figured I could handle my own class. I had to make the syllabus, do the marking, and interact with all the students. It was so much work, but it felt like freedom. Pure academic freedom, and I utterly loved it."

After a few false starts, Mona was in the middle of the story—which was the beginning of meeting Gabriel, a nineteen-year-old student who was five-foot-seven. Kerri placed a hand on her knee whenever the details became too difficult or squeezed when Mona needed assurance that she was here and not there.

An hour had passed. No one had come to investigate about the screaming. Mona was partly disappointed and partly relieved.

"Gabriel was obviously one of my students. And he was a good student, too. He sat in the front row. Asked a lot of questions. Did all the readings. Everything a prof could ask for. But his papers were strange. The syntax was bad. I thought it was because of a language barrier, but it turned out he never spoke French. English was his first language. He was just a bad writer, so I gave him a bad grade. I thought he would be mad. He was mad."

Mona remembered the flare of anger that had appeared across his face as she handed back the papers. His dark eyebrows fixated on the grade in blue pen—she never used red to avoid moments like this—and his entire body seemed rigid. She swore even the people around him were afraid. As quickly as the moment happened, the anger also disappeared. "He wanted to see me after class—which is honestly not that strange after a bad grade—and when he showed up, he just wanted writing advice and help. Since that was literally my job, I told him my office hours. And he was always there. We got his writing to work better, and he passed the class. He was one of my success stories, honestly.

"But then he kept showing up to my office hours. I told him I couldn't help with other work, but I gave him the info for the writing centre. His body went rigid again, but it soon disappeared. Meanwhile, the department loved the work I'd done, so they gave me the same section of Renaissance poetry the next semester. And so he showed up there."

"He took it again? Or he just sat in the class?"

"He walked into the class and sat down. He was easy enough to spot." Mona explained how the university had emphasized small class sizes, especially for the second-year courses that were more specialized. "At the time, I tried not to let it bother me. Sometimes, people slip into lectures that are not their own. I did it a handful of times in university, especially for women's studies classes. It was weird, sure, but if you like Renaissance poetry, where else are you going to find it? I tried to give him books on it, even sent him some academic papers—like my own—but it only made matters worse. I tried to draw the line when he came to the tutorial for the class. I told him he couldn't stay since it was an unfair advantage to other students. Then because he wasn't actually registered. All neutral excuses. I wanted to yell at him at this point—but I kept my cool."

"You were nice." Kerri's smile betrayed how much she hated the statement. "A good girl."

"*Petite joliecouer.* Pretty little heart." Mona sighed. "When I stopped going to my office hours and stopped answering his emails, he showed up at my apartment building and wanted to be let inside. He insisted we already had a relationship. When I told him no, that I was calling the police, he left. I reported him to campus security, told my advisers, and the problems seemed solved. I didn't see him for a month. But then the letters started. Violent ones, gross ones." She blinked as she remembered the first strange one filled with nonsense about poetry interpretation. She summarized the next one, where her image had been superimposed on an old Renaissance painting, turning her beauty into something sharp and painful. "Effectively, he was turning me into an object of the poem, constructing a story."

"It's what all stalkers do. Justification. You two are in love, but you don't know it yet."

"Yeah, except I called the police. I got him thrown out of school since he was barely hanging on by a thread anyway. The letters stopped. He seemed to finally get the message. I did everything right. Everyone told me I did everything right."

The last meeting she'd had with one of the sergeants at the police station had been so inspiring. He had commended her for everything she'd done, even asking her to come in and speak on behalf of other victims. She'd felt like a gung-ho feminist activist, an icon for stalked women who took no nonsense. There was something so alluring in that status, glorifying the wound so that she could be made stronger.

"It's okay," Kerri said. "You *did* do everything

right. If you had done nothing, too, you would have done everything right. Because these types of crimes are never about the victim and always about the perpetrator."

"Even if I'm a pretty little heart?"

"While I do think you're beautiful, that doesn't matter, either."

Mona nodded slowly. For months after all this had happened, she'd not put on makeup. She let her hair go into ruins, not using a brush for weeks at a time. She ate and ate and ate, hoping that she could make herself undesirable in some way. Her actions were all so transparent, but the only thing that made her stop was when she still got catcalled. In fact, the rate seemed to go up when she stopped upkeeping her hair, makeup, and when she gained ten pounds and filled out her jeans. So, she gave up and did what she always did, by rote habit, without ever really feeling pretty without guilt again.

Until Kerri, maybe. Hearing the word "beautiful"—not pretty—come out of her mouth was nice. Different.

"Maybe you're right," Mona said. "Maybe I should have done nothing...because a month after I thought it was all over, he was in a class again. I walked over to tell him to leave, and he put a gun on the table. In a room full of students."

The murmur of realization spread out in her

classroom in slow motion. His hand had always been on the gun, and though he never aimed it anywhere other than front centre at first, it seemed like it could go off at any moment. The barrel was so long. It seemed gigantic and heavy, a weight against her throat. Mona had stared blankly. She had never been trained in any damn TA session what to do if a gunman walks in. Her slides remained projected in the lecture hall. When one of her students started to cry, Mona snapped to action.

"He only wanted me," she explained. "So, I told him I'd go with him if he let the class go."

"And he said yes."

Mona nodded, though Kerri didn't ask as if it was a question. "He said yes, but only on the condition that the class stayed in the room. So, he grabbed me by the arm and walked me to the fire exit. He knew we didn't have a lot of time together, but he thought that by sealing the students in the room, our interaction could be prolonged. But there were at least thirty of them. Thirty witnesses. Even if only one of my students reported him, I figured I would be saved. Something would happen. They had cellphones. They had a means of communication, even if they were all scared to leave."

"Did they report it?"

"Yes. But it took so long. We walked across the campus, in broad daylight, and no one did anything.

The gun was concealed in his coat, but I thought it was so obvious that I was in fear. I tried to make eye contact with everyone I saw as we walked, but no one looked up from their phones or iPods or their friends. When I realized he was leading me to the underground tunnels of the school, I started to panic. It was harder and harder to move. So, he pressed the gun into me harder. We stepped into an elevator together. It went down."

Mona closed her eyes. She was dragging this out too long, she knew. But Kerri was on the edge of her seat, attention never waning. "When the elevator opened, I remember thinking that someone would be there to save me. Surely, someone had seen. But there was nothing. He directed me towards the parking lot, reciting poetry under his breath. My vision was a pinpoint in front of me. Everything else was fuzzy, all fear. I figured I was dead by the time we got out of the tunnels. So, when a gunshot sounded, I fell to the floor. I thought I'd been hit. I saw blood. But it was Damien—my ex-boyfriend had seen Gabriel leading me in the campus, through the library windows."

"Oh, wow. Was he…?"

"He lived. He was only shot in the arm. He had come up behind us, taking the elevator down afterwards, and I didn't even know. But Gabriel lost his mind after that. He pulled me up by my hair and tried to drag me the rest of the way through the tunnels to the parking lot exit. He kept shooting in the general direction where Damien had come from, but the other bullets only hit cement. I thought Damien was dead—on the ground, not moving—but he was faking. Gabriel was so focused on Damien, though, and dragging me as dead weight that he didn't realize people were on the other side of the tunnel. Cops arrived. He dropped me and tried to run, but they arrested him."

Mona shrugged. She didn't quite know how to finish the story because really, what was the ending? She and Damien were in the hospital for a few days. Damien needed surgery and physical therapy. They were both praised for their quick thinking. Articles were written. Gabriel went on trial and then was sentenced. A year and a half passed.

But Mona could never return to the school. "I could barely talk to Damien, either. Everything felt like my fault. Then the nightmares started a year after the event. I thought they were just panic attacks, but they soon morphed and changed. I tried therapy. I tried a lot of things. But eventually, the only thing that made the nightmares somewhat manageable was leaving. So much for that."

"I get wanting to leave. Sometimes, a change of scenery really does change everything." Kerri seemed smaller in that moment. "Thank you for telling me this. It makes a lot more sense now."

"Does it, though? Because apparently Gabriel is back. Apparently, he's after me."

"What makes you think he's here and behind all this? Because he sent letters in the past? And do you think he broke into your office, too?"

"How else would he have gotten the book?" Mona ran a hand through her hair. Her roots hurt, a sense memory of being dragged. "It's him...because who else would be after me? Who else wants to taunt me by tearing apart books?"

"And he drew x's over my eyes because...?"

"Because he's always good at taking down people who care about me. Damien and I dated during the semester that I first taught Renaissance poetry. He would sometimes wait for me after class. I know that Gabriel saw him, and that was why he shot him. He must know I care about you. That's why he's targeting you. It's a warning."

Kerri examined the book on Mona's desk. She seemed to run over several things in her mind, putting together another puzzle that Mona wasn't privy to. "Okay," she said after some time. "What if he's not out of jail, though? Does any of this change?"

"He was only charged with attempted murder. It's very possible that he's on probation or parole, especially if he was a model prisoner. And he's deceptive. Smart. Rich parents. The world is built for him." Mona shook her head. "And if it's not him, it's someone who knows him."

"Like a cellmate?" Kerri suggested.

"Yes. Either way. It's him. He's pulling the strings on this."

"Okay," Kerri said again. She rose from the bed and grabbed the book. "So, we do something about it. Let's call it in."

Mona's stomach flipped. Deep down, she knew she'd avoided calling for so long, in spite of her bad feelings and The Shadow People at the periphery of her mind because the police had been the first trigger for Gabriel. If she could just run and run and run, none of it would matter. She could start over again. Mona drew her feet to her stomach. "I...want to move. I just want to leave. Fuck psychology. Fuck this school. I can't stay here."

"No."

"No?"

"No. You've already been run out of one home. You're not leaving this one."

"My bug-infested home? Yeah, what a thing to hold on to." Mona's mind cascaded with all the terrible things that had happened since moving to Peterborough. Had she ever really had a break? She was never escaping him; she was only displacing him. The thought that she would never, ever run from Gabriel hit her like a punch because she knew she would really be running from herself. "I can't do this."

Kerri sighed. She sat on the bed again, rubbing Mona's back. "You will be surprised at what people can endure."

"You've said that before. And one of your characters says it in *The Wendigo Forest*."

Kerri chuckled. "You were reading it?"

"Yeah, the e-book. Since I couldn't read *Dante Under Ice,* I figured I may as well go to the nightmare book."

Another quiet fell over them. Kerri shifted, debating something internally before she spoke. "I told you my father was a survivalist. It's only half the story."

"Yeah?" Mona asked. "Can't be nearly as bad as what I told you."

"Well, he murdered my stepmother when Lee and I were twelve. Then he kidnapped us."

Mona shut her eyes. She shouldn't have spoken. At least no one died in her story. She was about to apologize when Kerri held up a hand. "This is not a competition or a game. We have shitty things happen to us. We internalize them and then can't fathom that other people have the same nightmare that we have. It's why I wanted to show you that documentary, though. Our nightmares are so personal, but they're also collective. The hag. The mares. Even The Shadow People are shared. We're not alone in fear. It feels that way, but we're not. My father... thought the world was going to end. So, he ended our stepmother's life because she got in the way. Her death—though he had caused it—became evidence that the world was out to get him. He called it The Redemption Arc, and she kept him from reaching that point. So, he packed me and Lee into his pickup truck, and we left our small town home to go to his bunker so we could wait out the rest of our own redemption."

"For how long?"

"Two months, give or take. It was for a summer. Almost like camp." Kerri chuckled; Mona flinched.

"That's so long."

"It is. But no one found our stepmother's body for such a long time. By then, he had gone completely off the grid. You're also forgetting that we were his kids. He wasn't going to hurt us. Only terrify us into thinking the world was over, which I admit is a different kind of injury, but one he did out of a strange sense of love. We were twelve and wanted to be together, and his theories on the world were nothing new. For a time, it was kind of exciting. Like hearing about Santa your entire life and then being told you get to go to the North Pole. You forgive a lot on the trip there, even if you never reach the destination."

"Did you see...you know?"

"Her murder? No. But Lee saw her body after the fact. He...always protected me." Kerri sighed and folded her arms across her chest, as if she was attempting to keep the emotions locked inside. "Look, our father was sick. And by the end of the whole ordeal, so was I."

"What do you mean?"

Kerri held up her elbow, right around the spiderlike scar. "This is from a burn. Our father got us sparklers for our birthdays. Lee held one too close to me and burned my skin. It got infected. I got sick. I was hallucinating and thought I was going to die. So, Lee told our dad. He convinced him that I was going to die, so eventually, we drove to get medical care. He came back on the radar. We were picked up, and the whole story was over."

Mona was amazed that Kerri could condense a two-month captivity down to a sparkler and infection saving the day.

"Where's Lee now?"

Kerri seemed sad. "I don't talk to him anymore. It makes me too sad."

"Because of the captivity?"

"Because whatever my father had, Lee now has. Schizophrenia runs in families, especially for men."

"I'm so sorry."

Kerri shrugged. "I should have seen it sooner. We lived with our birth mother's parents after this, where we were forbidden to talk about our father. Our grandmother thought it was best to move on from the horror through silence. Lee and I did not—so we spoke

Czech to each other, something our stepmother had taught us during homeschooling under my father's insistence. At the time, I hated it—but soon it became the only language where what we'd experienced was real. And it was horrific, paranoid, but also so loving. Lee would sometimes go on rants about the same things my father did—the government, aliens, clones. Things like that. He'd referenced the Redemption Arc, too. But it was so normal to me that it never registered as anything weird."

"What changed?"

"Our grandparents died. First our grandfather and then our grandmother. We were only sixteen, and we couldn't be on our own. We went to foster care—separately."

"Separately?"

"Yeah. It sucked. But we wrote letters. We could speak in English again to each other. Lee wrote a lot. It was…all strange and weird, but again, I figured he had a bad foster house. When we finally met up again at eighteen, we moved in together. He still had odd habits, but again, I thought he'd just had a horrible foster house and had his privacy invaded. I gave him space. He'd disappear for weeks at a time, not pay the rent, and then blame it on banks and the government. He was being paranoid, but paranoia was love for us for so long that I didn't see anything wrong with it. But he was descending. He started drinking. When he'd come home so drunk I could smell him down the hallway, it soon became clear that his insistence that he was being followed and listened in on was part of what our father had."

"What did you do?"

"I tried to live with him for a while. Be there for him to tell him that no, there were no spies living in our phones. But I eventually had to go. And so did Lee. He's in a hospital. He's been there for a while, whenever he's not in a shelter. When he's on his medication, he's great. But he's not good at taking it by himself. So, he usually stays at a place in Ottawa that regularly works with the shelter system. He's pretty close to Montreal, actually."

"I'm so sorry," Mona said. "Do you see him at all?"

"No. He told me to leave the last time I came. So, I did."

Kerri's voice was flat, but Mona could see the pain in her expression. Lee was part of her; he belonged to her and her to him in so many ways. They had shared the same experience of trauma, and when she wanted connection, he showed her the door. Exactly like she'd done when Damien knocked on her hospital room and wanted to talk. All she could do was turn away because the pain of the event was too fresh.

"And your father?"

Kerri flinched. "He writes. I...I was so worried that your office being broken into was him in some way. I hadn't written in a while. So, I feared he was trying to get my attention through one of his survivalist friends. I was getting some pretty strange letters, too. Exactly like yours."

Mona couldn't help but laugh. So much emotion and tension welled up inside of her it had reached a critical mass—and now she longed to dislodge it. Kerri caught a glimpse of Mona amidst her guffaws. Her brows were raised, perplexed—but also smiling.

"What's so funny?"

"We both thought we were being targeted, and we both didn't say a fucking word because we were too scared. We both became bystanders to our own pain and the other person's. Like Kitty Genovese. We tried to become strangers." Mona laughed again, a tear rolling down her cheek as she did. "I'm sorry. This is black humour. I'm ridiculous."

"But it *is* kind of funny." Kerri's guffaws were smaller, more tightly contained. "And laughing beats crying. I mean...we're both so used to thinking of ourselves as the problem that the mere idea that someone else could be the issue never occurs to us."

"Exactly. It's kind of perfect, right?"

Kerri nodded, her laughter now ebbing. Mona's did, as well. The humour had dissipated once they articulated it with words; the dread had twisted into actual danger rather than manic, nervous energy. They were still being hunted in some form or another—even if who the actual target was had been blurred. Mona was still certain it was Gabriel, or someone who knew him, who was the cause of all this—but now she was more determined than ever before to protect those she loved, rather than turning her back on them.

"We need to call this in," Mona said. "I'm ready now."

"I know we do," Kerri said. "But I think we're also forgetting something."

"What?"

"We've survived this kind of shit before. Even though my father scarred me for life, he still taught me things. I can live alone—with or without power or plumbing—and I know how to take care of myself. He drilled me relentlessly, even more than Lee, because I was so small and would need to rely on stamina more than strength. I know how to shoot. To stab. To fight."

"I took a self-defense class. And I have pepper spray. That's about it."

"This is how we work together," Kerri said. "I can teach you how to live alone and not be afraid. How to secure your apartment and keep your weapons close—not just a baseball bat or pepper spray or keys. As accessible as those are, they don't do what you need them to. Maybe you won't have nightmares anymore, either, if you know you can fight."

"And I can...?"

"You can show me how to file a police report," Kerri said matter-of-factly. "Because I've never done that before. My father was afraid of cops and all authority. I've gotten over a lot of his teachings, but my first response to any danger is still not to call the police but handle it myself. So, you'll show me."

Mona nodded along, liking the sound of their plans. Her hopeless, helpless feeling started to diminish. Like her dream, when she had finally rescued Kitty Genovese from the hands of Winston Moseley, she could rescue herself from Gabriel—while also keeping Kerri safe in the process.

Kerri grasped both of their hands together and raised them to her lips to kiss. "We're in this together, okay?"

"Together."

CHAPTER TWENTY-FOUR

When Kerri showed up at the police station, Absalom was far more relieved than he gave himself credit for. Ever since his aborted attempt to talk with her at the diner about the university break-ins, he'd been thinking of her possible insights into the case. She'd seemed tense, as well, which only made Absalom's insouciant interest dive into somewhat overwrought obsession.

When Mona appeared by Kerri's side, holding a box with an ashen expression, Absalom went back into pure business mode. There would be time for coffee and speculation. Now he was needed. He and Sandra met the two women at the front desk and continued their interview in an empty interrogation room. Mona's voice was reedy as she tried to explain the significance of the box. As soon as he realized it was connected to her office burglary, he'd donned gloves and retrieved a large evidence bag.

"Before you put it away, you have to see the book inside," Mona insisted. "It's Kerri's latest, but her author photo has been x'd out. I'm worried…I'm worried it's someone attacking her to get to me. We both think this is related to another case, one from—"

"Whoa now." Sandra held up her hand and set her pen down. "Let's not get too ahead of ourselves here. I think Detective Lincoln knows how to handle evidence, and then we can start to build a case."

"You're right. I'm sorry." Mona looked down, balling her fists as she did. "I think… everyone just wants to be a detective sometimes. In our life or in others. We think we know the right answer, so we jump in."

"Of course." Sandra's smile was saccharine; Absalom hoped Mona, and especially Kerri, didn't realize. "But we *are* the detectives. We know how to do our jobs."

"I wasn't insinuating—"

"She wasn't, either." Kerri squeezed Mona's shoulder.

Absalom bit back a smile when he saw Kerri shoot Sandra a look. All courtesy from the diner was gone. Kerri wasn't here with free coffee and hash browns. Another Kerri emerged, one that was made of stone and whose voice was like ice. "I think what Mona has to say is quite valuable, though, and I think the victim of the crime often knows how and why some things may have happened. Whoever is leaving these boxes around or breaking into universities isn't a genius. They're not all Ted Kaczynski. These are ordinary people who have ordinary experiences. All I'm asking you to do is listen to her experience."

Sandra seemed somewhat cowed by the response. "All right, then. Mona?"

Mona's gaze met Sandra before she started to explain the long and convoluted theory of the package. For someone who was small and had already consumed two cups of coffee from the station, Absalom was surprised Mona wasn't vibrating out of her seat. When he'd met her at the university, she'd been familiar enough to twinge his memory. It was only when she stepped into the station with Kerri, though, that he'd been able to place her at the diner—where she drank just as much coffee as she did now. No wonder her anxiety seemed to come in fits and starts; her experience of the world was already run through a filter of caffeine, so that when something truly anxiety producing occurred, it seemed like a far greater conspiracy.

But while Sandra seemed to fight rolling her eyes at the long chain of coincidences and bad feelings about bad men, Absalom found himself captivated by Mona's story. Whenever something seemed far-fetched, he'd looked to Kerri, who only nodded. She was stoic and silent—but she convinced him. This may not have been a Unabomber case, there may be no manifesto like Kaczynski, but there was something here between universities, between cellmates of a former school shooter, and they all better start paying attention.

Absalom was appalled when he looked down and realized Sandra had barely made any notes. "Mona," he said, interrupting her story temporarily. "Would you mind writing down a concrete timeline of events while you also write out your statement with Detective DeVos? You're doing a good job explaining, but with so many years, we would like to narrow down some dates at a glance." Absalom shot a quick look to Sandra. "And I'll process the evidence while you two are busy with that."

"Oh, sure. That's fine. Makes sense." Mona wrote down the starting date at nearly five years ago before she paused, pen in hand. "What about my apartment, though?"

"The package was found outside your door, right?" When she nodded, he went on. "Then it's not a scene. So, we don't have to block it off."

"But what if he comes back?" Mona asked, voice hinged.

"We will put a rush on your location. Do you have a landline?"

For once, Mona's expression betrayed some hope as she nodded.

"That's good. We can better track your location here. We'll also try to flag your cell number, too," Absalom went on, circumventing Sandra's ministrations. "If a call comes in from either one of your numbers, the officers on duty will know it's a priority. We'll also put an unmarked car close to your building. Here's my card to my direct line, too." Absalom reached under his jacket and produced two of his business cards. Mona grasped it like a lifeline while Kerri pocketed it easily. She gave him a curt nod, a subtle thank-you for taking this seriously.

Though Sandra was annoyed, the moment he'd stepped in and told Mona to do the writing, Absalom knew she'd comply. As he left the interrogation room with the box, he caught a glimpse of Kerri placing her hand on the small of Mona's back as she started her statement over again, complete with a directed timeline.

A deep pang of loneliness surfaced in Absalom. He shouldn't have been surprised by his emotion. Wasn't this what he felt every single night when he didn't have to work and he stared at the wall?—but it *was* different. He couldn't say how or why, but the shape of the pain inside of him was altered. Was it Kerri-shaped? He had to shake his head, but he wondered. How much of this feeling was stirred by jealousy? Over Mona or Kerri, or both of them, he wasn't exactly sure. He just knew that for once, he wasn't going to run to his phone for a hookup to solve it.

As he processed the box, he caught himself thinking of his last long-term girlfriend he'd had at twenty-four. He'd been so utterly destroyed when the two of them broke up—even if it had only been six months—that the only way he thought to make himself feel better was moving. He couldn't stand the thought of wandering around Kingston and possibly meeting her on the street. Each corner contained a memory that had twisted its form from comforting to painful, so he couldn't stay. It was almost—but not quite—like the memory of the Jane Doe. Scarborough was a place of decay from the start, though, the land of mountains and the looming legacy of Bernardo. Kingston had had potential—potential that had been marred with failure. Kingston, and Michelle, made him never want to start again.

So, he hadn't. He'd settled in Peterborough and dated through the internet, and then when he could, his phone. Everything had gotten so much worse when he could carry his escape around with him, rather than closing it off in a shitty silver laptop. There was zero need to start anything emotional again when he could just flick around instead. The urge for any kind of feeling subsided, a beast that had been fed by other means—until he met Kerri, anyway. She was the first person since Michelle who caught his interest. His attempts at flirting with her were so ham-fisted and out of practice that he couldn't believe she didn't kick him out of the diner. When she'd confided that she was gay, she seemed to be prepared to do just that if he made a fuss. But hearing she was gay had actually been the best thing, he told himself. Their relationship could remain perfect. Intact. And Peterborough, as the place where he met and formed half-imagined feelings for her, could also remain a utopia in his mind.

And who knew? Maybe if the world ended, things could change.

In one of Kerri's books, she'd written about a lesbian who falls in love with a man—basically a speculative fiction version of *Chasing Amy*. It didn't work out for them in the end, but they both survived the invading bug species from another planet. Near the end, the lesbian character jokes that it's damn near miraculous that she as a queer person and he as a black man both survived until the end of this horror world. If this had been aired on Fox, they would have been the first to go. What a brave new world this was.

Absalom had always wondered if the character was him. Outside of both being black men, they had absolutely nothing else in common. Daryl Simon was an Ivy League-educated professor of entomology who had two sisters and loved dirt biking. Jeanie Roux, the lesbian character, was almost six feet tall and covered in tattoos—definitely not like Kerri, either. But Absalom couldn't help thinking that maybe, just maybe, Kerri had written the scenario to see if they would have worked out. Maybe it was her way of letting him down easy but still also giving him a taste of something more. Her way of keeping what they had utterly perfect, even in the midst of horror.

But now she has Mona. And that's gotta be so much better than any fantasy.

Absalom finished processing the delivery box as evidence and moved on to the novel. When he opened the first page, he noted that it had the same redacted features of many of the other books they were finding in the burglarized places. There *had* to be a connection here. He hadn't been blinded by love or obsession at all. In fact, maybe they had just shelved the last piece of this puzzle.

When he stepped out of the evidence locker, he noticed Kerri by the coffee machine. She sipped from a paper cup. Her gaze fixated on a section of the wall, her thoughts in her own world. He walked over.

"Are you okay?"

She jumped but quickly replaced her stone-faced stare with a grin. "Oh, I'm fine. Sandra's making Mona go over the whole thing again from beginning to end, fussing on details. Sort of making the author in me bonkers. I needed a break."

"But at least it's down on paper now. Sorry

about Sandra before."

"It's okay. The whole thing is hard to follow sometimes. Hell, I'm not always sure I buy the motive." Kerri took another sip, and then eyed Absalom. "You think what Mona thinks? That whoever sent her the book wants to get me in order to hurt her?"

"I don't know, honestly. But I think we might have all the pieces now."

"What do you know? There's something you're holding back."

Absalom sighed. "I can't say much. You know more than most. The cat photos I showed you were only the beginning. There are so many more houses now. Things are trashed, like computers and books."

"Books? What kind of books?"

"All kinds." Absalom couldn't remember all the titles they'd filed away. He'd always focused on the redacted texts, not what they had been beforehand. "Are there any titles I should watch out for?"

"I was wondering if Edmund Spenser came up. Or any Renaissance poets or writers, especially if they're French."

"I can't remember. But I'll look into it." Absalom gestured towards his desk, and Kerri followed. He wrote down the name of the authors she listed, including the name of a group of seven variation from the sixteenth century. When a silence passed between them, he nudged it open. "Now you're holding back something."

She tapped the edge of her cup. "Maybe. But it's more of a favour than solid information."

"A clue is a clue is a clue. It all leads to somewhere."

After a moment of consideration, Kerri nodded. "Do a search for me?"

He nodded. His computer buzzed to life. For a second, he imagined a crack in the centre of the screen caused by a punch, one that radiated outwards. "What am I looking up?"

"If there is a record of a man named Gabriel Côte in any prison system. Could be in Quebec, but they get shipped around all the time, you know? Sandra said she'd do it after the statement, but I want to know now."

Absalom nodded and combed through some databases. There were a lot of security precautions and hoops to jump through, but he could do a very basic search on current prisoners.

"Current is fine. It's all I need, actually."

"All right." He typed in the name and waited. He tried the spelling several different ways and included a nickname, even though Kerri insisted this guy never went by any nickname. Each time gave him the same response: Nothing. "There is no one by that name in any current prison."

"Thank you," Kerri said. Her voice was thin.

"Do you want to do another name?"

"I…I'm curious about cellmates, but I don't know how to get their names."

"I can try."

Kerri nodded but remained silent. Absalom was about to ask more follow-up questions, but Mona came out of the interrogation room. Sandra's hand was on her shoulder, but it was awkward—an attempt to comfort gone awry. Sandra held the report in the other hand. As soon as Mona saw Kerri, both of their faces lit up. Their hands connected with a tight squeeze on reuniting.

"You okay?"

"Yes, yes," Mona mumbled.

Absalom felt awkward watching; even their small talk was intimate. So instead, he gave them another set of his cards, gestured to his own private line on his desk, and thanked them profusely. "We will keep you up to date as much as we can. In the meantime, know that this is not the end of the world. You will be all right. Just take care of each other."

"We will." Kerri smiled—and lingered in her stare. A day ago, it would have set hope alight inside of him. It would have reminded him of her novel and the possibility of something more. But now he'd seen them together. There never was, and never would be, a future between her and Absalom. It hurt a little, but it was okay.

"My God. *That* was confusing. Worse than any of your theories," Sandra said as soon as Mona and Kerri were gone. She flopped down at her desk with the handwritten statement. "Now I have to track down a bunch of names that may or may not have accents over them. Same goes for place names and a bunch of other stuff."

Accents. Absalom kicked himself, realizing he hadn't tried a different spelling of Gabriel's Côte name with accents. Was there an accent in it? And what kind?

Sandra's fingers pecked at the keyboard, attempting to make accents over vowels as she spoke to Absalom. "Not like it matters too much. For you, at least. You have any plans?"

"Plans?"

"Yeah. For the long weekend. Didn't you put in to have the next ten days off?"

Absalom's blood went cold. He checked his calendar with a sinking feeling—but he already knew Sandra was right. The August long weekend was a few days away, but he'd banked all his sick time and holidays to lead up to this moment, so he could actually feel as if he got a vacation. Last year, all he'd wanted to do in the summer was go for a run and not deal with the petty crimes that stacked up and ate all his free time away. The weariness of so many muggings wore into his bones.

So many things could change in a year. So many things were different. He was barely using his phone for hookups last summer, mostly because he'd been pining for Kerri after reading her book about the entomology professor who was not him but maybe could be him. He'd wanted all that time off so he could daydream. So he could go into the diner and listen to her thoughts on conspiracy theories and Canadian true crime. Back then, he'd thought it was cool she knew these things; it made her interesting and alluring. Now he wondered if there was an underside to what she wrote about—one that extended beyond keeping up interesting conversations with him. He'd never looked into Kerri's past. As much as he wanted to, as much as he could with the tools available, he'd stopped himself from doing so. Her past was so much better as an idea than a reality on his screen. She was so much better in the maybe fictional world than the real world of actual crimes and occurrences. He thought of her so vividly that he almost thought she'd walked back into the station. He turned around to be sure she wasn't standing there, asking for his help again. But there was no one.

Absalom kicked himself. He should have asked her more questions. He should have pushed her harder. He didn't even think of accents over letters— Sandra did. Which meant that he really did need to go. His feet were itchy for a run—but he also needed to leave before he started to daydream all over again and completely ruin a case he'd worked so hard on solving.

Absalom rose from his desk. "Are you okay on your own? If I cut out of here early?"

Sandra laughed. "I'm shocked you've stayed this long."

"Yeah, me too."

CHAPTER TWENTY-FIVE

Let me make one quick stop," Kerri said.

Mona stood on the street outside the police station, warming her hands in the early dawn light after spending the bulk of the night going over the story. She'd been shivering since she'd talked to Sandra, and her chills still persisted, even though the humidity outside was climbing with each passing minute. Kerri heard her father's voice, telling her that unnecessary shivering was the first sign of a perceived threat; the body shut down the heat system to get into fight or flight mode. The coldest Kerri had ever felt was in the car going into the woods, Lee's hand in hers.

"Sure," Mona said. "Where do you want to go?"

"A surprise." Kerri led Mona across to the street to her apartment. She didn't even stop in the strip mall to throw her off; she took Mona right to the door but asked her to stay outside. "I'll only be a minute. I promise."

Once inside, she grabbed her emergency kit from under her bed. The kit was always something she resented since it was one of her father's many lessons; as she lived alone for longer and longer, though, she realized its place. She hadn't touched it in nearly two years, not since a terrible ice storm made her huddle in a corner with the kit, candles, and the well-worn survival guide that also remained under her bed. Kerri grabbed all of it and headed down to her front lobby.

Another part of her father's routine niggled at her as she took the stairs. *Check every corner, every surface before coming or going. Especially home base.* She'd done no such thing this time around. As she reached her apartment glass doors, she almost expected to see Amos in his overalls in the parking lot, waiting for her with a heavy hand.

But it was only Mona. She smiled. She was no longer shivering. They were safe.

"I have a plan," Kerri said, holding up the kit. "And a small adventure for us. Roy has to give me his car again, but this could be fun."

"Oh, yeah?"

"Yeah. Nothing like the road trip we were planning to IKEA for some redecorating, but since when do they sell survival kits?"

Mona suppressed a small chuckle as Kerri

opened the kit. For a few minutes, they giggled like Girl Guides getting badges for the first time as they handled the material inside and the well-worn instruction manual. Then Kerri heard her father's voice again. *No lingering. No letting your guard down in public. You never know who is watching.* Kerri scanned the parking lot. She counted the beats. The stopwatch in the survival kit still had batteries, but she didn't need it to time herself. "We should go. I'll explain the rest on the way."

❧❧❧❧

"Like I said before," Kerri went on. "My father may have ruined my life, but he also prepared me for other people trying to ruin it. Thanks, Dad. Well done, Amos."

After picking up Roy's car, they'd driven another half hour to a wooded area in between Peterborough and Lakefield. Kerri gathered all the empty Coke cans and Tim Hortons cups from the back of Roy's car and worked on setting them up in a line. Mona followed along, helping in small ways when she could, but mostly listening. Though they were both tired from lack of sleep, the adrenaline from the last couple of hours kept them going.

Kerri talked in a quick clip, distilling many of the lessons her father gave her that were still useful while also guiding Mona in how to use the items in the kit itself. Many of them were easy to explain: first aid and fire starters, flares, and a Swiss Army knife, along with a bigger butterfly one. The survivalist guide wasn't one written by Amos or even one of his crackpot friends, but by the Canadian National Parks Services. The explanations and instructions were all neutral, useful. Plants you could eat, ones you couldn't. How to survive a bear attack. And so on. When the guide had been in Amos's possession, he'd littered it with sticky notes that pointed to a greater conspiracy, one that the government was in on. When she'd found the guide among the items she and Lee were able to keep after the arrest, she'd removed the sticky notes and kept the book. It made her feel better. She could always weed out the crazy, she was convinced, if she tried hard enough.

So, that was what they were doing now. Kerri's surprise gift to Mona was the basics of survival, from a survivalist, without the grand conspiracy holding it all up. Just information. Just ways to make it through.

Mona listened intently, wanting every last word.

"Rule number one is always depend on yourself. That means your own body. Know its limitations and its strengths. It's easy for us to think that just because we're short, we can't do anything. But we can." Kerri stood in front of Mona, her muscles flexed. Mona mirrored her without really grasping what was going on.

"Good, good," Kerri said. "You've taken a self-defense class, so I don't need to rehash much there, do I?"

"I don't know. It was a long time ago. I—"

Kerri raised an arm, and Mona blocked it right away. Mona took a step back, shocked she'd acted so quickly. She knocked over some of the cans Kerri had set up in the process, but it was worth it. Kerri was beaming.

"See? You're good."

"I'm on edge."

"In this context, that means you do well. You don't freeze. That's the toughest response and the one you have to push against the most in an emergency situation. Freezing is what many small prey animals do. It means you get away with playing dead. It does work sometimes—but it means you risk becoming prey."

Mona nodded, quiet and subdued. No doubt she was thinking of Damien or herself walking through the campus.

"You're stronger than you think you are. Use it. Fight," Kerri said. She ran through a couple of basic self-defense and counter-defense strikes before moving on to her next rule. "Step number two is always be prepared. If you can't use your body, then use tools. Hence the knives. And well, the gun."

Mona glanced at Kerri and then back at the car. "A gun?"

"A handgun, yeah. It was in a false bottom of the survival kit. So, I suppose I should probably add another rule: make sure to check all containers for false bottoms and all buildings for fire and emergency exits."

"Oh. *Oh.*" Mona looked at the cans, suddenly aware that she was setting up target practice. "Can we even do this here?"

"I can't see why not. Hunters do it. Jim, one of the diner regulars, told me about this place. And no one is here. So, let's try."

Kerri gestured to a far corner out in the field, a fair distance away from the cans. Mona followed, but her body was now stiffer and slower. As Kerri set up the gun and explained how to load it, Mona paid attention—but also seemed to be somewhere else.

"That's the basics of having a weapon. I don't keep this loaded because, you know, most of the time weapons kill the owner."

"So, why have one at all?"

"Because they used to scare me, quite frankly. I wanted to overcome that, so I bought my own." Kerri thought of the room full of guns in her father's bunker. In reality, it was only ten guns at most, but at twelve years old, they may as well have expanded and taken up the entirety of the room. Amos used them for hunting. She only saw him use them for hunting. But once she'd figured out what had happened to her stepmother, the room seemed like a death chamber. "I let the fear wash over me. And once I started to learn how guns worked, I didn't have to be afraid."

Mona nodded. She didn't say anything for a long time, and when she did, it threw Kerri for a loop. "What makes you think some people fall under certain spells while others don't?"

"What do you mean? There's no magic in all this."

"I know. But I keep thinking about Gabriel and his warped version of love. It was so similar to your father's. But Gabriel cited poetry while your dad wrote pamphlets. The survivalist guidebook..." Mona met Kerri's gaze. "Where did he take you? Was it close to here?"

Kerri laughed. "Oh, no, no. We grew up in a small town around Tweed, only a thousand people or so, so not unlike this area."

"But where did he take you? Was it not far from here?"

"It was...pretty far." Kerri sighed. She thought of the front cover of her survival guide, where she'd marked down the exact location like a memorial after the fact. The death valley—the literal Wendigo Forest. "There's a large survivalist movement in the Muskoka area. We were just outside of a village there, off the grid, only address being latitude and longitude points. Everyone in the town seemed to have a bunker and a story about aliens or the government. Or both."

"Isn't that more of a U.S. thing? I've never heard any of it in Canada."

"No, it's definitely over here, too. Almost the perfect place for it since so much of Canada is wilderness, especially in the Muskoka region. Our government issues may not be the same as the U.S., but the rhetoric infiltrates like a virus, you know? A word virus that gets into people's brains and makes everything they say infected."

"I don't want to be infected by it. But how could we not be, when we've grown up in the thick of it?"

Kerri had asked herself the same question over and over again as she pawed through the survival guidebook and removed every one of the sticky notes. "I can't tell you why some stories appeal to people and why some go off the edge with those stories. But I do know that both my dad and Gabriel used guns at the end of the day. So, we, in some way, have to learn their language. I know it sucks. But I promise you that the word virus won't get you. You won't start thinking about a Redemption Arc or that love can be bought with a .44 magnum."

"You promise?"

"I do. You are also not Kitty Genovese."

Mona looked away. She seemed to take a long

time before answering. "In my last dream, I saved her. I wasn't Kitty, and I know I'm not Kitty, but I had become a bystander that finally helped."

"Exactly. You have power and control. You can make a choice in all of this. I meant all of what I said last night."

Pain battled lingering desire on Mona's face. It was hard to believe, especially after being led through a campus—or through a forest for two months—that you had some kind of control over your life. It was so much easier to think of yourself as bestial and animal, a mess of systems and responses, because it was the closest thing to the feeling of fear.

But Kerri had a choice. Mona had a choice. Even Lee, in his strange brain, had a choice—and he went to the hospital. They did not have to cite poetry or redemptive arc at will to feel whole. They were going to use the same weapon—but use it as a tool of survival instead of ideology.

"Come on," Kerri said. "It's your turn."

Mona looked at the gun. When Kerri presented it to her in the flat of her palm, Mona looked away. Kerri understood the fear—but even more now that she heard Mona's story. Guns had been used against Mona. Guns made her walk. Made her leave her class behind. It was a weapon that commanded her, rather than the other way around.

"Go on," Kerri said. "You're in control here."

Mona shot Kerri a glance. Desire flicked between them. Kerri took a step forward and kissed Mona, who kissed back with a startling amount of alacrity. Kerri wrapped her own hand around the gun as she deepened the kiss with Mona.

Then Kerri slid her free hand over Mona's ribcage. When Mona gasped, Kerri knew she'd found the right spot. She held her hand there, and only her hand, anchoring their bodies together. She repeated, "You are in control."

Mona swallowed. Kerri slipped behind Mona so that their bodies could mirror each other. Kerri brought the gun up in her hand. Mona hovered just inside of her arm.

"I'm going to fire the gun, okay?" Kerri whispered the words in Mona's neck. "I'm going to do it, and then I want you to. Okay? Just follow me."

Mona nodded. Kerri fired. Mona baulked. Kerri fired again. Mona didn't move.

"See? Not so bad."

"Yeah. I guess."

"So, you try it."

Mona's breath became heavy as she took the gun. It was almost poetic how small her hands were against the gunmetal grey; Kerri wanted to write a dozen passages about how strong Mona looked, how petite and frail and yet so strong she was, but she stamped it all down. No poetry. No military. Mona was scared. But like everything else today, she was slowly letting it creep by and through her, without letting it take over.

Kerri stepped aside as Mona raised the gun. She stood behind her, watching with keen precision as Mona went through the basic drills Kerri had taught her moments earlier. She realized Mona had translated them into French. She fired once—and laughed as the gun knocked her backwards.

"You'll get the hang of it."

Mona nodded mutely. She raised the weapon and tried again. One of the tree branches bent and creatures skittered. She made a small O of surprise. The cans remained standing.

"I...don't want to hurt anything."

"To be alive is to hurt something. Crushing bugs with your shoes—like the bugs in your bed—is a fact of life. You just...have to be careful and only hurt what you intend to keep."

"Is that a hunting thing?" Mona asked. "Another mantra?"

"Yes and no. I think it's a human thing, too. It's something..." Kerri scanned her mind for the source of the line, then hesitated as she remembered it in one of her father's first letters to her from prison. Because of their bloodline, Kerri belonged to him. Their stepmother was nothing to Kerri and Lee, though, because she did not share that blood. But she did belong to Amos because he killed her. *Only kill what you intend to keep.* So in a way, it was a hunting mantra. When killing deer, you want to use it all, down to the bone. But he'd left her body behind and only taken her legacy.

"What's wrong?" Mona asked.

"Nothing. Just… My father wrote me a letter with that line when he was in prison. It was supposed to be an apology letter for killing my stepmother. Something like, *I'll never be able to shake her, I will pay for this the rest of my life,* type of thing. I figured it was posturing for parole or trying to taunt me because it sounded so creepy. He was hunting. She was a trophy. He was sick. And even when he was healthy, the pathways in his brain were the same. Different inflection, same words. You know?"

"I think I do. As much as I can."

Silence lapsed between them, only punctuated with bullets and the skittering of limbs. Mona made every attempt to aim away from the skittering of animals. Kerri wished she hadn't said a thing about her father; it still felt like a raw wound. She was so used to keeping secrets the truth still felt violent.

It *was* violent, she reminded herself. But now it felt like she was the perpetrator for her own memory.

"Was Lee like your father?" Mona asked. "In his...you know?"

"You mean did he have the words and phrases

he liked to memorize, too?" Kerri shrugged. "Yes and no. My father thought the world was going to end and was paranoid enough to prepare for it until he made it end and took us away. But Lee...Lee already believed it was done. So, he wasn't as much a survivalist in training as he was echoing a former time. It was why it took me so long to realize something was wrong. The world was a hologram around us, people were clones, and the real world that had ended was buried underneath the ice."

"But he wasn't violent?"

"No," Kerri said. "He was just confused."

Mona nodded. She looked down at the gun and raised it again to fire. Nothing happened. "I...think I'm done."

Kerri examined the tree and the cans in front of them. Mona's aim wasn't the best, but that was okay. She wanted Mona to get used to feeling powerful, to feel like she wasn't just a victim. And they'd done that. Kerri had to suppress the urge for perfection and settled on good enough. She retrieved the bullets from her back pocket as she stood and added it to the kit along with the gun. When she handed the box to Mona, her eyebrows rose.

"But it's yours."

"And I know how to use it. But you're still learning, and I think you should keep it just in case. If Gabriel is out there...then I want you to be able to turn the tables on him."

Mona tucked the box under her arm with a mumbled thank-you. "*D'accord.* But what about you?"

"What about me?"

"What will you do if he goes after you?"

"I have a knife." Kerri winked and gestured to the butterfly knife she'd placed in her back pocket. "And this is only temporary."

"Until when?"

"Until you register for your own. If it makes you feel better to have one, then get one."

Mona considered this for some time before she nodded. Kerri closed the distance between their bodies with another kiss. Gunpowder hung in the air, making Mona's mouth taste like ash and lightning. The embrace lingered, tongues together, before Mona put her forehead against Kerri.

"Thank you."

"Thank you. Now let's go get some food."

❧❧❧❧

"So, Carmen has a party tomorrow," Mona said after they'd finished a meal of bacon and eggs at the diner. "It's at a local pub to celebrate her MA graduation and successful thesis defense. I actually missed attending her defense today and feel like a heel for that, but—"

"You were busy. She understands." Kerri set her coffee down. It was odd to be eating with Mona, rather than serving her, and having the new waitress Tara get all she needed. But it was also kind of nice, too. "Her office was also robbed, so I'm sure she's grateful that you're finding clues."

"Yeah. I know...and I know it feels like a strange reprieve after all of this, to even think of a party, but—"

"It's fine. It's actually not that strange." A memory of Amos drinking the day before he murdered her stepmother sprung to her mind. He'd been partying because it was the end of the world. He'd brought Lee and Kerri with him to a bar, bought rounds for everyone, and then taken them to an arcade. It was the best night they'd ever had with him—because he was finally relaxed enough to have fun. The one thing he'd been waiting for was about to happen.

"What?" Mona asked. "Why are you smiling?"

When Kerri told Mona her memory, it was so much easier than before. "He would have never done anything like that if he didn't think the world was ending. I mean—an arcade? Where we could see popular culture? He homeschooled us to prevent outside influence like that. An arcade was another world to us. And in a way, though...he was right. The world was over. Our childhoods were. At least we got a party for it, you know? Most kids never get to celebrate before they lose it."

"I guess…I don't think Carmen's party is going to have an arcade."

"But there will be a bar. And we should definitely take advantage of that." Kerri slid her hand across the diner table, where Mona connected with her right away. It was so strange to think that she could share all this and the person didn't run in the other direction. Instead, they were running towards each other. Quotidian and the traumatic could exist at once. Kerri marvelled at this with another wide smile.

"Is that a yes, then?"

"Yeah, I'd love to go."

"Good. Great. Because I think Carmen'll love you, honestly. Just tell her you taught me self-defense today."

Kerri caught the slight gasp in Mona's words, as if she didn't even realize her feelings. Kerri didn't want to linger too long, though, before the good feelings fell away. Their lips met across the table. Love was somehow too strong and not enough. It was too soon and too late. So, Kerri kissed her, squeezed her hands, and then made sure she got home okay.

As Kerri walked back to her place, she thought of Mona—not her father. After hearing his voice inside her head for so long, it was a relief. She thought of Mona's body, her hair, and her silky pale skin. Even when Kerri set her keys at the front door and noticed the front hall mirror was off its hinges, she still thought of Mona.

And when he appeared from the front closet, Kerri still thought of Mona—and how to save her—without losing everything in the process.

CHAPTER TWENTY-SIX

Mona twirled a stir stick in her drink, her gaze fixated on the door. Each time an explosion of voices echoed through the bar, she turned to see if Kerri was among the students and town regulars pushing their way inside the pub. Each time so far, she'd been disappointed. She ordered another drink, not because she was necessarily thirsty, but because it gave her something to do with her hands as the bar filled up and she was still sitting alone.

Carmen's party had technically started an hour and a half ago, but there was always some leeway in events like this. Mona had said as much when she texted the start time to Kerri. She'd also emailed since Carmen had a nicer evite with the specific location. There had been no response, but Mona figured that was normal. They'd just spent all night together and were probably exhausted. Kerri was asleep.

Then Kerri was working.

Then Kerri was just aimless, not answering her phone. But she would come. She was running late, obviously. That was it. Mona stirred her drink again; she looked at the pub door when another burst of people came inside, and then she squelched her disappointment.

Mona was determined not to freeze or panic, only to let all her negative feelings wash over her. Perhaps Kerri taking a while was just a test. Maybe she wanted to see if Mona could keep the same control as the day before. She flashed back to the power she'd felt when she held the gun—and then how that power was a complicated monster in and of itself. Kerri had thought her hesitation with the weapon had been a flashback fear, and sure, that was part of it. Gabriel had used a gun, and now she was afraid of them. But he'd used a different one entirely, and since she didn't know that much about them to begin with, each make and model seemed separate. Holding one for herself wasn't exactly like conquering her fear of Gabriel—it was, in a strange way, conquering her own image.

She was not allowed to feel powerful with a gun. She was a woman, a feminist, a pacifist. A pretty little heart, a good girl. She wasn't allowed to be that kind of woman or even that kind of person who coveted weapons. All the memories she had of herself, given to her by her family or her exes, came back to her. All the reasons for not liking guns came to her, all based on logos. But fear was not logical, and neither was power. She *liked* holding the gun. She liked firing it. She was bad at using it, she knew that, but she wanted to get better. It was just a tool, right? A tool she could get better at, like learning to drive a car, and then she would know for sure she could defend herself if she needed to. The gun was still in her apartment, hidden under the bed with the survival kit, and that memory made her feel better. In control. As she waited and waited for Kerri to show, twirling her stir stick, she started to feel calm.

People from her Psychology Department passed her by at the bar with a gentle wave. Most didn't stay to make small talk. When the bartender produced a drink she didn't order, she looked up to see an older man across the bar. In the low light, she swore it was Dr. Conlin. Then man's jowls came around his face and replaced Dr. Conlin's trademark beard. Once the two of them had made eye contact, the man stood.

Before Gabriel, she would have humoured him. Maybe even given him her number if she'd been single. After Gabriel, she would have left the bar in fear, thinking that behind every man was a lurking boy obsessed with poetry and a penchant for violent obsession. But now she stared him in the eye and said hello.

"I hope it's not too forward, but I recognized you from the office. I'm the admin assistant."

"Oh. Right, of course. I recognize you now. Hello. I'm Mona."

He extended his hand and introduced himself as Nick. "I wanted to buy you a drink because of what happened at the office. I'm sorry everything got trashed. Are you still going to be able to give your talk tomorrow? Or were your notes backed up on a drive?"

"My talk?" Mona sighed as soon as she remembered the clipped conversation. Dr. Conlin had sent her a few follow-up emails for their talk together, most of which she'd glimpsed when she was looking for Kerri's response, but she hadn't responded to them. He'd gotten her to agree, she understood now, because he'd asked when she was at her most vulnerable. Her stomach quivered at the thought of delivering a paper on something she didn't care about—actually outright despised—and pretend to enjoy it. That was the worst part, she was convinced. Not the work anymore, but the pretending to enjoy it that came from something so public.

Nick took her reservation as upcoming jitters and lost work. He said she'd be fine. "You know, when I was in grad school, I lost the entire first draft of my dissertation."

"Oh, my goodness," she said, not faking her fear. "How did you manage that?"

"Long story. I was on the bus. Set it down. Fell

asleep. And then I arrived where I was supposed to be and got off. It was a Greyhound bus, too, so they threw it out without a concern. Even when I called back an hour later—it was already in Massachusetts and long gone."

"Hemingway did that," Mona said. "In my third year of undergrad, a professor told me his wife actually left one of his manuscripts on a train. He rewrote it from scratch. Said it ended up being better than the original version."

"Yeah, I think that's so."

"What did you do? How long did it take you to rewrite?"

"Oh, I never did it. I quit."

"Oh." Mona took a moment to process the information. She sipped her new drink, though her old one was half-full. The idea of quitting a PhD program was anathema. She knew anyone could, and she had watched several people attrition out in her English PhD in Montreal. But the man was so calm about it. It was in active voice, not passive. He wasn't kicked out. He *quit*.

"Yeah." Nick shrugged. "I know that's a bit of an extreme response. But I think I wanted to leave. It wasn't good for me."

"Neither is drinking, and we still do that."

"I suppose so." Nick laughed and took a drink of his own beer. His smile was jovial, making his rather jowly face seem quite young. She wondered how old he was. Unclouded by resentment and bar light, she could only see peripheral cues of his age in his dress: a small belly over his jeans, nice shoes and belt, but a rather ill-fitting shirt. She was so used to young faces in her program making her as the perpetual outlier since she was nearing thirty, but Nick could be anywhere from twenty-five to forty. His face and his attitude made it impossible to tell.

"What did you study? Were you in psychology, too?"

"I was. But what I studied doesn't matter. It could have been anything, and I still wouldn't have been happy. I wouldn't say this to any old academic here since so many are so gung-ho," he added, glancing around playfully. "But I think I quit because I had just gotten married, and I honestly just wanted to hang out with her all the time. I was on a bus to see her since she had started to work in Canada and I was still in the States."

Mona took a minute to process his words. *Massachusetts. A Greyhound.* When she asked if he was at Harvard, he confirmed it. He was studying in one of the best schools, and he *left*. For Canada. For an admin job in the Psychology Department of the school that everyone referred to as the "hippie" university. Mona was flabbergasted. She wanted to do a study on this man to figure him out, when she realized that she never could. Humans—like she'd always known—were never the best research subjects. They were human beings. We could never figure out their psychology in a complete way. To go on as if we could was never going to work.

And to give a talk on such a subject was never going to work, either. Especially without anything prepared and all the data gone.

"I don't think I can speak tomorrow," she said suddenly, interrupting Nick as he spoke about his wife's academic prowess. Apparently, she'd been the real "rock star" in the field, and he'd been more than willing to be her groupie.

"You'll be fine. The robbery could even be a good story to break the ice. But that's why I got you the drink. If you're still struggling with the talk, it never hurts to get the creative juices flowing a little more. Hey. Didn't Hemingway say something about that, too?"

Mona nodded. She sipped her drink again, only to see she struck bottom. Her stomach felt queasy. She reached for the nuts at the bar to cut down on her buzz. When the pub doors burst open again, Nick gestured to the new influx of people. "My wife is with Carmen. The people of the hour. Let's go say hello."

Mona was shocked to see Carmen standing with Jenny O'Connor, her supervisor, who was also apparently the rock star academic Nick had devoted his life to.

"Hello, everyone at my party!" Carmen said, bombastic and probably a little drunk herself already. "I am fashionably late because I have defended like a champ. And to everyone who is not at my party, come and join us."

She sauntered through the bar, Jenny tailing her. Jenny O'Connor looked ten times younger than her photo online, though she must have been at least thirty-five or forty. Her walk, her brightly coloured dress, and the way her eyes lit up when she saw Nick made them both seem like they were two grad students all over again.

The partygoers swarmed around Mona's place at the bar. Everyone chatted aimlessly about psychology case studies, queer theory, and the "so-called" transgender tipping point (as Carmen put it). Names dropped like rain and then discarded when their research meant nothing or had "been debunked and discredited worse than Freud." Mona had a hard time playing catchup, especially since her drinks had already gone to her head and the nuts at the bar did very little.

"Where are my manners?" Carmen turned to face Mona, smiling a toothy grin. "You should really officially meet Jenny."

"My manners have vacated, as well," Mona said. "I still haven't said congrats to you."

Carmen basked in the praise two seconds before she grabbed Mona's hand and led her to Jenny. Mona tried to straighten herself before she extended a hand and a quick greeting. "I've been chatting with your husband, and we've had a great conversation."

Jenny's grip was firm, strong. "Oh, yeah? All good things about me?"

"Of course." Nick reiterated his dissertation faux pas, and Jenny just laughed. She kissed his cheek as he slid an arm around her.

"If only I could remove knowledge from my brain so easily," Carmen said, lamenting dramatically. "But that's what alcohol is for. Come on now. Do your academic duty and wipe all my citations from my brain with shots."

"That's a great way to be," Jenny said, her voice flat. When the two of them exchanged a look and then erupted into laughter again, Mona understood it to be an inside joke she wasn't privy to. Two shots appeared in front of Carmen, as ordered by her defense party team, and she knocked them back easily. After some random applause and quips, Jenny and Nick disappeared deeper into the pub. Carmen plopped down next to Mona, nudging her side.

"Your turn?"

"Oh, no. I've reached my limit. But I'll get you another for later."

"Hmm. Later sounds good. But are you *done*

done for the night or…?"

Mona eyed the door. Still no Kerri. Still no messages on her phone. An email from Dr. Conlin popped up instead, making her blood go cold. She flipped her phone down and tried to ignore it. She was supposed to be here for Carmen. Not anyone else.

But Carmen saw through Mona right away. "What's going on? I thought your girl was coming tonight."

"I thought so, too."

"Trouble in paradise? So soon?"

"Has anything here ever really been paradise? I have to give a talk tomorrow."

"Ooh. Exciting. Wait. No. Not exciting?"

"Not exactly." With a sigh, Mona flipped over her phone and examined the email from Dr. Conlin. He wanted to meet tonight to go over the talk. It set her teeth on edge, so she deleted it without response. Mona ranted about the semantics of ownership versus belonging with Carmen while still covertly watching the door for a no-show Kerri. It wasn't too long before Carmen put her hand over Mona's, signalling her to stop. "Why is this even an issue? Jenny is literally free. Go over right now and get her as your supervisor."

"She's been free five minutes. Isn't there a grace period?"

"No! Not at all. This isn't like the academic version of buying a gun. It's just switching supervisors.

Now go make your life better and get your damn degree back on the rails."

Nick's words came to her, so strong and sincere. *I quit.* She pushed them aside. She caught Jenny in the crowd, but she was laughing with a group of other professors. Mona shook her head. "I'll send an email tomorrow or something. After I do the talk. Maybe I'll even bomb it, so Dr. Conlin feels relieved to get rid of me. Then I'll switch. The form I filled out months ago was destroyed in the robbery, anyway, so I have to start from scratch. It'll…be better for everyone this way."

Carmen rolled her eyes. Mona anticipated yet another sass-filled response, but Carmen sipped her drink. Angrily.

"What? What's going on?"

"Mona, I adore you. But you keep acting like shit is terrible all the time. And before you even bring up the shit at your old school, I know."

"Wait, what? How do you know?"

"Come on. You survived a school shooting. That's not exactly something you can hide. Not from the internet."

Mona felt exposed. Before she'd moved from Ontario, she'd attempted to scrub herself off Google, only to realize that no one ever really disappears from the internet. One story had reported her name. Only one—but it was enough for it to spread and hop languages, too. She'd tried flooding the search results with innocuous stories about herself or about a different Mona Ouellet, but there was only so much she could do. So, she gave up all social media presence and moved out here anyway. Pretending there was no such thing as the internet had worked for some time. She thought, however mistakenly, if people didn't bring it up it meant they never knew.

But obviously, that wasn't true. Mona sighed. "It wasn't a school shooting. It was a shooting at a school."

"Semantics. And yeah, it's shitty. But you're not making it any better. I get being sad. Oh, boy, do I get being sad. But when good things fall in your lap, it's insulting to those who helped it get there to ignore it."

Mona clenched her jaw. "I'm sorry."

"It's fine. I do get it. I was the same way. It's just... you need to stop wallowing, okay? I know that's not a simple command, but I also need you to understand that you are wallowing. A little bit. But that it's not always your fault. The people we're around affect us so profoundly, and life is so much better when you stop wallowing in toxic people and just get rid of them. So, dump him, please. Dump Roger Conlin and be a better version of yourself."

If this conversation happened two weeks ago, even two days ago, Mona would have broken down crying at Carmen's force. She wasn't blaming Mona, but she was still seeing through all of Mona's defenses and disguises. And she was right. Things were getting better. Even in the heat of the traumatic, there was Kerri. They'd laughed and kissed and played with guns. It was strange, but it gave her confidence. She knew that. Life wasn't all bad—but she kept making it bad when she focused on the wrong things. She had control in this matter. She didn't have to do anything. "You're right. I'm sorry. I'll go talk to Jenny now."

"Thank you. You deserve so much better than that."

"I'll probably still give the talk tomorrow. But that has more to do with not breaking my word."

"Oh, I know you. And I'll be there. Even if it is so damn early."

With a hug, Mona congratulated Carmen one last time. She stepped away from the bar and spotted Jenny in the crowd. As Mona walked towards her and Nick, she started to feel unmoored—not stronger like she thought. Each step she took got her closer to the psychology students who were her peers, but whom she felt nothing towards. She was walking away from the only friend she had in the program, a friend who was getting sick of her bullshit. And who was going to leave academia soon enough for a job elsewhere.

Meanwhile, Mona would still be here. She'd fucked up her proposal. Her experiments. Her degree—both of her degrees. Would talking to Jenny and signing herself up for another couple of years even matter? What did she even want to do after all this? She couldn't see herself teaching anymore. She couldn't stand up in front of a class and lecture on psychological case studies. The only thing she ever wanted to talk about was Kitty Genovese. The only thing she ever wanted to talk about was herself now, caught in her own nightmare. That wasn't what a PhD was for. She saw the outline of her life so clearly in that moment, alone in a crowded bar, full of strangers like citations.

She wanted to wipe it all from her mind.

Jenny caught her gaze in the crowd. She waved. So did Nick. Mona waved back. But she soon headed towards the back room and out the exit and walked to Kerri's place in the night.

CHAPTER TWENTY-SEVEN

Mona couldn't find Kerri's buzzer. Though each apartment unit had a name, Kerri wasn't on any of them—but K.T. Stellar was. Mona buzzed. She waited. There was no response, but soon a door popped open, as if her invitation had been accepted.

Mona's stomach sank as soon as she reached the apartment door. Kerri hadn't responded to her texts—so maybe she was just as sick of her bullshit as Carmen was. Maybe she thought Mona complained too much. Even if she knew the reason behind Mona's neurosis, Kerri had been through so much more. What if she thought Mona was just a pretty little heart, complaining about a schoolboy crush, like her mother had thought for so long? Mona almost turned around. She knocked when she remembered Kerri's hand on her ribcage, making all the pain and doubt disappear.

After two minutes of silence, Kerri opened the door an inch. Her face was hard, impassive, and free of makeup. She wore all black—it looked to be the same shirt as the last time they were together, but Mona wasn't too sure. Kerri's hair was pulled back in a tight ponytail. "Hi, Mona. What's up?"

"Um. Nothing. You...missed the party at the pub, though. Were you running late?"

"No, no. I was thinking of staying in tonight. Sorry."

"Oh. Why didn't you answer me then? I was waiting for you."

"Phone died."

"Oh." Mona tilted her head to the side. Kerri's voice was hard, as if her consonants had more texture to them. *Her Czech accent—or was it rage?* Mona wasn't sure, but she felt the sting of her own anger. "Were you going to charge your phone to tell me, or were you just going to stand me up?"

"That's the thing. We should talk."

"Can I come in then?"

"No."

Sharp tone, like nails on a chalkboard. Mona flinched. Kerri's face flashed with pain before she composed herself. "I mean I don't think we need to drag this out any longer than it should be. We should part ways. I think we've reached a natural endpoint, don't you?"

"A what?"

"An *end*point. I've given you all there is, and now this is the end. There's nothing else to say."

A pain ripped through Mona's chest, like a paper cut on the inside of her mouth. She glanced from Kerri to the floor, and then back at Kerri. Nothing had changed. The sharp pain continued. "Are we breaking up?"

Kerri nodded. A flicker of pain appeared on her face, too, but soon disappeared. "This was a nice story, but it's time for the last chapter. I think it's good to retreat back home."

"I...don't understand."

"Go, Mona. Go home."

"No." Mona took a step forward and put her hand on the door. Kerri's eyes bulged at her sudden movement, but she was strong enough to hold the door in place. Mona struggled, then gave up and grabbed on to Kerri's arm instead.

"No! Mona. Stop. Let go."

"No, no, no." Mona's voice was hinged. Her mind felt like it was unravelling. The pain and anger became sobs in her throat of utter desperation. Was this what Damien felt when she turned away from him in the hospital? God, it was awful. How could someone do this to someone else? How could love become this hideous thing? *We were lovers. Now we're strangers.* This was awful. Between heaves of her breath, Mona begged, "Please, don't leave me."

"I'm not leaving. You are."

"But I... But I...I wanted to belong to you."

Kerri sighed. Mona tried to scan her face for some recognition, some hint that she knew what she was talking about, but if it was there, it was gone just as fast as it appeared. Mona struggled to hold on, longer and longer, even as Kerri ripped her arm away.

"I'm sorry," she said in a whisper. "We have to end now."

Kerri closed the door bit by bit. When all Mona saw was the wood paneling, she stared for three long beats of her heart.

Then she turned and walked away.

❧❧❧❧

When Mona arrived home and found herself staring at the ceiling once again, she turned to Carmen's pills on her nightstand. She thought of Nick and his dissertation flying into the wind; she thought of Hemingway's wife leaving behind his book on a train. Both had turned out better for it, but Hemingway had still shot his brains out before he got too old. She thought of the readiness kit underneath her bed and The Shadow People that would surely greet her when she closed her eyes. She thought of the talk on ownership that did not belong to her. She thought of

Kitty Genovese, of course, but for once, she didn't pity her. She envied her.

In her mind, the worst thing Gabriel had done to her was not the shooting. It wasn't taking her across campus and then dragging her by her hair. It wasn't even the nightmares he birthed in her that made her flunk out of school. It was that he didn't just kill her. He'd let her survive. Her life was supposed to be some heroic gift, but all she'd felt in the days and weeks and years that had passed was an overwhelming numbness to her own life being spared. What was the point when everything else had changed? When everyone saw the scars and when no one knew their real story? That, at the end of the day, she'd gone with a madman. She'd said yes to his request, instead of steadfastly refusing, and then being shot for her disobedience.

She was always the good little girl. *Petite jo-liecouer.* Her obedience allowed her to walk away from Gabriel, but it also crippled her. She'd given up so much of herself in the process. Yes, yes, yes, I will walk with you. Just don't hurt the others. Yes, yes, yes, I will go to your car, just don't hurt Damien. Yes, yes, yes, please, anything! I'll do anything, just stop this. You're hurting me. Stop this. Please. *Aidez moi. S'il vous plaît. Mon Dieu. Je veux—je veux.* Then more yes, yes, yes.

Yes was the worst word she'd ever heard. But it had saved her.

She clasped the bottle of pills in her hands. With them, she controlled her dreams. She saved Kitty once, but that was part of the nightmare. If Kitty had survived, she would have dreams like this. She would be afraid like this. She would say yes, yes, yes over and over again like this. Mona thought of the case studies she'd read about people who had survived horrific encounters with gangs, serial killers, rapists, terrorists and wars. All acts of bravery, according to the authors who wrote a dozen think pieces about them. All acts of courage and resilience, just like hers.

But when the world did not actually end, how did these people make sense of their acquiescence? How did they forgive themselves for the inevitable "yes" that slipped from their mouths in their desperation? They were coerced, sure. All yeses were not considered equal. Mona understood that. But how did someone else manage to say "no" while others said "yes" as if it was the only word they ever knew? Why did this happen to her and not someone else, and why did it continue to happen to others? When did being ready for dangerous situations become not enough to avoid them? Did it ever get easier to say "yes" again and mean it?

Was this secret knowledge the cost of survival? Was that what being brave really meant?

If all this really was the true cost, Mona didn't want to be brave. Not anymore, though she doubted she'd ever been.

She swallowed five pills, one right after the other. She waited two beats and then took two more, finishing the bottle. She slipped back into a world that she was well familiar with, one she loved as much as she despised. It was starting to feel like home.

CHAPTER TWENTY-EIGHT

Even after his run, Absalom was still thinking about Kerri.

Not with youthful adoration like he might have in the past. He wasn't imagining ways she could be his detective sidekick or even fantasizing about a possible future with the two of them in a speculative fiction landscape. It was their meeting that bothered him. He was missing something, not grasping a nuance in her speech pattern. He used his old laptop to cross-check the name with all the accents he could think of—yet he still turned up nothing. Though he was off for the next ten days and someone else had picked up the case, he didn't trust them to see what he saw. He closed the laptop and dressed to go to work. He was around the corner from the police station, almost at the front steps, when he bumped into someone coming out of the library.

Then it all sank into place.

The books.

What type of books was this guy redacting? She'd been asking about genre, but Absalom had been so focused on the words the guy had been removing that he didn't bother to examine from a broader perspective. Genre communicated something, though. Genre was important. And if he could figure out *what* this guy was reading, maybe it would lead to the why.

Absalom slipped into the station without arousing too much suspicion. His first impulse had been to run the author names Kerri had given him in the evidence room. He soon found no Edmund Spenser or Rabelais at any of the crime scenes, not even a Norton Anthology of Renaissance Literature, which Kerri said were as common as dirt. So, what else was there, what else was common enough, and what else had meaning to this particular perp?

Absalom needed to rescan half the crime scene images to blow up the spines on the books at most crime scenes. From there, he tried to reverse Google search covers to obtain more information. It was at Tanya Winters's house, where the perp had stomped around in her bed, where he finally got his break.

She had a K.T. Stellar novel on her bedside table. The frisson of recognition excited Absalom, especially as he realized it was one of her earlier ones he'd read about a girls' trip into the forest. It was neat that she was being read, beyond just her diner friends and on the internet. On Tanya's floor, in the middle of the torn pages, was another K.T. Stellar book. He rotated the photo until the purple title was visible. *Dante Under Ice.* Her most recent one, one he hadn't read yet but was familiar with now because of Mona.

And the empty house he'd checked.

Absalom's heart beat fast. He was on Kerri's website in a heartbeat, examining all her covers and past works, even those out of print. He found one of her other novels at the cat crime scene, half-covered in blood. Another in the background of a more recent burglary. Soon, he was phoning the landlord of the first house he examined since the photos were too small and didn't take in everything. They hadn't known what they were looking for—how could they have? It was always just a mess of paper and books, then a mess of electronics. But he knew now that if he were to go back and do it all again, he'd find Kerri's latest work at almost all the crime scenes, heavily redacted, as if it was a top-secret document. He *knew* it. He just had to prove it.

When he finally got a hold of the woman who rented out the place, he asked her about the bookshelf.

"Is that yours or tenant property?"

"I own the first floor, and that's the only thing that's shared. So yes, that's mine. Why? Someone try to pawn my trashy romance?" She laughed with a smoker's hack.

Absalom ignored the bad joke. "Have you ever read anything by K.T. Stellar?"

"Oh, yes! I read her first mystery. I thought it was okay, but she didn't write anymore afterwards. Too bad. I didn't much like her dystopian one, though. Far too dark."

"Great. Thank you."

Absalom hung up the phone. Before his exhilaration took over, he called the lab to verify they'd not found a match of the print. And indeed, there was still no match. Whoever they were looking for didn't have a record, which meant that Gabriel Côte, Mona's former stalker and school shooter, was also out. So were any of his possible cellmates. This was *never* about Mona. This had always been about Kerri—or K.T. Stellar.

But who would want to hurt her?

A crazed fan? A rival author? Absalom paced the police station as he worked out his theories. He pulled up Kerri's latest interview circuit—but only came up with the podcast she'd done with *Can 9 From Outer Space*, which he'd listened to on one of his runs. She'd mentioned her brother in the podcast. What were the odds he was still alive? A quick search of Kerri and her brother, Lee, led Absalom to Amos Reznik. The murder of their stepmother, Layla Hunter, and the survivalist literature that Amos was famous for. When

Absalom found the same photo of Layla Hunter from the newspaper in the police file for the murder, an image of Lee and Kerri as kids was also there.

Absalom recognized Lee right away.

The man in the black suit. His shadow from his run.

The sun he was chasing all along.

CHAPTER TWENTY-NINE

Lee's mouth was ajar. It seemed as if it wasn't hinged properly, as if he had an underbite that never righted itself over time. If Kerri hadn't known him since birth, she would have guessed it had been this way all along. But his smiles had always been far brighter and bigger than her own. In the photo that would be plastered all over newspapers with them and Layla, Lee's smile had been so large it could make any onlooker forget any knowledge of what would happen to them all. When the press blurred their faces since they were still minors, Kerri had been relieved—but also saddened. With Lee's smile gone, the photo was just of Layla, a tense and fraught expression on her face. Layla had already been part of the survivalist movement when she met Amos; she'd eagerly taken on the role of their stepmother and wife of one of the most prolific writers and recluse figures in the movement. But a life off the grid, save for a handful of big gatherings in the warmer months, had worn on her. Believing in all this fiction guised as fact made her eyes tired. She was getting ready to leave Amos—and Kerri had a feeling, all along, that she'd wanted to take them with her.

All this came flooding back when Kerri saw Lee step out of her closet. It was as if time had never quite existed, as if she'd been waiting for this moment all along, when he'd come back into her life and they'd picked up where they left off. Though his jaw seemed unhinged, and he spoke from the side of his mouth because of it in a stilted voice, this was Lee. Her brother. Her best friend. She was so happy to see him it took her a moment to realize he wasn't making sense.

And when she had asked about his jaw, he looked at her as if she'd harmed him.

"My fillings," he said. "They had metal in them. They had to go. They get in through the metal. I read this article where a guy could get radio reception in his teeth. It was like he was seven million different people at once, except that they all wanted him to join the wrong cause."

Kerri didn't ask who "they" were. She was already well familiar. Lee was off his medication, so there were people listening in on the phones, people who lived in the phones, and there were messages through signs on the street that led to a cabal where he'd been singled out. If someone didn't say hello to him in a particular way, they were a clone and not a true survivor. They were not like the two of them, who had made it through the end of the world.

The moment she realized he was a different version of the brother she loved, she mirrored him—so she could remain a true survivor in his mind.

"Then we need to unplug the microwave."

Lee nodded. "Already did. And I have a car for us. We need to go. I have...so many plans."

Kerri stalled him as long as she could. She asked him questions that had been etched into her mind, as painful as her scar. Sometimes, she would try to guide Lee out of the thick dense of conspiracies and traumatic memories, but it didn't always work. When Lee showed her the gun, she knew she could only stall him for so long with chitchat before his stories started to have viscerally real consequences in the world.

"Lee, what do you have? Where did you get that?"

"Don't worry—it's not an automatic weapon. This one is inscribed and tested."

Kerri tried to keep her face placid. His words often made sense by themselves—his syntax was fine—but the semantic meanings sometimes slipped away. Schizophrenia wasn't about multiple personalities; that was one of her biggest pet peeves when someone mentioned it in the horror genre. It wasn't a way to create a bad villain. Schizophrenia was about shifting signification, hearing or seeing or even smelling things that weren't there due to a brain imbalance, and then ascribing meaning to all the sense data to understand the world the person was living in. It was about perception. The diagnosis made perfect sense to her when she read about it after Lee was admitted. Since it was so much about perception, it gave her hope that he would not become like their father because violence did not have to follow. If she could keep up with Lee's perceptions, even if they didn't quite track, she was convinced she could help him.

"Can I clean the gun?" she asked. "Sometimes, the radio waves get in between the bullets."

"Already did it. I got it." He smiled wide. When he opened his mouth, she could see that there were no back molars. He had only taken the visible fillings. Kerri knew he had more, but since they weren't metal, they were okay. Everything was going to be okay now, he went on in a kinetic speech because they were together. "Like before. And we can finish what Dad started."

"What?" Kerri leaned closer to him. As she appealed to familiarity with Lee, she'd also been trying to use her phone behind her back. He'd caught her off guard with this statement, though, and she nearly dropped the phone against the kitchen tiles. Lee had progressively stepped closer and closer to her, and she could only go so far without bumping into the sink.

"Dad's plan. The bunker. The Redemption Arc. The way to the end of the world."

"Lee, that was so long ago."

"And the world is different now, I know. But we can go back. I understand the time vortex now, thanks to you. There are reasons to believe the ice in the rivers will save us."

Kerri's face fell. That was a line from *Dante Under Ice*. *There are reasons to believe the ice in the rivers will save us.* Mickey Alan said it to his wife, Starla, before they ventured north, in hopes of staving off the end of the world. Lee produced her book from his bag and displayed his highlighted and redacted sections, along with intense notes in the margins. Everything cascaded in front of Kerri. She thought this visit was just a random interlude; he'd gotten out of the hospital because he took his medication and then he slipped. It had happened before. It usually ended up with him in a drunk tank and her taking him back to the hospital, but in this case, he had tried to find her. Kerri had even entertained the idea that it had been Lee who robbed the university, but it was just for her contact info. He'd seen her go inside for the experiment, and then he went, too. While that could still be the case, it was now clear he wasn't just trying to find her to say hello and be brother and sister again. He was trying to make the world go backwards, to find time's arrow like Mickey and Starla did in the book, so that multiple universes could open up, and the underworld could come forward.

Her book. He had found and read her latest book. Each time he'd come across a particular code word, he'd blacked it out or cut it out. His backpack contained stacks and stacks of torn pages with impenetrable writing smudged into corners. He had read everything she'd ever written, including the first failed book, but it was *Dante Under Ice* that captivated him the most. The book where she'd tried to expurgate all her father's survivalist nonsense now gave Lee a reason to believe again.

"It's like Dad, but you didn't call him by the right name. But there's a typo on page one hundred and thirty-three, and that leads me to another line where then I figured out how to unlock the time vortex, so we can go back. Except that, obviously, we're not fighting ice giants. You meant clones." He gave her a knowing look, as if she had spilled milk. "You mean clones, but I understand being coy. I get it. There are spies everywhere, and we have to keep it a secret. It's why you changed your name, too—but you still left your eyes on your books. So, I x them out to be safe."

Kerri's phone rang before she had a chance to say anything. Mona had been trying to text her, but each buzz was muffled by Kerri's pants and palms.

The ringing was too much, though. Now she was caught.

Lee's eyes flamed. "The airwaves!"

He lunged and snatched behind Kerri's arms. She was already backed into a corner, already found out, but she still resisted his advance. He was so much taller than her, though. That summer when they were both twelve had been the last time they'd seen eye to eye. It was strange, having this looming giant over her as he snatched her phone, twisting her wrist slightly until she let go. She gasped at how much pain he caused her—and how quickly he stopped. He was strong but not violent. Kerri still believed that because as he threw her phone and crunched it under his boot heel, she saw the care in his expression. The phones were toxic. He'd been trying to help her.

"You're trying to fight too many battles alone," Lee said. "I took care of your computer and everything else. But do you have more legions?"

Kerri shook her head. Her gaze darted to the gun that was on top of Lee's bag, discarded temporarily, as he explained his theories on her books. Lee noticed her glance. He reached down and picked the weapon up between his fingers. He took a step closer to her. "We have to stay together. We have to."

Kerri saw the blood on the edge of his shirt. It was barely noticeable before since he wore a giant Army reserve jacket over his broad shoulders, and everything seemed too big for him. It must have been their father's clothing because it smelled so much like tobacco. Lee's shirt underneath the jacket was sky blue, with an unfamiliar logo, and a line of red just around the edge. There was also a fine mist near the bottom. It was fresh, she was sure of it. *Blood spatter. From a gun.*

"Lee," she said slowly. "Who did you shoot?"

"You don't question. You don't understand." He clasped his forehead with his free hand as if he was in pain. "I heard you speak through the radio. And I knew I had to find you. I would do anything to find you, Kerri."

Kerri blinked. Her voice on the radio. For once, this wasn't a hallucination or his psychosis. Her interview. Her photo had been on telephone poles and in laundromats. On the back of books. She'd written her father's mythology down, thinking it was harmless now that he was locked away. But Lee had found it, and because they were the only people to speak about this for so long, and in a language that only the two of them shared, it had seemed real. It had fed the delusion. She'd made her brother mad again, taunting him with the past. Her heart broke as she met his gaze.

"I'm glad you found me, Lee. I spoke on the airwaves about you because I missed you a lot."

"I know, I know. But you are so far behind. Let

me tell you the plan, and then we'll go back in time to save the world."

Kerri inched closer to him, allowing herself to be led into her bedroom. She was fifteen minutes into his story when she remembered there was no survival kit. Only herself and her brother, their shared history, and a frantic quest towards the past.

❧ ❧ ❧ ❧

When Mona had shown up at the door, Kerri knew they had to leave the apartment. In spite of every single instinct telling her not to get into the car with Lee, that it would only make matters worse, Mona changed everything. Because if she'd come once, it didn't matter how awful Kerri made the breakup, she knew Mona would come back. And then Lee really would believe she was a clone, bent on destroying their quest, and Kerri didn't know what he'd do.

Lee saw her through the peephole. "The doctor. The experimenter."

"Yes," Kerri said. "But let me get rid of her. She doesn't understand the plan."

"But she does. I told her my name was Mickey. She believes in us. In you. The book was from her. We can save—"

"No." Kerri was sharp, persistent. Lee seemed hurt, his jaw off-kilter once again, but he let her answer the door as long as he was right behind her. He kept the gun in his hand. Though it was not pressed against Kerri, she became keenly aware of its presence.

The conversation was a blur. Kerri spoke as if she was two different people, trying to be as convincing as she could to get Mona to leave, while also planting all the clues she could for Mona to decode later. If she decoded it later. *The endpoint. A good time to retreat. I've given you all you need.* Inside the cover of the survivalist guide were the coordinates of the bunker. She'd removed each one of her father's sticky notes and then written her own legacy, like it was some silly school yearbook. June 14 to August 12, followed by the exact location. It was there, clear as day.

But would Mona look? Or would she toss everything that Kerri had ever touched now that they were broken up? If she did look, would she understand? Kerri had no time for doubt because the moment the door was closed, Lee was already in action.

"Come on now. Before the clones come. The sidewalk will open for them."

Kerri stared at the shut door. A small child's voice inside of her yelled and screamed. It told her all the bad things that would happen in the woods. All the demons that would surface and sit on her chest and scare her for a decade to come, when she thought she could write her way out of the bad memories and move on. Why hadn't she just stopped with *Wendigo Forest*? The Girl Guides' retreat novel had been her way of working her own trauma, the nightmares suddenly stopping after the last page was written. She could have moved on with her life. Left her father's nonsense alone, and by proxy, Lee's trauma.

But *no*. She had to write it all down. And now she was going to live it all over again.

"Come on." Lee opened his mouth again so wide Kerri saw his gums. "We need to get to base."

She sighed. *You could never write your way out of the trauma. Out of your family. You always had to go home.* She balled her fists and quieted her mind. She would go. They would leave. "I'm coming. Just give me a moment."

Kerri started to pack what Lee handed her in a small purse. He tossed the contents of most of her fridge, only selecting the jerky and canned goods. He tore her shirts into rags and then ripped apart two novels that she'd been reading. She made no sound as he moved. She focused on the line of red in the bottom of his shirt.

"Lee, who did you hurt?"

Lee looked down. He mumbled, "Clone," and went back to work.

Kerri trembled. Then she let her fear wash over her. *If someone had been shot, someone heard the shooting. Someone would call the police. Someone would help.*

"You ready?" Lee asked just before dawn.

Kerri followed him as an answer. She didn't lock her door. She squelched her sudden revulsion as she realized he had Roy's car, the rust so familiar and so painful to see. She closed her eyes again. *If someone has been shot, then someone heard the shooting. Someone was going to help.* She sat in the passenger seat. Lee started the car and drove. In the silence, Kerri remembered the first time she'd met Mona and their conversation about Kitty Genovese. The photo Mona had given her was now torn into shreds in her apartment.

And Kerri wasn't so sure about help anymore.

CHAPTER THIRTY

At first, the dreams were good.

Mona already knew she could control the scene, so she channeled her consciousness into adding new characters, which she then removed just as fast. She manipulated the landscape, trading city for city, for country for city again. Day for night and night for day. She made weeks pass. Snow fell and then melted into slush as winter became spring and then became summer. She lived an entire lifetime like this, before she turned her back on her creation to walk towards the city at the heart of herself.

When Gabriel showed up, she pulled the gun on him. She lined it up against his ribcage like he'd done against her, and she made him walk. She made him say "yes" over and over. Then she shot and struck him in the chest. The wound bloomed outwards like a flower. He fell to the ground, and the whole thing started again.

It was an endless loop, a video game with endless lives. In some, she kept killing Gabriel, while in other visions, she said no and waited for the inevitable death-null void. It never came. Even when Gabriel raised the gun and shot her, and she felt it against her chest like a pressure point, she never died. It all just started again.

When Kerri's dad emerged, Mona was ready. She had no idea what he looked like, but she knew he was a giant. She held her gun high, aiming up, and shot him point-blank. She watched him fall down, shaking the earth as he did.

Then he got up. He moved towards her, his spindly arms like machine rifles, and shot at her. It struck her arm. Then her chest. She was dying again, but it hurt worse this time.

Mona wanted to wake up, but she couldn't. Her entire body was pinned down. Her throat was stretched, as if the mares from her dreams before weren't just sitting on her chest but crawling out of her. She was a circus tent stretched to the limit as beasts flowed out of her body and into a cityscape. The Shadow People. The hag. Little demons. Then she wasn't in the city anymore; she *was* the city. Toronto. Montreal. Peterborough. New York. It didn't matter. Her body stretched and contorted as high-rises shot out from her arms. People and monsters coexisted in her nooks and crannies, lined every street corner, every elbow, every kneecap. She was awash in traffic, a cacophony of noise. A mythology of nightmares became contained inside of her, next to case study after case study of violence.

Nothing was anonymous anymore. Strangers did not exist. Everything was a part of Mona, and everything was familiar, even as it tore her apart. Familiarity was violence. Her body was not her own.

When she vomited, her refuse was in the shape of people. Her chest heaved. She retched again, ordinary and commonplace, and then felt peace.

The blackness of the city became darker. Each building fell apart. Mona understood deep down that the world was ending. That was why the city, and all that it contained, was disappearing. Dismantling, like a child finished playing house. As she drifted into the in-between space, Mona was relieved to no longer house its burden.

✦✦✦✦

When Mona woke, Carmen was at her bedside. Nothing was in the right place. All the lights were on. The shuffle of nurses' shoes blended with the beeps from her machines, signalling she was not in her house. She coughed and felt dust in her lungs. Her tongue was raw as a wound.

And she felt so utterly empty inside.

"Hey." Carmen put down the magazine she'd been reading and leaned closer to Mona's bed. "You're awake. They thought you'd be out longer."

"A city has been inside of me."

"What?"

"I'm thirsty."

Though Carmen still gave Mona a look, she grabbed the plastic cup by Mona's bed and extended it to her. A bendy straw met her lips. Water coated her tongue. Relief. Pleasure. She'd never been so happy for bendy straws in her entire life. What once seemed like an unnecessary item was now two more inches she didn't have to bend for the water to reach her mouth. Mona drank and drank and drank.

"Wow, okay. There you go," Carmen said, pulling the cup away when Mona took a breath. "Don't go too overboard."

"Thank you."

Carmen gave a weak smile. Her thin face was paler than Mona had ever seen it. Her hair was not done; her makeup seemed as if it had been on for too long, her lipstick worn around the edges of her mouth. Mona had no idea what time it was, but the thought that Carmen had been here long enough for her makeup to wear made her sad. If Carmen hadn't touched up what was already there, it must be an emergency.

Which meant she was an emergency.

"There was an entire city inside of me," Mona said quietly.

If Carmen heard her, she didn't comment on it. Mona looked at her hands against the hospital sheets. An IV was in her arm. From the hollowness she felt and the strain in her throat, she guessed that her stomach had been pumped. She braced herself for Carmen's lecture, her yelling, but after what felt like an agonizing long time, Carmen simply asked, "Why did you do it?"

"Do what?"

"Try to kill yourself?" Carmen's voice trembled a little. "I suppose I want to know solely because I need to be absolved."

"Oh, God, Carmen. This is not your fault."

"Even if they were my pills? Huh." Carmen shook her head. "I'm an idiot. I shouldn't have given them to you if you were upset. I just thought... It happens all the time with my trans friends. The medical system is out to get us half the time, so we share hormones. I just..."

"It's not your fault," Mona insisted. Each time she blinked, she saw the blackness she'd floated in. She saw her own death replayed again and again. It was terrifying. She didn't want to die. Even in her darkest hour, it was an existential question she sought in dreams. Not in reality. "I...I didn't mean to overdose."

"Yeah. Sure."

"I didn't."

"So you…what? Took half a bottle because you wanted to sleep?"

"Kind of."

Carmen let out a frustrated breath. Her hair danced across her face. Mona tried to parse out who had the right to feel guilty in this scenario, if anyone. Her mind pulsated with the questions she'd been trying to figure out before she went under. What was the cost of survival? Was it a city inside of her, all her experiences, good and bad, replaying on a loop? She'd take being a city over being brave. But how to explain that to someone who cared about her? How to explain anything that was beyond language, a pain that only saw its equivalent horror—and its solution—in dreams?

"I'm…I fucked up." Mona shook her head. "I'm so, so sorry. Kerri broke up with me. I was thinking about Gabriel, how I'd never escape him. And I was upset and wanted to sleep."

Carmen nodded, but a frown still fixated on her face. Mona debated whether or not she should insist it wasn't a suicide attempt again. Maybe it had been. Would it be okay to bear this weakness? Was that what Carmen wanted to hear? No, Mona realized. Carmen didn't want to be right. She wanted to be comforted. Mona shifted closer to her by the bed, extending her hand. Carmen took it.

"I...I'm sorry you found me. That had to be hard."

"That's the fucked-up thing about all of this," Carmen said. "I didn't find you."

"Who did? Oh, God. Was it Kerri?"

"It was Roger."

Mona gasped. Carmen only squeezed her hand in response. Dr. Conlin, the man she'd been avoiding for so long, had come to her apartment, found her half-naked in bed, surely covered in vomit. He'd taken her to the hospital. He'd saved her life.

"Apparently, he got worried when you didn't show up for the talk or answer his calls. So, he lied his way into your building."

After some time, Mona asked, "Were we wrong about him?"

"That's the thing...I don't know. Maybe my friends were wrong about him. Maybe his lack of personal boundaries and obsession made him go to your building and find you. Maybe he can be a creep and save your life at the same time, or maybe none of this even matters. I don't know. All I know is that I'm glad he did go."

"I am, too."

Mona squeezed the hand of Carmen, who returned the gesture. For a long time, they were quiet. Mona tried to remember if Dr. Conlin had been part of the city. Was he a Shadow Person? Was he a bad sensation or a good one? The feeling of familiarity or violence? Maybe he was just there, neutral, going about his life until they happened to intersect. More questions piled on more unanswered questions. Mona blinked and tried to right the world. It remained stuck, caught through a hospital filter of noise.

"I don't feel like my thoughts are mine anymore," Mona said. "I don't understand how this is happening to me. How this keeps happening to me."

"Roger? Kerri?"

"Both. Everything. And more. I remembered what you said at the bar. And you're right. I do act like things keep happening to me. Because they *do*. Why am I in the orbit of so many bad men? Surely, not all men are bad, but why do they keep finding me... you...your friends? Why does my office get trashed? Why does anything happen the way it does?"

"I don't know, sweetheart. That's a bigger question. And I don't know the first guy that fucked up stuff at your school, but I've had my share of trauma cycles. It'll pass. You'll get out of it."

"What now?"

"Trauma cycles. It's a theory. The latter half of my master's was focused on reducing harm in trauma cycles, so it's at the front of my brain. Our word trauma is derived from the Greek word for wound. The only way to heal the wound is to deal with it through treatment. But for someone who doesn't understand or know they're traumatized, they can't heal. So, they keep reinjuring their first wound. It's like walking on a broken leg. Falling down the stairs may have broken the bone, but if you don't understand that and keep walking, not only do you never fix the first issue, but you break at the smallest things. It's the entire basis for PTSD. It's also why some people seem utterly tragic and like they can't get a break no matter where they go. They literally *can't* heal because they don't understand how deep it may go. Other people, though, bounce back like nothing. They heal. And they break the cycle of harm in the process."

"Like Kerri…" Mona marvelled at her in that moment. She'd lost her mother. She'd lost her stepmother. Her father. And then her brother. She lost all these people, but she was still so strong.

"I don't think so," Carmen said, shaking her head. "If she broke up with you, then no."

"What do you mean? I thought it was my bullshit."

"You do have some bullshit. But we all do. If that's what made her leave, then she's not moved past her own, either. She broke up with you, probably, because it reminded her of her own pain. Not because she's healed and you're damaged. Never think that."

"Then why does she seem so strong?"

"I can't say because I never met her. But let

me put it his way. You, Mona, have broken your leg, and while you know it still needs time to heal, you keep trying to walk on it. You make it worse and then wonder why. But Kerri seems to know she's hurt. So, she just stops walking. She looks healed on the surface, but she's not testing herself. So, it doesn't count."

Mona wanted to insist that this was not the case, but she didn't. Not only did this make the pain of the breakup slightly easier to handle, but it made Kerri's secretiveness easier to comprehend. She was always half out of the relationship, not because of Mona, but because she was in pain, too.

"So, how do you heal then? How do you break the cycle?"

"Ha!" Carmen laughed. "I may have passed that defense, but *man,* I have not passed life."

"But you've done the reading."

"And so have you, sweetheart. I'm sorry, but it's not much different. There is no magic bullet here. It's just...you will have always broken your leg. There is no undoing that injury. And even after you've done your best efforts to heal, there may still be some pain. But you learn to live with it. Deal with it. I don't think we ever fully go back to normal. Wholeness is an illusion, anyway. But dealing with your injuries becomes easier to handle. It becomes your thing."

"My thing?" Mona laughed. It sounded like a quirk, like a snorting laugh or a coffee preference. Not an irrevocable reminder, something that never fades.

"Yeah. If you break your leg bad enough, you may always walk with a cane. But you will still walk, and the cane just becomes your thing that lets you live in the world. Maybe you'll always have shitty sleep. So, you learn to find the best ways to make sure you go to bed and get enough. You don't take it personally. You just deal."

Mona nodded. It sounded so simple. She wanted to believe in it like an advertising slogan, but she also resisted. There was something calming about the trauma, the wound itself. She knew it was unhealthy. But without it, she was left with her PhD, a broken life, and an empty apartment. All the reasons she became a city in the first place.

So, Mona focused on Carmen again. They slipped into inane chatter about Carmen's thesis and how she still had to finish some paperwork before submitting it to the graduate department. "Which reminds me… The grad office closes at four. I should head out if I want to file it. You need anything, though, call me, okay? Your phone is right there." Carmen gestured to the nightstand, behind the cup of water.

"Thanks. I don't think I'll be here too much longer. Or will I?"

"No note, no suicide," Carmen said, as if she was quoting something by rote. She sighed. "As far as the doctors know, this was an accidental overdose.

Another blessing from Roger is that he figured the whole thing could only be an accident since you were so nervous about your talk. You got too eager with sleeping pills, and since you're so small as it is, accidents in dosages can happen even faster. And I...I just went with the crowd, relieved that you were okay. And continue to be okay, right? Take care of yourself. If you need to stay longer, stay longer. Please."

Mona nodded, and then promised aloud that she would do just that. After waving goodbye to Carmen and wishing her luck, a nurse came in. Sure enough, the doctor was going to be around before the end of the day to discharge her.

Until then, she went through all her messages on her phone. The alerts were running off the top sidebar. She dealt with her parents first, speaking in French to calm them. She sent a thank-you to Dr. Conlin, though it felt strangely static over email. She didn't know what else to say, though, and how much longer she could run out the clock. An hour later, with no message from Kerri in the interim, Mona finally wrote her.

"Hey. I'm sorry about before. I don't think I conducted myself well, and I wanted to apologize. I want to talk to you, too. Even just as friends. We didn't finish *The Nightmare*, you know? And it feels like it's hanging there. I want to finish it."

She stared at the message. It was all about her,

nothing about Kerri. Mona didn't know how she could convey that she was here for her without seeing her face to face, though. She closed the message bar, the text still as a draft, and opened Facebook. Though she hadn't been on in a long time, news about her hospital visit had spread thanks to her parents. She now had messages to return and friend requests to comb through.

When she came across a message from Damien, dated six months ago, she baulked. How had she missed this? When she opened it, she read it in his slightly French accented voice.

"Mona, I hope you're well. I wanted to invite you to come to my first solo art show at McGill. If you're around and up for it. It's been a while. I know you've moved on and don't always want to see the campus, but I think it could be good for you. Especially since Gabriel is now gone. I don't know if you've heard, but he died in prison a few weeks ago. Apparently, a suicide."

Mona stared at the screen. She'd stopped reading after that point, not needing to see Damien's signoff because the most important part was there. Her eyes filled with tears. Then she laughed bitterly. It was so barbaric, delighting in someone's death like this—but it was the best news she'd seen in a long time. He was dead. Gabriel was dead.

For a brief second, she wondered if she had killed

him, if her thoughts had somehow become manifest. Were her dreams that strong? When disbelief set in, even for Damien's words, she double-checked the news online. A prisoner's suicide wasn't exactly going to make the newspaper, but she managed to find an obituary for a Gabriel Lucas Côte. The date of birth and death made him the right age. This was him. He was dead.

And he'd been dead for nearly a year. Mona cried in great gasping sobs. It felt like a city was inside her again, now purged of monsters.

When the doctor came back in and she was still crying, she had to convince him that she was okay. "Tears of relief, I assure you. Of joy."

He signed her release forms, and she gathered her stuff. Red-rimmed and shaking slightly, she left the hospital. The sun was out. The day was almost over, but she was okay. Maybe a little hungry and still thirsty, but these were small details. Easy ones to fix. She was going to be okay.

So, who had sent her a box?

She stopped on the sidewalk. Elation replaced with tentative fear. She looked around and saw nothing, no one. Only a bus stop. She walked towards the stop and hopped on the next bus.

No one followed her. No one bothered her. There was no need to be afraid. But what if it wasn't her that was the target? The x's over Kerri's eyes made

Mona's stomach sink. She dialed Kerri's phone but didn't get through. She found Detective Lincoln's card in her front jacket pocket and dialed his number. No answer. Desperate, she Googled all the information she could about Kerri's father but struggled to put a name to him (Andy? Arman?) and to find the appropriate spelling of Kerri's last name.

So, she broke the story down to its base components. Survivalist literature. Muskoka bunker. Murdered stepmother. Twins named Kerri and Lee.

She found an article about Layla Hunter. *Right.* The newspaper articles from her office, in the bottom of her desk drawer. Those had been about Layla Hunter's murder. She'd been posed with kids in one of the images, their faces blurred out for privacy. Mona swallowed and tried to find that image again. It took a while, but on a Reddit thread about survivalist literature, she found the image where the kids' faces had not been blurred.

Kerri was smaller, but her flat cheekbones and red hair were so quintessentially hers it could be no one else. Beside her was Lee—of course—who stood with the awkward gait of a boy about to hit puberty, his limbs and facial features not quite growing together yet. His dark hair and light-coloured eyes, along with his smile, was familiar. The longer Mona stared at Lee, the more a sinking feeling overwhelmed her. Lee was Mickey Alan, The Shadow Man from the

psychology experiment.
Kerri's brother, trying to find her all along.

CHAPTER THIRTY-ONE

Absalom's calls to Kerri went unanswered. He tried not to worry. He'd already phoned in his discovery, putting out a BOLO for Leeland Jonathan Reznik. His last known residence was a treatment facility in the Ottawa region six months ago. Since he'd gone there on his own volition, there was no need to keep him there, according to the staff member he'd called. As long as he had a prescription for his meds, Lee was allowed to leave. Absalom was disheartened when he realized Lee had put down the diner address as his own and his next of kin contact being Kerri. Obviously, Lee hadn't been living with her the last six months but on the streets of Peterborough.

It was a common narrative, Absalom knew, but he'd hoped it was better now. Didn't society tend towards progress? Towards better infrastructure and ways to help the community? He understood Kerri's kindness towards the homeless man who'd slept in the diner now—not that anyone needed a personal reason to be kind. It just helped to remember sometimes that the world was not out to get you. Instead, it could reach out to you with trust.

Absalom almost believed his own waxing poetic by the time he arrived at the diner. There were no cars in the lots. The doors were locked. The diner never closed, only for those Monday staff meetings at two p.m., the dead time where he often did his own paperwork. All his hopes were put on hold as he noticed a trail of blood. Small drops on the sidewalk, leading from a parking spot that bore the rust shadow of a car. Absalom pressed his face to the glass of the diner, struggling to see through the sun's glare. A pool of blood by the cash register emerged.

Absalom withdrew his weapon and called for backup. He walked around the back of the building, determined to go in. It could be Kerri's blood. It could be Mona's. Anyone's.

The back door was propped open by a rock. Droplets of blood mixed with the dirt and sand. He kicked open the door the rest of the way and stepped inside. No one was visible. He checked several corners, finding nothing save for the low rumbling of murmured voices.

"Police. Step out and show your hands."

The murmurs turned to shouts. They seemed to be coming from the large chest fridge in the kitchen.

Stepping closer, Absalom realized it had been blocked with a table. More people cheered and called from inside.

"I hear you. Let me check the rest of the diner. I'll be back."

Though the murmurs persisted, desperation obvious, Absalom tore himself away to finish his check. No one seemed to be here, though. Other than the fridge, everything was eerily quiet. The blood puddle seemed much larger than it had through the glass and spread around the corner of the cash register. Roy was sprawled against the tile. Absalom leaned down to feel Roy's pulse. There, but barely. The wound was on his leg and the amount of blood at the scene gave him the sense that this had all happened a while ago. Lee had been here, but he was long gone now—and with a car.

Satisfied there was no immediate threat, Absalom pocketed his weapon and opened the chest fridge. Several workers spilled out, along with one customer. Absalom recited the speech he'd memorized for situations like this, feeling his heart sink when Mona or Kerri was not among the crowd. Gone. And maybe gone with Lee.

Roy moaned. Absalom was by his side in a heartbeat. When Roy reached out, Absalom took his hand without question or qualm. "I'm Absalom Lincoln. You've been shot. Help is on the way. I need you to stay where you are."

"He took Roy's car," Tara said. She shivered while also hopping from foot to foot to keep warm. "He put us in there and was about to leave, but then Roy came and—"

When she started to sob, Absalom wanted to comfort her, as well, but he stayed by Roy's side. "It's okay. Everything is going to be okay."

Moments later, an ambulance and two police cars arrived. Absalom directed people to the officers, while he stayed with Roy. At first, he merely tried to be a comfort until he realized Roy was trying to speak.

"What was that?"

"My...baby."

Absalom was confused until he remembered an overheard conversation between Kerri and Roy. His baby was his car; he had no actual children. "Hey, Roy. What kind of car do you drive?"

Roy murmured. Words were harder for him to form. Absalom allowed him his quiet and instead reached into his pants for his wallet. He found the car's registration tucked into a zippered pocket, along with an image of a blond woman. He didn't have long to get what he needed before the EMTs came and took Roy away. He let go of his hand with a sustained squeeze and another plea that he'd be all right.

How do you catch a man who steals something no one owns? Absalom thought. You wait until he steals something you can trace.

He cursed Bill for being right. He gloated that Sandra was wrong. Everything was connected. He'd discovered all of it. He called in the stolen car's license, adding it to his original BOLO. As he hung up, he caught sight of a book wedged between one of the diner seats. Another one of Kerri's—which should have been no surprise, given the connection— but it was one he'd read. *The Wendigo Forest*. He thumbed its contents. The spine was broken over a passage. Nothing had been redacted like before, but a paragraph had been added. *No, corrected.*

In the section where the witch of the woods wants to help one of the girls, she tells her to go against the pine trees where they meet in the middle. It doesn't make sense to the girl, until she solves an equation. The numbers are latitude and longitude coordinates. In the margin, someone—*Lee?*—had written, "Wrong math. Right numbers. Clone equation."

The skin tightened on the back of Absalom's neck. He plugged in the coordinates on his phone. Then he was in his car, pulling out of the lot, and heading towards the sun in the dwindling daylight.

CHAPTER THIRTY-TWO

Mona knocked on the large oak door and waited. She adjusted her jacket and ran a hand through her hair, hoping she didn't look too dishevelled. She kicked herself for not having lipstick anywhere on her, but there was only so much she could do.

Mona left a dozen messages on Detective Lincoln's machine, and the weight of her guilt hit her like a train. She had been so stupid, so self-centred, that she had missed all the obvious signs. This was never about Gabriel. This was always about Kerri. Their traumas had intertwined until Mona's eyes blurred. Even her dreams had been telling her the answer through Amos. *This is not about you—for once. Maybe it never was.* Mona had been so obsessed with her own wound, so in love with her nightmares that she didn't even understand what Kerri had been trying to tell her. She just saw pain and pain and pain.

After pacing her apartment, Mona caught sight of the survival guide. Kerri's words floated into her mind, no longer tinged with the fresh pain of rejection. *I've given you all you need.* Was something in the survival guide? The false bottom in the box? Mona checked and found nothing among the items, other than what she'd already explored. When she'd thumbed through the survival guide in the car on the way to shoot, though, there had been an inscription inside. No names, only dates and coordinates. Since it was a park guide, she figured it was for a park.

She knew so much better now. She put the coordinates into her phone. Not for a park. But a random patch of wilderness in the Muskoka valley.

She dialed Detective Lincoln's number on her phone again, only to get voicemail once again. Who was next? She didn't want to call the other detective; she'd barely believed Mona's first story about Gabriel, and it was far stronger and more convincing than what she had now. All Mona knew were random coordinates. A possible break-in suspect. She could be wrong. She'd convinced herself she was wrong, that this was her looking for symbols in nothing, playing detective like everyone always wanted to do, until she arrived at Kerri's apartment. The door was unlocked. Everything was in disarray, smashed and torn. Though Mona shivered and hesitated on the threshold, she looked in every corner. No blood. No bodies.

But Kerri was gone. To the bunker. Towards her Redemption Arc or whatever Amos called it.

So, Mona was going to go, too.

Which meant she needed a car. Which was why, still running on adrenaline and guilt at her own bullshit, she ended up at Dr. Conlin's house. She recited the coordinates in her mind, bracing herself as he came to the door.

"Mona!" His voice was loud and gregarious. "You're doing better. I'm happy to see it."

"I'm feeling so much better." She tried to match his smile and enthusiasm. "And thank you. I wanted to come by and say as much."

"Well, this is a wonderful surprise." There was a slight pause as he glanced up and down her body. She had grabbed the only outfit that was clean in her apartment: the one she would have worn to the talk if she'd given it, except she swapped out the heels for flats. Dr. Conlin's gaze lingered on her cinched waist and v-neckline before he opened his door farther. "Would you like to come in? I think we have a lot of catching up to do."

"That sounds wonderful, but I'm going to have to decline. Truthfully, I came for a favour." She bit her lip, trying to act coy. It made her stomach flip—but only a little because now she was in control.

To go out to Muskoka by herself and to talk to Dr. Conlin in this way both felt like the same risk. Both amounted to potential bodily harm. Right? That was what Carmen had been telling her all along. *Roger likes to roger his students.* Mona had already felt gross about her degree, and Carmen's rumour just gave it a form. A monster it could become. It didn't matter if it was true because she already felt it anyway.

But she didn't have to be dictated by the monsters anymore. She could make them work for her. And if she could get Dr. Conlin to let her borrow his car, then maybe she had the upper hand all along. Maybe she could use her prettiness to her advantage, instead of letting it hold her down. If she could control the situation—using her assets instead of being used by her assets—then maybe she could save Kerri.

And break the damn trauma cycle.

"Of course, Mona. What kind of favour are we talking about, though? Can we talk about it?"

"I need to borrow your car."

"My car?"

"Yes. My parents are in Montreal, and they're really concerned. I talked to them on the phone, of course, but the hospital alerted them, and they want to be sure I'm okay."

"And they can't come to Peterborough?"

"They're so French," Mona said, painting her parents as a caricature of old world Quebeçois

Catholics. "And pretty old, too. My father is sixty-five, and his vision is going bad. It's a long enough drive that it'll be at night, and his vision isn't the greatest, so it's in a better interest for me to drive to see them. To assure them I'm okay."

Dr. Conlin crossed his arms and leaned against his doorframe, considering the problem. Though he lived in a two-story house in the nicer part of Peterborough, she wasn't sure if he had kids. She knew he had a wife from his casual remarks about her when he'd invited the class to his Christmas party, a woman named Natasha. Beyond the door frame, Mona spotted an image of a woman with dark hair and narrow features—almost exactly her own—in a photo frame inside the front hallway, standing with a younger version of Dr. Conlin.

"What's wrong with a car rental place? Or a bus?"

Mona blinked slowly. She waited just long enough for some kind of fear to cross her face. "I'm...I'm having a hard time with cash right now, so I can't rent a vehicle for that long. And the Greyhound bus doesn't quite go far enough."

Again, Dr. Conlin was silent as he considered. Mona wanted to scream at him that time was a factor here, and she needed to get to a bunker for the end of the world. She envisioned what would happen if she was late; what if her trip was merely following the cops to the woods, meeting Kerri with a hug and a shock blanket, and telling her everything was going to be okay? That was a good ending. A nice one.

But she didn't know what kind of state Lee was in. Kerri said he wasn't violent—and she had read enough to know that not all schizophrenics were—but so many years had passed. Everything was different. In spite of the survival kit she had in her bag and the gun at the bottom, she desperately didn't want to use it.

"I'm...I know this is strange. Especially since we're talking about ownership—and I'm asking to take something that's not mine. I could have gone to a dozen people for this kind of favour, so I think I went to you first because you would appreciate the irony of the situation." Mona looked down and made her voice quiet, purely passive. "You saved my life. So, now I'm asking you to make sure my parents know that I'm okay."

Mona chanced a glance. Dr. Conlin was smiling. She'd done it. He leaned back and grabbed the keys from behind his door. It was clearly a spare set, one that barely had anything but the key for the four-door sedan outside. He tossed it to her.

She caught the key and slipped it into her purse. Then she stepped forward and hugged him. He lingered a bit too long like she'd expected, but she didn't care. She had the car. She got into the car. She had survived.

As she turned on the engine, Dr. Conlin appeared by the window. She pressed the button so he could speak.

"Put gas in it before you return. Don't crash. Tell your parents I say, *prenez soin de vous.*"

Mona was startled by his French, especially the formality he used to address her parents, but she brushed it off. *Details to deal with later.*

"And I still want you to do that talk," he added. "I've scheduled it for next Thursday. So, try to be back before then. A lot of people wanted to see you."

Mona barely heard. She worked on adjusting her seat and let him ramble. Of course he was asking for favours as soon as he'd given her something. He was manipulating her as much as she was him. She considered toying with him, creating an entire PhD dissertation on the properties of ownership and the way in which people could use one another. It would be a battle of wills, and as she defended it, it would be like fighting one last battle.

Except that this trip, and these stupid coordinates, was her last battle. Not in academia. Not with a PhD. Gabriel had never won, so she didn't have to start again and again and again until she finished. She could just leave.

"And bring your friend by," Dr. Conlin said. "The one I met in the hospital. She's got some interesting theories on ownership, too, especially in terms of gender. I read it in her thesis. Fascinating."

"Uh-huh. Sure. That's great. But, Roger?"

"Yes?"

"I quit."

CHAPTER THIRTY-THREE

No one had followed them.

Kerri watched all the cars around them with wide eyes, hoping for a cop. Absalom, Sandra. Someone had to have figured it out by now. *Mona, please. Understand what I was saying.* By the time Lee merged off the highway and started to take back roads through the Muskoka territory, Kerri knew no one was coming.

She would have had a better chance of being flagged if she'd been in the trunk. Most cars now had the anti-kidnap button inside that blinked. There would have been more ways to escape then, too. Now they were too far away from any kind of civilization that running was a fool's errand. She'd freeze even in the summertime before morning. And deep down, Kerri knew she didn't want to leave Lee, even if she had no idea what the end game in all this really was.

Sure, he wanted to turn back time. He may have

even been successful in that endeavour in his own mind. Going into the woods like this did seem to throw the clock back to the early 1990s. He could live out his days here, growing his own food like Amos had taught them, and take refuge in an abandoned cottage along the way since there was no chance the bunker was still around. After the arrest, everything became evidence. When the trial was over, the bunker's contents were auctioned off or destroyed by police. Maybe they'd also sealed the bunker or let it grow over with weeds. Maybe someone else bought it and now lived out their prepper fantasy.

Either way, the bunker they were heading towards was not going to be the same one. They would be breaking and entering at the very least. Kerri hoped for nothing more.

She hadn't felt this deep sense of foreboding mixed with blind, amorphous hope in such a long time. *This is what staying in present tense is. Because present tense is all there is.* A new goal formed in her mind. She would stay focused on Lee and wait out his episode. Extreme breaks like this did not happen for long. If she could keep him calm and lucid, things were going to be fine. And honestly, Lee was logical enough if you didn't talk to him too long. If you didn't have electronics or say trigger words. He seemed like a kook in the wilderness, bitter about something—like every other survivalist out here. It was his notebook that made him seem out of touch, and only the gun made him seem dangerous. Kerri wasn't even sure if there were bullets inside, though considering the blood in the car, there probably was.

And if Kerri wasn't here, who would be with Lee? The months he'd surely been living on his own, without her or anyone, stretched out in her mind like a taunt. She hadn't been there for him. No one had been. And it hurt to consider all the what-ifs in that time period. What if she'd figured this out when she received the letter from Ashley? What if that publisher hadn't closed and it could have been delivered faster? What if she had sent Lee her actual address, rather than the diner? It was all too much to consider. So, she focused all her energy on the present, neglecting the past, and not worrying about the future.

When Lee pulled the car off the dirt path and parked it by trees, Kerri looked around. Nothing was familiar.

"Lee," she asked carefully. "Where are you going?"

Lee shook his head as if she should know. "We need to cover the tracks. There are sensors here. Radio waves."

"Of course."

Kerri got out of the car. She stood as Lee grabbed his backpack from the backseat. When she asked if they needed anything from the trunk, Lee shouted,

"Do not open the vortex."

She stamped down her panicked thoughts—what if Roy's body was inside?—and remembered that the only way to open Roy's trunk was through the sensor on the key, not the key itself. Lee had thrown it away before they'd even driven out from her apartment lot. Electronics. Triggers. Radio waves.

Everything was fine.

Lee walked quickly into a dense area with a lot of felled trees. There had been a storm not too long ago, and whoever's cottage this was hadn't cleaned up the broken limbs. Lee grabbed several in his arms and made a motion for Kerri to do the same. She did as she was asked, deliberately picking limbs that would not make a good fire. She didn't want Lee to start something too large and be unable to handle it.

The cabin they entered was small, quaint, and obviously for a family. No cars were in the driveway, and all the doors were locked. Lee used the butt of his gun to smash a window by the door. Kerri jumped, wondering if the gun would go off. Lee could have accidentally shot himself. He could have accidentally shot her. The amount of accidents spiralled in her mind and almost made her lose her cool.

"Come on."

Once inside, Lee moved through a routine he must have done a hundred times before. He turned on no lights as he walked around the cabin, only opened windows. When he saw a TV, he smashed it. A computer, he unplugged and threw it away. He commanded her to get more firewood for the night, which she did. Out in front of the cabin, she thought of running. This wasn't nearly as far into the Muskoka valley as they'd been before. It was still cottage country. She could probably get pretty far. Each time she added a branch to her pile, she repeated it like a mantra. *Run run run run.*

But she rejected it just as fast. She'd already run. She'd left him in a hospital when she was twenty-one and tried to move on. Except that her father found her. Lee found her. There was no sense of moving on. She gathered the branches and went back inside.

"Night's coming soon."

"I know." Kerri looked out the window. The sun sank lower on the horizon. There wasn't a single sound except for insects. No cars, no nothing.

Lee smashed a computer, interrupting the silence.

"We have to be quick," he said. "Time is going to go underground."

CHAPTER THIRTY-FOUR

Lee started the fire in the middle of the living room. He didn't even move the furniture out of the way; he merely stacked the branches over the couch and end table and went from there. The couch cushions were melting and stunk. Kerri waved her hand in front of her face, trying to dissipate the smoke. Lee was ranting, talking too fast and in a bunch of random syllables about the multiverse theory. Clones. Then about ice giants. Each time something from her books came up, Kerri felt a pang of guilt. Each time smoke tickled her nostrils, she wanted to puke.

"Lee," she said. "Lee."

"Hmm?"

"Why did you stop taking your medication?"

Lee shook his head. He went back to ranting. He put more wood on the fire. *He has to sleep sometime,* Kerri told herself, only to remember the time he'd gone three days without sleeping when they were both nineteen, like some enchanted creature from a fairy tale. Kerri was already exhausted, all of it etched into her bones. She wanted to curl up in the pile of blankets he had made for her, but she worried she'd die of smoke inhalation if she let go of her own hold on reality. She worried, from a primordial fear deep inside, that if she went to bed now, she'd wake up just like him. Just like her father. She was already close enough to Amos, penning the Armageddon without concern of those around her.

"Lee?"

"I am not on the radio waves. I will not eat the medication."

"I know, I know. I'm sorry I asked. But can we open a door? I'm coughing." When she shuddered with a full-blown cough that made her eyes water, Lee finally stopped ranting. His face tinted with worry. She traced her fingers along the scar on her elbow. He watched with fixation and then nodded.

"Sorry. I should have been more careful."

Kerri's fear dissipated. An exit plan formed in her mind. When she had become ill from her infected burn, Lee had been there. He got her soup, made sure she was drinking water, and when she was so cold, he threw himself over her like a blanket. Finally, when it became obvious that she was not getting better, he'd convinced their father to take her to a doctor. Lee always protected her. Even this strange jaunt to the wilderness was done under the guise of protection. Maybe now, if Kerri could become sick or pretend to be sick, Lee would leave the cabin.

And someone would help.

Kerri coughed again. Lee made subtle sounds of reproach as he walked around the cabin and opened more windows. When he got to the front door, he opened it without a second thought. Night air spilled in.

Mona stood on the stoop, her hand in her purse.

"Mona?" Kerri's voice betrayed her elation. She wondered if she was hallucinating.

But Lee saw her, too, and shouted that she was a clone.

"Do you see this?" Lee said, turning to Kerri. "She's a clone!"

In the split second that Lee turned away, Mona pulled out the gun from her purse. She held it out in the exact pose Kerri had taught her, legs splayed. The weaver stance. When Lee turned back, he pulled his gun, too.

And Kerri lost all hope entirely.

CHAPTER THIRTY-FIVE

Mona shook with the gun in her hand. She hadn't thought this far ahead. She really didn't think this would happen. Her adrenaline plummeted the moment she got off the highway and started driving in the wilderness. She doubted her ability to follow the coordinates, like a math equation in high school she couldn't quite master. When the GPS signal had dropped entirely, she used her phone for a panicked 911 call before she then lost her battery.

That was an hour ago.

Why was she the only person here? It wasn't the exact coordinates—not even close—but it had been hard to miss a house with a glowing orange orb in the centre of it. And the familiar rusted car in the front. Surely, she couldn't be the only person who thought this was odd and needed to check it out. She'd kept driving after the 911 call because it was the only thing to do, and now, so used to getting the wrong answer, she was here.

She had found Kerri. She had found Lee.

Now her gun was up, but her entire body shook. She and Kerri hadn't practiced like this. She barely understood the gun she'd been given, but she'd started to like the power it gave her. That was only when she was staring at the woods, some Coke cans to shoot at. When another gun was added to the mix, all the confidence short-circuited. It looped back and became fear, trauma; Lee became Gabriel, sitting in the front row of her poetry class, a gun on the table and fixated on her.

The next move was obvious, but it hung in the air unsaid.

"You are the clone."

"She's not," Kerri said. "She's real."

"You said you would get rid of her. But she found us here, so she must be in our heads. She must be a clone." Lee stared at Mona, though he spoke to Kerri. His jaw looked askew, as if he had broken it, but it didn't heal right.

"No, the one at the apartment was a clone. That's why I got rid of her. This one is real."

"How can you tell?"

"Because I love this one."

"Not good enough. How can I tell?"

Mona felt Kerri's gaze on her. Her gaze—like her touches at night—were a language, with its unique syntax and grammar. Mona desperately wanted to say something—but she had no idea what was going on. The words Lee and Kerri spoke were English, but their meaning was unclear. That was common in schizophrenic patients, right? She'd only done so much reading in psychology. So much of it was filled with abuse after abuse, asylums that locked people up and threw away the keys, drugs that induced catatonia as the only reprise.

But Mona knew translation. If she could parse out the implied meaning, connotation rather than denotation, then maybe she could speak with them. Maybe she could translate, pain for pain, and make the guns all go away.

"I destroyed the experiment," Mona said suddenly. Lee's attention on her seemed to narrow to a fine point. "Mickey, do you remember me?"

"*You* were the experimenter?"

"I was. But I destroyed the experiment. It's gone."

"Even the crystals?"

When Mona furrowed her brow, unsure of what he meant, Kerri jumped in. "The computers at the school were down. No information was sent in. Their crystal memory is not set."

"Yes," Mona said. "All that is gone. I'm here to tell you that the world is safe."

Kerri blinked. Mona's stomach sank. It was

the wrong thing to say. She wasn't sure how or why, but it was wrong. Lee started to yell again, his words too frantic to decipher. When something next to the fire popped, he jumped. His words stopped. The gun slipped from his hand—carelessly, ambivalently. Whatever had exploded in the flames now produced smoke; Lee searched but couldn't seem to find his weapon in the floorboards.

He bent closer to the flames as Mona took a step closer. She aimed her gun higher. She did not shake.

"Don't move. Don't pick up the gun."

"You will not take me into the square."

Lee stopped looking for his weapon and turned to Mona. His startling height of almost six feet four inches meant she was a foot under him. She cocked the gun instinctively. He was so big. He may have been sick, he may not have had a gun anymore, but he was tall enough and strong enough to break her in half.

Her fear overwhelmed her. Lee no longer became a shadow of Gabriel, he was Gabriel. She was looking at Gabriel, the man who'd ruined her life, only now she had the weapon. She wasn't going to be dragged across campus by anyone who spouted poetry. She wasn't going to let her ex-boyfriend be shot and her students scarred for life. She was going to fight back. This wasn't a dream anymore, either. Mona knew she could win for real.

"Don't." Kerri's voice broke through Mona's fog. "Please don't shoot him."

Lee had stopped his advance, Kerri's words also affecting him. He seemed to want to argue with her, to make a claim, but Kerri was wounded. She held her arm where her scar was. Blood seeped through her clothing. Mona didn't recall how it had happened—if it was the flames that got too close and the minor explosion from the centre—or something that had happened before she got there. But Kerri was bleeding. She needed to save her. She needed to—

"Don't shoot him. Please. He's..."

"No. I need to... No." Mona blinked. Lee was Gabriel again. Her breath was tight in her chest. Her finger slid around the weapon. She could end this. She could break out of the cycle. Except that Lee was not Gabriel, and Kerri was begging her. Kerri seemed to understand the glow that went over Mona's face, the temptation deep down, because she was begging again.

"Please don't shoot him. He's my brother."

Mona swallowed. She looked from Lee to Kerri and then back again.

"Please."

Mona almost put the gun down. She almost walked away. But Lee grabbed a branch from the fire, raising it in the air like a torch, and stepped forward. He charged.

A bang sounded.

Lee dropped the branch. Fire singed his pants before he fell forward onto the floor. The flames spread from his pants to his sleeve. Kerri screamed. She jumped up from her position and threw herself on his body, smothering the flames.

Mona thought Kerri's screams were her own. She looked down at the gun, her finger still on the trigger. All she smelled was smoke—but she was sure it wasn't gun smoke. She was sure she hadn't fired. She glanced behind her to see the flashing of blue and red on the horizon.

Detective Lincoln was behind her. He held up his weapon as he stepped inside, assessing the scene. "Is everyone okay?"

Mona shook her head. Kerri was on top of Lee completely, the flames now smothered. She continued to rock him, though, repeating a refrain of "I got you, I got you, I got you..."

CHAPTER THIRTY-SIX

Kerri had no memory of leaving Muskoka or her father's arrest. Her last conscious thoughts were of how safe she felt when Lee wrapped around her at night to keep her warm and how the scar on her arm from the sparkler was going to look like a constellation of stars.

After that, there was nothing but the Wendigo.

Four days after the burn, during the morning callisthenics their father insisted on, Kerri had collapsed. Amos thought she was faking. When he unbandaged her burn and saw pus-filled, angry red skin, he just thought she was weak.

"Not meant for survival."

Though it was still unclear what Amos had meant by these words, Lee had thought the worst. He tried to feed Kerri willow bark and whatever else he could find in the first aid kit. When nothing worked, he plotted to leave the forest with her strapped to his back, determined he'd hit some kind of civilization. Maybe an abandoned hospital. Either way, Kerri would be cured.

"But the Wendigo," she told him. "The Wendigo is the monster at the edge of the woods who eats people alive."

Lee had no idea what she meant. He listened, though, because it could have been real. The Wendigo was only a fever dream that attacked the base of her brain and made her see shadows out of nowhere; the bacterial infection mingled with her memories and twisted the boogeyman legends into something far more sinister. To Kerri, the Wendigo was a snarling creature with teeth as big as their arms; it chomped them down and turned them into kindling. It lived between the trees; it ate people; it was everywhere and nowhere at once.

Her vivid reimaginings didn't make much sense, but eventually, Lee had grown too scared to venture into the woods alone. Kerri's illness progressed. She was blacking out and not speaking, slipping into her own dream world of monsters and destruction. Lee wrapped himself around her, trying to keep her warm, while also begging Amos to help. When Kerri felt the pickup truck's wheels against the dirt road, she thought she was flying. Then she thought she had died.

Instead, her life was being saved. The local hospital gave her antibiotics and set her up in a room with Lee by her bed. An hour later, the police showed up and arrested her father. He was hiding in the parking garage.

All the monsters were gone.

Mostly, anyway.

Decades later, when Kerri wrote her novel about the girls in the woods, she remembered the original dream that had been the inspiration for the story all along. It came to her in bits and pieces, snarled teeth, the peaty scent of decay, and the feeling of her brother's arms around her. As she wrote the novel, her chest ached and her elbow smarted from the old wound, as if she was reliving it all again. At the time, it had been too frightening of a prospect. She shut out her recollections. She focused on research. In indigenous folklore, the Wendigo was a man who was made into a beast by consuming human flesh. Though her father had never been so desperate to consume flesh of his own kind, he used people as if they were meat. *Only kill what you intend to keep.*

As a child, she'd grown used to seeing the people she loved hollowed out inside by some unknown force, so no wonder her fever dream had managed to conjure something so vicious. The Wendigo was the creature that took her father, his first bite of survivalist literature that fueled the sickness in his brain. The Wendigo was the hereditary sickness that Lee now had as his legacy—a legacy that had somehow skipped her. She was never going to be eaten by the Wendigo because she'd shed blood, like the girls in her story. She'd suffered her wound in a pattern of stars on her arm. But she would still be forced to watch her friends and family be consumed.

For Kerri, it was a far worse fate.

"Not meant for survival."

Maybe Amos had been right.

෴෴෴෴

When Kerri woke up, her arm ached. She tried to make a fist, but it felt as if her skin was being ripped from the bone. She must have cried out because a nurse appeared at her side and shot her through with something that felt like liquid honey in her body. The pain went away. She went back to sleep.

This time, instead of the Wendigo vision that made her arm flare in pain or her father's voice, she dreamt of Mona. Mona's white bedsheets, her dark hair, and red lips. Mona had worn a skirt to the damn cabin, as if it was a conference instead of a survivalist ploy. Each time Kerri thought of Mona that night, though, she also cried. Then all she could do was cry. She woke up in tears again, seeing a nurse by her side, who shot her through with more drugs.

The sad dreams went away, the good ones remained, and when Kerri opened her eyes next, Mona was actually there. She was slumped over in a chair, her dark hair tucked behind her ears. She wore a red shirt and black pants. A stain was on one leg. An empty coffee mug next to her. She had been here a while.

"Hey," Kerri said. Her throat was raw. The smallest crack of her voice sprung Mona awake, who appeared with a drink with a bendy straw.

"Good?"

"Yes, thank you." Kerri nodded as the water went away. Mona went on for a while about the bendy straw, how it was so simple but so effective. She rambled in a way that Lee rambled when he was excited. Kerri's face must have twisted in pain because Mona slid a hand over hers.

"I'm sorry," she said. "I can stop talking and give you space."

"No. All I've had is space." Kerri blinked. She rubbed the sleep from her eyes with her right hand, her left one still smarting. White bandages were wrapped up and down her arm.

"You'll recover from that," Mona said. "It's just going to hurt like hell, and we need to ward off infection. Most of the burns are second degree."

"I'm familiar with the process of infection." Kerri braced herself before asking, "And Lee?"

"I...I didn't shoot him."

"I know." She remembered the entire display,

like a broken-down theatrical performance, and this time, she didn't cry. "I know you didn't. And thank you."

Mona nodded. Relief etched her face. After a sigh, she reported Lee's status was good. He was alive, thankfully, but still away in recovery. "Detective Lincoln only got his shoulder. Shattered the bone and gave him some pretty bad burns on his legs and arms in the process, but he's going to be okay. He's just… in a different part of the hospital."

"I figured he would be chained to the bed. Breaking and entering, attempted murder, and…?"

"Roy is okay."

With a sudden burst of tears, Kerri let go. Roy was okay. He was shot, Mona went on to tell her, but he was fine. "Lee confronted him and took his car because he thought it was yours. When Roy put up a fight and tried to grab the gun, Lee shot him in the leg. He hit nothing major, but since it was a long time before Detective Lincoln got to the diner, it bled a lot. He was touch and go for a while. Needed a lot of blood. Rare type, too, but apparently, I was the same type, so that helped." Mona smiled before realizing she was rambling again. "Apparently, Detective Lincoln figured out where we were because of your book."

"*Dante Under Ice*. Not my favourite work right now, I tell you."

"No. The Wendigo one."

Kerri closed her eyes. The moment she conjured her own private Wendigo monster, the plotline sprawled in front of her. A math equation where the answer was the coordinates. Of course. And if Lee got his hands on that book, too, it was a freaking sign pointing to where they all ended up.

"And you," Kerri said. "You figured it out, too."

"Not using that book…But yeah. I got there."

A quiet settled between them that was only broken when Roy showed up on crutches. Mona stood to help him inside, greeting him with a wide smile. She was so cordial and upbeat, their meeting was far more like a high school reunion than a teary "thank God you're okay" in a hospital room. Kerri wiped away her tears and held on to Roy's hand with her only good one fiercely. Without his bandanna and standard work clothing, he seemed so much slimmer and paler. His hair that much greyer. Or maybe that was the loss of blood and near death experience. *Maybe a little of both.*

"Oh, it is so good to see you." Roy leaned back on his crutches, a devious smile replacing his earlier worn-down expression. "Now if I don't get to be a character in your next book after all this, then we are totally not friends."

Kerri laughed. It hurt somewhere deep inside how easy this was. It wasn't the shooting. Not the attempt on his life or the theft of his car or her brother that made Roy not want to be friends. It was her books and not being allowed in them. "Roy, I will let you be seven characters. It'll take place in a strange city in Orangeville where everyone's name is Roy. All I need is a title, and I'm basically set."

"*Everybody Loves Roy*?" Mona suggested.

"No! *A City of Clones*!" Roy boasted. "I love it. Please do exactly that. And maybe let me be on the cover."

"I can't do that last part. Publisher's discretion. But everything else? You got it."

Kerri didn't realize she was crying until Mona placed a hand on her shoulder. The tears fell down her cheeks silently but relentlessly. She thought it was more relief stacking on other relief, but it was the clones. She didn't know if she could ever write about them or apocalypses or anything to do even remotely with her life ever again. Maybe she couldn't even write horror anymore. Maybe this book for Roy would have to be a romance—or like the manuscript from *The Shining*, with Roy's name endlessly repeated to fill the pages. What made Kerri cry even more was that Roy would probably still love that. As long as it was from her, it didn't really matter.

"But anyway," Roy said, clearing some of the tension in the room. "I look forward to your next book, K.T. Stellar, but do take time to recuperate. I can always read my old favourites."

Kerri nodded, her mouth sealed. If she let out just one sound, she worried an entire cascade of emotions would come out of her and not stop or make any sense. Mona helped Roy to the hallway and gave him a hug as he left. She returned to Kerri's bedside and took her hand again. Silence surrounded them. Kerri's tears had stopped, but it was still hard to breathe and speak.

"I didn't shoot him," Mona said. "I know that I already said that, but I need you to know."

"I know."

"But I also wasn't going to shoot him, either. I wasn't."

"You don't know that."

"I do, though. I said no. Finally." Mona took a breath. "It was so similar to what happened with Gabriel. Time slipped, and I did see Gabriel. But then I *didn't* see Gabriel anymore. I didn't shoot—but I also wasn't scared. At the end, I made the choice, not fear or anything else. I made it. I said no, not yes, and I feel like I'm finally out of the cycle."

"What cycle?"

"It's something that Carmen told me—who, by the way, already has a job." Mona chuckled lightly but soon grew serious as she explained how people repeated their trauma through different scenarios until they finally understood their pain and were able to heal from it. "I couldn't understand that Gabriel had treated me like an object, so I kept putting myself in shitty situations where people were treated like objects in hopes that I could somehow fix the first pain. But instead, I couldn't process it. I couldn't heal from it. I kept running and running without understanding. So, I took Dr. Conlin's car. I told him a lie, and I made him give me what I wanted."

"And it healed your pain from Gabriel?"

Mona sighed. "I know it sounds ridiculous. Maybe it is. But I needed to do it to prove to myself that I could ask for something from the world. It wasn't just all take, take, take. And I got the car. I drove to meet you guys. And it was so difficult. But I didn't shoot Lee. I thought I was going to, but I didn't. I was in control, like you said. I wasn't in the past anymore."

Kerri wanted to shake her head. It all sounded too simple like a fortune cookie. Her editor would have underlined it and said "save it for bumper stickers; we don't do self-help books" or something like that. But Kerri also felt it intuitively, in the place where the Wendigo lived inside of her. *What you can't control consumes you. So, control what you consume.* "I think I understand," she said slowly. "I was trying to do the same thing with my books. I thought I could let the fear wash over me and then pin it down like a butterfly in a shadow box display. I thought I had won by writing it out. But…it only made Lee sicker as I got better."

"That's not true."

"Come on, Mona. He saw my face in a book, and then heard my voice on the radio. I wrote out my father's Redemption Arc and slapped a horror cover on it. I caused his fucking breakdown. I'm no better than Amos. Not…meant for survival."

"No."

Mona said the word with such conviction Kerri was struck mute. Mona ran her hands along her jeans, sighing. "No," she repeated, slightly cowed. "Not taking his meds caused Lee's breakdown. Not finding the right combination of meds. You are not your father. And neither is Lee. I saw him, you know."

"You did?"

"Yeah. I wanted to be sure they were treating him well."

"And are they?"

"Yes. I mean, he's handcuffed to the bed, and that's shitty, but they're treating him well. I even talked to the doctor for a while. I played myself off as a psych student, though I don't know how much longer I can do that, but I tried to get a sense of his medications without violating a privacy clause. From talking to Lee, though, it seems like he stopped taking his meds because of some side effects. Near catatonia. The hospital he was at discontinued his standard medication, I think, because it got more expensive. So, he didn't want to stay there anymore—but it's not the only option for him. Either way, we have something to look into now. A better problem to examine and maybe plan for the future."

Kerri wanted to be mad. To hear Mona talk about her brother in such a casual, intimate way was maddening, mostly because Kerri had borne witness to Lee's catatonic states, his drinking, and endless cocktail of meds—all alone. Without help. Mona's knowledge felt violating, like the breaking down of a boundary, and Kerri wanted to weep again. But the more Kerri went over the scenario in her mind, the more she realized she was only mad because she'd been alone in all this for so long. Mona was breaking down a boundary, not to be violent, but to be intimate. She wanted to know Kerri as much as she wanted to know Lee—and she wanted Lee to get better. Kerri was only mad at Mona because of time itself. Where had she been when she was nineteen? Or twenty-two? Or even six months ago, when Lee's doctors first stopped the meds that worked and effectively kicked him out the door?

These questions could not be answered, though, because even if they had met when they were nineteen and twenty-three, they would not be the same people. They would now bear the same bodies with the same marks. As Kerri grasped Mona's hand, she wondered if

Mona would trade her own experience, to have never met Gabriel at all in her life, if it meant giving up any of this in the process. Would she pay that price?

Kerri didn't voice the question. Time did not bend that way. And she didn't want to worry about what-ifs anymore. Not when she didn't have to go through any of this alone anymore.

"There's also the matter of Lee's sentence," Mona said. "I called a friend through Carmen who knows of a good legal office that will most likely take him on as a client. He won't escape the charges, but there's a high chance he'll serve whatever time in a facility."

Kerri wanted to cry. The relief she felt was so powerful but so deceptive. She didn't want to say anything in case it fell apart.

"What I'm trying to say is," Mona added, after going on for some time about Lee and his after care, "is that you never made him get sick. You saved him."

Kerri nodded, but it was strained. She didn't know if she could believe that because no matter what she did, she always felt as if she was making up for lost time from when he saved her. Luckily, Kerri's silence didn't slow Mona down, as she kept adding stray thoughts of interjections about Lee, medication, and the future.

"And you know," Mona said after a while, "there was something else Carmen told me about trauma.

We may break out of those cycles, but it never actually gets better. Not completely. But that's okay—it's just we have to deal with it. So, I'll have nightmares again someday, and Lee will have episodes, and you will...write a bajillion stories until your limbs fall off. Because I think that's your thing, even if it scares you. Whatever it is, though, we will deal with it."

We. The more Kerri heard it, the more she liked it. She squeezed Mona's hand, not daring to do more. But Mona squeezed back, seeming to understand. Maybe she was right about Lee, too. It was a thing. Not good or bad—but they would do it together.

"I think..." Kerri said after some time had passed. "I think I want to sleep some more. If that's okay."

Mona chuckled. "You know, sleep for once actually sounds good. I think I'll go home and do the same. You'll be okay?"

Kerri nodded. She would be. Eventually. She always would. Mona leaned down and kissed Kerri gently. Kerri opened herself to the embrace, attempting to overwrite whatever had come before. There was no breakup. They belonged to each other, even more than before.

"I love you, I'm pretty sure," Mona said. "But we can talk more later."

"I love you, too."

With a small wave, Mona disappeared around the corner. Kerri breathed in and out. Fear didn't wash over her; it moved through her, tangling with her insides and making her feel as if she would vomit like she did when she was twelve and the bacteria created a monster in her brain. But she didn't vomit now. She held the pain inside of her because it was hers. Her life. Her memories. And she wasn't alone with them anymore.

She turned over onto her side, another monster already blooming in her brain, another story for another time.

CHAPTER THIRTY-SEVEN

When Mona arrived home, she went right to bed. She did not dream.

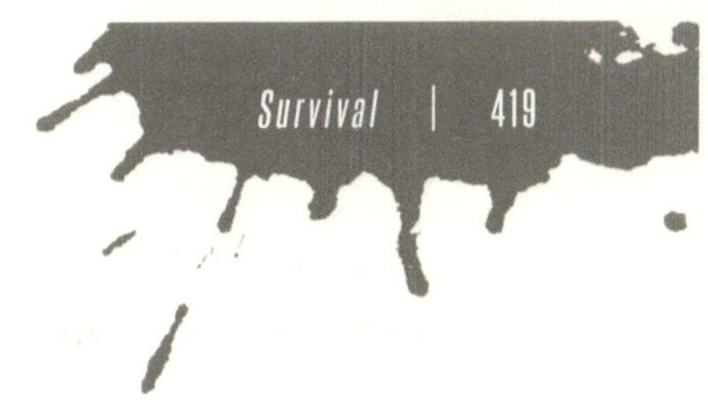

CHAPTER THIRTY-EIGHT

Absalom set down his transfer request. As he'd driven away from the Muskoka cabin, Absalom knew this was what he wanted to do next. He still had a week off, though, so he kept the notion of transfer like a silent secret in the back of his mind. On his runs in the morning, he woke earlier than ever before to chase the sun right out of a pitch-black darkness. He ran all the way to Parkhill every time, his heart in his throat as he ran down and down and down. The run was elating. Wonderful.

But he still thought of Scarborough.

She was always going to be there, a scar and a blot in his mind. He'd not helped someone when he should have—but more than that, he'd not helped someone who had asked. That was the worst injustice. He couldn't keep paying for it with hookups and fixations. He either had to let her go or go home.

So, he was going to try to go home.

When Sandra saw the transfer request, she raised her brows. "Huh. You get back from break, close your unclosable cases, and then want to ditch? Why not stay and be king shit for at least a week and a half?"

Absalom smiled but shook his head. "This has nothing to do with those cases."

"Could have fooled me, Anansi." Sandra's gaze hovered over the transfer request. Absalom knew she wasn't reading it; she was stalling for time, trying to find a suitable way of expressing her emotions. "This isn't because of me, right?"

"What?" Absalom asked, genuinely shocked by her question. "Why would it be about you?"

She shrugged. "I'm your partner. So, I suppose I should have figured you were leaving. Or figured out if something was wrong. I don't know…Doesn't everyone think the world kind of revolves around them?"

Absalom only smiled. He was about to tell her that no, he was well aware that the world was heliocentric and that he worked hard to chase the sun, rather than begging the sun to chase him as if he was the centre of the universe. He stopped, though. He'd constructed his entire mission around Jane Doe, assuming that she thought of him as a villain. Assuming that she, in her worst moments, still remembered a random kid who was too scared and turned around.

But she might have forgotten who he was. She might have no idea her effect on him. She may be okay now, too, living a perfectly okay life. She may already trust the world again, even more than him.

"I suppose you're right," Absalom said. "But trust me—I don't think this is about either one of us."

At the end of the day, when Sandra offered to go to the diner for a bite to eat, Absalom declined. He'd seen Kerri—and Mona—in the hospital on his days off. They were slowly working back to their own equilibrium, and he didn't want to get in the way. Maybe it was being self-centred again, but he didn't want to wear out his welcome. Kerri had forgiven him for shooting her brother, and even Lee seemed to hold no grudges once he came around. But Absalom had finished with Peterborough. It was still a perfect city in his mind, and he did not want to tarnish it anymore.

He walked to Parkhill as the sun was going down. He trailed behind the old university dorms, where he'd first caught sight of Lee, and then back towards the campus. He stood in front of the Otonabee River. He held his phone in his hands, staring at the screen. His image stared back at him.

He tossed it in the water. It hurt, like getting a thumb stuck in a door. Nonthreatening, but urgent and piercing, and fading just as fast.

EPILOGUE

Kerri appeared at Mona's side, coffeepot in hand. She raised her eyebrows to ask if Mona wanted another.

"Please." Mona held up the cup and murmured a thank-you as Kerri filled it. She'd been back at work for only two days, but she'd fallen into the routine as if it was second nature. Mona supposed it was.

The only difference between the Kerri she'd met months ago at the beginning of the spring semester was that this one smiled at her a bit more and now had to wear longer sleeves as her arm healed. Her burn was better, for the most part, but there was a latticework of red wounds that would soon be scars over her elbow and arm. Roy, too, was back at work, though he had a stool brought to the kitchen so he could sit when his leg pained him. He had waved at Mona as she came into the diner.

"Anything to eat?" Kerri asked.

Mona debated a grilled cheese, decided on the special instead, and reported to Kerri. When the bell rang at the front, both their gazes rose to see Sandra—but not Absalom—come into the diner. While Sandra gave them a perfunctory nod, Kerri waved. She leaned close to Mona, kissing her forehead before leaving to take Sandra's, and all the other customers', orders.

Mona opened her laptop on the diner table. She had filed her paperwork to leave school the week before. While Dr. Conlin and Carmen had tried to convince her to stay, she simply ignored the emails. She cut her student card in half and returned all her library books. She'd reached out to Damien on Facebook, thanking him for the message and then informing him all about Kerri. She responded to a message from him now, still cautious, still hopeful for friendship—before she shut all internet tabs to stare at a blank Word document.

Kerri had begun work on a new novel the night before. She was secretive as she slipped out of bed and cracked open her own laptop, but Mona knew the joy across her face could only mean one thing. A new monster. A new fear.

"I think I might try a mystery this time," Kerri said after writing for a couple of hours and returning to bed. "You know, see if I can redeem that earlier one."

They'd talked into the morning, brainstorming ideas. Kerri eventually concocted some long, convoluted version of *Murder on the Orient Express*, but on Greyhound, before they both fell asleep.

Kitty Genovese remained in the forefront of Mona's mind, but it didn't bother her as much anymore. When she was packing up her stuff for Kerri's place, Mona had stumbled on one of her early Kitty Genovese books. She skimmed it long into the night, soon realizing that the ending—Kitty's death—was told differently. She still died, and no one stopped Moseley, but she hadn't died alone. Sophia, a neighbour in the Kew Gardens apartments, heard the commotion and came downstairs. Moseley had just slipped out the door. Her choices had been to run after him or stay with Kitty—and so she'd stayed with Kitty. She held her as she bled to death, telling her everything was going to be all right.

Mona read the passage at least six times. She couldn't believe it. She'd thought that Kitty had died alone. Wasn't that what the city was known for—the violence in anonymity? But Kitty had died in her neighbour's arms, the definition of community. The story, in some way, proved Mona's point about her original dissertation. Kitty Genovese's death didn't break down the community; it didn't turn us all into strangers who didn't care about one another. Her death banded people together.

She had not died alone.

Mona wanted to tell someone this. But who? She didn't want to do a PhD, not even in poetry anymore. She'd applied for an admin position in the English Department at the school since it was far enough away from psychology, but that was just for money. That was like Kerri's diner job. The real stuff that kept Kerri up at night—in all the best and worst ways—was creating monsters.

Mona's was always Kitty. Mona would always wonder if something good could come from survival, even if it was only the survival of an idea. Community. Hope. That was what kept her up at night; that was what her city dream was made of, when all the world was inside of her. It was a good dream; now she understood. Even if it haunted her.

She stared at her blank Word document. There was still a niggling doubt, still something that she had left unfinished.

"Here you go," Kerri said moments later, placing her lunch in front of her. "Anything yet?"

Mona shook her head.

"Well, don't worry. It'll come. Sometimes, these things take a while."

Mona nodded. If anyone knew her frustration, it was Kerri. She appeared again moments later, topping off her coffee. When Mona looked at the clock, she realized hours had actually passed.

"We still good to see Lee later on?" Kerri asked. "Will you be done here?"

"I might not be done—or even started—but we will go. I promise." Each Tuesday and Thursday, they made a point to visit him in the medical facility where his plea deal had landed him. They'd only gone a handful of times, but it was already better than before. His medication was covered there. He was adjusting. It would take time, but time was no longer a threat. It was a promise.

"Great. Sounds good. And good luck." Another refill, another peck, and Kerri was gone. Mona wished she'd stayed a second longer, so she could at least tell Kerri about Kitty's actual death. So she could receive some kind of validation before stepping into the abyss of a blank page.

But Mona knew she'd be back. She'd tell her this revelation soon enough. A new routine had settled around her, a new cycle filled with quotidian details among the darkness but never overshadowing them. A routine that let her go to bed by midnight and be up before ten in the morning. A routine that gave her someone in the bed at night. A normal routine. Boring, really. But one she liked more than she thought possible.

Mona stared at the blank document in front of her. She swore the eyes of Kitty Genovese stared back at her, begging to be witnessed.

So, Mona started to write.

IF YOU LIKED THIS BOOK...

Share a review with your friends or post a review on your favorite site like Amazon, Goodreads, Barnes and Noble, or anywhere you purchased the book. Or perhaps share a posting on your social media sites and help spread the word.

Join the Sapphire Newsletter and keep up with all your favorite authors.

Did we mention you get a free book for joining our team?

sign-up at - www.sapphirebooks.com

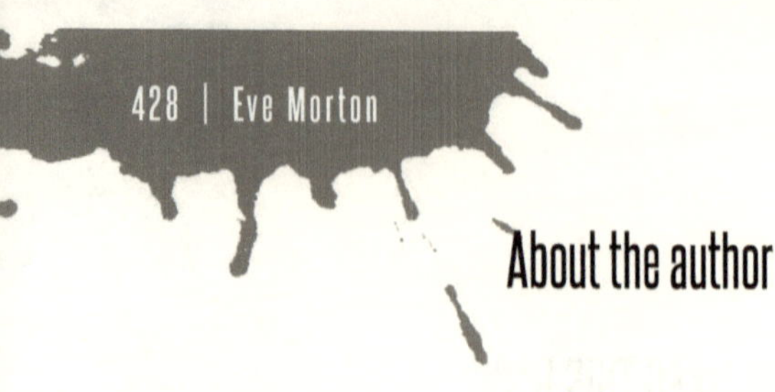

About the author

Eve Morton is a writer living in Ontario, Canada. She teaches university and college classes on media studies, academic writing, and genre literature, among other topics. She reads tarot, has a lot of tattoos, and loves all things occult and supernatural in nature. She also loves true crime, especially the forensic side of it, and is often swayed by a really good podcast (even more when it's funny). She received a PhD in 2019 and continues her research work on LGBTQ communities and film, in addition to other topics related to addiction and mental health. Find more information on authormorton.wordpress.com.

Other Sapphire Books from Sapphire Authors

The Dragonfly House: An Erotic Romance - ISBN- 978-1-952270-14-7

On the outskirts of a small, picturesque Midwestern town, sits a large, lovely old Victorian house with many occupants. This residence, known simply as The Dragonfly House, is home to Ma'am, the proprietor, along with several young women in her employ. One such woman, Jame, is very popular among the female clientele. One such client, Sarah, fresh from a divorce and looking for a little adventure, as well as some gentle handling, becomes one of Jame's repeat clients. Once Sarah enters the picture, Jame and Ma'am, as well as the brothel, will be forever changed.

Keeping Secrets – ISBN – 978-1-952270-04-8

What would you do if, after finally finding the woman of your dreams, she suddenly leaves to fight in the Civil War? It's 1863, and Elizabeth Hepscott has resigned herself to a life of monotonous boredom far from the battlefields as the wife of a Missouri rancher. Her fate changes when she travels with her brother to Kentucky to help him join the Union Army. On a whim, she poses as his little brother and is bullied into enlisting, as well. Reluctantly pulled into a new destiny, a lark decision quickly cascades into mortal danger. While Elizabeth's life has made a drastic U-turn, Charlie Schweicher, heiress to a glass-making fortune, is still searching for the only thing money can't buy. A chance encounter drastically changes everything for both of them. Will Charlie find the love she's longed for, or will the war take it all away?

The Coffield Chronicles – Hearts Under Siege: Book One – ISBN – 978-1-952270-12-3

The year is 1862. The war between the states has been raging intensely for a year now. The country is in complete and utter turmoil, and brother is fighting brother to the death, dying for what each believed. It seems it's all the townsfolk of New Albany, Indiana can speak of, and Melody Coffield is paying attention. Through a series of heartbreaks and sorrow, she settles on the decision to cut her hair and don men's attire. Going under the alias of Melvin A. Coffield, she leaves her childhood home, the only home she had ever known, and enlists in the United States Army. Chewing tobacco and drinking liquor were ways of men, and she learns quickly how to behave like one. She would soon know the horrors of battle, and what was called the glory of war, through roads that led straight to Vicksburg, Mississippi. However, her biggest concern was making sure she was not detected by the others. Keeping her secret would not only be challenging, but trying as well. Will she remain in this solitude the rest of her life, never allowing anyone into her heart again? Or will she find love, once more, in a world that was intolerant and unaccepting of who she truly was?

Diva – ISBN – 978-1-952270-10-9
What if...you were offered a part-time job as the

personal assistant to someone you have idolized for years? Meg Ellis has just completed the school year as a nurse in the Santa Fe school system. It isn't her first choice of profession, but a medical problem derailed her musical career years ago. The breakup of a bad relationship is still painful. The loving support from her close-knit family and good friends has buoyed her spirits, but longing still lurks below the surface. She can't forget the intoxicating allure of the beautiful diva who haunts her dreams. Nicole Bernard is a rising star in the world of opera, adored by fans around the globe. When Meg learns that Nicole is headlining a new production at the renowned New Mexico outdoor pavilion—and then is asked to accept a job offer to be her personal assistant—she is beside herself. After a short time learning the routine and reining in her hormones, Meg discovers that Nicole's family will be visiting for the opening. Her responsibility to the charismatic singer immediately becomes more difficult when Nicole's young husband Mario shows up and threatens the comfortable rapport between Meg and the prima donna. The two women brace for a roller-coaster interlude composed by fate. Will the warm days and cool nights, the breathtaking scenery, and the romance of the music create summer love? A heartbreaking game? Or something very special?

Finding Faith: When you're lost, Wynter will find you –
ISBN – 978-1-952270-16-1

Faith Fitzgerald thought that if she got an education and became a high-powered attorney in Manhattan, maybe—just maybe—she'd gain the attention and respect of her absentee father. Considering he was the only parent she had left after her mother's suicide when Faith was just a child, she thought that's what it would take. She was wrong. What she dreamed would be glamorous and satisfying turned out to be grueling and thankless. Since she wasn't willing to play the game between the sheets, she was forced to stay in the cubicle jungle doing all the heavy lifting while the men got the credit and the rewards. Deciding she is done, Faith packs up and, with the flip of the bird to the rearview mirror, leaves New York and heads home to Colorado. She has nothing there: no job, nowhere to live, no relationship with her father. Truth is, she barely has a relationship with herself. On the drive home, she finds herself in Wynter, a tiny mountain town at the foot of the Rockies. Looking more like it belongs in a made-for-TV Christmas movie than on the map, Faith is utterly enchanted. When she tries her luck and buys a raffle ticket at Pop's, Wynter's charming café, her prize is far more than meets the eye—or the heart. Enter Wyatt, a feisty, sexy southerner and waitress at Pop's, who just happens to be married to a local sheriff's deputy. All is not as it appears with the All-American boy and his Georgia peach. A colorful cast of unforgettable and charming characters will teach the jaded attorney that sometimes to find yourself all you have to do is go back to the basics...and have a little Faith.

Broken - ISBN - 978-1-952270-08-6

Even the sturdiest of people have their limits. For Captain Melinda Morris, USN, that limit came in the form of a bomb that violated the peace of a Baghdad café. Her career ended, her body damaged, her marriage finished, her home lost—a strong woman learned what it meant to be broken. She remembered her father's words from over two decades before. "If you ever need us, the ranch is here. Come home."She did. She left the sea that had been her life to return to her first love—the land and horses. Her father was long dead, but the ranch was there, as well as the memory of his reminder that a Morris never gives up. Those words held her fast as she dealt with the nightmares that never quite ended, leaving her with the mystery of an unfilled promise to a dying mother whose name she never knew. The ranch, the horses, the love of family, and a promise to her brother, Hoyt, gave her an anchor to hang onto.When Addie Romero returned home to the neighboring ranch, she brought home a history of success and her own nightmares from a story she could tell no one, at least not until she saw Mel again. Former three-time World Champion Cowgirl—an accomplishment that was her springboard into a successful career in the world or horses, movies, and the California high life—Addie was ready to return, perhaps to heal an old and deep wound that never lost its grip on her heart and mind. Together, Addie and Mel would seek the gold to mend the broken, to create something even more beautiful than before.

www.ingramcontent.com/pod-product-compliance
Lightning Source LLC
Chambersburg PA
CBHW061342190726
48288CB00005B/1566